ENTRANCED

PRINCE OF THE DOOMED CITY:
BOOK I

FIRE WYRM BOOKS

ENTRANCED

PRINCE OF THE DOOMED CITY:

BOOK 1

© 2021 by Sylvia Mercedes

Published by FireWyrm Books

www.SylviaMercedesBooks.com

All rights reserved. No part of this publication may be reproduced, stored in a retrieval system, or transmitted in any form or by any means—for example, electronic, photocopy, recording—without the prior written permission of the publisher. The only exception is brief quotations in printed reviews.

This volume contains a work of fiction. Names, characters, incidents, and dialogues are products of the author's imagination and are not to be construed as real. Any resemblance to actual events or persons, living or dead, is entirely coincidental.

Cover illustration by Amira Naval

This book is for Clara Darling,
Always an inspiration.

PROLOGUE

OBLIGATES LIVE BY THREE SIMPLE RULES:

Never anger the fae.

Never trust the fae.

Never love the fae.

If we can honor these rules, then we have a chance. A chance to serve out the terms of our Obligations. A chance to atone for our crimes against our fae overlords.

A chance to return home.

It should be simple enough. Keep my head down. Don't draw undue attention. And don't let my heart do anything stupid.

I will survive this. I will get home.

Then I will pretend that my life here was nothing but a bad dream . . .

A nightmare.

1

I'VE BEEN HUNTING PIXIES SINCE DAYBREAK.

It's one of the less agreeable duties of a junior librarian in the Court of Dawn. A family of pixies got into the library last night. Technically this shouldn't be possible, but when I unlocked the doors and stepped into the bright white-and-gold foyer, I sensed the disturbance right away. The library is always quiet, especially first thing in the morning.

But this was *too* quiet. A hushed, hiding sort of stillness brimming with stifled giggles.

They probably got in using a gnoller hole or a window left open by mistake. Some point of access that doesn't fall under the official library rule of "No Entrance without Library Card." I'll have to find it later and either block it up entirely or make certain I write a caveat into the rules. The various beings of Eledria are sticklers for written rules. Even pixies. I'm not sure they even *can* break a rule if it has been properly written down. But they are all of them—from the lowliest pixie to the highest, most glorious elfkin lord—experts in finding workarounds.

I'll deal with rule-writing later, however. For now I need to catch those pixies.

My ears, though not as sharp as a fae's, are quick and keen for any slight sound that might disturb the hallowed quiet of the library. Thaddeus has trained me over the years so that I can detect the indrawn breath of an impending sneeze from ten shelves away. "Librarian Ears," he calls it. I should be able to pick up the buzz of pixie wings before they know I'm coming.

My slippers whispering on the polished marble floor, I creep through the stacks. I've got an iron-laced cage in one hand, hidden beneath a cotton cloth so they won't smell it coming and bolt. In my other hand I grip a mesh net on a stick. Pixies are my nemesis. I've learned to keep tools on hand to deal with them.

Turning a corner, I step from the Goblin Histories section into the east wing—Prophecies. Signs of pixies are immediately apparent. The shelf on my right is lined with the Complete Works of Benjamin Aged, Soothsayer Esq. There are bite-marks out of each and every spine. Tiny wadded mouthfuls spat out on the ground mark a trail of destruction. Did they think old Benjamin's work would improve in flavor as the series progressed?

I follow the trail of bites and munched leather to the end of the shelf. There I turn a corner, peer around into the next aisle, and gasp in horror. Apparently the pixies found something they liked. Piles of books lie strewn on the floor, most of them fallen open, pages torn out and scattered. I set aside my cage, crouch, and pick up one book, turning over the spine. It's *The Marvelaur*, by Mage Zummaer Jhaan of the Miphates Order. An original edition, written in ancient Araneli characters, a volume more than five hundred years old.

My stomach sinks. This book is priceless. Irreplaceable. And now the pages have been gnawed down to the spine stitching.

A curse bubbles up in my throat. I swallow it back. Mama always said a lady never curses. A lady controls her feelings, puts them all in their proper places, and shuts the doors fast where necessary. She certainly doesn't give vent to unseemly emotion, not even when there's no one around to hear.

So I don't curse. I grind my teeth and hiss, *"Pixies!"* with all the vehemence of a curse instead. It helps a little.

Pixies live under the delusional belief that they can accumulate power by devouring books. They are innately magical, of course, like all the natural denizens of Eledria. But they are singularly *un*powerful creatures, unable to spin or cast spells or direct their magic in any way. Thus they are always on the hunt for ways to improve their lot and rise in Eledrian society.

A futile wish. Really they're just pests.

A growl in my throat, I brandish my net and continue down the aisle, stepping carefully around damaged books. It's my job to open the library this morning, but my fellow librarians will be joining me shortly. Then we'll spend the day trying to repair what damage we can—salvaging the torn-up remnants of pages and attempting to recopy at least some of Mage Jhaan's great work. Which will be challenging, considering none of us speaks or reads Araneli. But I'll worry about that later. For now . . .

My ears prick. Is that buzzing I hear?

Narrowing my eyes, I step to the shelf on my left and cautiously—oh-so cautiously—push aside books until I can see through to the other side.

There—a flash of sparkling pink and green. That's a pixie, all right. Can't mistake their glimmer. I set my teeth. My prey is close now. Stepping back, I roll my head and shoulders and grip my pole with both hands. I tiptoe to the end of the aisle and crane my neck to look around into the next. I'm just in time to see a book being pulled from its shelf and dropped with a *thud,* falling spine-open, pages on display. Three small, flashing glimmers descend upon it, squeaking with glee. The pages flutter in the breeze generated by their buzzing wings.

I steel myself. I don't want to see a book destroyed right before my eyes. But if I wait just long enough, I might be able to catch all three of them in one fell swoop.

I close my eyes, let out a slow, careful breath. Count *one, two, three* . . .

A battle cry bursting from my lips, I whirl into the aisle, lunge three strides, and bring my net smacking down over the open book and the voracious book-eaters. The netting—woven of spun-silver and mermaid hair—settles around them, too fine a mesh for even their tiny teeth to chew through. For an instant I stare down into three ferocious faces. Their eyes are like burning marbles, their teeth like viper fangs, bared at me.

With a sudden surge they take to the air, all three at once, dragging my net with them. I cry out, nearly lose hold of the pole. They yank me right off my feet, but I land hard, brace myself, and tug back with all my strength. I've battled pixies before; I'm not about to give in now.

The three of them relent. For a moment.

Then, wings buzzing like a swarm of bees, they take off, making for the end of the aisle. Though I try to dig in my heels, they drag me along behind them. I let go of the pole with one hand, attempt to grab hold of a shelf with the other. In the process I knock several books flying. That's no good! I'm supposed to be preventing further damage, not causing it. I let go and grab hold of the pole again as the pixies reach the end of the aisle and burst out into the open space beyond.

A hand reaches out. Catches hold of the pole.

We all come to an abrupt stop.

I gasp for breath and stare at that hand. Strong and yet elegant somehow, with long tapered fingers. My eyes swivel in their sockets, following the line of a wrist to a muscular forearm then to a silken, embroidered sleeve, all the way up to a set of broad shoulders. The front of the jacket is open, and a loose white shirt hangs open in a deep V, revealing rather a lot of manly chest, all chiseled definition and warm olive skin. I lift my gaze to a clavicle and throat, a square jaw, a wide mouth with distinctly sneering full lips.

At last I look a little higher. Up into a pair of vivid, violet eyes.

A shock of fear lances through me. Or . . . not fear exactly. Something else. Something I cannot name. A sort of dreadful, stomach-sinking familiarity. But that can't be right. Because I've never seen this man. I'd remember if I had; his is not a face one would forget easily.

He's one of the elfkin—a lord, judging by the cut and quality of his clothing and the perfection of his face, which indicates potent magic. It takes a good deal of magic to produce glamours so convincing one almost believes the projected beauty is real. But surely no man could be so beautiful without magical aid.

His eyes—such an intense, unnatural color—scan my face slowly. His sneer deepens and somehow, it only increases his attractiveness. His gaze travels briefly down the lines of my body. Not a slow, lascivious study such as I've too often been subjected to by lusty elfkin men. No, just a quick up-and-down inspection, before his eyes fasten on mine once more.

"You're shorter than I remembered," he says.

Like that, the spell is broken. I drag in a breath. How long have I been standing here, staring at him? Gaping like a goggle-eyed frog with my mouth hanging open? Hastily I shut my jaw, pull myself together. In that same moment, the pixies utter a joint squeal and give a tremendous tug at the net, nearly pulling the pole free of both my grasp and that of the stranger.

He whips around, adjusts his hold, and yanks them back into submission. Then with one hand he grips the net itself and holds it up to his face. "Pixies, eh?" he says, as they jeer and spit and make obscene but futile gestures through the netting fibers. "Nasty blighters." He turns another disdainful look down at me, one eyebrow tilted. "In Queen Dasyra's day, pixies weren't allowed in the library. It would seem things have gone lax around here in the five years since last I visited."

"Oh!" The word blurts from my lips, a pathetic little bleat. I shake my head, blinking hard, and force my voice to steady. "Oh no, pixies are not permitted in the library. That's why I'm hunting them."

The stranger looks over my head, no doubt taking in the damage left in a trail behind me. "One might wonder how they managed to get in in the first place."

"I don't know." I'm still gripping the net pole. Though it's quite useless now, it feels like a lifeline I dare not let go. "But I intend to find out, just as soon as . . ." I reach for the net, but the stranger holds it a little higher, beyond my grasp. I swallow thickly then offer what I hope is a submissive smile. "Thank you, sir, for your assistance. I'm sure I can manage from here."

"Are you?" I wouldn't have thought it possible for his expression to turn more contemptuous, but he manages it and then some. "It looked to me as though they were pulling you right off your feet. What are your intentions for these little beasties anyway?"

My mouth is dry. "I . . . I have a cage."

"Show me."

"Oh really, sir, I can manage well enough—"

"All evidence would point to the contrary." He dips his chin, his gaze hard beneath the ledge of his brow. "I said, *show me*."

Never anger the fae, I remind myself firmly. And this particular fae already seems to have a peculiar dislike of me. Best not to antagonize him further. "This way, sir," I say.

Still holding onto the end of my pole, I turn and lead the way back through the carnage. It's awful—all those books damaged and scattered, all those torn pages and chewed spines. His sweeping gaze seems to take in everything and accumulate it as further evidence of my incompetence. I can almost hear his teeth grinding. I won't let him see my discomfort though. I keep my head high and my face carefully masked in a calm, meaningless smile.

"Where are the other librarians?" the stranger asks abruptly. "This place feels positively abandoned."

I turn my head about but don't quite dare to meet his eye. "There are no others. Not at this hour."

"What?" The word is short and sharp, like the crack of a whip.

"Later on Mister Thaddeus Creakle will join me," I continue. "Most days there are a few others as well so long as their masters and mistresses don't have other tasks for them."

"How many?"

"Four. Five including me."

"You're telling me the staff of Aurelis Library has been reduced to nothing more than Thaddeus Creakle and five come-and-go Obligates?"

He sounds angry. I couldn't guess why. The fae don't generally care about books and written words, incapable of reading as they are. "Mortal magic," they call it, the ability to capture thoughts and ideas with ink and page and preserve them for generations to come. It's as mysterious to them as the glamours they spin are to humanity.

The stranger seems to be waiting for some sort of answer. I shrug. "Yes, sir."

He scoffs then, tossing his head. Long locks of raven black hair gleam across his shoulders and down his back. "In the queen's day, there were twenty dedicated librarians on staff in Aurelis."

"Yes," I respond meekly, "but Queen Dasyra died before I came here. You must understand, the queen was *human*. King Lodírhal's Fatebound wife. This whole library was built in her honor, but since her death—"

"I do not require a lecture on the history of either this library or the late queen."

His tone is so sharp, it could cut iron. I bow my head and murmur an apology. The Lords and Ladies of Aurelis are a condescending lot, but they generally don't bother taking notice of the human Obligates running around underfoot. I don't remember the last time I was the object of such intense fae scorn.

To my relief, we reach the end of a row of shelves where my iron cage sits under its cotton cloth. I lift the cloth, then freeze.

Iron, after all, has an unpleasant effect on fae blood. I glance at the stranger, prepared for him to snarl at me for my carelessness. Instead he answers my look with one of total indifference. The iron does not seem to influence him in the least. Does this mean he isn't fae? No, he must be—no ordinary man could wear such glamours. Part-human perhaps.

He catches my eye. One eyebrow slides up his forehead. "Is it my incredible beauty that so captures your attention, or do I have mustard on my shirt?"

"Oh, no!" I blurt.

"You're saying you *don't* find me extraordinarily beautiful then?"

"Well, of course!" Heat roars up my neck and floods my cheeks. I drop my gaze. "That is, I mean, you are very beautiful, of course, and . . . and your glamours . . ."

"You think all this beauty is due to a little glamour?"

I lick my lips. How have I put myself in this situation? I've lived in Eledria long enough to know how dangerous it is either to admire or to compliment any of the Lords and Ladies. They like it rather too much. "I wouldn't presume to venture an opinion, sir," I murmur.

He is silent for a long moment. Then: "That was a well-spoken, little Obligate. Very proper and deferential. They've got you well trained by now, haven't they?"

The next moment, to my utter astonishment, he reaches out and takes hold of my chin. His grip is firm, and I freeze at his touch, too startled even to pull away. He tilts my face up, forcing me to look at him. Forcing me to stare into those incredible violet eyes of his. The black pupils are dilated, like two endless wells into the depths of his soul. He tips my head this way and that, studying me so intently. I feel as though he's digging into my head. I can do nothing—neither yank away nor retreat nor even draw a breath.

Finally he clucks softly and shakes his head. "What has my cousin done to you?"

I blink and draw a little inhale. "What?"

"Your powers," he continues musingly, as though not speaking to me. "They've been locked down fast. Such a waste."

He lets me go. I stagger back several paces, nearly tripping over the iron-laced cage. What in the worlds is he talking about? What powers? I have no powers. I'm nothing but a librarian. I may have a gift for organization and a knack for pixie-hunting. Beyond that, I've no skills or talents to speak of.

Hands shaking, I pick up the iron cage and open the top. "Here, sir," I say. "For . . . for the pixies."

He grunts. To my great relief, he upends the net and its contents into the cage. The pixies put up a stream of shrieking, cursing, chattering protest as they drop inside one by one. I slam the hatch and latch it even as they fling themselves at the bars. When they hit, the cage rattles. I smell burning pixie flesh.

"Settle down and sit in the center," I say sternly, glaring inside. "It won't hurt you if you don't touch it directly. And I *know* your head hurts," I add to one particular pixie, who gesticulates wildly and grips its bald little scalp. "Serves you right, eating *The Marvelaur* like that. Greedy things."

I look up at the stranger again. He stands with his arms crossed, leaning against a bookshelf, watching me still. Analyzing my every move. It's desperately unnerving.

"Thank you for your assistance, sir," I say. "I really must be going now . . ." My voice trails off as my gaze darts to the small book he has tucked under one arm. It's nothing much, just a slim volume with a red leather cover. Not one I recognize and yet . . . there's something strange about it. Something which draws my attention and holds it. An energy, unseen, nearly undetectable to human senses. An uncanny, pulsing aura.

"What is that?" I ask.

"What?" He raises both eyebrows now, then looks down at the book as though surprised to see it there. "This?"

I frown. "Do you . . ." I hesitate even to ask the question. "Do you *read?*"

"No," he replies dryly. "I carry books around for their aesthetic properties." I stare at him, uncertain whether to take his answer seriously. He smirks. "Close your mouth, girl. You look disconcertingly like a herring when you gape at me like that. Yes, for your information, I can read."

He must be half-human then. It's the only explanation. Hybrids—*ibrildians*, as they're called in fae tongue—are rare but not unheard of in Eledria. There was a time when their very existence was against the law, and many of them were hunted down and slaughtered. I read about it in one of the many histories collected in this very library. Somehow this one survived that perilous era. Whether or not he's accepted among fae kind, I cannot guess.

None of that is my business, however. So I say only, "You cannot take a book from the library, you know. Not without a card."

His lips quirk. My heart makes an odd flutter, but I take care to reveal nothing on my face. "Good little librarian," he says, his voice a purr, "guarding your collection like a dragon it's hoard."

"It's not my collection," I say quickly. "It's the king's. And it's the rule, the *written* rule, I might add." Half-fae though he may be, a written rule should still be enough to bind him.

His smile only grows. He slips a hand into the front of his jacket and withdraws a battered rectangular card from his pocket. This he passes to me. "Satisfied?"

I blink several times. The faded words on the card seem to swim before my gaze, finally resolving into: *Official Library Pass: Aurelis Library, Court of Dawn.* These are printed in a blocky, distinct script. Underneath it is a scrawled signature: *Castien Lodírith.*

My eyes widen. I know that name. I've heard it before, whispered here and there among both Obligates and courtiers alike.

I jerk my head up, staring at the stranger before me. "But . . . but you're the—"

"Prince Castien!" a ringing, golden voice cuts me off. "Do my eyes deceive me or is that really you?"

I WHIRL, MY SKIRTS SPINNING ABOUT MY ANKLES. Another tall, broad fae appears at the end of the stacks, standing in the dawnlight streaming through the nearest window. To compare him to the stranger beside me would be like comparing the dawn itself to deepening twilight. Where the stranger is all dark intensity, this man is brightness and brilliance, a true golden son of Aurelis Court. He's built like a warrior, but moves with utmost grace and ease, his long pale hair falling in waves across his massive shoulders.

"Ivor, old chap," the stranger says, leaning nonchalantly against the shelf once more and crossing his ankles. "Fancy meeting you here."

"I could say the same to you." The glorious fae lord strides toward us, the smile on his face like the rising sun itself. "Are you not needed on that little troll rock island of yours, Prince? Or have the insurgents finally had enough and booted you out once and for all?"

The Prince—Castien Lodírith, King Lodírhal's son. That's who I've been talking to. That's who I've been scolding about books and making fetch and carry pixies around in nets for me and . . . and . . . lecturing about his own mother's death!

Oh, gods above. I wish the floor would open up and let me sink down into it.

At least for the moment his attention is fixed solely on the approaching Lord Ivor. "Would that I was so lucky," he says around a knife-like smile. "No, the trolls are content for the time being at least, and all is well in Vespre. I'd heard my father was hosting a little get-together this evening. Thought I'd come join the fun."

My gaze swivels from one tall elfkin man to the other. Am I mistaken, or is there a frisson of animosity in the atmosphere between them? I have not seen so much as a glimpse of the Prince in my five years of service here in Aurelis. Though he may be the king's only son, he has fallen from favor somehow. I don't know the particulars. Lord Ivor Illithor, however, is King's Champion, a favorite both with Lodírhal and his court.

He takes a stance now across from the Prince. And here I am, caught between them, with my little cage full of cursing pixies. This is not how I anticipated this day going. Not in the least.

"And what are you doing here, Ivor?" the Prince asks and

tosses a hand to indicate the mess of shredded books and pages all around us. "This is not the usual haunt of my father's bravest warrior. Come to soak up the ambiance, have you?"

"No indeed." Ivor smiles. Suddenly his gaze shifts from the Prince to me. Pins me down. Captures me in the warmth of eyes like two twin suns. "I've come for my reading lesson with Clara Darlington here."

My insides go all hot and liquid. I can't help it. I know the rules, but . . . but it's not my fault! It's not my fault that, of all the librarians available in Aurelis Library, Lord Ivor singled me out. My Obligation does not belong to him. He shouldn't even know I'm alive.

And yet, somehow, just about a year ago—if one dares to calculate time here in Eledria by such human measurements—he found me at work one day and asked if I would teach him how to read. In my surprise I'd dropped a whole stack of books I was busy shelving. At first I couldn't say a word in answer. After all his kind *cannot* be taught to read. They simply haven't the ability to comprehend how markings on a page can be made to hold meaning. It's an altogether *human* magic, possibly the only power humans can boast over the exalted fae.

To be asked for help by Lord Ivor of all people was terrifying.

I'd noticed him, of course. Many times since my arrival in the Court of Dawn. Indeed it's impossible *not* to notice him. Even among the painfully beautiful members of the king's court, he stands out. Unlike most of his kind, he favors simple dress—

light colors and plain cuts, which somehow only emphasize the perfection of his beauty. The elaborate robes and jewels of his brethren cannot compete. He wears glamours, but not so thickly as the other warriors either, opting instead to let his scars show, like badges of honor for each victory dearly won.

He is breathtaking. I mean it—he took my breath away when he first made that request. He takes it again now as he gazes down at me, unblinking, those golden eyes of his just a little too knowing.

I'd tried very gently to explain that I couldn't teach him to read. Of course I'd said it was because *I* wasn't qualified. I wasn't stupid enough to imply any insufficiency on *his* part.

He'd smiled, however, and said, "You forget, Clara, that I do have a drop or two of human blood in my veins. While I possess no more than a trace of *ibrildian* magic, I may prove a more apt pupil than you think."

I'd gaped at him again. Stupidly. Wordlessly. It probably took a full minute for me to realize I'd not yet answered. Even then I only managed to blurt out an idiotic, "Oh!"

He'd taken that as an agreement. Our lessons began the very next day.

It's been a year now. Ivor, an eager and willing student, has made a point to meet me in the library at least three times each month. During those sessions, I've found him to be not without ability. He can recognize a few simple words by sight, though the concept of sounding out a word based on the combination of letters presented is still entirely foreign to him. I don't think he has enough human blood in him to progress beyond the most basic level, comparable to a four-year-old human child. But he never complains. He never gets frustrated. And he always comes back.

The last year has given me time enough to adjust somewhat to his unsettling beauty and the overwhelming aura of sheer charisma that follows him everywhere. That doesn't mean I know how to catch my breath in this moment, however.

"Well, Clara?" Ivor tilts his head slightly. A lock of golden hair slips over his shoulder, and the smile on his lips grows. "What do you say? Do you have time for a lesson?"

Suddenly I'm very aware of the Prince's gaze hard upon me. I dare a glance his way only to find a strange expression on his face. I don't know how to describe it. Angry, irritated. If I didn't know any better, I might call it . . . *possessive?* But that's ridiculous, of course.

"Really," he says, grinding the word through clenched teeth. "*Really.* You are attempting to teach this lout to read?"

I am so far out of my depth, I might as well be drowning. I offer a quick nod.

"And how much progress have you made?" The Prince angles that toothy smile up at Ivor. He looks like a tiger, eager to hunt. "Have you mastered that great literary epic, *See Spot Run*? Or are your tastes not so elevated as all that?"

All the warmth in Ivor's eyes has vanished, replaced by something cold and dangerous. His hand goes for his belt, reaching for a dagger there. My gods, are they going to fight? Pixies have caused enough damage for one day! The last thing I need is two posturing fae lords bashing each other against the shelves.

"There may be no brawling on library premises!" I blurt, holding out one hand as though to push Ivor back even as I turn and fix my gaze on the Prince. "It's . . . it's in the rules. Written down," I add for emphasis.

The Prince's gaze shifts from me to Ivor and back again. His eyes burn with strange fire straining to be unleashed. On me. On Ivor. On the whole world for all I know. I don't pretend to understand it. Or him. But at last he lets out a slow breath and takes a slight backward step.

I turn to Ivor. He too seems to have shrunk back into himself somewhat, no longer the bristling animal ready to launch an attack. He trains another heart-melting smile my way. "I would never dream of thwarting any library rule," he says, "nor of bringing you personal discomfort. As you are occupied at present, I will come back some other day to resume our lessons. Until then, Clara."

He bows deeply. Which discomfits me no end. I'm an Obligate—he shouldn't bow to me. When he straightens, I don't know which way to look. But Ivor merely casts the Prince another narrow-eyed stare over my head. "I will see you later."

"I look forward to it," the Prince replies. When Ivor turns to leave, he mutters, "Ass," so low, I almost don't catch it. Ivor does, however. He pauses, half-turns his head. My shoulders tense. But he merely sniffs softly. Then he continues on his way, disappearing around the stacks.

I draw in a great lungful of air. I'd not been able to breathe normally so long as Lord Ivor was near. It's both a disappointment and a relief to have to put off our reading lessons. I won't deny how much I look forward to those interludes, but . . . but I dread them equally.

The Prince is watching me. Much too closely, I might add. I flick a glance his way. Why is he still here? Why did he come to begin with? "Will you be checking out that volume, Your Highness?" I ask quietly, and nod to the book still tucked under his arm.

"What? This?" He turns the book over several times then shrugs. "I haven't decided. I'll probably peruse the shelves a bit more. If it's all the same with you of course."

There's a snideness to his tone which I don't like. I merely lower my lashes. "As you wish, Your Highness."

"Hmmm." He grunts. "And what about you? Will I be seeing you at the king's feast this evening?"

"Oh, no." I shake my head hastily. "No, I am an Obligate. I'm not invited to such things." And thank the gods! The last thing I want is to spend time in company with the Lords and Ladies of Aurelis Court. The more I can avoid their notice the better.

The Prince, however, doesn't seem to realize the absurdity of his question. He merely studies me from beneath half-closed eyelids, his gaze once more sweeping over me from head to toe. I maintain my bland demeanor, determined not to let him see me flustered.

"You really are shorter than I remembered," he says at last.

Then he turns and sweeps away in a flutter of long embroidered coat and glossy black hair. Leaving me standing there, a cage full of angry pixies in one hand, surrounded by chewed-up books and broken spines. Wondering when or where we possibly could have met before. Or how I could have forgotten it.

3

I BELIEVE I SAW MY MASTER LEAVING THE LIBRARY THIS morning. Was he here during all the commotion?"

A flush creeps up my cheeks. I try to ignore it, and try as well to ignore Thaddeus Creakle's gaze, which is, as always, just a little too incisive. Or perhaps *intrusive* is a better word.

Granted, Lord Ivor is Thaddeus's master, so the senior librarian does have some vested interest in the fae lord's comings and goings. Still I can't help but wish those watery old eyes of his didn't notice quite so much from behind those neat, square spectacles perched on the edge of his nose.

"Yes, well—" I hear myself beginning to stammer and have the good sense to stop, clear my throat, and carefully turn over the chewed page on the stack in front of me, pretending to inspect the damage. "Lord Ivor was interested in pursuing another reading lesson this morning."

"Oh yes?"

There's something in the way he says it. As though he knows I'm keeping something from him. The last thing I want is to tell him about the unexpected appearance of the Prince. Or the friction sparking between him and Lord Ivor, the near-insults, the posturing. All of which had felt strangely as though it had something to do with . . . me.

I shudder. It's all nonsense of course. Just my imagination getting away with me.

But I don't feel the need to communicate any of this to Thaddeus Creakle.

"Yes," I reply and offer a smile. "I informed him of the pixie damage, however, and we agreed to meet at a later date."

Thaddeus grunts and narrows his eyes. We are both comfortably ensconced in a back workroom tucked away from the main library. The shelves are strewn with tools for book upkeep and restoration, not to mention numerous books in various states of disintegration and repair. I'd spent all morning collecting the sorry remnants of the pixies' work. Thaddeus and I discovered several more places in different wings of the library where they'd gorged themselves on the written word. How three pixies could cause so much destruction in just a few short hours is nothing short of amazing! I loathe the little blights.

At first I'd been pleased when Thaddeus invited me to join him in the workroom and begin the delicate process of organizing the strewn and torn pages, creating separate stacks for each book. It's nice to think that he trusts not only my reading and comprehension of the various languages represented within Aurelis's collection, but also my passion for the proper care and keeping of such delicate and valuable material.

Now, however, as I writhe beneath his too-knowing gaze, I wonder if he had another motive entirely in mind when he asked me. I know perfectly well Thaddeus does not approve of my tutoring sessions with Lord Ivor. But what does he expect me to do? Deny the fae lord's request? I'm an Obligate; I do what I'm told. Ivor might not own my Obligation, but he is still my superior.

Taking care to show nothing in my face, I scan another page. It's written in Old Araneli, and I recognize Mage Jhaan's spidery script. Another sorry shred of *The Marvelaur*. I place it in the appropriate pile. Only then do I dare glance Thaddeus's way. Why is he still looking at me? I blink impassively and paint a faint smile on my lips. I've learned over the years that a smile is a much more effective mask than a non-expression. Every non-expression is ultimately a blank canvas inviting unwanted feelings to flash into momentary visibility. But if you're wearing a smile, it's easier to hide that which you would prefer to remain secret.

Thaddeus dips his head, creating three extra chins beneath his fringe of white beard. His spectacles teeter on the edge of his nose, just clinging to the pointy tip. "I hope, my dear Miss Darlington, that you have not forgotten Mary West."

My stomach tightens. "I . . . Yes, I do remember Mary." My voice is deceptively light and airy. "She arrived in Aurelis a few years before me, didn't she?"

"And you remember what happened to her?"

All too well.

Mary West was an Obligate of course. All humans living in Aurelis are these days. She served under a fae by the name of Kiirion the Fair, one of the more glamourized members of King Lodírhal's court, gifted with a silver tongue and a charming demeanor, which left fae ladies—and not a few fae gentleman—swooning in his wake wherever he went.

The rules of the Pledge prevent the owner of an Obligation from compelling his Obligate to love him, so I know Lord Kiirion did not use magical influence to persuade Mary West into his bed. He didn't have to. She went of her own free will, Obligation or no Obligation. And for a time she enjoyed the fruits of Kiirion's favor. He dressed her in gorgeous gowns, escorted her on his arm to grand occasions, treated her to fine wines and fine foods, swathed her in glamours to make her as beautiful as any fae damsel. She, in her turn, loved him madly.

When he tired of her within a year, that love turned to poison.

For another six months, she continued to serve just like the rest of us—fetching, carrying, mending, scrubbing, even occasional stints in the library, where I interacted with her. But as the days, weeks, and months wore on, she became a mere shadow of her former self. She did not survive to the end of her Obligation.

Mary West's name swiftly become a byword among the

Obligates. A tragic example of our third and most important rule: *Never love the fae.* It should go without saying of course. They are our captors, our masters. They control our fates at their whims. Loving them should be no more tempting than loving the wild winds and waves and storms that rule the sea.

But then someone like Lord Ivor comes along. Looks at you in a certain way. Makes you feel important. And suddenly the line between glamour and attraction is blurred.

I shudder but keep my smile in place. "I remember Mary West," I say again firmly. "Don't worry, Mister Creakle."

He narrows his eyes. Telling him not to worry is a sure way to make him worry more. But he drops the topic for now, thank the gods, and turns back to the stack of pixie-chewed pages in front of him.

My heart hammers so loudly in my throat, I'm almost afraid the senior librarian will hear it in the silence between us. The truth is, I'm not as immune to Lord Ivor's charms as I'd like to believe. The stammering and the breathlessness are all well and good—no girl in her right mind would be entirely at ease around a being of his great beauty. If I'm flustered by his presence, it's only natural.

What's dangerous is the growing, insidious belief that he sees something *special* in me. The moment I let that belief take root, I'm already halfway down the same road Mary West trod to her doom.

A shiver ripples down my spine. I sit up a little straighter, check to make certain my smile is still fixed, and concentrate on my work. It's good work, focused work. The perfect distraction I need. Soon I am caught up in it—so caught up, I don't notice the delicate knocking on the workroom door until Thaddeus says, "Come in!"

I turn in my chair. The door opens. Instead of one of my fellow librarians, a meek little face covered in short gray fur and framed by long, velvety ears like a rabbit's peeks in. She's dressed in a prim blue maid's uniform, and her delicate little hands, tipped with long claws, are folded in front of her apron. She bobs a curtsy to Thaddeus before addressing herself to me.

"Miss Darlington," she says.

"Hello, Poppin," I answer. "Is something the matter?"

The little bunyi blinks her soft brown eyes at me. "The princess requires your presence in her chambers at once, miss."

A frown pulls at the edge of my smile. Though I spend most of my working hours in the Aurelis Library, I am officially *obliged* to Princess Estrilde. She doesn't often remember me—my skills are best suited to library work, and the princess has no interest in libraries whatsoever.

"What does she want?" I ask, casting a look back at the stack of pages on the desk. Even this slight resistance is a mistake; I already feel the beginnings of the headache that always accompanies any defiance of my Obligation. I am meant to leap and run the moment I am summoned.

But it doesn't make sense. I'm no use to the princess in any practical capacity. I don't cook or sew or mend, and she has Obligates enough to do all those things for her. Not to mention, she simply doesn't like me. Not that the fae truly like any of us, per se. But I've had the strong impression many times that Princess Estrilde actively dislikes me, finds my very presence offensive.

"It's not my place to say, miss," Poppin answers, bobbing another deferential curtsy. "I am merely the messenger."

A sharp stab in my temple tells me I'd better get moving or be sorry. I heave a sigh and turn to Thaddeus. "I'll return as soon as I can," I say, sliding a couple of paperweights onto the various stacks in front of me.

"No, no, away with you," Thaddeus says, without looking up from his work. "Oblige your mistress as you must."

The headache dissipates the moment I step from the workroom and follow Poppin out into the main library. She doesn't know the ins and outs of this space as well as I do, so I take the lead and guide her through the Lunulyrian Mythologies section out to what I think of as the highway—the broad aisle that cuts straight through the ground floor of the library, leading past all the various wings straight to the shining golden foyer. Two librarians sit at the reception desk there—my associates, George Nobblin and Lydia Trewet, both longtime denizens of Aurelis with years of Obligation left to serve. Lydia nods as I pass; George doesn't even pretend to notice.

Poppin and I progress out to the passage beyond the library and on through Aurelis Palace. The walls here are more of the same gold and white as the library foyer, set with vast windows and skylights and sometimes open arcades to let in as much light as possible. The Court of Dawn exists in a golden, dawn-like glow much of each year—though we do experience midday, afternoon, dusk, and even full night upon occasion. There are overcast days as well, but in this world, the gloom only seems to emphasize the shining loveliness of the palace interior.

Everything is built on a positively enormous scale, large enough to accommodate even the dragons and giants who sometimes pay visit to King Lodírhal's court. I remember being totally overwhelmed, even terrified by the vastness of it all when I first arrived. Now, five years into my Obligation, I hardly notice or think of it as I trot along behind Poppin. It's amazing how quickly one can grow used to one's own insignificance.

The little bunyi maid leads me to Princess Estrilde's apartment suite in the north wing of the palace. We pause a moment before the door, and I take the opportunity to straighten my skirts and comb my fingers through my hair. Not that it matters—Princess Estrilde is unlikely to offer me more than the barest glance. Humans are far beneath the notice of King Lodírhal's only niece. But Mama always taught me to put on the best possible front, particularly when going into a difficult situation.

Taking care to fit my firmest smile in place, I give Poppin a nod. The bunyi nods back, opens the door, and announces in a high-pitched squeak, "Miss Darlington, Your Highness." Then she bows her head, steps back, and motions me through.

I step into a lounge—not quite as grand in scale as the library foyer, but ten times more opulent. Every item of furniture is gilded and draped with silks in various shades of pink trimmed in mounds of lace. Living roses climb the pillars and walls, framing the windows like curtains. The atmosphere reeks of their perfume.

Ladies, a few gentlemen, and at least one being for whom I cannot begin to determine a gender, drape the furniture in attitudes of languor that somehow never quite diminish the sheer power of their natural being. Glamours pulse from them in auras even my un-magical eyes cannot ignore.

In the center of this gathering, Princess Estrilde sits on a gilded chair only a little less glorious than a throne, sipping a shining liquid from a tall, clear glass. Three human Obligates are hard at work brushing her hair, which is astoundingly long. When not styled in one of her preferred elaborate arrangements, it drags a full meter behind her, like a shining golden train. It takes all the efforts of those three Obligates to keep it healthy and maintained. I do not envy them the task.

I approach, stepping through the center of the gathering, very aware of the way the members of the princess's entourage don't look at me as I pass. I am less than nothing in their eyes. But I don't mind; my irrelevance is my greatest protection here in the Court of Dawn.

I sink to my knees before Estrilde's chair, bow my head, and murmur, "You summoned me, Mistress?"

Estrilde does not answer. She's studying her face in a handheld mirror, humming softly and tilting her head at various angles, her mouth pursed. She's experimenting with a new glamourized lip-color—a pure, shimmering gold. It's quite garish, in my opinion.

But one of her companions declares, "Perfection, my love! You pull off that shade as no one else can."

"Hmmm," Estrilde grunts noncommittally. "Is *perfection* quite what one wants on an occasion such as this?"

"But, darling," another sycophant interjects with a trill, "on you, even imperfection becomes perfection. You simply cannot help yourself."

Estrilde's eyebrow rises slightly, but I can tell she's pleased.

"You may depend upon it, sweetness," the first lady says, reaching out a fluttering hand and patting the princess's arm conspiratorially. "Lord Ivor will surely declare himself tonight. Once everything is settled."

Something turns over in my gut.

Which is stupid. Completely stupid. I am well aware of the delicate dance which has been taking place between my mistress and Lord Ivor since long before I came to Aurelis. It only makes sense. The favorite champion of the king and the king's only niece? They are a perfect, beautiful, undeniably well-suited match by every possible standard. While I'm a human. An Obligate. Nothing. Less than nothing. I have no business even thinking about someone like Lord Ivor.

So I won't. I'll stop right now.

I keep my chin tucked, my head bowed, hoping to the heavens no one in this room detects the way my knees suddenly start trembling. Estrilde finally sets her glass down in her lap and turns her cool gaze upon me. Me, the lowly creature crouched before her. "Ah," she says, as though only just realizing that I've arrived, though I've been kneeling here several minutes now. "I require your services tonight, Obligate." Her voice is like a breath of springtime, slightly chilly but full of sweet perfumes. "King Lodírhal, my exalted uncle, has requested I provide entertainment at the feast this evening. You will give a reading."

My mouth drops open. I can't even draw a breath. *Me?* Present at one of King Lodírhal's feasts? I've never, in all my years of service, been called upon for anything of the kind. "A reading, Mistress?" I repeat.

"Yes. I require you to select a wondrous work of human poetry. Something exciting and romantic with a tragic ending. You will read it before the assembly."

I am not and never have been a performer. And before such a company? Before King Lodírhal and all his guests? I feel the beginnings of a headache just on the edges of my awareness. This is no request; I don't have a choice here. "I . . . um . . . if my mistress is certain this service would please her," I say, putting as much doubt into my tone as I dare. I cannot overtly question Estrilde's command, but perhaps I can maneuver her into reconsidering.

No such luck.

"Off with you then," the princess says, and waves the hand holding her tall glass, nearly sloshing shining liquid over the brim. "There's a dress for you in your chambers. Wear it. And remember, something with a tragic ending. I want to see the whole company in tears by the time your reading concludes."

I duck my head, stand, and back away. My smile is still bravely in place, the only armor I possess. I keep backing up, trusting pure instinct to keep me from colliding with one of the lounging guests, and make my way at last to the door, which Poppin opens for me. There I whirl and dive for safety.

Poppin shuts the door behind me. I sag back against it, my knees trembling so hard, I'm afraid they'll give out entirely. For the second time that day, I feel a curse bubbling on the back of my tongue. With an effort of will, I fight it back, and simply tilt my head up, staring hard at the arched ceiling far above.

"Oh, gods," I whisper in prayer. "Oh, gods in heaven, I'm going to *die*."

4

THE DRESS PRINCESS ESTRILDE HAS CHOSEN FOR ME to wear tonight is very much of the Aurelis style. Which is to say, not at all to my taste. The violet blue cloth mounds in multiple layers of sheer, shimmering skirts, but the bust is little more than a corset, the boning uncomfortably pressed right up against my bare skin. There are no straps or sleeves, leaving my shoulders and a great deal of my bosom exposed. No lady would dare be seen in public wearing such a garment back home. But here in Eledria, it's fairly tame.

I sigh as Poppin helps me to settle the skirts. Princess Estrilde sent the bunyi to make certain I was properly readied for the feast tonight. "I don't know why she bothers trying to make me look like a fae," I sigh, turning my shoulders and trying to see the back skirt of the gown. "No one's going to be fooled."

The bunyi tuts and pins a headdress to my hair. It's styled in two small, coiling horns with clusters of dainty violets around the base. Horns are all the rage in Aurelis this season. My mistress started the trend when she attended the Glorandal Dance last season sporting a beautiful pair of spiraling gazelle horns that sprouted directly from her forehead to rise in elegant curlicues a good two feet over her twists of golden hair. From that day since, I've watched more and more elfkin, male and female alike, adding horns to their daily glamours. Some subtle little things, no more than goat-kid nubs. Others massive, circular ram's horns or even the broad, curved, dangerous horns of a bull.

I can't glamour myself to look as though I've grown horns naturally. A headdress is the most that I can manage.

"There, Miss Darlington!" Poppin says, stepping back and giving me a satisfied once over. "You'll not disgrace the mistress, I think."

"From your lips to the gods' ears, Poppin," I mutter. I already feel foolish enough being called upon for this impromptu performance. Having Estrilde dress me up like a toy doll is not helping my confidence.

The time has come, however. I've no choice but to honor my Obligation.

I pick up the book I've borrowed from the library. It's a collection of poetry by human author Magdelita Bronwin. She's not a favorite of mine; altogether too sentimental for my tastes. But her best known work is a ballad of two mortal lovers who are separated by various cruel twists of fate and ultimately end up killing each other in a tragic—if somewhat idiotic—misunderstanding. Communication is not their strong suit. But the story should be suitably romantic for my intended audience. The fae love a properly catastrophic romance.

I turn, clutching the book to my breast, and offer Poppin a fleeting smile. "Wish me luck!"

She dips a little curtsy, her long ears flopping over her shoulders. "Gods go with you, Miss Darlington. Gods go with you."

It's the sort of thing you'd say to a soldier about to step into the battlefield.

King Lodírhal holds his feasts and revels in Biroris Hall. I've seen it a few times, but never for a feast. I, of course, will not be part of the merrymaking in the hall itself, but will take my place in the upper gallery among the other entertainers, only stepping into visibility long enough to give my reading. That, at least, is a mercy.

I creep along the back passages used by servants and Obligates such as myself. I'm ridiculously overdressed for this part of the palace and catch more than one disapproving glance from pinch-lipped matrons—and, more embarrassingly, several admiring eyebrow-waggles and low whistles from the footmen and waiters. I ignore them all.

The upper gallery is a long, curtained space overlooking Biroris Hall. It's already full to bursting with musicians, dancers, singers, jugglers, tumblers, and other such entertainers waiting to perform for our Lords and Ladies. Some of them are fae creatures from across the various Eledrian worlds. Most of them, however, are human Obligates. Like me.

The musicians and their instruments dominate one side of the gallery, plucking away at their strings, puffing away at their pipes, and making a gentle, lulling sort of noise that underscores the rumble of conversation and click of horns from below. I spot two empty chairs just on the other side of a young lute player and make my way through the gathering to take my place, leaving an empty chair between us. From here, I peer through the gauzy curtains into the hall below.

There are nine great, low tables with lounging cushions on which the Lords and Ladies sprawl in elegant ease. Their glamours are shining—so many different sets of horns, some gold-plated, some draped in garlands or jewels. Their garments are all revealing, making my own dress seem quite demure by comparison. Most of the men are bare-chested, and the women wear gowns that somehow combine copious amounts of fabric with very little practical coverage.

King Lodírhal's table is set higher than the rest, and the king himself sits in a throne-like chair. Unlike most of his guests, he wears a robe of claret velvet trimmed in gold, with wide bell sleeves that fall from his elbows and spill over the arms of his chair. His golden hair is braided back from his face, emphasizing the severe lines of his cheekbones and jaw.

I rarely catch a glimpse of the King of the Court of Dawn. When I see him now, my throat tightens and my veins throb with a sudden onrush of fear. I can't explain it. Something about the king immediately triggers every flight instinct in my body. It's all I can do to grip the edge of my little gallery seat and keep from leaping up and elbowing through the other performers in a bid for freedom.

Instead I turn my gaze from Lodírhal to my mistress, seated at his right hand. Princess Estrilde isn't wearing horns tonight—she's chosen to sport a pair of delicate antlers, each prong tipped in silver and dripping with little gems. By the way she sits, I can tell how aware she is of all the watchful gazes of the guests, studying her, cursing themselves for not anticipating this newest current in the tides of fashion. By tomorrow, the halls of Aurelis palace will be crowded with antlered fae.

Ivor sits on the king's left hand. I try not to look at him but . . . gods above, I'm only human! Like the other lords, he's not wearing a shirt, but has donned nothing more than an intricate gold chain and capelet that brings even more attention to the breadth of his shoulders. As always, his glamours do not disguise his scars, which are prominently displayed across the chiseled muscles of his torso and arms. His hair is long and loose, parting gently around a pair of subtle ivory horns.

I can't help but notice how neither Ivor nor Estrilde look at each other. They both seem to be utterly engrossed in conversations taking place on their opposite sides. I'm sure this is a pointed maneuver on Estrilde's part—she would die before she let anyone catch her *trying* to command Lord Ivor's attention. As for Ivor . . . I really can't tell if he's as indifferent to Estrilde as he seems. Or am I foolishly letting my own wishes misinterpret what I'm seeing?

I drop my gaze to the book in my lap. I must not indulge myself. Just because I'm hidden away up here doesn't mean Ivor won't somehow learn of my secret scrutiny. This gallery is stuffed with Obligates, several of whom no doubt belong to him. Any one of them might bear tales. The last thing I need is for the gorgeous fae lord to learn that I spent the whole of the feast ogling him.

There's no sign of the Prince anywhere, I note somewhat belatedly. Had he not said he'd come to Aurelis specifically for this event? Perhaps he intends to make a grand entrance of some kind. That would be in character, I suspect.

"Can you see it?" someone whispers behind me.

"Not sure," someone whispers back. "I mean, perhaps he doesn't look wholly well. But *dying?* I didn't think a fae king *could* die."

"It's because of his Fatebound," says a third voice. "You know, the queen? When she died, everyone said Lodírhal wouldn't last much longer."

"Five years is a good bit of time."

"Not for a fae, it's not. He's withering fast by their standards." This voice belongs to a woman, low, husky, and lightly accented. "I'm told he won't last the year out. That's the price of the Fatebond."

My brow puckers slightly. I peer out through the curtains again, down at the king. I can't see any signs of sickness or withering about him, but then, I don't have any magic. Perhaps it's more visible to magically attuned eyes.

"They say," someone whispers behind me, "the king has ordered the feast tonight because he intends to name his heir."

Now that is interesting! I sit up a little straighter, carefully turning my head just slightly to better hear. I don't usually take much interest in the courtly intrigues of the Lords and Ladies, but my mistress, Princess Estrilde, is the king's only niece. I know she hopes to become Queen of the Dawn Court. Tonight could well prove the culmination of all her hopes and schemes.

"His heir?" a third voice butts in. "Doesn't the king have a son?"

I catch my breath. I know that voice.

My blood runs suddenly cold.

"Oh, yes," the woman answers. I can almost hear her sneer. "But no one expects him to make the *prince,* of all people, his heir. What a notion!"

"And why not?" that new voice demands. "Is he unsightly? Uncouth? Does he have two heads or a rat's tail?"

"He's half *human,*" the woman replies. "How can a hybrid rule the Court of Dawn? Surely the Lords and Ladies would revolt."

"Well, if the fellow is as *revolting* as all that, I suppose we can't blame them."

"I didn't say he was—"

"Are you going to keep plucking away at that same note over and over again, boy? You're like a little fly, pluck-pluck-pluck, buzz-buzz-buzz. And what is this dolorous tune? Are you playing for a funeral or a feast? I'd heard the king was *dying,* not *dead.*"

There's a sudden bustle behind me, and something bumps the back of my chair. I turn, catching my breath, just as a blue sleeve flashes before my eyes.

The next moment, Prince Castien himself has snatched a lute from the hands of a musician two chairs away from me and plunked down on the seat between us. He leans back in the chair, his legs stretched out, crossed at the ankle, and begins tuning the lute with expert fingers. "Gods above me, what a sour-faced lot you are!" he exclaims, casting a glance around. His eyes flick over me only momentarily, hardly long enough to see me, before sweeping back to the folks clustered behind me instead. "Aren't you supposed to be the entertainment? You look about as lively as a rain-drenched peacock, all your pretty plumes dragging in the mud. No wonder the folk below are such dull company."

He strums the strings of the lute, making them sing out far too bright and loud above the ongoing lull of music from the other musicians. The music director, standing a little to one side, squawks a wordless protest and waves his baton in sharp, shushing moments. The Prince casts him a quelling glare and strums on even louder. Then he bursts into song:

> *"I strolled through the fields, tra la, tra la*
> *And she strolled at my side, so fair.*
> *I patted her rump, and she swatted my face*
> *With her bounty of chestnut hair.*
> *Then she jumped o'er the hedge and galloped apace,*

And that's how I lost my brown mare, tra la!
And that's how I lost my brown mare!"

His voice rings out from the gallery, echoing out over the hall below. A susurrus of voices erupts below. The Lords and Ladies, interrupted from their dignified feasting, begin to growl and grumble.

"My lord!" The music director nearly falls over himself, his voice hissing with an effort not to shout. "My lord, this is the entertainment gallery. For *humans*. If you intend to join the feast, the stair is just over—"

The Prince lowers his lute and fixes the director with a stare. I can't say exactly what kind of stare. It isn't stern, it isn't dismissive. Perhaps faintly amused. Whatever it is, it stops the poor man mid-sentence. "I haven't been invited to the feast," the Prince says smoothly. "But not to worry, my good fellow! I am, in fact, part of the entertainment, though not until later this evening. In the meanwhile, don't let me disturb you. Carry on with your little funeral dirges."

With that he tosses the lute back to the boy beside him. The boy scowls darkly, but the Prince answers this with a grin that brings a wrathful flush to the boy's cheeks and makes him drop his head. He hunches over his lute and, at the director's beckoning, begins playing the slow, solemn chamber music once again.

Down below, sounds of disturbance subside. The feasting returns to its decorous patterns.

The Prince crosses his arms and heaves a sigh. "It's not every day one attends a feast in Aurelis quite so tedious," he says, speaking out of the side of his mouth. "Ordinarily, I expect the pretty folk to be in a mad flurry of frenetic dancing and battling and battle-dancing, with copious amounts of drink on the flow, and far too much noise to be able to hear these fellows at their work." He spins a finger to indicate the musicians.

Is he talking to me? He must be. As though our little encounter in the library has made us . . . acquaintances? I don't know how to respond. Does no one else here realize who he truly is?

He peers out through the curtain. The line of his jaw hardens slightly, and his lips thin. He draws a slow breath through his nostrils and tilts his head back. Then, without looking at me: "You look very nice this evening."

"What?" I blink. "Did you . . . Do you mean . . . ?"

He waves a vague hand, still without actually looking. "The color. It suits you."

Heat roars up my skin. Before I can begin to think of a response, a sudden sharp clap of hands sounds below. The musicians stop playing at once, and the next moment, Princess Estrilde's voice echoes against the walls and ceiling:

"Lords and Ladies of Aurelis, honored brethren, fellow servants of our great and glorious King Lodírhal, may he shine with the life of a thousand suns! Tonight, I bring you a simple entertainment, token of my esteem and affection for all of you, and most especially, for my beloved uncle."

She's laying it on thick. Everyone knows her affection for King Lodírhal is mercenary at best. But then, that pretty well sums up the vast majority of alliances and intrigues within the Court of Dawn. I doubt Lodírhal takes offense.

"For the delight of your ears and the invigorating of your imaginations," Estrilde continues, "I give to you a work of human poetry. A tale of love and longing and ultimate loss, performed by my own Obligate."

There's a murmur below. It sounds approving. The fae do love a good reading.

My stomach plunges.

"You're up." The Prince beside me elbows me in the arm. I give him a startled look, but he's still not looking at me. *Distinctly* not looking at me. "Break a leg."

From a human, it would be a well-wishing. From him . . . is that a threat?

I rise, pulling my bounteous skirts to fall a little more gracefully, my book of poetry held tight against my pounding heart. The other entertainers make way for me to the end of the gallery and the little stair that leads down to an empty place below. I wish I could stay up in the gallery to do my reading, tucked out of sight. But it's simply not how things are done.

Princess Estrilde waits for me at the base of the stair. This surprises me. I expected her to return to her seat. Does she intend to give me some last-minute instruction? To check my choice of poem before letting me perform? She doesn't look at me, but very carefully looks over and around me. I am far too unimportant to merit a direct gaze.

But when I come to a halt before her—my head only just reaching the top of her shoulder—she reaches out suddenly and catches me by the throat. I start and try to draw back, my heart thudding. What is happening?

"Hold still, little fool," Estrilde growls.

I feel the force of my Obligation freezing my limbs. There's no resisting her. So I stand in place, and her fingers tighten around my throat, and her eyes, usually so resistant to seeing me, stare into mine.

Something reaches inside of me. Like a knife digging into my head. A gasp escapes my lips, and with it a strange *tension* I don't quite understand. It's as though I've been flexing a muscle for years without realizing it, and suddenly it's relaxed. Something moves in my veins, a warmth I can't describe. The sensation is momentarily very strong, but fades with the next breath.

"There," Estrilde says, withdrawing her hand and stepping back a pace. "That should do it. Read on, Obligate." She turns from me and wafts back to her place at the king's table, smiling and nodding to friends and foes alike as she goes.

And I'm left in that empty space below the stair, very aware of all the eyes not *quite* on me, very aware of the bright light focused on my face, casting my shadow long at my back. I touch my throat, feeling that place where her icy fingers had gripped.

What did she just do to me? Or . . . or *undo* to me?

The silence has lasted too long. I can't just stand here. It's time to read.

Fingers trembling, I fumble to the marked place in Bronwin's book, dropping the bookmark to the floor. I stop myself from crouching to pick it up, remembering my dignity just in time. Holding the book out on my arm, I clear my throat. Then I lift my gaze. Just a for a moment.

Ivor is watching me. The only pair of eyes in that whole room, fixed right on me.

He smiles.

Heart pounding, I focus on the swimming words on the page. Oh gods, help me get through this!

"The Sorry Tale of Devdon and His Ladylove, Rosalin the Fair." I read, my voice trembling. I clear my throat again, adjust the set of the book, and begin the first few words:

> "The breeze was a lilting lullaby
> Among the lilies bright
> The moon was a lady's mirror
> Reflecting the pale starlight."

Though my heart is still racing, soon the familiar cadence lulls me, and I fall into the rhythm of Bronwin's language.

> "The stream was a dancer's ribbon
> Trailing o'er green-grown hills,

> *And Lord Devdon's heart was a-dancing,*
> *Dancing, O! a-dancing.*
> *Lord Devdon's heart was a-dancing*
> *As he strode 'cross vale and rill."*

Something is happening.

At first I hardly notice it, caught up as I am in the stanzas on the page. But as I read on, line after line, a sensation burns inside me, bubbling along my veins, across my tongue. I keep on reading without pause. Thankfully I know this ballad by heart, because more and more, I'm finding my eyes flicking up, glancing out at the folk I'm here to entertain.

They're watching me. With rapt attention.

Me—whom they never look at unless absolutely necessary.

Almost every pair of eyes in that room is fixed on my face with such concentration, it could burn me up like fire. King Lodírhal alone keeps his gazed downturned, but even so, I am painfully conscious of his *awareness*.

Something is moving around me. Shadowy images seem to be taking shape on the walls, in the air. Silhouettes, almost like paper puppets, but more lifelike, more nimble, acting out the words as I read them. Is it magic? Is Estrilde doing this? A little trick to augment my performance? But this doesn't feel like fae magic. It feels like . . . like . . . like it's coming from me . . .

BOOM!

I choke on a yelp. Immediately the shadowy images fade to

nothing, and the room is once more bright with shining lantern glow. Much to my relief, The Lords and Ladies turn their gazes from me to the door which has just slammed open. I look as well, my mouth still open with unspoken words.

In the doorway—looking rumpled and small, his square spectacles perched on his nose, his beard a cloud of frizz and his hair a wild mane—stands Thaddeus Creakle.

"Noswraith!" His voice echoes across the hall. "There's a Noswraith in Aurelis Library!"

5

THE FEASTING HALL ERUPTS. LORDS AND LADIES alike scream as they surge to their feet, goblets crashing, cushions flying, skirts flaring, horns clattering against one another.

I stand mutely in place, staring at the confusion. What is going on? I can't see Thaddeus anymore; when all the feasting guests jumped up, they blocked my view of the door. What was it he said? Something had gotten into the library? Something worse than pixies, I'd wager.

"*Silence.*"

The word rebounds off the walls. Not a shout, but a command spoken with such force, everyone in the room freezes.

King Lodírhal rises from his place at the table. He plants one fist into the tabletop to support himself. For the first time, I glimpse the weakness the others whispered about. It takes him a great deal of strength simply to maintain an upright position. But there's nothing weak about the look of disgust he shoots his assembled guests.

Estrilde stands beside the king, gripping a long knife which she must have hidden on her person somewhere . . . though where in that skin-tight gown of hers, I can't begin to imagine. Ivor is on the king's left, his eyes wide, his jaw set, his nostrils flaring. I don't know that I've ever seen him look afraid. I'm not convinced he's afraid now. But he's definitely uneasy.

Lodírhal opens his mouth. "Be seated, all of you." His words fill the air with more of that potent authority, almost like a spell. "There's no good to be had in a palace-wide panic. Be seated and let us hear what this human has to say for himself."

One by one, the guests return to their places, casting resentful glances everywhere but at the king. Soon I'm able to see Thaddeus again, still standing in the doorway. His face is white as a sheet, and he mops his brow with an already damp handkerchief.

"Whose Obligate is that?" Lodírhal demands, indicating the senior librarian with a wave of one hand.

"Your pardon, my liege." Ivor bows his head. "That one is mine."

"Then bid him approach and explain himself." Lodírhal sinks into his seat, managing to make it look like a graceful slouch and not a sudden giving out of his knees. He leans his head back against the headrest and half-closes his eyes. Golden irises gleam through the slits as he watches Thaddeus, responding to Ivor's gesture, trot into the hall.

"Great king! My master!" Thaddeus says, bowing to Lodírhal and Ivor by turns, then adding an extra bow to Princess Estrilde for good measure. "I have terrible, terrible news. There is a—"

"A Noswraith, yes." Lodírhal sounds bored, an unnerving contrast to the fear-stricken glances his guests are exchanging. "So you said. But are you quite certain of what you think you've seen? I do not hear an uproar of screaming terror outside this hall, nor do I hear walls breaking and foundations shattering to the core. Pardon my incredulity, but I don't wholly believe you."

Thaddeus mops his brow and bobs another quick bow. "It is but a small wraith, great king," he says, his words shaking through his teeth. "But I fear none of my librarians nor I have the skill with which to bind it! It will cause untold destruction unless . . . unless . . ."

"Unless what? Out with it, human!" Lodírhal snarls.

Thaddeus turns. He looks right at me standing at the base of the gallery stair. One trembling finger rises, pointing. "Unless you unbind *her*. Let her catch it for us."

My blood runs cold.

What is he saying? *Unbind* me? Does he mean from my Obligation? No, that doesn't make sense. No fae would ever end an Obligation before its time.

And what is a Noswraith? And how am *I* supposed to catch it?

"Impossible." Lodírhal's cold voice draws my attention back to him. To my horror, he's looking at me now. Once again, I feel that terrible urge to flee, to turn and run with blind terror anywhere but here. I don't know why the king hates me above all other Obligates in his court. But he does. In that moment, I have no doubt that he does.

"That one's powers have been restricted for the safety of all Eledria," the king continues. "By rights, she should have been done to death years ago."

A small gasp escapes my lips. I feel as though I must not be here, as though the king and the senior librarian and all of those staring guests must be looking at someone else. Someone whose skin I might wear, but who certainly can't be *me*.

"It is the only way!" Thaddeus clasps his hands, sinking to his knees. "Please, great king! Think of your wife! Think of good Queen Dasyra! Would she want her beloved collection to fall prey to the ravenous destruction of a Noswraith?"

"Do not invoke my wife's name at me." Lodírhal turns such a look of disgust Thaddeus's way, I'm half surprised the poor old man doesn't transform into a worm on the spot. The king opens his mouth as though to say something more, but Lord Ivor interjects.

"My king, if you would hear my humble opinion?"

Lodírhal gives him a sideward glance. He does not like to be interrupted, but for his favorite he is willing to be lenient. "Yes, Ivor?" he says coldly. "What have you to say to all this?"

"Only that Obligate Clara's loyalty is certainly as great as any power she may possess. I have interacted with her myself on numerous occasions and can personally vouch for her trustworthiness."

I don't dare look at Estrilde. I don't dare look anywhere. I drop my gaze to my feet and keep it there. But I'm all too aware of the eyes fixed on me. My mistress. The king. Other guests crouched in fear at their places round the tables. And Ivor. Ivor is looking at me too. With an expression I cannot bear to see.

The king's voice breaks through the thundering in my ears. "Estrilde," he growls, "you hold the control of this Obligate's powers, do you not?"

"I do, Uncle," Princess Estrilde responds. Her words sound like slow-dripping poison.

"Then lift it."

Estrilde's eyes flash to his face. "But Uncle—"

"Do not question me." Lodírhal raises a hand like a shield, deflecting her protests. "Do as you're told. We can't have a Noswraith loose in Aurelis, can we?"

Estrilde looks as though she wants to say more. She holds her uncle's gaze for a long, terrible moment. In that moment, I see anew the power that simmers inside her. She may not be queen yet. But looking at her side-by-side with her uncle, you can see that queenship is her right, her destiny. Beside even the glorious Lodírhal, she is breathtaking. And terrifying.

But Lodírhal does not break her gaze. Finally, Estrilde rises smoothly. Still holding the knife in one hand, she turns without a word and approaches me. She's so graceful, like a panther stalking its prey. I fight the urge to drop my book, pick up the edge of my skirt, and scramble to the gallery above. But I can't flee my own mistress. I am her Obligate."

Estrilde reaches me, her eyes burning into mine. I'm so unused to her looking directly at me that it's almost worse than the feel of her fingers once more gripping my throat in a chokehold. I try not to struggle but can't help a little whimper. "Silence," she snarls, and the command is enough to stop any further sound I might make. I feel again that sense of something stabbing down inside my head. Something sharp, sleek, and sure.

And then, I am . . . *unlocked.*

I'd felt a small swell of sensation before, right before the reading. This is different. This is like a rush, a flood through my veins, burning with light and eager destruction. It's so overpowering, were it not for Estrilde's hold on my neck, I would surely drop to my knees and begin convulsing. As it is, I stand there, staring into her eyes. My limbs go numb, and I distinctly hear my copy of Bronwin's poems fall to the floor with a *thud.* There's so much power and, simultaneously, so much weakness coursing together inside me, enough to tear me in two.

Then, like the sudden silence after a clap of thunder, it stops. I stand there, sweat on my brow, blinking dazedly into the eyes of my mistress.

Estrilde nods, her mouth grim. She lets go of me, shaking her hand as though she's just touched something disgusting. "It's done," she says, her lip curling slightly. "For now. Go. Do what this little bearded person wants of you. Then return to me directly."

"Thank you!" Thaddeus Creakle yelps. He turns to the king

once more. "May I have your leave to depart, great king?"

Lodírhal nods and waves a dismissive hand. It's enough to send Thaddeus scampering to me. The senior librarian squeezes my hands. I try to focus on him, try to make my dizzy vision take the double image before me and bring it into one whole. All I can see are glinting lights shining from two pairs of spectacles and the blur of two white beards.

"Come, Miss Darlington," he says, tugging my arms. "We haven't a moment to waste."

"But Mister Creakle," I gasp as I trot behind the senior librarian, holding my skirts out of my way with both hands. "What is a . . . a Noswraith?"

"You don't know?" He casts a nervous look over his shoulder, then shakes his head, his lips bunching behind his mustache. "No, of course, you wouldn't. They took that memory from you too."

A cold feeling washes over me, like a phantom passing over the site of my future grave. Gooseprickles run up and down my bare arms, and suddenly the twilight purple that passes as night here in Aurelis feels much deeper, darker.

All of us Obligates are aware that the fae suppress our memories. We're all of us Pledge-Breakers—somewhere along the way, we managed to fall on the wrong side of the delicate treaty lines set in place between our world and the wild, wicked, wonderful worlds of Eledria. Most of us probably didn't intend any wrongdoing. The treaty was established so very long ago, no one really remembers it in the human world anymore. But the laws still stand. And they are binding.

Our Lords and Ladies do not want us to remember exactly *how* we broke the Pledge, however. Such knowledge is dangerous. Such knowledge might indicate vulnerability on their part. So those memories are simply locked down inside us, inaccessible. I've never thought of myself as one with particularly manipulated memories. After all, they didn't remove any of my family—Mama or my brother, Oscar. And I still remember Danny and his sister, Kitty, vividly enough. Even Dad is there in my brain, lurking. Much as I sometimes wish he wasn't.

What else is down in there, suppressed behind my mistress's enchantments? Suppressed like this strange new sensation I find bubbling in my veins. This thing that feels like . . . *power* . . .

We pass few others on our way to the library, but the closer we come to the library doors, the more Obligates cluster in small groups, whispering furtively behind their hands. They eye me in my glamourous gown and my foolish horned headdress. What a sight I must look to all of them, wearing the garb of our Lords and Ladies! Like a pig trying to pass for pretty by wearing a strand of pearls.

Lydia and George stand at the library doors and seem to be holding them shut. "Is it still in there?" Thaddeus asks, wheezing heavily. That trot across the palace was nearly too much for a man of his age."

Lydia nods, her eyes very wide. George merely blinks dully.

"Very good. There's still a chance then." Thaddeus turns to me, takes a few panting gasps, then says, "It was last seen in the modern poetry section, second story. I don't know how much damage it's caused." He wrings his hands again, rolling his eyes ceilingward as though in prayer. "Gods on high, it shouldn't have gotten through at all! Something must be wrong for it to have escaped the Doomed City."

He tosses these words at me as though I have any idea what he's talking about. I open my mouth, trying to decide which question to ask first, but he's already reaching into the front of his vest and pulling something out. The next moment, he shoves a fountain pen and a small leather-bound book into my hands. "Here," he says. "Write it back into the pages."

I look down at the book, the pen, then gape back at Thaddeus. "Write . . . write it . . . *what?*"

"Write it back into the pages," he repeats. "The Noswraith. It needs to be bound again. So write it back into the pages."

I'm not sure my jaw could open wider if I tried. I close it with a *clunk,* lick my dry lips, and shake my head. "But Mister Creakle, *how do I do that?* I don't even know what a Noswraith is! Much less how to . . . how to . . ."

"It's a Nightmare." Thaddeus's eyes are pitying. Which is unnerving under the circumstances. "Don't worry—some of the knowledge will creep back now that the suppression is lifted.

You'll know what to do when you see it. At least, I hope you will. I've never done it myself."

"You've never . . . Mister Creakle!" This last comes out a weak protest, for the senior librarian has suddenly motioned to my associates. They pull open the doors, and Thaddeus takes hold of my arm, ushering me through with surprising strength for a man of his age. I just have time to gasp another "Mister Creakle!"

Then the doors shut in my face.

I stand alone in the gold and white foyer of the vast Aurelis Library.

It's amazing how quickly a familiar space can turn foreign and threatening. The library has become my home in this strange world in which I find myself. A haven in a realm where otherwise I don't belong. I've been in the library alone plenty of times. Only that morning, for example, when I'd come at daybreak to open it before my fellow librarians arrived.

But I've never been here past sundown before. In this weak, purpling, twilit gloom pouring in from the high glass dome overhead, what ought to be familiar suddenly feels terribly unknown. Dangerous.

And somewhere in here with me is a Noswraith. A . . . a nightmare? A shiver rolls down my spine. I look at the book Thaddeus handed me and, chewing on my dry lips, flip the cover open. It's blank inside. Each page, totally blank.

"Write it back into the pages," I whisper and shake my head. "What in the worlds does that *mean?*"

As though in response to my question, sudden heat burns

in my veins once more. I tense, but the feeling isn't exactly unpleasant. Along with the heat, there's a strange sort of itch. In my brain. In my fingers. An itch I can't understand, though it does feel oddly familiar . . .

Well, I can't stand here dithering all night. I close the book with a snap, tuck it under one arm, and set out across the foyer, past the big front desk and on to the center of the circular space beneath the dome. Here the library branches off into six main parts, like the points of a star. Behind me lie the foyer and front entrance. Straight ahead of me lie histories—mostly human, as they are written by humans, but with a good scattering of Eledrian sagas as well. Fiction resides on the righthand side, non-fiction, on the left. A stairway leading up to the second level will take me to poetry, both ancient and modern.

I turn my gaze up that way, peering at the balcony rail and the shadowy impression of shelving beyond. Thaddeus said the Noswraith was last seen up there. Is it still—

A growl ripples through the stillness.

I shrink back, hands clutching my pen like a dagger. There was something strange, something wrong, something . . . *gloopy* about that growl. I don't know how else to describe it. It wasn't animal, not at all. It sounded vaguely wet. Slimy.

I stare up at the railing, my heart ramming in my throat. Is that a shadow I spy, lurching along on the other side of the banisters? Something long, low, and ponderous.

Oh, gracious heavens above me. The last thing, the very last thing I want in all the worlds, is to climb those stairs.

I swallow, feeling once more the tightening of Princess Estrilde's fingers around my throat. *"Do what this little bearded person wants of you,"* she'd said. That's enough to call upon the bonds of my Obligation. To fight, to resist, will mean to suffer pain and, ultimately, lead to an increase in my terms of service. Then I'll never get home.

I draw a long, slow breath and hold it. Thaddeus has faith in me. Faith enough to send him running across the palace and risking King Lodírhal's wrath by bursting in on a feast. He believes I can do this, thinks I can stop this thing. So why shouldn't I believe in myself?

Gathering my skirts, I make for the stairs, moving quickly so I won't have time to change my mind. They spiral up into shadows, and my hand trembles as I grip the polished rail. My slipper-shod feet make no sound, and I hope the thing waiting on the floor above won't hear me coming.

I reach the top of the staircase and peer around the banister into the second floor. Before me, a series of two dozen bookshelf ends stretches into the distance; and between the bookshelves, long aisles lead into more labyrinthine turns and passages. A narrow walkway runs between the shelf ends and the balcony rail overlooking the circular space below. For visitors inclined to curl up for a little page-turning or a nap, a few comfortable chairs nestle into odd corners here and there. It's all so familiar. And so ominous.

I hold my breath, straining my librarian ears. Is that grunting I hear? Just down aisle five? I swallow hard, then step from the stair into the walkway. It feels foolish to be stalking some unknown monster with only a book and a pen in my hand. But would I feel any better if Thaddeus had handed me a sword? I'd probably end up cutting my own leg off.

I reach aisle five and, heart thudding, breath hitched, peer into the shadowy space. Something is there.

It takes a moment for my eyes to adjust enough to see it. At first, all I can get are impressions. Impressions of size—about the same size as a large dog. Then a vague sense of shape—long, squat, dragging on the ground. Like a fat slug. But at one end, two shoulders and two long arms emerge. One of those arms ends in a long-fingered hand, the other in a broken stump. A head of sorts hangs from the end of a long, skinny neck. It's vaguely humanoid, but without hair or ears or any defining feature that I can see from this angle. Just sagging flesh. It's turned away from me in that moment, so I can't see a face. If it even has one.

A Nightmare.

Thaddeus wasn't kidding. This thing—whatever it is—is like something out of the very darkest dreams.

It noses its way along the lower shelves, now and then lifting its stump arm to nudge at the volumes, leaving smears of slime or blood or pus as it goes. It doesn't seem to know what it's looking for, but hisses and burbles wetly, pulling its heavy body along behind it. I think it's . . . *melted*. Like maybe it used to be man-shaped but has been slowly sagging into a puddle of living wax.

Suddenly it stops, pulls out one volume, which drops to the

floor in front of it. The creature—the Noswraith—turns pages slowly with dripping fingers, grunting, and dribbling slime from its sagging jaw. The book itself begins to melt, the pages and cover puddling until there's nothing left but a pool of soggy pulp.

Then the Noswraith reaches for another book.

My heart hitches in my breast. I can't let this go on! I can't let this . . . this *thing* destroy any more of my books right in front of me.

"Write it back into the pages."

What if . . . what if . . . ?

My fingers burn, trembling as I adjust my grip on the fountain pen. I clench my teeth, step back a pace, and open the blank book across my arm. With a quick shake of the pen, I plant the nib to the top of the page, hesitate a moment . . . and begin to write:

I discover the Melted Man in the fifth aisle. He's pulling books from the shelves and seems to be trying to read them. But everything he touches melts.

With a few flicks of my pen, I dash off a description of the thing before me. Doing so doesn't seem to help anything. Or maybe it does? Maybe there *is* something happening as I put words to page. I'm not sure what, exactly. It's like *threads*. Little filament threads stretching out from me into that aisle, reaching for that awful creature. Is this what Thaddeus had in mind? Is this the skill he thought would come back to me when the moment came?

Maybe I can work with this. Maybe I can do more than capture the moment as I see it. Maybe I can alter the moment itself.

All of a sudden—I write—*he begins to shrink. At first, it isn't much, so little the Melted Man doesn't even notice. Slowly, slowly, the long fat tail contracts, and those awful forelimbs retreat into the shoulder sockets.*

It's working. I don't know how. But as I glance up from the page, I can see the effect of my words. The Noswraith *is* shrinking—slowly at first, then more quickly.

Soon—I write—*it's no bigger than a cat.*

I've scarcely lifted my pen from dotting that last period, when the Noswraith abruptly lifts its head. It snuffles, a hideous, wet sound, turning its heavy head on the end of its long neck one way then the other.

Then it turns that neck all the way around over its shoulders and looks directly at me.

It snarls.

6

THERE USED TO BE FEATURES ON THAT FACE. I CAN still just see the barest impression. Two eyes. A nose. A mouth.

Now one eye drags halfway down a sagging, dripping cheek. The other eye is nearly lost behind the drip of a heavy brow. The nose is nothing but a long dark streak, the nostrils blended into one another. And the mouth . . . the mouth . . .

The mouth drops open. Instead of teeth, it has long drips of slime. But somehow, I know they'll bite just as hard all the same.

For a moment, I can't do anything but stare. I can't believe it. I *don't want to believe it.*

Then, it's lunging straight at me.

How it moves so fast, I can't begin to guess. It hauls itself on those two, bowed arms and slithers that fat, blob of a body, quick as a snake. Before it reaches the end of the aisle, it crouches, its chest close to the ground, then pushes off, somehow propelling itself through the air. Streaking straight at my face.

On impulse, I pull up my book like a shield. But the Noswraith sails right over the top of the cover and connects with my head, knocking me flat. I lay sprawled on my back, the world spinning around me. But wait! Why am I not covered in melted, slimy body? Why am I not pressed beneath weight? Why am I—

A shudder ripples through my body, through my soul. I'm slowly torn in two.

I try to scream. But it's no use. The breath is completely stolen from my body as I'm split between realities. Half of me is still in the library, standing with book in hand, pen at the ready, trying to write.

The other half of me is on my back in a world of darkness.

I blink, gasp, turn my head. I can still discern the impression of bookshelves and the balcony rail behind me. But it's all through a haze of whirling shadows like smoke. I shake my head, trying to clear my vision. It's no use.

Where is the Noswraith? It hit me straight on . . . then vanished. Is it . . . ? Could have . . . ?

Gods help me, did it jump *into my mind?*

Before I have time to think this through, I hear that wet, gurgling growl. Pushing onto my elbows, I turn and see the Noswraith snarling at me from the end of another aisle. Its melted face is the only thing clear in this whole dark world. Bracing its forelegs, it pushes off again, rushing at me.

I just have time to sit up. My flailing hands catch up my book beside me. The Noswraith bears down, and I swing my arm as hard as I can.

The book hits the monster's face with a thick, squelching sound. The Noswraith shrieks and falls to one side. Its ugly form shrinks into itself until it's once more the size of a cat. It lifts its head. The half of the face that I struck is smashed flat. One eye flashes with ferocious hatred.

Back into the pages . . .

I don't stop to think.

Acting on pure instinct, I open my book wide and shove the pages down over that misshapen head. All my weight in my arms, I push and push. Is it working? I think it is! I think I feel the being disappearing, absorbing into the pages.

With a shriek and a spurt of slime, the Noswraith shakes itself, throwing off my balance. I fall to one side, pulling the book with me. In that moment of reprieve, the creature streaks away, disappearing down the nearest aisle.

"No!" I snarl and struggle to my feet, fighting against the long golden skirts tangling my legs. "No, no, no, you don't!"

My feet slipping and squishing in blobs of slime, I run down the aisle in hot pursuit. It's got a good start on me, however. I watch its fat tail end disappear at the end of the aisle. Snarling, I redouble my pace. The world around me loses more and more definition as I focus on the end of the aisle. I'm surrounded in shadows, in blackness.

But I'm going to catch that monster if it's the last thing I do.

I reach the end of the aisle and turn right. To my surprise, the Noswraith is just the next aisle over, using its misshapen hand to scramble up the shelf. It reaches the top and cranes its neck around to snarl at me again. Its smacked face is partially settled back into natural lines, but the eye, glaring and savage, is still out of place, positioned over its nose.

With a shake of its hairless head, it turns and gallops—for lack of a better word—along the top of the shelf, out of reach.

I clench my jaw, a growl squeezing through my teeth. I run as well, keeping pace with the fiend, until we reach the end of the shelf. There the Noswraith makes a flying leap for the next shelf over, its fat tail wagging in the air behind it. It miscalculates the distance, however, and hits about a foot too low.

The whole shelf teeters, tilts. Then it falls, crashing into the next shelf over, which crashes into the next, on and on in a cascade of destruction. I scream, covering my ears. Shadow-books fly and disintegrate into the darkness all around me.

But when the last shelf falls, the Noswraith is still lying where it landed, stunned.

With a snarl, I leap. It turns to me, but I whack it again across the head and bring one foot down hard on its tail. It squishes under the pressure. So gross! A horrified yelp bursts from my throat.

But I don't let up. I open my book again and, flinging myself bodily over the slimy mass, shove the open pages down over that awful head. It struggles, squirms. I won't let up. I force the book down further, further, covering the head, down the neck, to the shoulders. Soon there's nothing left but wriggling tail.

With a desperate heave, I drag the book the last few inches and slam it shut.

I come to with my back up against the balcony rail.

My feet stick out at angles in front of me, one foot bare. A tear in my slinky skirt reveals bare skin all the way to the knee. I clutch the book up against my stomach, and my whole body heaves, trying to breathe.

With a choking gurgle, I let out a gust of air then drag in another lungful.

What just happened? What did I do?

Images dance in my head—strange images, nightmarish and unfocused. I think I see a hideous, melted face and writhing shadows overlaying the world. It's all so dark, so terrible, I squeeze my eyes shut and try to force those images out and away.

When I dare look around again, I'm still just sitting on the second floor of the library. The bookshelves in front of me aren't toppled over, their contents aren't scattered. I see the melted book lying on the floor partway down the aisle. Otherwise there doesn't seem to be any major destruction.

Slowly, carefully, half-afraid of what I'll find, I drop the book from my stomach into my lap and peep under the cover. The words written there are my own looping handwriting:

There used to be features on that face. I can still just see the barest impression. Two eyes. A nose. A mouth. Now one eye drags halfway down a sagging, dripping cheek.

My jaw slowly drops open. Everything I'm reading . . . it's all what just happened. To me. Isn't it? I'm not entirely certain. What was dream and what was real? I don't know. But I *know* this story, even though I don't have any actual memory of *writing* it. I *know* this story because I just *lived* it.

Or did I? How could something so bizarre be real? And how could I have lived it *and* written it down? Or had the act of writing it somehow made it real?

Something ripples. I jump and stare. There's a lump of movement pushing against the page, just under the words. Like it's *inside* the book, trying to burst out.

I don't stop to think. I slam the cover shut and press the book to my chest, both arms wrapped around it tight. There's another bulge, a push. Then stillness. For the moment.

I sit there, mouth open, breath ragged, questions raging in my head. So many questions for which I can find no answers.

Thaddeus, Lydia, George, and the other librarians watch in wide-eyed silence as I emerge from the library. I come to a stop in the doorway and look slowly around at the lot of them. What do they know? About me? About this thing inside the book I'm carrying tucked under my arm? About these sensations coursing in my limbs which sprung to life when Estrilde did . . . whatever it was she did to me? Do they know anything? Or are they as ignorant as I am?

Why do they keep looking at me *like that?*

Carefully fixing my usual non-committal smile in place, I march over to Thaddeus and hold the book out to him. "Here, Mister Creakle. I wrote it into the pages. The Noswraith, I mean. Just like you asked."

He makes no move to take the book. He stares at it like I've just offered him a spider.

"The damage to the library doesn't seem to be great," I continue, pleased with how brisk and businesslike my tone is. "A few books lost, I'm afraid."

Thaddeus nods slowly. "Th-thank you, Miss Darlington. You have my gratitude and that of every Aurelis librarian."

He's definitely not going to take the book.

I tuck it back under my arm, wincing a little when I feel another disconcerting ripple of movement beneath the cover. "I think I ought to return to my mistress now," I say, recalling Estrilde's final instruction.

"Of course, of course." Thaddeus waves a hand, licking his

lips nervously beneath his brush of beard. "I wouldn't want to delay you."

Apparently he's not going back with me either.

I set off on my own back through the cavernous passages leading to Biroris Hall. I don't meet anyone as I go, but I have the creeping suspicion people are ducking into hiding just seconds before I round each turn. Why they would do this, I can't explain. I'm nothing but a lowly Obligate. Not worth their notice, certainly not worth their fear.

I shake my head and grit my teeth hard. It doesn't matter. It doesn't! In another few moments, Estrilde will put back into place whatever restrictions she's bound me with these last five years. With any luck, she'll suppress my memories of this evening as well, and I won't have to think about any of this. About that awful, melted, monstrous face. About that shadowy world lying so close to this one. About the hatred in King Lodírhal's eyes when he said that by rights, I should have been killed long ago.

About the look on Ivor's face when he vouched for my loyalty . . .

No! I don't want to think about any of it! I know my place here. I know the rules of the Obligates: Never anger the fae. Never trust the fae. And, sure as the gods are living, never, ever, ever *love* the fae.

I'm not doing too well with any of those rules just now.

All the noble guests are still seated at their various tables when I reenter the feasting hall. No one is eating. No one is laughing or talking. All are waiting in silent suspense, their eyes fixed on the door. Stepping into that space is like stepping into a giant spiderweb waiting to ensnare every limb.

I keep my head high. Still holding the book against my heart, I march across the hall to the table where King Lodírhal sits, my mistress and Lord Ivor on either side of him. I don't look at them but sink into a deep curtsy before the king and slide the book onto the table without a word.

"It is done then?" King Lodírhal asks. For a moment, I almost catch a trace of trembling weakness in his voice. But I might be imagining that.

"It is done, great king," I reply.

"There now!" Lord Ivor declares. I can feel him smiling at me, though I cannot raise my face to see it. "What did I tell you? The loyalty of this Obligate is surely beyond question!"

"It doesn't matter," Lodírhal snarls. "She is, as I have already stated, far too powerful to keep. Estrilde, my dear, I'm afraid you must give her up."

Estrilde snorts. "Though I would never dream of contradicting my esteemed uncle," she says, in a voice that strongly implies the opposite, "I have a contract with this human. A *signed* contract. The laws of Obligation are binding. Not even you, most beloved king, may gainsay them."

"Is that so?" I glance up and see the king's hands curling into fists on the armrests of his chair.

"It is a *written* law." Estrilde smiles prettily. "The spell is unbreakable save at great loss to he who breaks it."

"Perhaps," Lodírhal growls, "the loss would be worth the gain."

"Come now!" Ivor interjects, his voice a welcome relief from the tigerish growls of the other two. "Surely we cannot feel anything but gratitude to the Obligate who has done us so great a service. It has been many a long age since a Noswraith penetrated the boundaries of Aurelis. Were it not for her abilities, we should even now be at the mercy of unimaginable terrors."

"There is truth to what you say." Lodírhal turns his gaze from Estrilde back to me. I really wish he wouldn't. I can't see any gratitude in his expression. "A Noswraith. In Aurelis! It should not be possible. How did it come to pass? How did it—"

"I may have the answer for you."

At the sound of that bright voice echoing from above, every head in the room turns, including mine. Every neck cranes, every eye gazing to the top of the gallery stair.

There stands the Prince in full view of the assembly. Though it may be a trick of the light and the angle, he looks taller, broader, more generally impressive. His hair flows thick and dark over his shoulders, and his robes, which I had taken before as humble, simple, are now exquisitely cut and elaborately embroidered in intricate patterns of silver and gold. He wears a dark stone crown on his head, the points rising like a mouthful of teeth. Beneath that crown, his brow is slightly puckered, and his mouth curves in a grin that doesn't quite seem pleasant.

"Good evening, Father," he says, his voice ringing against the ceiling and high walls. "I seem to have arrived at a most propitious moment. This is quite the little gathering you've assembled here. Was I not invited? Or was my invitation simply lost in transit?"

The king's lips pull back, revealing sharp canines. "Castien," he growls.

7

THE KING INDICATES THE BOOK LYING ON THE table before him with a wave of his hand. "Are you behind this? Is this one of yours?"

"Indeed," the Prince says with a casual shrug. He begins to saunter down the stair, taking each step slowly and holding himself in such a way as to draw every eye in the room. "Through a trick of fate, it managed to escape Vespre, despite the best efforts of my librarians. I've come to fetch it, only to find you have taken care of the matter quite nicely on your own."

I gape at the approaching Prince, my mind spinning. Why would the king ask if the Noswraith belonged to him? I remember suddenly the little volume he'd had tucked under his arm when I met him in the library that morning. Could it be it had held this same monster captive between its pages? Had he purposefully set it loose in Aurelis, just to disrupt his father's feast? The same feast during which Lodírhal intends to name his heir . . .

Before I can begin to fathom any more of this mystery, the book containing the Noswraith gives a sudden lurch, nearly falling off the table. I lunge from my kneeling position and grab it, hold it down fast. The cover bulges and bucks under my hands. My eyes widen. It's getting stronger by the minute.

"Allow me."

I dart a sideways glance. Somehow, the Prince has appeared at my side. He must have moved like lightning to cross the hall and reach me so quickly. His large hand deftly moves mine off the cover, and he slides the book out from under my nose. Even as he hefts it, the whole back cover bulges. For an instant, I see the outline of the Melted Man's face right through the leather. A scream squeezes my throat, and I press both hands to my mouth.

But the Prince quite casually opens the book and flips through the first few pages. "Ah!" He nods, his mouth quirking to one side. "Unusual technique. Not quite the polish one would hope, but then, you've not been given opportunity to practice. *The Melted Man.* Interesting. And effective insofar as it goes." He turns another page.

I shriek as the Melted Man's face and shoulders lunge out from the book, screaming just inches from the Prince's nose, wet teeth dripping, one eyeball slipping down its cheek. The Prince, unperturbed, holds the book back a few inches and shuts the cover. The nightmarish image vanishes with a snap. I'm left blinking, my mind seared with a dark afterimage of horror that I'm not entirely certain was real.

Reaching into the front of his robes, the Prince withdraws a quill—a lovely, plumy white feather affixed with an elaborate silver nib. "You cannot complete a binding," he says, his voice one of casual instruction, "without the name. The name is the lock which keeps the rest of the spell firmly in place. Without it, even the strongest of spells will eventually break down. Allow me to demonstrate."

I open my mouth to protest, but the Prince has already opened the book once more. This time a long-fingered half-melted hand stretches out, reaching for his face. He tilts his head to one side, dodging the swipe, and applies his quill to the paper. With a few quick scratches, he jots something down.

There's an awful, ear-splitting shriek. Then the hand withers away, disintegrates into little motes of darkness and is gone. The book lies still.

"There!" The Prince shuts the cover and tosses the little volume lightly to me. "That should hold your Melted Man for a good long while."

Mouth hanging open, I look down at the book. It feels perfectly ordinary. I turn it around, crack the cover, peek at the pages. Pages of my own writing, detailing my confrontation with the monster in the library. Turning to the very last page, I find there a single word penned in a large, strong, flourishing hand that takes up most of the page: *Yinzidor*. Something about the word makes me shudder and close the book again quickly. I look up and catch the Prince's watching eye. He is, I notice with some surprise, a bit gray in the cheeks. Shadows I hadn't noticed before ring his eyes, and beads of sweat dot his brow.

Before I have a chance to consider this oddity, the Prince turns from me to Lodírhal and sweeps a deep bow. "There, Your Majesty! My little party trick for your entertainment this evening. Does that, at the very least, earn me a place at your table? Or will you cast me out of your noble company?"

Lodírhal looks as though he's just swallowed a bitter pill. But he simply waves a hand, saying, "Sit down, Castien, and let us have no more of your theatrics. Estrilde, beloved niece, your Obligate is still in my sight. Bind it and send it away."

Princess Estrilde beckons me closer. I obey reluctantly, coming around the table to kneel beside my mistress's chair. Once more, Estrilde grabs me by the throat. You'd think I'd be used to it by now, but it's such a singularly humiliating sensation. I feel powerless in her grasp.

I wince as something sharp but unseen pierces my head. Try as I might, I can't prevent the pathetic little whimper. Estrilde's enchantment clamps down—a relentless vice around that place inside of me which had, moments ago, brimmed with so much life, so much strength. I blink a few times, gazing into my mistress's hard eyes. By the third blink, I'm not even sure I remember what it is I just lost. Just as well. Better not to question these things.

Estrilde releases my neck and wipes her hand on a napkin, her gold-tinted lips curled in a grimace of distaste. "Go," she growls. "Out of my sight, Obligate. Don't let me set eyes on you again unless summoned."

Her command jolts through my limbs, activating my Obligation. I scramble to my feet and swiftly turn, duck around the table, and make for the gallery. But before I've taken more than a few paces, a blue-robed form steps firmly in my way.

"I'll take that off your hands, Clara Darling," the Prince says smoothly.

I look up into shadow-ringed eyes. For a moment, he commands my gaze. I can't explain it, a sudden feeling of steel edge and bitterness that the lightness of his voice only seems to emphasize. Something is there in the depths of his eyes, in the pits of those dilated black pupils—a darkness so deep, so desperate, one could easily tilt over the edge and fall, never to recover.

Why does he look at me like that? Like when he sees me, he sees the worst of monsters?

I realize I'm still clutching the book. His hand is out, but he's not going to snatch it from me, not this time. I'm expected to hand it over. Is this some sort of a test? If so, I have no idea what for or why. I draw a deep breath and carefully place the book in his grasp.

He tucks it away under one arm, turns to one side, and inclines his head in something not quite as polite as a nod. It's definitely a dismissal.

Catching up the edge of my skirt, I flee to the gallery. The other humans in the gallery draw back, giving me a wide berth. I ignore them and creep to the rail, peering out through the gauzy curtains to the tableau still in play below.

The Prince drags a chair up to the king's own table and plunks it down beside Estrilde's. She gives him a disgusted look, which he ignores. He helps himself to a platter of sugar-sparkling fruit, selecting a plump peach which he turns several times before taking a bite. Still chewing, he leans forward to look around Estrilde at the king. "So, Father," he says, "what's this I hear about you naming your heir tonight?"

The whole gathering of silent guests sits up a little straighter. Were they not all aware of the purpose behind tonight's assembly? Or are they simply pretending ignorance? One never knows here in the Court of Dawn. Everything could be part of the ongoing game.

Lodírhal picks up his goblet, swirls the contents, then sips delicately. "Indeed," he says after a slow swallow. "The time has come. My decision is made at last."

"How thrilling!" The Prince takes another few bites then tosses the peach pit to clatter into Estrilde's empty cup. She shoots him a withering stare, which the Prince answers with a smile. He pushes back his seat, props his feet on the table, crossing them at the ankles as he leans his chair back on two legs. Lacing his fingers behind his head, he half-closes his eyes. "And who's it to be? Not, I trust, my fair cousin Estrilde here. That would be much too expected."

My mistress's face goes pure white. If she looked disgusted

before, she's positively seething now. But there's more than mere hatred in her face: there's fear. Real fear. I don't think it had occurred to her until this very moment that Lodírhal might choose another for his heir. Certainly not this son of his.

The king heaves a great sigh and sets his goblet down hard. A drop of red slops from the lip, staining the white tablecloth like a bloody smear. He looks at his son long and hard before sweeping his gaze out to take in the rest of the company.

"I have dwelt many a turning cycle upon this choice," he says slowly, each word carefully chosen and beautifully enunciated. "I have considered the good of Aurelis and the strength of her standing among the courts of Eledria. I have pondered the question of who should best take up this mighty mantle and lead my people into the future. And though the inclinations of the heart may often try to lead one astray, a great king must always know when to heed the bidding of wisdom above all else."

He stands then, stretching out his right arm in a gesture of blessing and strength. His hand comes down to rest upon Lord Ivor's head beside him.

"In the sacred name of the Great Goddess Anaerin, and the names of her three brothers and three sisters, who sit enthroned above, I declare before all of you—Ivor Illithor shall be my heir, sovereign king over all Aurelis."

THE PRINCE

"AND HOW WAS THE BANQUET, YOUR HIGHNESS? Was it everything you anticipated?"

Lawrence, my loyal Obligate and valet, bends to pick up the elaborately embroidered coat I've left in a pile in the middle of the chamber floor, then deftly catches the pair of cufflinks I yank free and toss over my shoulder. I don't bother to look back and make certain of this. I've known the man long enough by now to trust his reflexes.

I lean heavily against the footboard of the great bed in the center of the room. My breath is tight, and I grimace at each attempt to properly fill my lungs. "Indeed, Lawrence," I respond through gritted teeth. "It was everything and then some."

A clink of glassware. The next moment, my man approaches, offering me a nip of something bracing. Though my stomach knots, I accept the glass and down its contents in a single draught. A shiver rolls down my spine, and I send the glass flying over my shoulder as well. There's no shatter; apparently Lawrence managed to catch it.

"Everyone was displayed to best advantage in their god-awfullest glamours and finery," I continue when I can find my voice again. "It was just the medicine I needed to cure me of any desire to return to Aurelis."

The image of Ivor and his smug face appears unbidden before my mind's eye. He'd known. He'd known, damn him, what my father intended. Estrilde had not. In that, at least, I may take both comfort and pleasure. The image of my cousin's visage suffused in murderous glow was worth whatever other knocks the night afforded me.

But Ivor. Of all people, Lodírhal had to choose Ivor . . .

I close my eyes. But it's no use. Because this time I see him, not in Bioris Hall, receiving the fawning adulation of Aurelis Court. No, indeed. Instead he stands in the library. Gazing down at *her*. With that look his eye. A look of confidence, of triumph.

Of ownership.

My hand clenches into a fist.

"I've prepared a bath for Your Highness." Lawrence's voice breaks through the throbbing in my head. The man is busy about his usual bustle, setting my disorder to rights, hanging my coat up in the wardrobe, depositing my cufflinks in some nook or cranny. Unaware of the storm inside me. Or perhaps more aware than I like to credit him.

"Excellent." My voice is an ungracious growl. "Let me wash some of this Aurelian filth away before it gets in my blood." I push away from the footboard. The floor spins underfoot. Gritting my teeth, I move slowly across the chamber, making for the washroom. It feels like swimming through fog.

I've just reached the open door and inhaled my first breath of scented steam when Lawrence calls after me, "And the young lady? The librarian? Did she live up to your expectations?"

I stop. My gut jolts, a sickening tension. Probably another aftershock of the evening's exertion. Nothing more.

It's a fair question, after all. Did she live up to my expectations? Did all the doubt and worry and rage I'd felt at the prospect of seeing her again find any relief when I laid eyes on her face this morning? That determined face, screwed up in concentration, intent upon her pixie quarry . . . melting into shock at the sight of me. Shock and just a glimmer of fear.

She should have been far more afraid. Considering our last encounter, she should have been trembling in her shoes. But of course she doesn't remember. Estrilde saw to that, locking down her memories along with her powers. Perhaps it's just as well. Just as well that she's not thought of me these five long, dreadful years.

Not as I've thought of her. Every night. Every waking hour. Haunted by those doe-brown eyes. So wide, so frightened, and yet so fierce.

My lip curls. I hate her. Far more than I should, perhaps. I hate that look in her eye, all the innocent confusion and wariness upturned to me. I hate the mild gentleness of her voice, a determined disguise for her true feelings. She's neither so innocent nor so gentle as she would lead everyone to believe. Of that at least I am certain.

But most of all, I hate the way she looked at Ivor Illithor. Like he was her rescuer. Her hero.

He'd not rescued her though. No one could. Not from the monster I'd unleashed tonight. Instead she managed, despite all odds, to rescue herself. Thrown to the very jaws of the beast, she'd somehow not only survived but conquered.

"She is not without talent," I say at last. "Something may be made of her yet."

"I very much hope so, sir," Lawrence replies. "For your sake."

I turn sharply at that. But my Obligate is already moving on, cleaning up more of the debris I've left scattered around the room. His face is a mask of guilelessness, impossible to penetrate.

Lip curled, I stagger into the washroom, strip off the rest of my banquet apparel, and sink into the steaming scented water of the in-ground bath. I try to relax, try to let my shivering limbs release their pent-up tension. But I cannot.

Because I cannot get those eyes of hers out of my head.

CLARA

8

I WAKE WITH A GASP, CLUTCHING MY BLANKETS TO MY chest, my heart racing. For some moments I simply lie there and stare at the ceiling above me, panic whirling in my veins, with no idea why. Then the memories creep back in.

Last night.

That *thing*.

That *Noswraith*.

And that indescribable sensation of *opening* when Estrilde reached inside me, followed by the pain of once more being slammed shut.

With a groan, I rub the heels of my hands into my eyes. It's all over now. However strange the events of last night may have been, they're done. Done! I don't need to remember anymore. It's best not to dwell on unsettling events while serving out a term of Obligation. Everything about this life is unsettling if you think about it too closely. Best just to keep my head down, stay focused on the day-to-day tasks, ask no questions, seek no answers. And besides . . .

A slow smile manages to pull at the downturned corners of my mouth. I let out a small breath and whisper, "Today you're going *home*."

It's one of the agreements written into my Obligation. Once a month—according to the human count of time—I am free to return to my own world from sunup until sundown. Free to see my family and any friends who might still remember me after such a long absence. Free to try to maintain those bonds that keep me attached to that world.

I know some of the Obligates have ceased to bother returning home on their days off. George, for instance, hasn't traveled home in years. I'm not sure Thaddeus ever did. But some of us with shorter terms of Obligation still make the effort. I've got more than one reason to try to keep a grip on my home world, after all. I've got Oscar. And I've got . . .

My smile grows as an image clarifies in my mind—an image of summery blue eyes beneath a shock of tousled, honey-brown hair shot with strands of gold. Of brows always just a little puckered with unresolved sadness, but a dimple in the corner of the mouth ready and willing to emerge with each smile.

Danny. *Doctor Gale* as I should call him now. It will be good to see him. And I know he'll be glad to see me.

Even as that pleasant thought warms my chest, another intrudes, bringing with it an unwelcome chill. Across the familiar, comforting face of Danny, another image manifests. An image of sharp, chiseled angles, strong jaw, piercing golden eyes. An image of perfection to make the heart break.

Lord Ivor.

How beautiful he was last night, standing beside King Lodírhal, receiving the cheers, the laud and acclaim of the assembled guests. In that moment, gazing at him from the gallery, I saw clearly how wasted the king had truly become, and how *right* it was for Ivor to be his successor. Soon now, he would be Lord Ivor no longer, but King Illithor of Aurelis, Master of the Court of Dawn.

And what of my mistress? I'd scarcely dared look at her following the king's announcement. She'd masked her face swiftly, but not before I glimpsed the shock in her eyes. The horror. The rage. Will her feelings for Ivor survive this new betrayal? Will she blame him for stealing away her uncle's favor and her throne?

Or perhaps she'll simply redouble her efforts to snare him. After all, queen consort is still a queen of sorts.

Huffing a short breath, I toss back my blankets, sit up, and swing my legs over the edge of the bed. None of these things matter. None of them are my business. It's far too easy to get caught up in the intrigues playing out all around me, but none of this world is *mine*. I must only survive here another ten years. The best way to survive is to make no connections, form no bonds, take as little interest as possible.

I must not think about Ivor.

I must think of Oscar. And Danny. And home.

I pull myself together quickly. Instead of my regular work gown, I don a neat, simple day dress—a present from Danny's sister Kate a few visits ago, sweet friend that she is. The fabric is soft but durable and a lovely mulberry shade that compliments my complexion. I pull on my shoes and grab a cloak, knowing it will be much colder in my home world than it is here in the perpetually clement weather of Aurelis.

Morning light is already breaking through the windows when I step out of my chamber and close the door behind me. That's no surprise—the semi-darkness that passes for night in this world only lasts a few hours at a time. But the hours of my day off are dictated by sunrise and sunset of my own world. I've still got plenty of time.

A spring to my step, I hasten down the passage. My room is part of Princess Estrilde's elaborate suite of rooms, but it's tucked off to one side and is neither large nor ostentatious. I can easily use byways to avoid bumping into either Estrilde or any of her entourage. The palace itself is more like a city, with halls and passages instead of streets and highways, but over the last few years, I've learned my way around well enough.

My goal is one of several hundred gates that line the outermost walls of Aurelis. I don't know where the other gates lead, but the one I'm heading to serves as a portal to my own world. Straight to my own kitchen, in fact. It's a bit of a hike to get there, but I don't mind. I'm careful to avoid bumping into anyone on my way. The last thing I want is to meet any of my fellow librarians. I don't want to face their questioning stares following the events of last night. Their questions only make my own questions seem all the more unanswerable.

I don't need that right now. I need simplicity. Focus.

Trotting down a last stairway, I step through a side door and out into a swath of green garden on the western side of the palace. All is shaded and a bit gloomy here, which I appreciate. I feel almost stealthy as I steal down one of the winding paths. Ahead I can see the palace wall and the topmost arch of the Between Gate. Not long now and I'll be breathing the air of my own world again.

All my attention is fixed on my destination . . . so I'm not prepared when suddenly a figure steps out from behind a line of shrubs and stands in front of me. I yelp and leap back three paces, clutching my bundled cloak against my chest.

"Your pardon, Clara," a smooth, calm voice says. I can only just discern a gentle smile playing across strong features half-hidden by shadows. "I did not mean to startle you. I thought you heard me coming."

"Lord Ivor!" My heart is racing, pounding in my throat. Oh gods on high! This is not what I need right now. I've got to get away from this man, away from these feelings he sets pulsing in my blood at the mere sight of him. I drop my head and dip a quick curtsy. "Allow me to offer my congratulations. I . . . I heard, of course, about the king's declaration. May you enjoy a long and prosperous reign."

Ivor snorts and shrugs dismissively. "That? Well, I'm not king yet, and there are more than a few who would prefer I remain uncrowned. But let us not worry about that."

He takes a step toward me. Is he . . . is he reaching out to take my hand? No, I must be mistaken. I half-turn away, holding onto my cloak like a shield. For an instant, I think I see a flash of hurt in his face. But that might be nothing more than the play of shadows.

"I was hoping," he says, "you would have time for one of our lessons today. It has been some while, and I've missed our conversations. Besides, I would dearly love to hear more of your adventures from last night. Rumor has it you were quite the valiant heroine."

This is not what I need. This is not at all, on any level, even remotely what I need. That look in Ivor's eye . . . the way he's gazing at me, as though to drink me in . . . it's dangerous. Completely dangerous.

Don't forget Mary West!

I open my mouth. I'm about to give some answer. Some stupid answer, no doubt. I'm about to give away my one day, my one chance to return home for a month. I'm about to tell him that I've got all the time in the world and it's entirely at his disposal—

A flicker of movement catches my eye.

I glance to one side. An arbor of trailing vines half-hides another path close by. Is that a golden head I spy among the greenery? I'm almost sure of it. Has my mistress followed me out here? Or followed Ivor?

I take another step back, draw myself up to my full height, and meet Lord Ivor's gaze straight-on. "I'm afraid I cannot help you today, my lord. I am . . . I am obliged to be elsewhere."

Ivor's eyes narrow slightly, and some of the warmth goes out from them. He turns his head suddenly, peering back at the arbor where moments before I could have sworn a tall figure in a pale, diaphanous gown lurked. It's empty now. But the line of Ivor's jaw tightens.

He turns and looks down at me. "Clara, tell me the truth: is Princess Estrilde making your life difficult?"

The bluntness of the question takes me aback. I gape at him, try to speak, but can't make anything like a coherent sound.

"Tell me, Clara. Please," he urges. "I know she is your mistress, but the terms of Obligation don't permit her to torment you. If she is treating you harshly, if she is punishing you for perceived infractions, tell me. I have some sway with the princess. I will speak to her on your behalf."

No! No, no, no, no! I want to scream the word, shake my head, clasp my hands, and beg him to do nothing of the kind. Oh, gracious heavens, how much worse will my life become if ever Estrilde begins to suspect . . . to suspect . . . what? What is there to suspect? Nothing! Nothing and more nothing. And I must remember it. I must be wise. I must keep my head on straight.

I must remember Mary West.

Inhaling deeply, I force my habitual smile disguise into place. A blank, sweet, small smile that allows no room for a more traitorous expression. "Thank you for the offer, my lord," I say primly and dip my head. "Princess Estrilde is a good and just mistress. I have no complaints about my treatment at her hands. I pray you would not trouble yourself in any way concerning me."

Ivor studies my face. I feel the questions brimming in the silence between us. Questions to which, I fear, he has already guessed the answers. To my relief, however, he simply bows. "Good day then, Clara. Enjoy your time in your own world. Your absence from Aurelis will be . . . noted."

Why does he have to bow to me? Why, in that sincere fashion, without a trace of irony or derision? Why does he have to look at me like that? As though I'm something unusual, something extraordinary. Something . . . *desirable.*

All too aware of unseen eyes upon me, I bob another curtsy. The moment Ivor steps to one side, I hasten up the path, head high, smile firmly in place. I can only hope I look carefree and disinterested, focused on nothing but the gate ahead of me and the prospect of a day-long holiday.

I can only hope Princess Estrilde can't sense the turmoil roiling in my breast.

9

THE GUARDIAN OF THE BETWEEN GATE IS AN ANCIENT fellow by the name of Lyklor. He may or may not guard the other numerous gates surrounding Aurelis as well, but as I've never visited any of them, I can't say for certain. He's an intimidating presence—at least eight feet tall, with massive hooves, bent, hairy legs, and a bone-white head set with yellow, horizontal-pupiled eyes. A massive rack of antlers sprouts from his skull, not a glamour in his case. I'm never sure if that head is his actual face or a mask. Sometimes it seems one way, sometimes the other.

He never speaks. He stands by an immense stone dial carved with intricate symbols, which he turns according to the traveler's intended destination. The dial of this particular gate has at least a hundred symbols carved in it, and one of them belongs to me.

The gate itself is really more of an open arch in the wall. There are no bars, no doors, nothing visible that would prevent anyone from coming or going. Perhaps someone with magic senses would be able to perceive something invisible that I cannot. All I can see through the two-story opening is a landscape bathed in golden sunglow. A whole beautiful, lush world lies out there beyond the boundaries of the city-palace, but I have no idea what it's like. Perhaps it's as idyllic and peaceful as it looks from this side of the wall. Perhaps it's all a deadly ruse.

Hopefully I'll never have to find out.

"Good morning, Lyklor," I call out cheerfully. The guard stands somberly in his usual spot by the dial, awaiting my arrival. He's always there when I arrive, as though he knows to expect me.

He regards me through those strange yellow eyes of his, a swath of long lashes blinking slowly. Though he makes no move, I sense the faintest trace of expectation in his gaze.

"I have something for you today," I continue, reaching into my pocket. I withdraw a pretty golden apple, something I'd collected and saved from a meal two days ago. I hold it out to the antlered being, who turns his gaze from my face to the offering.

He bows and delicately takes the apple in his huge teeth, like a horse might. Straightening, he crunches solemnly, the whole apple in a single mouthful. Though I can't read any expression in his strange face, I think he's pleased. I always make a point to bring a little treat to Lyklor when I visit. I like to think I'm one of his favorites as a result.

His munching complete, Lyklor beckons. I move to stand in the gate arch. The wall itself is ten feet thick, and every time I move to stand in the center, I'm reminded all over again of my own tiny insignificance.

I look back over my shoulder to Lyklor at his dial. He nods slightly, the barest inclination of his white chin. I nod back, then face forward into the landscape I'll never enter and close my eyes. Behind me, Lyklor turns his dial.

A shudder ripples through my body. Through my soul.

It's difficult to describe the sensation of being propelled between worlds to one who has never experienced it, but I would say it feels as if someone plants the tip of a sharp knife straight into the top of my head and then, very carefully, very precisely, draws a series of hair-thin lines all the way down my body from the top of my head to the soles of my feet. None of these "cuts" are deep enough to draw blood . . . but each one hurts *just* enough to make me wince, to make my fists clench and my breath catch. My head fills with a white light, and a sensation of cold air runs right through me, whistling among my bones. Then the light begins to fade, and the *whooshing* calms. I blink a few times, trying to force the dancing shadows surrounding me into clearer definition.

Slowly, slowly, the room around me solidifies. It's a small, square living space, with a few humble sticks of furniture. Mama's old rocking chair, one runner broken, is tucked away in one corner. A little stool with uneven legs stands near the hearth. A threadbare rug—much-mended, its color long since washed away, leaving behind mere hints of russet and green—graces the hard stone floor. On the mantel stands a little china shepherdess, her face smashed, but her frock nonetheless offering a bright splash of cheerfulness in the gloom.

I breathe out a sigh as I take it all in . . . and in my mind's eye, I see myself, once more a girl crouched on that hearth with Oscar beside me. My hands are busy darning a sock, but my eyes are bright as I spin stories for my younger brother—stories of monsters and dangers and the fae. Stories of terror and turmoil and triumph. Stories that take us momentarily out of this room, out of this house, out of this town . . . and into realms where monsters can be fought and defeated with magical artifacts or ancient blades. Mama sits in shadowy silence in her rocking chair, her hands quiet in her lap, rocking, rocking. She smiles down at us fondly, occasionally reaching out to stroke my hair or touch Oscar's cheek, and we turn our faces up to hers, smiling our adoration.

Then a footstep sounds at the door.

Silence falls on the room.

We crouch, our breaths caught, our muscles tense and still.

I swallow hard and shake the image away, returning to *this* moment, this empty space. It's best not to live back in those days, best not to remember. Or, if I must remember, to dwell only on the good times . . . and draw a firm boundary around anything more.

I look around the space now, pursing my lips at the sight of the dead, cold hearth. There's been no fire lit for days, maybe weeks. A few dry sticks lie across the andirons, but the coal scuttle is empty.

I check the kitchen. It's also bare. A bit of stale bread, a hunk of moldy cheese. Sighing, I cut away mold and slice the bread into pieces small enough to gnaw. In the bottom of a basket, I discover a wrinkled but edible apple and add it to my tin plate. Carrying this meager meal in both hands, I approach the rickety staircase leading to the bare rooms overhead.

"Oscar?" I call softly up the stairwell. "Oscar, are you there?"

No answer. But then, I didn't really expect one.

Each tread creaks under my weight as I climb the stair. Sometimes the whole house feels as though it will topple around my ears. But then, it's always felt that way and somehow never toppled. Perhaps it's like an old dead oak tree, the life inside long since gone, but the roots still anchored so deep, not even the strongest storm winds can blow it down. This house will likely remain standing much longer than any of the rest of us.

I reach the landing. There are three rooms up here. Two doors hang open, revealing the blank spaces inside. Anything of value was long ago sold, all the pathetic sticks of furnishing or window treatments. Nothing is left but trash and emptiness.

The third room's door is shut. I knock softly. "Oscar? It's me, Clara. Are you awake?"

A thump. A clatter like tumbling glassware. A curse, another thump. Then a sound of padding feet.

I wait, my lips pressed in a thin line.

Finally the door creaks open. A face that once was so handsome but is now far too drawn and pale and thin peers out through the crack.

"Clara," my brother croaks. "You're back again, are you?"

"I always come back. You know that." I push the door, meet a little resistance. Then it swings inward so fast, it slams against the wall. Oscar stands before me, clad in nothing but his nightshirt. His bare legs are all knees and bones, his bare feet almost blue with cold. Though I wouldn't have thought it possible, he looks even worse than he did a month ago.

"Let me in," I say, my voice gentle.

Oscar tosses his hands and turns away. He stomps back into the room, collapses on his bed, and tosses a hand over his face. "Just when I started to think I was rid of all remaining nagging relatives!" he sighs. "Have you come to express your disappointment? Or will you simply give me *that look* this time?"

Ignoring him, I take the plate to his desk, which is covered in random sheets of paper, all a mass of indecipherable handwriting and blotches of ink. A whole pot of ink has spilled across several pages and drippled over the edge of the desk in a spreading dark puddle on the floor. It looks like an old bloodstain.

I push a few things to one side, set the plate down, then pick up the topmost page. "You've been hard at work, I see." I try to discern something from the illegible scrawl. "A commission? Or are you writing this one on spec?"

"What do you think?" Oscar growls. He turns and glares at me from under his hand. "Ever since you cast your curse on me, I've not been able to get a contract. Hope you're satisfied, witch!"

I set down the page and move to perch on the end of the bed, my hands folded in my lap. There's no point in protesting Oscar's accusations. Though once a promising young novelist, he's not penned anything successful in five years. Five years, which of course coincides with my own disappearance into Eledria.

I'm never quite certain how aware Oscar is of my comings and goings. Looking around the room, I see empty bottles, glasses, and, worse still, dustings of white powder and little silver spoons, all of which speak to my brother's foulest habits. He lives his life in an angry fog of pain and self-medication.

I struggle to suppress a sigh. What's the point of scolding? It does no good. But I reach out and take Oscar's hand. For a moment, his fingers are limp in mine. Then, almost imperceptibly, he offers a little squeeze. "I wish you wouldn't go, Clara," he says pathetically, still with his other hand over his face. "When you go, it's all so . . . dark."

"Maybe you should write me a story? Something to tempt me back again."

"I was never as good as you. Dad knew it. Everyone knew it. I can't write like you do."

I shake my head. "That's not true, Oscar. You're the family genius, remember? You inherited Dad's . . . his . . ."

Oscar drops his hand, fixes me with a dirty look. "His vices? Go on, I know you're thinking it."

"I was going to say his gifts."

Oscar snorts. With a tremendous effort, he sits up. His shoulders sag, his chin hangs to his breast. "Dad never had any gifts. Just curses. Even his gifts were curses."

And that's probably true. Our father, Edgar Darlington, was renowned for his dark and ingenious tales of horror. He earned himself a reputation for literary brilliance that far outstripped his reputation for debauchery and cruelty. At least, in the public eye.

In private, well . . . that was a different matter.

I squeeze Oscar's hand a little tighter. "No one ever said you had to *be* him. Be yourself! Be your own writer. You've got great things inside of you, beautiful things. You just need to . . . to clear out some of the debris. Then you'll see it."

"Stop with the drinking and the smoking and the rest of it, you mean?" Oscar smiles wryly. Despite the bitterness in the look, I catch a glimpse of his former beauty. What a sweet boy he once was! My precious little brother, my heart, my joy. There's so little of him left now, all wasted away. Languishing in our father's shadow.

"Well," I say, knowing better than to let him bait me into a fight, "I see you've been hard at work lately. What is this newest work of brilliance? Something to tempt the editors over at *Starlin?*"

"*Starlin?* No." Oscar spits a foul curse and pulls his hand out of mine. He rises from the bed and totters over to the desk, pushing aside the untouched plate of food and rifling through the pages. "No, I'll publish it myself when it's done. That'll show them. That'll show them all! When the whole city is bursting with talk of Oscar Darlington and his newest tale, they'll regret how they once laughed at me."

His hands are shaking so hard, the pages shiver as he holds them up to his face. I sigh. And I don't ask him where he thinks he's going to get the money for printing costs or distribution. There's no point in talking reason to Oscar. There never was, really.

"I'm stepping out for a bit," I tell him instead. "Going to pop around to Kitty's."

"Going to make eyes at your pretty doctor?" Oscar says meanly.

"I'm going to have a cup of tea with my friend." I rise from the bed. "I'll bring a few things when I return. Some food. Milk and eggs. Please try to remember to eat them before they go off."

"And then you'll disappear again?" Oscar looks at me, his mouth twisted into an unpleasant sneer, but his eyes sad. "You'll flit away and leave me wondering if I dreamed you up all along. Leave me wondering if you're truly dead. Just like Mama. Just like Dad."

I take a step, covering the short space between us, and grip his shoulders hard. "I am *not* dead," I say with all the firmness I can muster. "I swear to you, Oscar, I am alive. Alive and well and doing *everything* in my power to get back to you. And *you* must live until then. Do you hear me? You've got to figure out how to survive on your own. You've got to, Oscar. For both our sakes."

He tries to meet my gaze but can't. "I'm sorry, Clara. I'm sorry for being what I am."

"Sorry for being my beautiful, brilliant little brother?" I draw him to me and kiss his forehead, forcing my smile to disguise any prickling tears. "*I'm* not sorry. Not for a moment."

10

"OH, I KNEW YOU WOULD COME TODAY!"

I take a step back, my hand still upraised to reach for the lion-head door knocker. The door swings open before I touch it, and I'm met by Kitty Gale's smiling face. She catches me in an enormous hug, right there on the doorstep, her arms squeezing so tight it steals my breath away.

"I saw you coming up the street." Kitty steps back, still holding my hands, and gives me a once-over as though to make certain I really am there. Then she looks into my eyes, and her smile falters. "You look troubled, Clara. What's wrong?"

"Oh!" I toss my head and offer a dismissive smile. For a moment all the many dozens of wrong things crowd my tongue, wanting to be spoken. The strange discovery of powers I had no idea I possessed—the realization that those powers have been kept under enchanted safeguards all these years—Princess Estrilde—Ivor—all of it.

But I can't speak of any of this to Kitty. Kitty only partially understands my situation. She can accept the concept of another world well enough, but when it comes to me, she takes that concept and places it under lock and key, never to be acknowledged save at direst need. Instead she acts as though I simply work as a governess for some distant landowner out of town. I try not to contradict this pretense. It's more comfortable for both of us.

"It's Oscar," I answer instead. Which is at least partially true.

Kitty's face softens again. "Is he in a bad way?"

"When is he not?" I sigh and shrug. Then, with a quick shake of my head and a brighter smile, "But enough of that. I want to hear all *your* news. And I would just about die for a proper cup of tea!"

Kitty calls out to the housemaid, requesting tea in the parlor as she leads me into the house. It's a lovely gray stone townhouse on Elmythe Lane, once considered a fashionable part of town. Now fallen into the emerging "middle class" of Wimborne society, it still maintains a stolid respectability. The original Doctor Gale's practice allowed him and his wife to move in exalted circles . . . which is how they met the celebrated novelist, Edgar Darlington.

When my father suffered his fall from grace and moved our family to a less reputable side of town, the Doctor and Mrs. Gale officially dropped the acquaintance . . . but not so the Gale children. Danny and Kitty clung to our friendship with such ferocious devotion, it warms my heart to this day. I'm not sure how I would have survived some of those dark years without them.

Kitty sits me down in a lightly faded upholstered chair, her tongue already busy with chatter. "Lindella Stroldin is engaged, did you know? No, of course not, how would you? It was just announced in the Gazette last weekend. A fine-looking young lawyer with a small fortune to his name as well as his work prospects. A good match for Lindella, if not the duke or lord she once aspired to."

I nod and smile. Lindella and all the other names tripping so lightly from Kitty's lips are familiar to me. But the people themselves seem like faraway phantoms, figures of some alternate reality which I might once have shared, but which now feels more fictional than real. When I picture the newly engaged Miss Stroldin, I still see the pimply-faced girl I knew five years ago. I've not witnessed her blossoming into the sophisticated society climber Kitty describes.

When Kitty runs out of her usual chatter and pauses long enough to take a sip of tea, I set my own cup down in its saucer. "And what of . . . of Doctor Gale?"

"Oh! *Doctor Gale.*" Kitty chuckles, rolling her eyes. "How formal you sound, my dear. Danny is quite well. As you know he's finished his second year of proprietary school. They keep the third years practically as *slaves* down at Westbend Charity. Got to give the new doctors all the low-income patients to practice on. There's always more of those. But Danny's much loved down there, as won't surprise you a bit. He's got a reputation for healing more than he harms."

A glow of pleasure warms my heart. "We've always known he would make a fine doctor."

The look Kitty shoots me is a little too knowing. She sets her cup aside on a near table and glances at the clock on the mantel. "He ought to be home any minute now. They kept him overnight, but his shift ended at seven o'clock, so I would think . . . oh! That should be him now."

I hear the front door opening and a murmur of voices as Danny hands his hat and coat off to the housemaid. A flush rises in my cheeks, and I just *know* Kitty sees it. But Kitty merely laughs and goes to the parlor doorway, calling out, "We're in here, Danny! Guess who's come to visit!"

Another minute and Danny appears.

Just that mere sight of him fills me with an overwhelming sense of *rightness*. In that moment, I can almost—*almost*—forget about Ivor and his enigmatic looks. I can almost forget about the darkness and dread of the shadowy otherworld library in which I walked last night. I can forget about Estrilde and the intrigues of the Dawn Court. All of it. None of it really matters. This is my world. This world of labor and day-to-day toil, lived alongside people I care for. Looking at Danny—seeing that smile of his momentarily wash away the sadness in his eyes and bring out that dimple in the corner of his mouth—I know where I'm meant to be. Only . . .

Only I still have ten years left to my Obligation. And who knows what ten years will bring?

"Miss Darlington." Danny steps into the room and takes my

hand as I rise to greet him. A dart of pain passes through my heart. When did he stop calling me *Clara* and revert to this more formal mode of address? Probably around the same time I started calling him *Doctor Gale*.

"Good morning," I say, squeezing his fingers just enough to remain within the bounds of politeness, not enough to be considered a flirt. "Kitty tells me you're excelling down at the Westbend Charity Hospital."

"Oh, I don't know about all that!" The haunted look returns to his eyes. "There's been an outbreak of gray fever. It affects the children mostly, which is . . . hard."

He doesn't go into more than that. I know better than to press him. Instead I say simply, "Well, for the children's sake, I'm glad they get to benefit from your comforting presence as well as your skill."

Danny smiles again. It's amazing to me how eyes as blue as his never seem cold.

"The pair of you!" Kitty laughs suddenly. She catches Danny's arm and gives him a tug. He, realizing he's still holding my hand, drops it at once and turns to his sister. "Before you both start going all soppy," she says, "why don't you escort *Miss Darlington* to the market? She needs to pick up some things for home."

"Oh, but doesn't Doctor Gale need to rest after his long night?" I protest.

Danny and Kitty both deny this with absolute vehemence, and within another few moments, I find myself back out on Elmythe

Lane, walking beside Danny. He offers his arm, and I accept it gladly. "I can call a cab if you like," he says, still in that formal tone. But then what do I expect? Once-a-month visits are hardly enough to maintain the same closeness I once enjoyed with the Gale siblings. In a few more years, who knows what our dynamic will be?

"I quite like the walk." I smile up at him and hope he can't sense the tension in my tone. "Sloaner Square is only a few streets over, is it not?"

"Indeed," Danny responds. He sets a leisurely pace; he's in no rush for our time together to end. My heart warms again, chasing away some of the hovering sorrow. "How have you been this last month?" he asks after a few minutes.

Once again, I'm stumped. How can I possibly answer a question like that? A question so simple and yet so fraught.

"I've been well," I say. Even as the words slip out, I know they sound like a slamming door. A door between me and Danny. A door preventing him from entering into life as I know it. His arm stiffens in my grasp. For the first time since my Obligation began, I realize why it is that many Obligates no longer bother returning home on their off days. Is it really so impossible to maintain bonds to my own world?

We exchange pleasantries as we go. Danny tells a humorous anecdote about his work at the charity hospital, deftly steering around the darker truths I know he must be facing on a daily basis. I have no right to pry for those stories, for I have no right to offer him comfort or support. How can I, when I have only until sunset before I must go, not to see him again for many weeks?

All too soon our conversation trickles away into silence. It's a relief to reach Sloaner Square and the bustle and busyness of market day. The Gales, of course, would ordinarily send their maid to do the shopping, but Danny always makes a point to escort me personally. He and Kitty have also offered on multiple occasions to give money to help Oscar meet his basic needs—an offer I staunchly refuse. Oscar is my responsibility. Whether or not I'm currently inhabiting the same world as him.

I take the lead in the market, guiding Danny through a series of stalls and booths until I come to Farmer Gavril's cart. The ginger-haired man recognizes me, his eyes lighting up with interest at my approach. "The usual today, miss?" he asks, touching the brim of his cap politely.

"Yes, thank you." I reach into the little purse attached to my belt. I don't have money of course; Obligates aren't *paid* for their services. But no one in Aurelis seems to mind any of us Obligates harvesting leaves off the *lurrea* shrubs that line the walkways of the eastern garden. Lurrea are common enough in Eledria but cannot thrive in the soil of this world. Which is probably just as well, for lurrea leaves turn to gold the moment they touch our air.

I pull out a handful now. They're tiny, scarcely larger than my thumbnail, and so delicate, but because they are pure gold, they're surprisingly heavy. I've had difficulty finding sellers in Wimborne willing to exchange goods for such unusual currency, but Farmer

Gavril has always been eager to make a trade.

Danny silently observes my deal with the farmer. I'm uncomfortably aware of his thoughtful gaze. I never quite know what he thinks of these few stray glimpses into my new world. We don't talk about it. Ever.

And the barriers between us continue to grow.

The exchange complete, I bid good day to Farmer Gavril and allow Danny to take the basket of eggs and milk for me. We continue through the market, and I add some fruit and a fresh loaf of bread to my purchases. I wish I could buy some fish or meat, but I know Oscar will just let them spoil. He only eats things he can grab and cram into his mouth between spurts of frantic writing and still more frantic drinking.

Our market mission complete, Danny offers his arm, and we turn again for home. Our footsteps are even slower now, for once we reach the tidy townhouse, Danny will have to slip away and catch up on sleep from the night before. Kitty and I will visit a little longer, then I will set off for home. The bulk of my day must be spent with Oscar, after all. I can't neglect him.

So Danny and I don't hasten our return. When Danny takes a sudden detour down a side street, I offer no protest, even though I know it will take a good ten minutes longer to reach our destination. I simply adjust my grip on his arm and fight the urge to lean my head against his shoulder.

"Clara," he says suddenly.

The sound of my given name on his lips startles me. I look up and find those sad, sweet eyes of his gazing down at me.

"Clara," he says, "I can't bear this. I can't bear what we're becoming."

I bite my lip. "I know. I don't like it either."

"Ten more years!" Danny's voice cracks on the edges, raw with emotion. "Ten more years of barely seeing each other. Ten more years before we can have any hope of . . . of . . . of anything."

My throat thickens, and I swallow with some difficulty. Lifting my head, I meet his gaze straight on. "Danny." I try to be firm, but my voice comes out scarcely above a whisper. "I would never ask you to wait for me. You are free. Free to live your own life and—"

"No, Clara. I won't hear it." A flash of ferocity crosses his face, both surprising and a little frightening. I've always known that Danny cared for me; I've depended on that care for years now. But this intensity is something new, something unexpected. Something that wouldn't be out of place among the passions of the Dawn Court.

"Clara, I've been . . . making inquiries." Danny sets the basket of purchases down so that he can turn me to face him, holding onto both of my hands. I glance to either side, aware that passersby can see us. But no one is paying any attention.

Face burning, I force myself to meet his gaze. "What kind of inquiries?"

"There are places here in the city where certain folk live. Folk who *know* about things. About other worlds. About Eledria."

My heart feels as though it's turned to stone and dropped from my breast to my stomach. "Oh, Danny—"

"No, hear me out." He squeezes my hands a little tighter. "I've found people who've told me a thing or two about Obligations. I even met a man who claims to have once been an Obligate. He claims there's a way to break an Obligation."

I shake my head. When he continues to look at me with that same intense gaze, I shake it harder. "You mustn't think of it."

"Why mustn't I? If there's a chance of bringing you home sooner, oughtn't we to take it?"

"The risk is too great."

"The risk?" Danny's eyes narrow and he bows his head, trying to force me to look at him. "Clara, have you known about this? All along?"

I lick my dry lips. Then I nod slowly.

"Why didn't you tell me?"

The pain in his voice is enough to break my heart. "I couldn't. I couldn't bear it if you came and tried. If you failed." With an effort of will, I force myself to meet his gaze. "If you ended up Obligated too."

His expression is almost enough to melt me on the spot. "But even if the worst happened, we'd be together, Obligated to the same mistress. It wouldn't be the same as the life we've always meant to build together, but at least . . . at least . . ."

I pull my hands free from his, take a step back and cross my arms tightly. "You don't know what you're proposing. You don't *know*. I won't have you throw your life away on something so hopeless." I hold his gaze, silently begging him to hear me, to understand.

"You have a place here. The work you do at the hospital, the people you help. The children. This is where you're meant to be. I can't risk that, not on a selfish chance. No!" My voice sounds so sharp in my ears. I try to soften it as I add, "It's my choice too. I choose to live out the term of my sentence. To pay for my crimes, whatever they may be. And I choose for you to have your life. Your *real* life."

He takes a step nearer, reaching for my hand. I turn away quickly, putting my back to him. "Clara," he says.

I shake my head, fighting to hold back the tears brimming in my lashes. "Please, Danny. I would rather you forget me entirely than do something so foolish."

He stands very close behind me. So close, I can feel the warmth of his chest against my back, can hear the rhythm of each breath he takes. He speaks low, in a tone so heartbreaking, it threatens to tear me in two.

"I could never forget you, Clara. Not even if I wished to."

11

AN OBLIGATE'S FIRST TASK UPON RETURNING FROM an off day is to report to her mistress. A task I am *not* keen on fulfilling as I step through the shimmering thinness in the worlds back under the shadowed arch of the Between Gate.

Immediately, I'm hit with the warm, sweet air of this world. I shrug out of my cloak and bundle it under my arm, even as dread pools in my gut. "Thank you, Lyklor!" I remember to call to the gate guardian, who stands at his stone dial and offers me a solemn nod in response as I pass.

The western garden paths feel more ominous to me now than they had early this morning. Every shadow makes me jump, and I can't help peering into the arbors and round the shrubberies, half expecting either Ivor or Estrilde to jump out at me. While I was in my own world, breathing unenchanted air, I could more easily forget the growing paranoia that plagues me here in Aurelis. Now I wonder how I can possibly survive another ten years of this.

Maybe I'm just being overly sensitive. After all, Aurelis has always been a perilous place, but I've managed to keep my head down and avoid any real trouble. The last few days have been stressful, yes. But real life is back home. Back with Oscar and that last forlorn look he cast over his shoulder when I stood in his bedroom doorway and bid him yet another goodbye. Back with Danny and the expression in his eyes when he told me he wanted to break my Obligation.

I drop my cloak off in my room and make my way to Estrilde's reception room. The princess is there, of course, as she is most evenings. She lounges with her entourage around her, her three human maids once more dressing her hair. This time, there's a gaming table pulled up close to Estrilde's chair, and she's bent over the pieces, involved in some intricate strategy against an opponent who knows how to carefully lose without being too *obvious* about it.

Estrilde doesn't look up when I enter, curtsy, cross the room, and kneel beside her chair. "I've returned, my mistress," I murmur, "to serve my Obligation. Obligate me as you wish."

I bow my head. Ordinarily speaking, Estrilde spares me less than half a glance before waving me on to my business at the library. I can't remember the last time she had any specific instruction for me upon my return from a day off.

This time, however, Estrilde's silence lasts much longer than usual. She lingers over her game, fingers trailing over different pieces as she considers various moves. Her silence holds the entire room captive. At last, she selects a beautifully carved marker and moves it three paces diagonally to the right. Then she sits back in her chair, her three maids scampering to adjust so they won't inadvertently tug her hair with their combs. Without looking at me, Estrilde picks up a glass of clear, sparkling liquid and takes a single sip.

Only now, her lips moistened, does she speak: "Prince Castien Lodírith of Vespre has requested your presence in his suite upon your return. You are to attend him."

I blink.

Did I just hear her correctly? No, surely Estrilde must be addressing someone else, someone standing behind me perhaps.

Then I feel the choking hold of my Obligation wrap around my throat, as tight as Estrilde's fingers had been last night. This is a command then. A command meant for me.

But it doesn't make sense!

"Mistress?" I quaver. I want to ask why. I want to beg for clarification, for further details.

Estrilde simply turns and, for the first time since I entered the room, looks directly at me. "At once."

I have no choice.

In a daze of confusion, I rise and barely manage to curtsy without stumbling. Then I back from the room, my hand reaching behind me for the door latch. I find it, turn it, crack the door open, and spin on heel to make a swift exit.

"One more thing, Obligate."

Arrested by my mistress's voice, I stand frozen in place for three heartbeats. Slowly I look back over my shoulder. The princess is bowed over the gaming table again, seeming to inspect her opponent's newest maneuver. But I know her attention is actually fixed on me.

Estrilde selects a piece, picks it up, and turns it around in her fingers, studying it idly. "I don't want you speaking to Lord Ivor again." Her voice a smooth purr. The next moment, her eyes flash, meeting my gaze with lance-like precision. "Ever."

A noose of Obligation tightens around my throat. I nearly choke right there and then. My eyes bulge, and only my grip on the door handle keeps me firmly upright.

"Yes, mistress," I murmur, bowing my head.

Then I duck from the room and shut the door silently behind me.

What just happened?

Head spinning, I stumble down the passages of Aurelis, my hands occasionally reaching to feel my throat, trying to loosen the constricted cord that isn't there. Most of the time I can dismiss and ignore the Obligation. I must obey my mistress's commands with promptness and precision, of course, but I can do that without being overtly *aware* of the Obligation itself.

Now I'm reminded all too clearly what the Obligation truly is: a curse. A curse I cannot escape until all has come to fulfillment.

I shudder, tucking my chin in and wrapping my arms around my middle. Oh, gods on high, what am I supposed to do now?

Well, the answer is simple enough: I must obey my mistress. That's all.

Don't talk to Ivor. Fine. I shouldn't be talking to him anyway. It's dangerous. Every interaction with him has only made me more aware of the danger. Estrilde's command? It's for the best, really. It will simply reinforce what I already know I must do—avoid the handsome fae lord and put him out of my mind entirely. Or as entirely as I can while living in the very city-palace he will one day—sooner rather than later—rule.

I should see Estrilde as an ally here, not an enemy. Because really, that's what my mistress is. A shield between me and doing something I will forever regret.

"Keep your eye on the goal," I remind myself in a whisper. "Ten more years. Never anger the fae. Never trust the fae. Never love the fae. Ten more years."

I lift my chin and put my shoulders back. I can do this. I *will* do this.

I realize suddenly that I don't know where I'm going. I'm meant to attend upon the Prince of Vespre, but where is he staying exactly? Does he have his own set of rooms in Aurelis? Is it part of the family wing, close to Estrilde's own suite?

"Pardon me," I say to a young Obligate hurrying in the opposite direction. "Can you tell me where Prince Castien is staying?"

The Obligate shoots me a wary look. There's recognition in his gaze, though I don't know him in the slightest. He offers no answer save for a quick shake of his head, then hurries on his way. On some business for his lord or lady, no doubt. I shiver, wondering at that look he'd given me. Has word of last night's little misadventure spread beyond the library to the rest of the human inhabitants of Aurelis? Will I be shunned and feared for the rest of my stay here? For something I don't even clearly remember doing?

I try three more times before I finally find someone who can tell me where the Prince is staying. Apparently, he's taken up residence in the queen's suite. Which is a surprise. No one has lived in the queen's suite since Queen Dasyra's passing. I've heard rumor that her rooms are grander, more sumptuous even than Estrilde's, which is hard to imagine.

Though I've never been there, I know the way to the queen's suite well enough, and quickly turn my feet that direction. The door leading into the apartment is a good fifteen feet tall, white, and gilded and decorated with a repeated pattern of delicate blue flowers of some variety I don't know. I feel very small standing in front of that door. But that's not a new feeling. I've felt small ever since coming to Aurelis. The only time I don't is in Ivor's presence. Which isn't good. Much better for me to stand here. Small. Mousy. Insignificant. Aware of my place in this world.

After first clearing my throat and brushing out my skirts, I lift my hand, knock smartly. And wait.

Nothing.

I knock again. And wait again.

Still nothing.

Perhaps the Prince isn't in. Perhaps I should go away, report back later. But no. Estrilde's instructions were clear: I'm to attend upon the Prince in his suite. Even if he's not in, I must present myself and wait. And wait and wait and wait.

I bite my lip. Then, drawing a short breath through my nostrils, I knock one more time, calling softly, "Excuse me? It's Clara Darlington. I've been summoned by the Prince of Vespre. My mistress, Princess Estrilde, sent me to be of service."

There's a sound on the other side of the door. Footsteps? I draw back, straighten my skirts again, then clasp my hands behind my back. The latch moves. The door opens. I prepare myself to meet some servant of the Prince's.

Instead the door swings wide, and the Prince himself stands before me. Shirtless.

My eyes widen. I stare straight at a bare, muscular, golden torso. Tight-fitting trousers hang low on his hips and wrap his legs only to the knees, leaving his calves and feet bare. Glossy strands of black hair hang over shoulders which are almost impossibly well-muscled and strong.

I shut my sagging jaw with a quick *clunk*. Lifting my eyes to his face, I meet his strange, violet gaze. My heart shivers.

He's looking at me with an expression of unmasked loathing.

"You," he snarls.

I open my mouth again, try to speak. No words will come.

The Prince's teeth flash in a grimace. He lifts one foot, takes a step toward me.

And to my utmost surprise, his legs buckle, his eyes roll back in his head, and he collapses. Into my arms.

12

I STAGGER AND TRY TO CATCH MY BALANCE EVEN AS I struggle to hold onto him. It's no use. He's too heavy. My legs fold. I crumple to the ground, crushed beneath his weight.

I'm only too aware of all the bare skin my trembling hands are clutching.

"Help!" I call out, turning my head this way and that. "Someone? Anyone!"

There's no answer. Of course not! Everyone in Aurelis is avoiding the pariah prince.

I look down into his face. His head tilts back on my arm, his jaw partly open, his eyes closed. How unexpectedly long and dark his lashes are, fanned across his tanned cheeks! Only now, those tanned cheeks have taken on a grayish hue, and his eyes are framed in deep, dark circles.

What in the seven secret names of all the seven gods am I supposed to do now?

Gritting my teeth, I ease out from under him, trying to be gentle as I let his naked torso slide to the cold, hard ground. I can't very well leave him in the hall and go running for help, can I? No, no. I grab hold of his wrists and slide him along the floor. Grunting and puffing, I drag him through the open door into the queen's suite. I'm vaguely aware of opulence and elegance surrounding me, but my attention fixes on an upholstered lounger not too far from the door. With more puffing, I slide the prince along the polished floor up to the lounger, only to realize there's no way I can get him up two feet onto the cushions. Maybe if he were at least partially conscious . . . but as it is, he's a dead weight.

I growl softly in my throat, suppressing a curse. Snatching a tasseled pillow from the lounger, I tuck it under the prince's head. Now his neck crooks at what must be an uncomfortable angle, but at least if he wakes, he will see that I tried.

Sitting back on my heels, I scan the room, searching for inspiration, and spy a pretty painted table with cut-crystal decanters and glasses in the shapes of blooming flowers. Among the bottles, I spy what looks like a bottle of *qeise*, a strong drink favored by the fae. That might serve my purpose.

It's the work of a moment for me to hasten across the room, pour a measure into one of the flower glasses, and carry it back to the prince. Kneeling beside him, I lift his head and tip a little of the bright, clear brew between his open lips.

He twitches. His mouth closes. Then he coughs violently and surges upright into a seated position for a few seconds before collapsing once more on the pillow. His eyes flash up at me, bright violet and livid. Then they roll again, and he fades.

"No, wait! Stay awake!" I set aside the glass, catch him by the shoulders, and pat his cheek with one hand. "Is there someone here? Some servant I can call?"

His lashes flutter, and he looks up at me again, his eyes swimming in and out of focus. "Bottle," he gasps. "Blue . . . bedside table . . ." He sinks back into unconsciousness. No amount of cheek-patting can stir him.

"Seven gods!" I mutter, looking up and around the room. It's some sort of receiving space, not unlike Princess Estrilde's own chambers. Simultaneously grander and less elaborate than Estrilde's, according to the tastes of the queen who once lived here. There are several doors leading into adjacent chambers, and a stairway leading to upper floors and rooms. The apartment is bigger than the whole of the Gale's townhouse. By a long shot.

One of the doors is opened. I think I can see the foot of a big bed from here.

I scramble to my feet and race to the door. It is a bedchamber—a beautiful, sumptuous bedchamber, truly fit for a queen. Blooming flowers climb the walls and bedposts, and woven, living vines create bedcurtains. Unlike the stink of roses that permeates Princess Estrilde's rooms, these flowers come together to form a harmonizing blend of perfume, like a delicate orchestra for the nose. Whoever encouraged their growth knew what she was doing when she paired them.

For several moments, I simply stand there, staring. One would think after five long years of service in Aurelis, I would grow used to fae grandeur and spectacle. But there's always room for yet another surprise. And this room certainly surprises me, for despite it's great size and the obvious wealth of every article of furniture, there's an unexpectedly *welcoming* atmosphere in the air. As though anyone could be at home here.

The Prince has certainly made himself at home. I blink and look a second time, spying signs of his habitation everywhere—strewn garments and shoes, books, quills, cloaks, all dropped and left wherever they happened to land. If he has a servant, the poor man must be at his wits end to keep up with this level of dishevelment.

But I haven't come to gawk. A blue bottle stands on the bedside table, just as the Prince said. I dart across the room, snatch it up, and hastily return to the receiving room and the prone figure on the floor.

He looks worse than ever. Gray and haggard. Even his hair seems to have lost its lustrous shine. I pop the top off the bottle and prop the Prince's head again. How much am I supposed to give him? There's no label on the bottle, no instructions. Shooting a swift prayer to the gods, I stick it between his lips and pour. Then I set the bottle down, tilt his head back, close his lips and nose. "Swallow!" I urge him. "Please!"

The muscles of his throat tighten and relax.

The next instant, his eyes flare open.

He sits upright, one arm flailing wildly. His hand clunks my jaw. I tumble over, pain radiating through my face. Sparks burst on the edges of my vision, and I glare through them at the Prince, who's bent double, coughing and retching. Is he going to vomit up everything I just gave him?

I pick myself up, clutching my jaw, and watch him narrowly until the spasms subside. He shudders, his bare shoulders bowed, his head hanging heavily. For some moments he simply breathes one ragged breath after another. Then he turns, peering at me through lank locks of black hair. "Looks as though I'm not going to die this time after all." His brow puckers slightly. "Did I . . . ?" He waves a vague hand my way.

I realize what he's asking and lift a brow. "Knock me silly? Yes, Your Highness."

"Oh. I beg your pardon. I certainly didn't intend to initiate a brawl. These fits take me, and there's little enough I can do about them, other than feel shame for my behavior after the fact."

Am I mistaken or does he actually look chagrined? "It's all right." I offer a weak sort of smile. "No harm done."

"Yes, well, let us be grateful for small blessings," the Prince answers dryly. He starts to rise, but his knees give out almost at once, leaving him in an awkward heap and breathing hard. He twists his jaw to one side. "I don't seem to be in full mastery of my limbs. May I beg your assistance a little further, Clara Darling?"

I wince at the misuse of my name. It sounds so wrong coming

from a man who obviously despises me. But there's no point in correcting him. I shut my lips and offer him my arm. He drapes himself over my shoulder, and I am once again painfully aware of the near proximity of naked flesh pressed up against me. I've never been this close to a bare, manly torso in my life! My palm splays across a well-toned abdomen, and I can feel heat creeping up my arm, all the way to my cheeks. Gods above, how did I end up here? This is no place for a lady!

But now he's awake, I can get him onto the lounger. He sinks into the cushions, his head tilted back, his throat tense and exposed, his chest heaving. It's impossible not to notice all over again the fine-tuning of each muscle, the cording in his arms as he so casually rests them across the back of the lounger. I think he's doing it on purpose. I think he knows *exactly* the sight he makes. It's not quite a glamour, but it's equally effective.

I turn away quickly, my face burning. "Shall I summon a servant, Your Highness?" I ask, taking care that my voice registers nothing but brisk politeness.

"My servant is away on his off day," the Prince replies, his eyes still closed. "He won't return for some hours yet, as I am a more lenient master than some." He cracks an eye and peers up at me. "I don't think I like that look on your face. What? Do you disapprove? Or does it simply surprise you do know not all princes like to travel with a large bevvy of caretakers? Lawrence has always served my needs admirably. And I can generally contrive to bumble my way through a day without him."

I raise my eyebrows.

"Yes, well," he growls in answer to my unspoken comment, "I'm not bumbling along so well at the moment, obviously. It's this place. Aurelis. For some reason, it always makes the curse I carry act up more than usual. Especially after any exertion of human magic. Gods!" He leans his head back once more, groaning. "One little written binding, and I'm left weak as a kitten a full day later! This is why I never come to the Dawn Court."

"You're cursed?" I know I should mind my own business, but the words slip out before I can stop them.

"Didn't you know?" His eyes open in slits again, vivid violet peering through that thicket of black lashes. "I should have thought rumor of me and my foibles abounded! I suppose I'm old news by now, long since shuffled off to Vespre. Out of sight, out of mind, as you humans like to say. Yes, Miss Darling, I am in fact cursed. Or at the least, part of me is. I'm not entirely clear on the details. But it acts up any time I use the *human* side of my magic. Been that way for . . . oh, the last five-ish turns of the cycle I should say."

I really shouldn't show any interest or encourage his chatter. With another meaningless smile, I pick up the pillow and the flower-shaped glass of *qeise* and the blue bottle. The pillow I plop on the lounger beside the prince, and the glass and bottle I take to the table full of decanters. This done, I cast a quick glance around, but see no other signs of disturbance in the peaceful, elegant room.

"Are you quite through bustling?" the Prince calls from his seat.

I return to the lounger and stand demurely in front of him, hands folded, head bowed. He's sitting up a little straighter now, though his eyes are still ringed with dark smudges. I bob a quick curtsy. "If that will be all, Your Highness."

"No." He snorts. "That jolly well isn't *all*. What, did you think I summoned you here just so you could manhandle me and pour bitter brews down my throat? No, no, I'm afraid you're not getting off that easily."

My masking smile slips a little. "I . . . I thought—"

"I certainly wasn't *expecting* to faint into your arms. That was an unfortunate accident. No, I had another purpose in asking my fair cousin to send you my way. Look." He lifts a languid hand, pointing across the room. I turn obediently and see a book lying on a long table between two potted plants. Not just any book: *the* book. The book Thaddeus Creakle gave me last night when he pushed me into the library and slammed the door behind me.

My mouth goes dry.

"Do you remember what you did?" the Prince's voice breaks the thudding in my temples.

I swallow. Slowly, I first shake and then nod my head, uncertain how to answer. I do remember some of last night. I remember the Noswraith vividly! And I remember being sent to deal with it. I remember Estrilde's fingers around my throat.

Beyond that . . . I'm not sure.

"I thought as much." The Prince grunts. "It's not enough merely to suppress your powers. One must suppress the *memory* of them as well, or risk you fighting to reclaim them. Go on. Pick it up. Have a look at what you did."

I cast him an uneasy, sideways glance. I don't have to look, do I? No, surely not. He's not my master; I'm not *obliged* to do as he says. And maybe I don't want to look. Maybe I want to pretend whatever happened last night never happened at all. Go back to life as I knew it, which is complicated enough.

Yet somehow I find myself crossing the room and plucking the little volume from the table. I crack the cover.

"Careful!" the Prince calls out. "Take care you don't read the last page. You'll risk setting it free again."

For a moment I freeze. Then, slowly, I open the book across my arm. My own handwriting appears before my vision. Slowly I read my account of entering the library last night, of how strange and foreign and dangerous it felt. I turn a page and read of climbing the stairs to the second floor, of encountering the Noswraith. All written in my own hand, though I have no memory of writing it.

It's good reading, if I do say it myself. Gripping even. I keep turning pages, experiencing as though for the first time the fear, the horror, the struggle. The chase through the stacks. The moment I tackled that hideous creature and pulled the book down over its head, physically forcing it into the pages. Caught up in what I'm reading, I begin to turn the last page.

A horrible, melted, waxy face rears up before me, roaring with rage.

I drop the book and leap back, a scream frozen on my lips.

But it doesn't hit the floor. Instead a pair of hands deftly catches and slams the volume shut. Heart pounding, breath catching, I look up to find the Prince standing before me, his eyes narrow and watching me closely. I stare into those eyes, unable to think straight, unable to draw air into my constricted lungs.

"Your method is inelegant," he says, his voice pitched lower than before. "But the containment spell is effective insofar as it goes. Without the name to bind it, however, you couldn't possibly hope to keep the wraith contained."

"I . . . I gave it a name." I don't know where I find the strength to speak. The words seem to come of their own volition. "The Melted Man."

"And an evocative name it is." Those lovely full lips of his quirk to one side in a smirk. "But unfortunately not good enough. Only the original creator of the Noswraith may truly name it. This one was written into being centuries ago by a fellow named Zhoron. Mage Zhoron of the Miphates. Have you heard of him?"

I shake my head.

"Yes, well, the Miphates seem to have slipped from history into the stuff of legends in your world, I'm afraid. Poor fellows. In his day, Zhoron was a respected member of his order. Or so I'm told. My mother met him once or twice."

My head is spinning. I can't seem to take in any of what he says. Instead my gaze fixes on the book in his hands. The book that contains a spell. *My* spell. So I'm a magic user? Impossible! Then again . . . My hand creeps to my throat, still feeling the pressure of Estrilde's fingers gripping fast. It must be true. I have magic. Magic Estrilde suppressed, along with all memory of it. Could this have something to do with my Obligation? With how I broke the Pledge, calling the wrath of the fae down upon my head? With why I was dragged from my home, my family, my world, and plunged into this terrifying new existence?

The Prince is watching me still. I feel his gaze like a weight, ready to crush me. I glance up and, for an instant, catch a glimpse of that unguarded viciousness, that hatred. He blinks, however, and the expression vanishes behind one of bland indifference.

"I can teach you, you know," he says. "I can teach you how to write a binding on a Noswraith's name. I can teach you how to create much stronger bindings than this. You have the talent. All you require is the training."

I gape at him. What exactly is he saying? The words are clear enough, but I can't seem to make them make sense in my head. Is he truly offering to instruct me in magical arts? "I . . . I . . ." I shake my head, frown, and tear my gaze from his, focusing on the book in his hands once more. "I have no interest in learning such things. There's no need. Noswraiths don't come to Aurelis."

"Not until last night, you mean."

"Yes, but . . . but didn't *you* let this one out?"

"What an ugly suspicion!" He chuckles softly, like a growl. "Really, Clara Darling, yours is such a mistrustful young mind. You quite wound me."

I flash a swift glance up at him again. "You did." My conviction grows with each word I speak. "You let it out. You turned it loose on Aurelis Library, because . . . because you *wanted* Princess Estrilde to release my magic. You *wanted* me to hunt it down, to see what I can do." It's all so clear now. I see it in his face. But I still don't understand. "Why?" I demand, the word blurting from my lips.

He smiles a slow, unhurried sort of smile. But the bitterness never leaves his eyes. "Because I needed to show them all—my father, Estrilde, even that pasty-faced Lord Ivor—that you don't belong here. You belong in Vespre. With me. Where you can be of great service to all Eledria."

"*What?*" I take a step back, then another. "You want me to leave Aurelis?" I shake my head, slowly at first, then faster and faster. "No, no, no. I'm Obligated to Princess Estrilde. I can't go anywhere. I must serve her. Here."

"Obligations can be bought and sold." The Prince tilts his head slightly to one side, his eyes once more narrowing. "You know that, right? And even Estrilde, stubborn though she may be, has her price. And her limits."

I keep shaking my head. This is a nightmare, a total nightmare! I've barely survived five years here in the Court of Dawn with all its intrigues and back-stabbing. I can't go to Vespre, wherever the gods'-only-know that is! I can't be turned into some sort of wizard, learning binding spells and battling Noswraiths like the one I saw last night. I just have to keep my head down. Survive.

Never anger the fae, never trust the fae, never love the fae . . . that's all. Then I can get home, home, *home.* I close my eyes and call to mind Oscar's face. And Danny's. They need me. They both do. I won't let them down.

A chuckle rumbles in my ear. The sound is so bitter, so dark, my eyes fly open again, meeting the Prince's too knowing gaze.

"Gods above, girl, don't look so horrified," he says. "I may loathe the very sight of you, but I'm no monster. I won't carry you off to the Dark Isles and devour you! You have something I need. You can serve me far better than you can serve my cousin, and the term of your Obligation will be no longer than it was before. Besides, you'll find life in Vespre more *stimulating,* shall we say, than this stifling court of sunshine and sparkles."

My stomach dips and plunges. I see the truth in his eyes—both the truth of his inexplicable hatred and the truth of his purpose. His determination.

"Don't," I whisper. "Please."

"Don't what? Talk to my cousin? Too late. Negotiations have already begun. She's putting up some fight, but it won't take long to wear her down. After all, Estrilde doesn't care for *competition.*"

My eyes widen. I want to pretend that I don't know what he means, but . . . but if I'm honest . . .

I whirl on one heel and flee for the door. Even as my hand reaches for the latch, the Prince steps in my way. How he moved so fast when just minutes ago he looked ready to collapse again I cannot begin to guess. His long fingers catch hold of my wrist, and he's suddenly very close. So close I can feel the heat of his body, almost vibrating with inner power.

"You can't run from who you are." His words fall on me like a curtain of darkness, closing around me, hemming me in. "One way or another, the truth always catches up. And you, Clara Darling, were born to be more than a fetch-and-carry girl for my cousin."

He lowers his head. Warm breath tickles my ear, and gooseprickles run along my neck, down my spine. I can't move. I'm caught, not just by his grip on my wrist, but by the very magnetism of his presence which overwhelms my senses.

"You were born to be a warrior," he whispers.

I close my eyes. My lips quiver as I let out one desperate plea: "Let me go."

To my surprise, his fingers immediately relax their grip. He steps to one side, and I lunge for escape. The latch gives, the door swings open, and I stumble out into the passage beyond, slamming the door shut behind me.

13

I MAKE MY WAY BLINDLY DOWN THE HALL, HEAD throbbing, heart pounding. My mind spins with the Prince's words, his threats.

Gods on high, this can't be real! Estrilde holds me in no great fondness, but she is a woman who likes to keep tight hold of all that *belongs* to her. She won't be parted from an Obligate easily. Not for anything less than a stupendous price.

So I should be fine. Yes, I should be just fine—

I hit something solid.

"*Oof!*" the breath bursts from my lungs, and I stumble back, nearly falling, before strong hands catch hold of my forearms, righting me on my feet.

"Your pardon, Clara. It seems I cannot help running into you today."

Ivor.

My blood runs cold. I crane my neck back to stare up into the beautiful face of the golden fae lord. In the same instant, I feel the force of Estrilde's last command clamp down on me like a vice.

"Clara?" Ivor's brow, which had been alight with a smile but a moment before, darkens into a frown. "Clara, what's wrong?"

I open my mouth, try to answer. But Estrilde's injunction closes my throat. I gasp, choke. My eyes widen. I'm going to . . . Gods above me, I'm going to suffocate!

"Clara?" Ivor bends his head, staring into my face. "Clara, what is this? Is it . . . is it Estrilde? Has she done something to you?"

I can do nothing but nod desperately and hope he understands. Oh gods, oh gods! I'm going to die! I'm going to choke to death right here in this beautiful man's arms. All because my mistress doesn't want me to speak to him. I struggle to get free, to put any distance at all between us. But without air, my body goes limp. Darkness closes in on all sides.

Ivor's face, swimming before my tunneling vision, grows ferocious. He bares his teeth in a snarl. Then, to my horror, he suddenly presses me close to his chest, enfolding me with devastating tenderness. "Don't worry," he murmurs into the top of my head. "Don't worry, sweet one. I will speak to her. I will put an end to this."

With that, he draws back, meets my eyes once more. Then, to my utmost relief, he lets me go, turns, and retreats down the hall. The moment he's out of sight, my throat opens. I collapse to my knees, dragging in breath after ragged breath. Tears run down my cheeks as I sob with sheer relief. Shuddering, I curl into a ball, holding onto my midsection as though I can somehow hold myself together.

"Never anger the fae," I whisper.

Too late. Ivor is going to my mistress. He's going to try to help. Estrilde is going to be so, so angry.

I should report back to my mistress's suite, but the idea fills me with such dread. Especially if Ivor is even now making good on his word and speaking to the princess on my behalf.

Since Estrilde gave no specific command, I decide to make for the one haven I know—the library.

Evening has come to Aurelis, and the library is already closed, the few librarians dispersed to various parts of the palace where they will either enjoy some leisure or will continue to serve their masters and mistresses in various ways. That's just as well as far as I'm concerned. I don't want to deal with their frightened stares.

"*One way or another, the truth always catches up to you.*"

The Prince's words, spoken with such subtle menace, slide like razor blades across my mind. But he's wrong. None of *this* is real. None of it! What's real is the world I just left behind, the world that contains Danny and Oscar and Kitty. All of this? It's nothing but madness. Madness I must survive, but not actually part of *me*.

I won't let the madness drag me down. I won't.

I wander through the quiet aisles, gazing at the books nestled in their shelves. The shelves themselves are made up of white branches, densely intertwined. From some angles, they look as though they've been carved from marble, but from others, they seem to stir with life. Here and there gold-edged leaves sprout and waft gently in the air. I trail my fingers along the spines of certain books, seeking comfort from them as I would from old friends. But tonight, there is no comfort. I feel only cold. And fear.

What I need is a task. Something to concentrate on, something that will distract me from all the whirling thoughts crowding my head. I make my way to the back workroom where the stacks of pixie-chewed books still await attention. Thaddeus has made some progress since yesterday, but there's plenty of work to be done. Piles of unsorted page fragments sit in various baskets.

I take a seat, pull one of the baskets close, and begin to go through the pages. Some of them are little more than scraps, most of the knowledge once contained therein lost to a pixie's belly. How will we ever fill in the gaps? Ventures into the mortal world will have to be made to find replacements, but King Lodírhal rarely sanctions such expeditions, especially now that Queen Dasyra is no longer alive to urge him.

Dasyra . . .

Why does the thought of her seem to spark something in the back of my mind? Is it a memory? Maybe. Or maybe just an impression.

"Miss Darlington?"

I start, dropping the page I hold, and turn in my seat. Thaddeus Creakle stands in the doorway. His face, usually so carefully moderated into pleasant, uncommunicative lines, looks worried. "I thought this was your day off, Miss Darlington."

"Oh, it was." I fix my smile firmly in place, determined not to let him glimpse the anxiety simmering inside me. "But I thought I'd make a little start on tomorrow's work before I turn in."

He knows I'm not speaking the truth. He knows I'm avoiding something. I can see it in his eye. But old Thaddeus simply takes a seat at his own desk, where a large volume sits disassembled, the spine unsewn, the pages neatly stacked. He selects a quill and writes a few lines in a notebook, and I realize that he's not going to say anything more. He's simply going to *be* there. Which is unexpectedly kind of him.

I return to my work, carefully lifting chewed-up pages from the basket, inspecting the remains, and setting them into appropriate stacks according to the book. In this way, I manage to distract myself for a good five minutes. But at the end of those five minutes, I turn in my chair, facing the senior librarian again. "Mister Creakle?"

He grunts without looking up.

"What do you know about Vespre?"

His eyebrows slowly rise. His gaze lifts from the work in front of him to meet mine. "Why do you want to know?"

"I just . . ." I lick my lips. "I know the . . . the monster from last night came from Vespre. And I understand that there are more monsters like it kept there. So I wondered . . ."

Thaddeus draws a long breath through his nostrils and leans back in his chair. His fingers twirl his quill, the only indication of nerves he betrays. "Vespre," he says at last, "is an old troll city located in the Umbrian Isles. There is no king uniting the isles anymore, but each is ruled instead by a prince who, in turn, serves the king of his own court. Vespre, the largest of these isles, is ruled by Prince Castien Lodírith."

I nod. I wonder if the Prince was given this island to rule in lieu of his father's kingdom. A sort of pacifier for not being deemed worthy to be named true heir.

Thaddeus continues: "Vespre is known throughout Eledria as the *Doomed City*."

My stomach pitches. "That doesn't sound good."

"No. Not good at all." Realizing how quickly he's twirling his quill, Thaddeus abruptly sets it down and folds his hands tightly in front of him. "There's a library in Vespre—a vast library that puts this one to shame. There, Noswraiths have been collected and are contained by the Doomed City librarians. Hundreds of Noswraiths. Thousands perhaps."

The horrible image of the Melted Man flashes across my memory. Are the other Noswraiths as bad as that? Not a pleasant thought.

"Wh-why is it called the *Doomed* City?" I ask.

"Because," Thaddeus says, his tone a little too placid, a little too calm for comfort, "one day, it is said, there will be a reckoning—"

Before he can finish, there's a knock at the door. Thaddeus closes his mouth tight, picks up his quill, and bows over his work. "Come in!" he calls.

The door opens to reveal Poppin. The little bunyi bobs a curtsy, her furry hands neatly folded in front of her. "Pardon me, miss," she says in her polite, squeaky voice, "but your presence is required in Princess Estrilde's chambers."

I stare at her, my mouth open, unable to give an answer. I knew it was coming, of course. I knew I couldn't hide in the library forever. There's no escaping my mistress's wrath. Even so, I can't seem to find the will to speak, to answer. To move.

Within a few seconds, the pain begins—creeping into my head, trickling through my veins. The Obligation won't allow me to resist for long. If I try to hold out, soon the pain will be unbearable. I must honor the law.

Knees trembling, I rise. Thaddeus won't meet the quick glance I cast his way but remains bowed over his work. "Thank you, Mister Creakle," I say. I'm not sure what I'm thanking him for. My words sound more like a farewell than anything. "Thank you for . . . everything."

He grunts. He doesn't look up.

My legs are so unsteady, I'm half afraid I won't be able to follow Poppin from the room. But I manage to steady myself against the table and then, squaring my shoulders, take a few firm steps. Poppin bobs and scampers ahead of me, leading the way through the silent library. I refuse to look around me as I go, refuse to take in what I suspect will be my last glimpses of this place I've grown to love. After all, I could be wrong. Estrilde will be mad, certainly, but that doesn't mean . . . it doesn't mean . . .

I can't bear to finish the thought. Hope is too painful.

Neither I nor the bunyi speak as we go. The halls of the golden palace are silent and lonely, and though the shadows are few, they feel denser than usual. We pass only a handful of other living souls on our way, none of whom will look at me. Do they know I'm a condemned woman on my way to the gallows? Would they take more interest if they knew?

We turn a final corner, and I'm startled to see the door of the princess's suite open suddenly. My heart lurches . . . then lurches again when Ivor strides out. His face is a study in absolute fury, a face that would belong more naturally on the battlefield than here.

My worst fears are confirmed. He's spoken to Estrilde.

The fae lord doesn't see me or the bunyi where we stand at the end of the passage. He turns the opposite way and strides off, his fists clenched, his head angled forward as though he's about to charge into a brawl. Where is he going? To seek out King Lodírhal? But not even the king can command Estrilde concerning her own Obligates.

My heart shivers. I appreciate that Ivor would try to help me, but . . . oh gods, how I wish he had never taken an interest in me to begin with! Never looked at me in *that* way, never spoken to me in *that* voice. Never singled me out from among the many hundreds of humans serving in the Court of Dawn. Too late now.

Poppin leads on. She opens the door to Estrilde's suite and announces me, just as she did yesterday. All of this feels like a weird, mirror-image of that day—but a murky image in a darkened carnival glass.

I step through the door into the receiving room. And stop short.

The lovely lounging furniture has all been overturned, some of the more delicate pieces broken. There are spatters of red wine like bloodstains on the floors and walls, and shattered glass strewn every which way. The climbing roses have withdrawn their buds, and even the usual stink of rose perfume is deadened into a musk of pure rage.

At the head of the room, Estrilde sits above this destruction in her throne-like chair. She has thrown a golden, fur-trimmed cloak around her shoulders, and the effect is unmistakably queenly. She may not be Aurelis's ruler in fact, but she'll playact the part with all the vigor she can summon.

But as impressive and terrible as she is, my gaze is inexorably dragged to one side. To him. The Prince of the Doomed City.

He lounges in one of the few unbroken chairs, his leg slung over one of its arms, his elbow resting on the other, his hand cupping his chin. One would never know to look at him that less than two hours ago he was gasping for breath on the floor. He's donned some clothing, at least—a loose-fitting coat, unbuttoned, revealing his still-naked torso. Embroidered slippers grace his feet.

He idly turns his head when I step into the room, his lips curling in a smile that never reaches his eyes. "Welcome, Clara Darling," he practically purrs. "We've been eagerly awaiting your arrival."

My limbs tremble so hard, I fear they'll give out. Somehow, I find the will to tear my gaze away from the Prince, to cross the room, to sink to my knees before Estrilde's chair. "Mistress," I say, my head bowed, my heart hammering.

"There you are." Estrilde's furious gaze doesn't quite rest on me. Which is a relief. I'm fairly certain if the princess actually looked directly at me, I'd go up in a puff of smoke. "I have sold your Obligation to my cousin here. You are to pack your things at once and leave Aurelis."

No preamble. No explanation. No time for me to hope she'll say something else. Anything else.

And yet—as I kneel at the princess's feet, feeling my lungs tighten up, feeling the walls closing in—I can't quite believe it.

Estrilde turns from me and addresses herself to the Prince. "Remember, I retain Breaker's Rights. But the rest of the Obligation is yours to do with as you please. Though I must say, you have spent far more on a ten-year service than you ought."

"It's your own fault, fairest cousin," the Prince answers demurely. "You drive a hard bargain. I am powerless against your subtle arts."

Estrilde's face clouds. She knows he's mocking her. "Well," she says coldly, "the creature is yours now." She rises, pulling the folds of her cloak close to her body as though afraid it will brush against me. "Take it away and let me not set eyes upon it again, if you please." With those words, and without so much as a last glance for me, she sweeps from the chamber, entering some inner room of her suite and closing the door firmly behind her.

I remain in place, kneeling before the princess's empty seat. My palms press into the cold floor, and my hair falls in a thick curtain over one side of my face, blocking my view of the Prince. Of my new master.

I hear him unfolding himself from the chair, rising.

The next moment, a hand appears in my line of sight.

"Go on," he says. "Take it."

I lift my gaze slowly, meeting his. His eyes spark with an unpleasant light that doesn't reach the depths of his dark pupils. "Is that a command?" I ask, the words grating between clenched teeth.

"Not necessarily." He shrugs. "A suggestion, perhaps. But one you ought to heed, considering you seem to have momentarily lost the use of your limbs."

I shake my head slowly, refusing to blink or look away. "Why?" I whisper. "Why did you do it? Why?"

"I already told you." The Prince retracts his hand and folds his arms. "You were meant for greater things than Aurelis Court can offer. You were meant for Vespre. You were meant for battle."

He leans in, bringing his face close to mine. His pupils are so largely dilated, I can scarcely see the violet irises ringing them. A perfume of darkness, of shadow-grown flowers and secrets wafts from his hair, an intoxicating blend that stings my nostrils and makes my head spin.

"I'll make you pay for what you've done, Clara Darling," he

whispers. "I'll make you pay tenfold for the evil you've wrought upon the worlds."

He straightens then, turns from me, and strides from the room, calling over his shoulder as he goes, "Gather your things quickly now and report back to my chambers. We leave for Vespre tonight."

14

THE PRINCE IS TRUE TO HIS WORD.

Two hours later, I find myself walking through the western garden of Aurelis, bathed in the purple haze that passes for night in this world. I wear my regular work gown and my cloak and carry a small bundle of belongings against my chest—my mulberry gown from Kitty, an extra pair of shoes, humble shell hair combs, a few other oddments. Nothing much. Obligates don't keep many personal belongings; we are provided with all necessities by our Lords and Ladies.

The Prince leads the way through the gardens to the outer palace walls. He's dressed for travel in an elaborate, swirling cloak, tall boots, gloves, and a hat with a dramatic plume. He scarcely gave me a second glance when I showed up at the door of the queen's suite, but strode passed me, saying only, "Keep up!"

His manservant is more friendly. "Good evening, miss," he said with a bright smile as he stepped out of the room and shut the door behind him. "My name is Lawrence. I am a fellow Obligate." He spoke the words lightly, as though naming his profession. I've never heard anyone speak so casually of their Obligation before.

It's difficult not to return Lawrence's smile. He's a tall, spare fellow with a long face covered in freckles and pleasing gray eyes. Striding a few yards ahead of me at the heels of the Prince, he strikes me as being in a particularly fine mood. Perhaps his own visit to the mortal world that day had been enjoyable. At any rate, he hadn't returned to find his life utterly upended.

I trot along several paces behind Lawrence, feeling as though I'm moving through a dream. None of this seems real. I keep revisiting key moments of the last forty-eight hours in my mind, trying to decide what different choices I could have made along the way to end up in any situation other than this. But it all has a certain inevitability about it. As though the gods themselves have conspired to drive me to this place.

"I'll make you pay tenfold for the evil you've wrought . . ."

What could the Prince mean by those words? The evil *I've* wrought? There must be some mistake. I've never met him before, and I certainly haven't done anything . . . I haven't done . . . I haven't . . . I grimace. After all, my memories were suppressed. I don't know what I've done. I only know I've done *something* bad enough to land me in this position as an Obligate. The fae don't dole out fifteen-year sentences for nothing.

"Keep up!" The Prince's imperious voice rings out through the gloom. Lawrence casts a sympathetic look back at me and motions with a jerk of his head. His arms are full of two large carpet bags, presumably stuffed with the Prince's belongings. Other servants carry several large trunks between them, preceding us up the garden path. How much luggage had the Prince brought along for a single night's stay?

The palace walls loom in the half light. And a gate as large as the Between Gate I'd used earlier to travel into my own world but constructed of darker stone and not in very good repair. My heart gives a painful thud. I've never traveled anywhere else in Eledria, never left the relative safety of Aurelis Palace save to return to my own world. Will this gate take us directly into the Doomed City? Will I step through into the middle of a library full of Noswraiths?

The servants drop the chests beneath the stone arch then scurry away quickly. A shadow moves, and Lyklor's tall form seems to manifest from nothing to stand before the great stone dial. His strong, muscled arms spin the dial, and the next moment, the chests disappear.

"Thank you, Lyklor," the Prince says, offering the gate guardian a flashing smile. "Tell me, how's the family these days? The little ones still giving you trouble?"

Lyklor opens his mouth and utters a sound I've never heard before—a kind of sawing bray that, weirdly enough, seems to have words in it.

"Well," the Prince says with a shrug, "my father would tell you *discipline, discipline, discipline.*" He spreads his arms, his cloak sweeping like a pair of wings. "And see how well I've turned out! He must know something about the subject."

I observe this exchange with mute fascination. While I've always tried to be on friendly terms with the gate guardian, it simply never occurred to me that he might be a family man, er . . . family creature.

Lyklor grunts and spins the dial again until it comes to rest on a certain mark that looks uncomfortably like a single, staring eye. The Prince steps under the arch, tossing back over his shoulder, "Lawrence, take care my new Obligate doesn't try to bolt the moment I'm out of sight. I expect to see her on the other side anon."

Lawrence chuckles like this is some sort of joke. I, for one, fail to see the humor in it.

Lyklor moves the dial again, and the Prince's form shimmers, becomes translucent, then vanishes altogether. I let out a breath. Not much of a breath, for my lungs are still tight with tension. But it's a relief just being out of the Prince's sight for a moment.

Lawrence turns to me, offering another of his surprisingly sweet smiles. "After you, miss," he says with a sweep of one hand. Lyklor is already spinning the dial, getting the gate ready yet again.

I draw a deep breath. My stomach shudders with nervous terror of all the unknowns lying ahead. Though I promised myself that I wouldn't, I cast one last longing glance back to the palace. What am I hoping to see? Ivor's face in one of the windows, looking down at me? Watching my departure with regret? *Would* he regret my going from Aurelis? Though I try hard not to let it, memory creeps back into my mind—memory of Ivor's strong arms wrapped around me, pressing me close to his heart. In the moment, I'd been too distracted by the horror of my airway being cut off. But in retrospect, that moment of closeness had been . . . revealing.

Or had it? Who knew with the fae? Who knew what Ivor was thinking, feeling? Plotting? He may look upon me as nothing more than a well-liked pet, one he'd prefer to keep around but would quickly forget once I'm out of sight.

Lyklor rumbles something deep in his throat. I turn swiftly just as he sweeps an arm to indicate that the gate is ready. I set my jaw and take a step toward the arch.

"Wait! Miss Darlington! A moment, please!"

I spin around. "Mister Creakle?"

Thaddeus Creakle is sprinting across the garden, holding his long robes out of the way of his feet. His sandals slap in the gravel path, and he's waving something over his head. In the twilight I can't quite see what it is. The old librarian draws near, puffing and panting hard. I've never seen him move so fast and hope he hasn't winded himself too hard for a man of his age.

"Miss Darlington," he says between heaving breaths. "Before you go, I want you to have this." He holds out the object he'd been waving. It's a quill pen. A large, lovely, red plumy thing from some bird I've never seen before. Certainly not something from my world. The nib is gold, delicately engraved with a swirling pattern.

"I can't take this!" I protest. But even as the words slip from my lips, I set down my parcel and carefully lift the quill from Thaddeus's palms. I turn it over, admiring the rich color, vibrant even in the twilight. "Surely this belongs to Aurelis Library." I look up sharply and catch the old man's eye. Is he even allowed to give this to me?

Thaddeus's expression is difficult to read through his breathless puffing. He simply shakes his head. "It belonged to a powerful mage," he says. "A Miphata. Some say the power of the Miphates is transferred to their quills over the years and lingers long after their deaths. If so, this quill is one of the most powerful seen in many an age."

I hastily try to hand the quill back. "In that case, I absolutely cannot take it! I'm not a . . . a . . . whatever it was you just said. A mage." And I have no desire to become one.

But Thaddeus pushes my hand away, making my fingers curl around the quill. "Please, Miss Darlington. It will give me peace of mind to know you have taken this with you to Vespre. I believe the mage to whom it once belonged would be satisfied as well."

Part of me wants to protest further, but before I can even shape the words, Lawrence appears at my shoulder. "Pardon, Miss Darlington, but it's best not to keep the Prince waiting."

A shiver ripples down my spine. I look into Thaddeus's solemn eyes and blink back sudden tears. Then, giving in to a sudden impulse, I wrap my arms around the old librarian, squeezing tight. "Thank you," I whisper.

Before he can answer, I let go, turn on my heel, and hasten to the gate, snatching up my small parcel as I go. I tuck the quill into my parcel, hiding it within the folds of my mulberry dress where I hope it will be protected. For some reason I can't rightly explain, I don't think it would be a good idea for the Prince to see Thaddeus's gift. Not yet anyway.

I turn around under the arch, facing Thaddeus and Lawrence. Lyklor begins to turn the dial, and the air around me shimmers and moves. I close my eyes—and experience again that sensation of tiny knives peeling away the topmost layer of my skin. Only this time, I think the knives dig a little deeper, down several layers. The pain is more than I expect, and it seems to increase with each passing moment. If I could, I would scream. But I can't move, not even to open my mouth. Has the Prince tricked me, betrayed me? Was all of this just an elaborate ruse to get me to this place where he can *accidentally* bring about my death without breaking the terms of my Obligation? The thought flashes through my mind in a split second of sharp agony.

Then the split second is over.

I stand blinking into a world of gloom.

The gate arch is gone. A rocky shore stretches out on either side of me before a dark sea. The sky overhead is richly purple with twilight, not quite night but close. Stars spangle that expanse in glittering profusion, more stars than I've ever seen at once, dazzling my eye. Vertigo overwhelms me, as though I might fall upward into those stars, dragged into the vastness of space.

Hastily, I pull my gaze down to the shore again. A long pier stands not far from my current position and stretches out over the water. Glowing orb lanterns suspended on long poles every ten feet or so light the way from one end to the other. No ship awaits at the far end of this pier, however. But there's something there, something I can just discern, illuminated in the pale orb light. A carriage.

I frown. What in the gods' seven secret names—

"Oof!" I stagger as something strikes me from behind.

"Oh, Miss Darlington!" Lawrence's voice bursts in the stillness, and a hand catches my elbow, keeping me from falling to my knees. "I *do* beg your pardon." I turn to him, meeting his sheepish grin. "I assumed you would have moved on your way by now or I would have waited to step through. It can be difficult to judge these things, you know."

His plain face and cheerful voice ought to be comforting under the circumstances. But in truth, I find that the sheer contrast of an everyday sort of fellow like Lawrence only makes the strange atmosphere of this world seem stranger still. I shiver, and murmur politely, "It's quite all right. My fault entirely."

Lawrence doesn't argue the point. "Shall we then?" he says and sets off along the shore to the pier. I have no choice but to follow. He navigates the rocks with nimble ease, and I try to step where he steps. As I go, I can't help feeling that many eyes are watching me from various nooks and crannies and shadows, but when I try to catch sight of these watchers, there's never anything there. What sort of beings would live in a desolate place like this?

"Miss Darlington!"

I lift my gaze from the rocks close by and see Lawrence up ahead, waving me on. The Prince stands beyond him, on the near end of the pier. His face is shadowed by his large-brimmed hat, but everything about his stance breathes impatience.

Picking up my pace, I hasten to the pier, grateful to be out from among the sharp rocks. By the gleaming starlight, I can just discern the Prince's glittering eyes looking me over but cannot read his expression. "Quite through sightseeing, Clara Darling?" he asks coldly.

I don't answer. My gaze flicks from him to Lawrence and back again. Lawrence simply stands there smiling. He's truly mastered that smile-mask that I've worked so hard to perfect over the years.

The Prince's eyes narrow. He doesn't push me to answer, however, but grunts and turns, striding out along the pier. For all his billowing cloak and stomping boots, he doesn't move quickly. He's panting, limping even. Still weak from whatever curse-ailment plagued him earlier. But though Lawrence offers his arm, the Prince waves him away with an impatient hand.

I follow behind the two men, trying not to let myself look back at the shore and the unseen watching eyes I've left behind among the rocks. We pass in and out of the globe lanterns' light, like wanderers between small worlds.

The carriage at the end of the pier stands fully in a pool of pale lanternlight. It's quite ornate, all black with silver trimmings, and large enough to fit six comfortably inside. The driver's seat is enormous as well, and as for the driver sitting there, holding the reins . . . I stop in my tracks, blinking in surprise. It's a troll. A great rocky lump of a troll, with a face that looks as though it were battered into shape by a hammer. He wears an oversized suit that strains across his absolutely massive shoulders, and an incongruous top hat sits tilted at a rakish angle atop his domed head.

He catches my staring gaze and grins, flashing what look like raw gemstone teeth, sharp and multi-faceted. Then he winks.

I'm still trying to recover from one surprise when another strikes me with equal force. Six beasts stand in their traces, hitched to the carriage, beasts which I took at first glance to be horses. Then one of them snorts, drawing my attention, and I realize they aren't horses at all. Their necks are too long, their heads too short. Their hooves are cloven like a bull's, but they aren't bulls. They're something different, something I've never seen before. Spines protrude from their backbones and through the thick, braided manes on their necks. Their tails are long and serpentine, studded with what look like barbed stings at their tips. One of them tosses its head and champs its bit, flashing the sharp yellow teeth crowded close in its jaw.

"Morleth."

The Prince's voice breaks through my stunned senses. I turn and find him watching me closely, observing my reaction to the creatures.

"Morleth," He says again. "Darksteppers. They walk on darkness, a useful skill under the circumstances."

With this enigmatic explanation, he moves to the carriage. A figure jumps down from the back and holds the door for him—another troll, I note, though not quite as huge as the driver. Still massive, awkward, lumbering, and incongruously dressed in footman's livery, complete with shining silver epaulets. He pulls out a box step then makes a stiff bow.

With a single nod of acknowledgement, the Prince climbs into the carriage, disappearing into the shadows within. After handing his two carpet bags off to the footman, Lawrence climbs in as well. The footman turns to me next, his tiny eyes glittering beneath a heavy stone brow. I hesitate, holding my parcel tight. I don't want to go anywhere near that carriage, its driver, or its hideous team of six. I'm not sure what the Prince means by *walking on darkness,* and I really don't want to find out. But I can't very well stand here forever.

Chin up, parcel pressed to my chest, I approach the carriage door, trying very hard to ignore the footman's stony gaze. I plant a foot on the step.

"No." The Prince's voice freezes me in place. "Up to the box seat with you." I peer through the door and catch the malicious flash of his eyes in the shadows. "I can't stand to be in close quarters with you for the length of this flight. Go on! You'll have a better view from up there anyway."

I step back, knees trembling, and peer up at the box seat. I'm to ride up *there?* Beside that enormous troll, watching those six awful beasts walk across *darkness* all the way to some distant shore

I can't even see?

"Oh, gods," I breathe.

Somewhere in the back of my mind, I notice that the Prince hasn't yet asserted my Obligation over me. There's no pressure in my head forcing me to comply to his will. But he could start at any moment. And I don't want to wait around for that.

Swallowing back the curses mounding in my throat, I move to the front of the carriage. Little bars lead up the side to the box seat, incongruously tiny for the size of the driver waiting up above. He looks down at me from beneath the brim of his top hat and grins.

"*Har rorturk?*"

I jump and turn to find the footman at my elbow. He holds out his hands for my parcel, and I reluctantly hand it over. Then, first wiping my sweaty palms across my hips, I scramble up the little handholds to the box seat. The driver politely scoots to one side, but even so there's only the barest sliver of space for me to sit. Gods on high, I'll end up crushed to death by a troll long before we reach our destination! Still, I settle into place, gripping the edge of the seat with both hands and leaning away from the troll. My spine already hurts. If I get through this without permanently contorting something, it'll be a miracle.

The footman finishes securing the luggage to the top of the carriage, then springs lightly onto the back. The two trolls exchange a few growling words before the driver says, "*Yark yark!*" and slaps the reins.

The morleth lurch into motion.

My stomach pitches fearfully as the creatures step right off the pier out into the empty air above the water. For an instant, my brain is absolutely convinced we're falling, tumbling, crashing into the waves below. But it doesn't happen. Instead the carriage finds a smooth rhythm, and the morleth's cloven hooves make sharp, clopping noises as they step on absolutely nothing discernable. Another *"Yark yark!"* and a crack of the driver's whip, and they pick up their pace into a quick trot up a sharp, invisible incline.

Soon we're a good fifty feet or more above the water.

I close my eyes before we get much higher, trying to force the contents of my stomach to settle. I'm painfully aware of the unexpected warmth of the troll beside me. How can someone with such a rocky hide be so *hot?* It's like his blood is molten. Maybe it is. I really don't know anything about trolls.

After a while, I open my eyes again briefly to gaze out over the bobbing heads of the morleth. Is that a distant shore I see on the horizon? Vespre? Or one of the other Umbrian islands? I have no way of knowing. I've never bothered to research this part of Eledria. I certainly never expected to see it.

Determined not to look down, I instead turn my gaze upward to the star-strewn sky. Wispy clouds drift overhead like gossamer veils across the purple vastness. Will I adjust to this eternal twilight the way I adjusted to Aurelis and its incessant sunshine? The idea of living in such relentless gloom is depressing.

I close my eyes again, bow my head, and try to think of words to pray. I can't. I can't even decide which god to petition. The clop of morleth hooves beats a jarring rhythm in my skull, and I allow it to carry me into a mindless lull where I don't have to *think* anymore. I barely even *feel*. I simply exist. Exist a little longer until I reach the far side of this watery expanse. Until I see Vespre City for the first time and can begin to grapple with the new realities of my life.

A shriek rips the sky.

The driver grunts. Then it growls, *"Rortro dra!"* It sounds like an expletive, spat between his gem teeth. Hunching my shoulders, I peer up into the sky once more. At first I see only the clouds and the stars.

Then I realize that one patch of clouds is a little darker and denser than the rest. And it's banking oddly. Turning toward us. The shriek sounds again. Only this time, it isn't one voice but many. A whole swarm.

"What is that?" I gasp.

Before I can get another word out, the swarm is upon us, surrounding the coach. A dark cloud of beating wings, flashing claws, slashing beaks. The morleth bellow and snort, rearing and pawing, lashing out at the shrieking cloud. Fire dances from their eyes, and sparks spring from their cloven hooves.

The troll driver stands in his seat, waving his arms. I glimpse razor talons slashing at his stony hide, unable to pierce it. He is safe enough. It takes me a moment to realize through my terror that he's trying to defend me.

Something catches my shoulder.

I look down and see a creature no bigger than a bat, with

black feathered wings, a body like a hunched old man, enormous lantern eyes, and great, curving snake fangs. Those fangs have latched onto my cloak, piercing through layers of fabric to scratch my skin. With a cry, I knock it loose with my fist. It rips my cloak as it wheels away. Another appears in its place, grabbing hold in the same spot. Before I can react, another and another and another fly at me, catching my clothes, my hair, tiny talons digging into my skin.

Suddenly, I'm yanked from my seat and lifted high into the sky. Tiny evil faces and beating wings surround me. I throw one arm up in front of my face, warding off slashing attacks at my eyes. But other attacks rip into my arm, my neck, my back, my kicking legs. My flesh tears and blood rolls down everything, soaks through my clothes. I'm being shredded alive.

I scream. Fight. Flail, desperate to escape, knowing if I manage to get free of the monsters' clutches, all that awaits me is a death-plunge into the sea. Any death is better than this death. I scream again, hopeless, terrified.

A burst of light.

Vivid, glowing.

Violent, hot magic, piercing through the swarm in lance-like streams.

The creatures shriek and disperse in a burst of feathers and blood and pain. I hang a moment longer, suspended in the talons of those who can't quite work themselves free of the fabric they've grasped. And I look into a face.

A golden, shining, magic-burning face.

The Prince rises in the air in a whorl of light that takes the shape of wings at his shoulders. He stretches out one hand, and another burst of light shoots through the swarm, blinding me, but knocking the last of the monsters free. They wheel away into darkness, and I . . .

I fall.

I fall and fall, air whipping my face, my shredded arms and legs. It's almost a relief. A relief to know that everything is going to end in just another instant, when my body hits the water, when every bone breaks, and I sink beneath the waves. I'll be dead then, and the pain flaring through my senses from all those deadly cuts will be over. The fear of the future will be over as well, and my ten years of enslavement. All will be done.

The Prince is there. Just above me. Powerful wings of light beat the air, speeding his streamlined body straight toward me. I stare up into his eyes, which glow with more of that strange, otherworldly light.

He really is beautiful, I think.

Then darkness closes in, and I hit—

Cushions.

With a choking cry, I bolt upright. My movements are ungainly, and I fall, only a short way, however. I land hard on a narrow strip of floor and stare down at my hands, very pale in the light of a single globe lantern hanging overhead.

"There, there, Miss Darlington." Lawrence's soothing voice touches my ringing ears. "There, there, you're all right now."

My hands. They should be shredded. Flayed to bits of blood and bone where the monsters slashed into me.

But my skin is unmarked. Not even the faintest scrapes remain.

My lungs exhale a painful breath, then drag in a huge gulp of air. I was falling. Wasn't I? Falling to my death. But now I'm . . . I'm . . . I'm inside the carriage. This is all wrong. The Prince barred me from entering the carriage with him. I remember that part clearly enough. I was supposed to ride on the box seat with the troll, and then we were attacked . . .

Warm hands grip my shoulders. Startled, I look up into Lawrence's long, freckled face. He smiles. "Come, Miss Darlington. Let's get you back in your seat."

Shivering so hard I fear I'll break into a thousand pieces, I allow myself to be assisted into the upholstered seat across from Lawrence. A small globe lantern swings back and forth overhead. By its light, I see the Prince sitting opposite me. He's slumped in his seat, his head lolled to one side, his body limp, but not exactly relaxed. He almost looks as though he's sleeping.

But his face is gray and drips with sweat.

15

For a long time I sit frozen, my limbs braced, my hands gripping the seat cushions. The clop of morleth hooves echoes in my head, accompanied by the whoosh of sea air all around us.

Lawrence, after settling me comfortably in place, pulls out a bit of reading. It's a magazine, the *Starlin Gazette*. An old edition, but I recognize the bold, elaborate typeface. My father used to write for them. I blink and look again. It's difficult to read by the swinging lanternlight, but I'm half convinced I see the name *Edgar Darlington* just visible beneath Lawrence's long fingers. The moment is strangely surreal—that blend of my old world with this awful new one.

Aware of my gaze, Lawrence looks up over the edge of the

magazine and offers another pleasant smile. "Feeling better, miss?"

I glance from him to the Prince, who is still slumped awkwardly beside his manservant. Lawrence has done what he can to make the Prince comfortable, propping him up with pillows and occasionally mopping his brow. But he still looks horrible. Shrunken, almost.

"What happened?" I ask in a whisper. I can still *almost* feel phantom talons scraping across my skin. Or was that just a dream?

Lawrence puts aside his magazine. "Frights," he says simply. As though I'll understand. "Small nightmares, little things, but dangerous in a swarm. They must have escaped the library in the Prince's absence. Ordinarily, they prey only on the sleeping and wouldn't dare an open attack. They must have sensed his current vulnerability. Thankfully, it was only one flock."

I blink stupidly at him. His words clatter in my head, meaningless, an explanation that is no explanation at all. "I . . . I was caught," I stammer, trying to figure out how to phrase the question. How to overtly say, *How come I was being torn apart and falling, then somehow I'm not anymore?*

Lawrence, however, nods his understanding. "Oh, the Prince was forced to use magic. Human magic. See?" He reaches between seat cushions and withdraws a book. A battered old volume of red leather that looks as though it's seen better days. "He keeps it on hand for occasions such as this. When he saw the frights swarming you, he set to work writing at once. He is *very* talented, the Prince is. Not that I know much about it, of course. But everyone says he's the most gifted of his kind ever known."

I stare at the book. Something stirs in my mind, a vague memory of standing in Aurelis Library, writing . . . watching my writing become true . . .

I realize I've been silent for a very long while. I glance at Lawrence again. He's gone back to reading his magazine. "Why does he look like that?" I ask.

Lawrence raises his eyebrows and lowers the magazine, only the faintest trace of impatience visible in his expression.

"The Prince," I persist, waving a vague hand. "He looks so sickly."

"Oh, well, that's his curse you know," Lawrence says, as though it's the most obvious thing. "His human blood is cursed, so it takes it out of him to use human magic, especially in a big spell like that. He should be all right after a rest." The manservant's brow puckers slightly as he looks at his master. He pulls a handkerchief from his front vest pocket and wipes the Prince's brow again, all tenderness and concern.

I shrink back into the seat cushions and press as deep as I can into the shadowed corner. My mind rattles with the effort of trying to comprehend what Lawrence has just told me. So the fright attack was . . . real? Or was it a dream? And the Prince had *written* it away? But I'd seen him rising up on those shining wings, had seen him fling that bolt of magic, shredding frights to pieces! It had felt so real. As real as the cuts in my flesh that are now nonexistent.

My head aches. I peer at the Prince from under my lashes. Even shrunken and gray and worn out as he is, the lines of his face are finely drawn. And yet not *perfect*. In this weakened state, the perfection of the fae has melted out of him again, leaving behind only natural human beauty, imperfect but undeniable.

"Jar tarka!"

The bellowing troll voice startles me, and I press back into my seat again. But Lawrence, with a little, "Ah!" closes his magazine and tucks it inside his jacket. He leans forward and pulls on a cord, lifting the silky black curtain that covers the carriage window. "We're approaching Vespre now. I always love this sight!"

I swallow. After the horror of that fall I just experienced—or didn't experience; I'm still not sure what actually happened there—I don't relish the idea of looking out the window from so great a height. But my curiosity gets the better of me at last. I sit forward in my seat and dare a peek.

Vespre City spreads before me.

It's unlike any other city I've seen. While there are streets and towers and houses, much as one would expect, it all seems to have been carved directly from rock and stone. Not built, but *etched*, somehow. Under the twilit sky and millions of stars, that stone gleams a pale white, but the shadows between each building are deep and dense.

The whole city seems to be arranged in a series of concentric circles with all the winding streets eventually leading to the center, where a great palace rises like a mountain looming over all. Unlike Aurelis Palace, no walls separate it from the rest of the city. Instead it gives the impression of having sprung up from among the smaller buildings so that all is part of one great whole. The palace consists of many tall towers, and the one at the very center is tallest of all, a colossal citadel with a clear, domed roof.

"Who built this place?" I ask.

"Trolls," Lawrence answers. "Below you see a prime example of classic Second Age troll architecture. Impressive, no?" He gives a modest cough. "Back in my old life, I was training to become an architect. But humans haven't even *begun* to dream up cities like this!"

I don't want to be, but I'm impressed. At first glance, Vespre is an ugly place, but the more I look, the more I can't help appreciating its unique form of beauty. Rough-hewn, ragged, yet majestic, the pale stone luminous beneath the starlight.

Then I see one portion of the city where the pale stones have been blasted black. All the structures are flattened, ground down. It looks almost like a gaping wound. "What's that?" I ask, pointing at the desolate spot as the carriage passes overhead.

Lawrence's face goes grave. "That happened last year. A Noswraith got free. The librarians went out to fight it, but it was a big one. It took them time to contain it." He shakes his head, and his expression darkens still more. "We lost one that day. One of the librarians, I mean. A good man, Soran Silveri. He'd been with the Prince for nearly three hundred years." He sits back in his seat, letting the curtain fall back across the window.

I too lean back, relieved not to see any more. I feel cold, and a shiver ripples across my shoulders. A single Noswraith worked *that* level of destruction? In the glimpse I had, it looked as though an entire street was decimated. Maybe more. I think of the Melted Man, tearing into the books at Aurelis Library. I thought he was terrible, but he couldn't have wrought anything like that level of damage.

"Why . . ." I hesitate. Do I even want to know the answer to my next question? "Why is Vespre called the *Doomed* City?"

Lawrence meets my gaze. When I met him just a few short hours ago, I wouldn't have believed him capable of such a solemn expression. "It's the Noswraiths," he says. "All those Noswraiths accumulated in one place. It's too much magic, too much concentrated power. They feed each other, and their containments break down over time. I don't pretend to understand it all, truth be told. I'm no magic-user. But Mixael—that's one of the librarians—he's tried to explain it to me a few times. The belief is, the containments will all break down eventually, unleashing the entire horde of Noswraiths on Vespre at once. The city will certainly fall and be lost, and the rest of Eledria will have no choice but to cut off the island and let it drift into the Hinter, away from the rest of the worlds."

I stare at him, hardly able to believe what he's saying. "Why do they keep all the books in one place then?"

"Where else would they be kept?" Lawrence shrugs. "None of the kings and queens of Eledria are willing to have Noswraiths stored in their courts. And they can't very well leave them in the human world; that would be asking for disaster! So it was decided they should be sent here. No one cares much for Vespre and its inhabitants. No one cares much for trolls. No one save the Prince, that is."

I glance from Lawrence to his unconscious master. The Prince's breathing seems to have eased somewhat, but he's still quite gray and sweating through his garments. I wonder . . . does he truly *care* about the trolls? About *anyone?* It's hard to believe, hard even to imagine.

Within another minute or two, the driver growls something overhead. Lawrence translates, "We're about to land," and stretches one arm across the Prince's chest, braced against the carriage wall. Then he props one foot on the seat beside me. "I'd make ready if I were you, Miss Darlington."

I barely have time to register what he's saying before the carriage pitches and rumbles and rolls so hard, I'm convinced the whole thing is about to capsize. I let out a yelp and flail my arms and legs, trying to brace against anything and everything I can. It makes one last great lurch . . . and I land in the Prince's lap.

Blinking fast, my swimming gaze refocuses just inches from his unconscious face, with my nose almost touching his. Heat flares up my cheeks. Scrambling and utterly undignified, I push against his chest, somehow find my footing, and plop back into my seat just as the carriage resumes a regular rhythm. It's not as smooth as when the morleth walked on darkness; now the carriage wheels seem to catch every bump and divot in the paving stones of whatever road we're now traveling.

Lawrence is looking at me. Did he see how I blushed when I

practically sat in the unconscious Prince's lap? When I glance his way, he offers the same bland smile. But something sparkles in his eye.

I look away again quickly.

The carriage lurches to a stop, the springs creaking and wheels groaning as the footman jumps down from the back. A moment later, the door opens, and the lantern illuminates an ugly troll face. He pulls out the box step, then backs away, bowing.

"After you, Miss Darlington," Lawrence says.

I do *not* want to get out first. To face this new city, this new life all alone. I haven't known Lawrence long, but I would still much prefer to know that he's standing out there before I climb down myself. But I don't have a choice.

Summoning the dregs of my courage, I duck out of the carriage, ignoring the troll footman's proffered hand. I brush out my skirts . . . then turn my gaze up at the looming edifice before me. The road has brought us to the front doors of the central city palace. I'd known even when glimpsing it from the air that it was truly massive. Now, standing here, I feel positively miniscule. Like a bug crawling up to the foot of a mountain. The double doors, at least ten times the height of a fully grown man, are intricately carved in patterns of dragons and monsters devouring each other. Fifteen enormous block steps lead up to those doors. They're much too big for me; I'll have to jump up each tread and will be hot and sweaty by the time I reach the top.

Bustling movement behind me draws my attention back

to the carriage. I turn to see the footman helping Lawrence pull the unconscious Prince out. The footman slings the Prince unceremoniously over one shoulder, even as Lawrence bleats, "Careful there!"

The huge door at the top of the stairs opens. I whip my head around to see six trolls emerge—six trolls, marching two by two with a seventh figure at their head. A figure that is . . . not a troll.

But what is it? A fae? She's not like any fae I've ever seen before. Seven feet tall, pale as the moon, and clad in golden armor, she radiates beauty without the added aftertaste of glamours. Strangely, though, something about her is indescribably *trollish*.

The beautiful figure precedes the others down the steps. I fight the urge to duck behind the carriage and hide. I've simply never seen anyone so beautiful, or so terrifying! She would stand out in King Lodírhal's court, outshining all the Lords and Ladies, even Princess Estrilde.

Sparing not a glance for me, the armored figure fixes her gaze on the footman. *"Hortar! Korikarshor!"* she barks when she sees the Prince slung across his shoulder. Her voice is deep, guttural.

"Torar for gart," the footman responds peevishly, even as the armored woman rushes toward him. He turns to one side, keeping the Prince just out of her reach.

"Now, now!" Lawrence jumps between the two massive figures. He's tall for a human but looks positively puny by contrast. "There's no reason to get all worked up. We met with a little trouble on the crossing, that's all. Frights. The Prince contained them with a spell and wore himself out, as you see. But he's well, I assure you, Captain Khas! Or he will be once he's slept it off."

The formidable Captain Khas casts Lawrence a dubious look. Judging by her expression, she holds Lawrence personally accountable for the Prince's health and wellbeing. Lawrence merely meets her gaze with his blandest smile.

Growling in her throat, the beautiful woman turns and motions to the six trolls on the steps behind her. At her command, two of them spring forward, hands outstretched. The footman scowls and looks for a moment as though he'll resist handing over his burden, but ultimately shrugs the Prince off his shoulder. The two trolls sling the Prince between them and climb the stairs quickly, followed by the other trolls, Captain Khas, and Lawrence last of all.

And I'm still standing down below. Watching them go.

I open my mouth, try to call out after Lawrence. My tongue cleaves to the roof of my mouth. Should I trail after them through those gigantic doors? I can't make my feet move. I look back at the carriage, and part of me wants to climb back inside, into that shadowed safety, and stay there.

A rough grunt startles me. I look up at the footman standing on the carriage roof. He gestures me out of the way. "Oh!" I gasp and skip to one side. The next moment, something lands on the ground in front of me. I stare at it several moments before recognizing my own little parcel of belongings. Hands shaking, I pick it up, then back away a few more steps as the footman and driver unload the rest of the luggage. Now that I'm out of their way, they ignore me completely.

Once the carriage is divested of its burden, the footman gathers up all trunks and carpet bags, somehow managing to balance them on his shoulders and head, tucking the rest under his arms. He climbs the steps to the open front door while the driver resumes his seat and slaps the reins. The morleth lurch into motion, tossing their ugly heads and snorting. Eager to return to their stables, perhaps.

I swivel my head, gazing first after the carriage, then up to the footman ponderously climbing the steps. Well, I can't be meant to go to the stables, now can I?

Holding my parcel tight, I begin the arduous climb, sometimes jumping, sometimes using my hands to help me clamber from one step to the next. By the time I've scaled all fifteen, the footman is long gone. But the door is still standing open. I approach nervously and peer inside. "Oh, gods!" I whimper.

At first glance, I feel as though I'm looking into a cave. A vast dark cave with stalactites studded with crystals high overhead. But a second glance reveals that this is no mere subterranean dwelling. The crystals, gleaming with their own inner light, illuminate a floor which is beautifully smooth and inlaid with a mosaic of black and white stones in an intricate, circular pattern. That pattern feels familiar, somehow, like I've just seen it somewhere else recently . . . and I realize that it's a recreation of the city itself.

The scale is vast. A scale not intended for humans or even for fae like those I left behind in the Court of Dawn. Even the intimidating Captain Khas I just glimpsed, with her great height and her golden armor, is not big enough for a space like this. There's a strong but inexplicable sense of *ancient days* here, and I wonder what kind of beings dwelled within this palace long, long ago.

Breathing out slowly, I peer this way and that. There's no one here. No watchman at the door, no footman, no servants. Nothing. All is empty. When I strain my ears, I *almost* hear what I think might be the echo of footsteps. The troll guards carrying the Prince away, presumably.

As no other plan presents itself, I decide to follow that sound.

I scuttle across the giant open space beneath the stalactite crystals. There are many different passages leading in all different directions out from this hall. I choose the one from which the echo of footsteps seems to be coming. This passage is a little less cavernous than the foyer, at least, though still overly large for someone like me. It's dark here too, without the crystals to illuminate it. The only light comes from the pale starlight shining through high, arched windows. Maybe enough for troll eyes, but I'm left nearly blind.

I hurry on, picking up my pace, determined to catch up to those retreating footsteps. Suddenly, a door opens in the wall to my right, and a huge figure lurches forth. I scream and leap back, narrowly avoiding being crushed beneath the feet of a massive troll. The troll casts me a disinterested glance and continues on its way. It carries something heavy on its back, its stride slow but purposeful. Whatever it's doing, wherever it's going, it has no time to spare for a puny human.

It takes me a few minutes to recover my breath. By the time I do, I can't hear the footsteps anymore. I'm lost. Lost somewhere within Vespre Palace in the middle of the Doomed City. Completely and utterly alone.

"Well," I mutter, even as my arms clutch my parcel a little harder. "Well, I'm getting my bearings. That's all. Discovering the . . . the . . . the lay of the land."

It sounded better in my head than spoken aloud.

I grind my teeth and press on down the passage until I come to a place where it forks. I can either continue straight on or turn left or right. I hesitate, then, with a shrug, choose the righthand passage at random. This one is even less cavernous than the previous, and I'm immediately more comfortable. I wonder if it was built onto the palace later, when the inhabitants no longer needed such enormous spaces. There are lanterns set at intervals here. Maybe I'm nearing the part of the palace where humans live. Surely there must be any number of folk living in a huge palace like this. Then again . . .

Then again, who would want to live where all the Noswraiths of the worlds are gathered?

The bone-shivering thought has no sooner crossed my mind than a thin cry catches my ear. I stop short, trembling, my first thought of Noswraiths and nightmares and razor-taloned monsters. Another cry follows the first, and a third.

"*Ror! Sis taror!*"

"*Kah mer lorat! Sis! Sis!*"

Those are troll voices. At least, I think they are. Only these voices are higher, softer. Almost sweet in a way. Are they . . . could they possibly be *children?*

16

I STAND STILL, LISTENING TO THOSE VOICES, DOUBTING my next move. Part of me wants to follow, see what I find. But who knows what that will be in a place like Vespre? For all I know, those little voices, lisping and frightened though they are, could be Noswraiths trying to lure me to them.

But they don't *sound* like Noswraiths. There's an altogether earthy quality to them that simply doesn't feel nightmarish.

Finally, I shrug and turn in the direction of those voices, making my way through a series of baffling passages. I come to a staircase and climb to the top, where I face a long hall with huge floor-to-ceiling windows on the right side, offering a sweeping view of Vespre City. I stop, and gaze out on that view. The concentric streets lead down ring after ring after ring into the deeper city below. Up in the carriage, it had all seemed so far away, I'd not had a strong sense of the actual depths of the city or the towering heights of the palace itself. Now the sensation is enough to take my breath away.

I realize there's no discernable glass between me and a precipitous drop into darkness below. My breath catching, I step back quickly from the window.

"Sis! Sis!"

"Kah mer lorat! Sis!"

The little voices drag my attention back to present. Frightened voices, I realize now. The sound of their fear gives me an unexpected jolt of courage, and I hurry on down the passage, take a turn . . . and come upon a strange little scene.

Three rock-monster creatures leap and flail around one of the open floor-to-ceiling windows. They climb on each other, climb the window frames, fall to the ground, roll around, then rise and stamp their feet, clasping their overlarge hands to their overlarge heads.

Troll children. They must be. And as ugly as their adult counterparts. But also rather cute in a way, with their enormous eyes and their tiny gem teeth and their big wailing mouths. From those mouths, a continuous stream of babble emits, one word standing out from all the rest. *"Sis! Sis! Sis!"*

One of the little creatures starts to climb out the window. The other two quickly grab him and drag him back inside, even as he wails, *"Sis! Sis!"* Great tears pour down all three of their faces, splashing to the floor and leaving puddles in their wake.

What in the seven gods' names am I supposed to do? I look

around, trying to discern the source of their distress. There's certainly no Noswraith here, not that I can see anyway. They must be upset by something they see outside the window. But what?

Suddenly, one of the three turns and blinks great white, tear-swimming eyes at me. We freeze, both me and the monster, staring at one another.

Then that ugly little face breaks into a wide grin, showing a collection of sparkling teeth with big gaps in the gums between.

"*Mar! Mar mar!*" the goblin cries and scampers toward me on all fours like an animal. I brace myself, resisting the urge to turn and flee. It is, after all, just a child. Even when standing upright, it barely comes up to my knees. It collapses in a little rocky bundle at my feet and catches hold of my skirt hem. "*Horar tah lorat, Mar!*" He tugs hard enough to nearly pull me over, dragging me toward the window.

The other two troll children have gone silent and watchful. The smaller of them sidles behind the bigger, eyes so huge they seem to take up most of its face. The three of them look like perfect stacking dolls—only discernable from one another by size. Otherwise I can't tell their features apart. The one holding onto my skirt is the smallest of the lot. The largest one's head might come as high as my heart, and the middle one up to my waist. But they are all shockingly broad, like little living bricks.

"*Horar tah lorat!*" the littlest one prattles. "*Mar, mar! Horar tah!*"

"Yes, yes, I'm coming," I say, allowing myself to be pushed and prodded toward the window. For a stomach-plunging moment, I half-wonder if the child intends to push me right over the edge. I resist his pull and feel the tremendous strength in his tiny arms. It's truly terrifying.

I drop my parcel, put out a hand, and catch hold of the window frame. My stomach pitches at the dizzying drop suddenly spinning below me. This part of the palace towers a good five stories or more above the very distant ground. Terror thrills in my veins, and I hold on for dear life.

"*Sis! Sis! Sis!*" the little one holding my hem cries. It's no longer trying to pull me along, at least; it merely yanks and tugs and points frantically. With an effort, I pull myself together and look where it's pointing.

A series of flying buttresses arch before my vision—stone supports creating numerous arcs that support this wing of the palace. Some of them swoop down at perilous angles, while others span high over my head. The one just before me, just beneath the lip of the windowsill, creates a gentle incline, however, all the way to its far support pillar. One could almost walk it were it not so terrifyingly narrow.

I blink and look again. At the far end of this buttress sits a dark, hunched form. A gargoyle. I can't see its face, only its spiny back and outspread wings, and the long, stone tail carved so that it looks as though it's coiled around the buttress.

Climbing up the spines is a small, pale figure. Another child.

"*Sis!*" the troll at my feet cries.

The child turns, looks back over her shoulder.

My breath catches hard in my throat.

She's stunning. Absolutely stunning. I'd been struck by the beauty of the awful troll captain on the front stair, but she had absolutely *nothing* on this perfectly delicate little creature! Her features are so lovely, even compressed into an irritable frown, it could almost make one weep with joy at the sight. She's pure white, from the top of her head to the soles of her feet. White and shining like a star. And stark naked.

The other two trolls crowd close to me now. All three pull at my skirts, pointing and weeping, "Sis! Sis!"

Almost unwillingly, I tear my gaze from the girl to look down into those ugly faces, made all the uglier by sheer comparison to that vision I'd just witnessed. "Is that . . . is that your sister?" I ask. It doesn't seem possible that these lumpish, awkward things could be in any way related to such an angelic being.

"Sis!" they cry, tears rolling down the crags of their cheeks.

I look out along the buttress once more. The pale child has climbed to the top of the gargoyle's head and is kicking her feet, perfectly at ease. The drop below her is dreadful. It's too easy to imagine a sudden breeze picking up and knocking that delicate little frame from her perch, sending her plunging, plunging, breaking on the stones below.

I shudder, close my eyes. This is not good.

"*Horar tah lorat? Mar! Mar!*" the littlest troll pleads, pulling my attention back to him. Ordinarily, when I listen to fae language, the words alter themselves to become understandable in my ears. It's part of the magic of Eledria. Apparently, troll language doesn't work the same way. The words are just a series of grunting, growling sounds.

But I can't mistake the meaning: *"Help her! Help her, please!"*

What can I possibly do? I look again along the buttress with its gentle decline leading all the way to the gargoyle at the end. I look at the dizzying drop on either side. I can't very well climb out there, can I?

The troll children cry out together. My gaze snaps up in time to see the beautiful child swinging from the edge of the gargoyle's outspread wing, her feet kicking over the drop. She laughs, lets go with one hand, and turns to flash a brilliant smile back at the other three, who sob and grab their heads and pound the floor in dismay. The littlest troll catches my hand with crushing stone fingers and looks up at me, his eyes huge and pleading. *"Sis!"* he wails.

"All right, all right!" I push all those hard little hands away from me. The three trolls hold onto each other and back away, blinking solemnly. I turn from them, face out the window, and brace myself. "All right. I'll get her. You just . . . just wait here . . ."

I get down on my hands and knees, gripping the edge of the windowsill. Somewhere in the back of my head, my own reason clamors: *This is not a good idea! You can't be serious! You can't be sane!* But it's as though some spell has me in its grip now. I *cannot* refuse to help.

Scooting forward, I ease my body out over the edge of the sill and stretch out one foot to plant on the buttress below. It's a little wider than I initially thought. Just like a bridge, or so I try to convince myself. A perfectly fine, stable bridge. Nothing to worry about.

My gaze tries to drag to the awful drop on either side, but I refuse to let it. Instead I focus on my foot. Then I bring my second foot down beside the first and stand there, gripping the edge of the window, both feet firmly planted on the buttress. I look over my shoulder. The pale child has climbed back onto the gargoyle's head and sits there cross-legged, watching me. Her perfect little face puckers in an incredulous frown.

Still holding the windowsill with one hand, I reach out to her with the other. There's only about fifteen feet between me and the girl, but it feels like a mile. "Come on!" I wiggle my fingers, gently coaxing. "Come here, little one. Your friends are worried about you."

The child holds onto her toes and rocks backwards. For a heart-stopping moment, I think she's going to rock right off the gargoyle. But she straightens upright once more, head tilted at a fetching angle. A breeze picks up and blows her long white hair out like a streaming cloud.

I harden my grip on the windowsill. Every instinct tells me to climb back inside, to make excuses, to go search for other help. But when I look back, the pleading faces of the three troll children meet my gaze, their eyes full of unshed tears. They're so ugly and so pathetic! My heart twists at the sight.

Biting down on a curse, I face the pale child again. I move one foot out along the buttress. Then the other. Then the first one again. Now I'm at the fullest reach of my arm. I can't go any further without letting go. But why shouldn't I let go? It's perfectly wide enough to walk on, and the downward slant is almost nothing at all. I'm fine. Totally fine. I can do this.

The pale child stands up. Her arms wave wildly as she catches her balance, and my heart jars to a stop, certain she's about to pitch over and plumet to her death. Behind me, the three trolls cry out in unison, *"Rortar, Sis!"*

I take another step. Now I'm beyond the reach of the windowsill. I stretch my arms out to either side, take another step, then another.

My head swims.

Darkness closes in, tunneling my vision.

A whimper in my throat, I sink to my hands and knees, gripping the buttress hard. This is better! I can crawl to the gargoyle, right? What I'll do once I get there I can't honestly say. Maybe I can get the girl to cling to my back and neck then turn and crawl back again. Yes, that should work. That should work splendidly!

I'm not thinking like a sane person. But I can't seem to stop.

"Wait right there!" I call out to the child, my voice only trembling a little. I move my hands, make another tentative crawling push forward.

Something latches onto my ankle.

I just have time to gasp out a scream before I find myself roughly dragged backwards. I try to grip the buttress with both hands, but there's no resisting that pull. My palms scrape on the stones until

I'm forced to let go. The grip on my ankle shifts, takes hold of the back of my dress.

The next moment, I'm lifted like a kitten held by the scruff, pulled back through the window, spun wildly around. Suddenly I'm face-to-face with the hard, cold, pale, perfectly beautiful visage of Captain Khas.

"What," the pale woman says in perfectly clear *human* language, "do you think you are doing?"

I hang a good two feet above the floor, staring into that terrifying face. I want to struggle, to fight for my dignity. But I can't. I've gone limp.

The troll children dance around the huge captain's feet, singing, "*Sis! Sis! Horar tah lorat! Sis!*"

With a growl, the captain plunks me down on the floor. I sit hard, my legs splayed out in front of me, my skirts askew, my breath tight in my chest. I watch, gape-mouthed, as the captain peers out the window, looking where the troll children are pointing.

The white child stands on the gargoyle's head, dancing a little jig. Her hair whips wildly in the wind.

"*Herar tak!*" the captain barks and gestures impatiently.

The little girl sits cross-legged again and shakes her head. Her lower lip protrudes in a pout.

"*Herar tak!*" the captain says, even more ferocious this time. Then, to my surprise, she climbs right out the window and onto the buttress. She's so big, I would not have thought her capable of navigating that narrow space, but she runs lightly from one end of the buttress to the other. The pale child, seeing her coming, utters a shriek and makes a wild dive straight out into midair. The troll children and I all gasp together.

But Captain Khas extends one long arm and neatly catches the child by her ankle. She holds her upside down in front of her face. Unlike me, the child doesn't go limp, but flails and kicks and tries to scratch, all to no avail.

"Jertok!" Khas says.

At this, the child finally goes still.

Captain Khas retraces her steps along the buttress and climbs back in through the window, all as neat and confident as though she's walking down a broad, level road. She marches up to me, still seated on the floor, legs outspread, skirts rumpled to my knees.

Khas holds the child out to me. "Is this yours?"

I nod. Then I frown and quickly shake my head. "I've never seen her before!"

The pale captain's brow darkens. "Her brothers say you are their mother."

"What?" I gasp and stare around at the three troll children, who have clustered close. The smallest of them clutches me by the shoulder, stony fingers digging painfully to the bone. "No! No, I only just happened upon them a moment ago. I'm certainly *not* their mother."

Khas's frown deepens. Then she addresses the children again, still dangling their sister upside-down in front of them. *"Kak kak! Korat ta mor far?"* There's a questioning lilt at the end of the harsh sounds.

"*Mar mar mar!*" the three troll children say, shaking their head and dancing around me, gesturing wildly, showing all their diamond teeth in great grins. Even the upside-down little Sis joins in, kicking her one free foot and throwing out her arms as she cries, "*Mar! Mar-mar-mar!*"

Khas's deep, rumbling voice speaks above the noise. "They say they asked you to be their mother and to save their sister. They say you agreed."

"But I . . . I . . . I didn't know—" I break off with a gasp as the smallest troll throws his arms around my neck, hugging hard enough to choke me. I pull at his arms, struggling to breathe.

"What seems to be the trouble here, Captain Khas?"

At the sound of that new voice ringing down the stone passage, everyone turns. To my great relief, the hold on my throat lessens, and I'm able to draw a deep breath. Then I turn as well to see someone striding down the hall toward us, smiling broadly. He's a tall, rangy young man with a mop of red hair and slightly stooped but broad shoulders. His face is surprisingly delicate, almost pretty, though the jaw is firm and masculine. He's definitely human.

He turns his beaming smile upon the pale captain and . . . and am I mistaken? Or did I just see the faintest, most delicate of lavender flushes rush in Khas's pristine cheeks?

"The new human is causing trouble," Captain Khas says, her voice even rougher than before, though she continues to speak in human language. She holds out the upside down, naked little girl, dangling her in front of the newcomer's face. "She's adopting waiflings."

"What? Oh dear, we can't have that, now can we?" The red-haired fellow plucks the child from Khas's grip, turns her right side up, and plants her on her feet. Immediately the three troll children surround her, catching her up in their arms and covering her with hugs and kisses. She looks annoyed but submits to their embraces, only half-heartedly pushing them away.

Then all four turn to me.

I just have time to gasp a short "No!" before they swarm like frights. I throw up my arms for defense as all those little hands reach out and all those little bodies crowd close.

"Oh, I say!" the red-haired young man cries. He forges into the midst of the milling herd, swatting and prodding, even kicking, though he only succeeds in stubbing his toe on those stony hides. "Get out of here, little pests! How'd you get into the palace anyway? Really, Captain!" He tosses a glance the pale woman's way. "You're letting down the watch disgracefully if we're to be invaded by trollettes like this! Can't you do something?"

The captain draws herself up, towering a good foot higher than the red-haired young man. *"Ukar toh!"* she barks.

At once, the troll children back away from me. They catch up their pale sister and scamper down the hall without so much as a backward glance. I watch them disappear around a corner, my last sight of them the pale child's face, slung over her largest brother's shoulder. She sticks her tongue out at me, then vanishes from sight.

"Well now, that's better, isn't it?" The red-headed fellow dusts his hands off and grins at me. "I do apologize about that. Miss Darlington, isn't it? Waifs from the city are forever trying to creep into the palace. Like rats! Looking for food, making nests. It's all but impossible to keep them out." He lifts an eyebrow, shooting Captain Kha a look. "Our good captain of the guard here does her best, but there's only so much one can do, isn't there?"

The captain's face has gone completely stony. Without a word or look for me, she offers a short nod to the red-haired young man, then pivots on her heel and marches off in the same direction the troll children went. I look up at the young man just in time to notice how his gaze follows after the tall captain, how his smile has slipped into something more thoughtful. An earnest expression. Possibly even *longing*.

I raise an eyebrow.

Then the stranger turns to me, smiling broadly, and all trace of that earnestness is gone. He extends a hand. "Welcome to Vespre, Miss Darlington! I'm Mixael Silveri, junior librarian of Vespre Library. I must say, I'm very pleased to meet you."

17

I LET THE YOUNG MAN HELP ME TO MY FEET, HASTILY straightening my skirts and trying to assume some measure of dignity. Mixael gives me a moment to adjust myself and goes to fetch my parcel lying on the floor near the window.

"So sorry about the troll waifs," he says again, holding my parcel out to me. "There's a bit of an orphan crisis in the city, you understand. Trolls don't like taking on other trolls' children, so the little ones are most often left to fend for themselves. They'll form packs like feral animals and can become quite vicious. And they're always bound and determined to find new mothers! They can get quite aggressive about it."

I blink, taking this all in. "But . . . but the poor things!" I protest. "You mean those four are orphans? And no one will take them in?"

Mixael shakes his head and shrugs. "No reason to get knotted up about it. Troll children are tough—much tougher than you'd think. They can eat rocks at a pinch, and there's always plenty of those around. They don't *like* it, mind, but rocks are a perfectly natural part of any troll diet, so they don't starve. And with those stony hides, they don't get cold or hot too easily. They're really quite sturdy and self-sufficient almost from birth, not at all like human children."

"But what about . . . about . . ." I'm not entirely certain how to put my next question.

Mixael, however, seems to guess. "The pretty little sister?" He chuckles. "She's just as much troll as the three boys, don't you worry. She looks delicate, I'll grant you, but if anything she's the sturdiest of the lot."

"Wait." I struggle to make sense of this, frowning hard. "So she . . . the little girl . . . and the captain . . . you're telling me they're trolls too?"

At this, Mixael laughs outright. "Of course, they're trolls! What else would they be? Oh, I see: you thought all trolls were big lumps of rock. I suppose I can't blame you. Most folks do who haven't grown up around them. We call trolls like Khas and the little sister *throwbacks*. According to legend, trolls were one of the original beings of Eledria, formed by the god Lamruil at the height of the Creation Age. They were all beautiful then, extraordinarily beautiful, without any magic or glamours. Completely natural. But then they suffered a fall from grace. I'm a bit hazy on the details, but as a result, Lamruil cursed them, turning them into the stony beings we know and love today. Every so often, however, a *throwback* is born. They're hailed as a sign of good luck and given special eminence among their families."

This I believe, remembering the overwrought weeping and wailing I saw from the three troll brothers over their little sister's peril. Though, really, I begin to doubt she was ever in any real peril at all.

Then I frown, remembering my own reaction to that little girl—that strange, overwhelming urge to risk my own life in a bid to save her. "Did the child put a spell on me?"

Mixael gives me a look. "Why do you ask?"

Hastily, I describe the mad impulse that took me, the climb out the window, my attempt to crawl along the buttress. As I talk, Mixael's ginger brows climb further and further up his forehead, and his eyes round with disbelief. "Gods on high!" he says when I finish. "It sounds a bit like troll magic got into you, all right. Probably happened when the boys asked you to be their new mother and you agreed. That would make you part of their family, so the need to protect the throwback child would become more urgent."

"But I didn't agree! I didn't even know what they were asking!"

"I'm not entirely certain that matters. It's more about the *spirit* of the request and the *spirit* of your response, if that makes any sense to you." Mixael offers another shrug. "I'm sorry, Miss Darlington. I've lived among trolls my whole life, but they are an enigmatic race. Quite taciturn and unwilling to let outsiders into their inner circles. I probably know more about them than most humans, and what I know barely scratches the surface of all there is to know. Sometimes I wish . . ."

His voice trails off, and his bright, lively face takes on a momentarily wistful expression. I remember the way he'd watched Captain Khas striding off. Perhaps the beautiful captain has something to do with his wishes just now.

"But, no matter!" Mixael says, coming back to himself with a toss of his head. "Now then, you needn't fret about waiflings, Miss Darlington. Captain Khas will drive them off, and once you've been apart from them a few days, any bond between you will wither on its own. That's the nature of these kinds of magics; nothing to worry about." With that, he offers his arm, a gallant gesture. "The senior librarian has sent me to greet you and bring you to the library for introductions. Sorry I wasn't quick enough to meet you at the door! I was in the midst of a binding when word came that you'd arrived, and it never does to leave a binding unfinished. You know how it goes!"

I take his arm gratefully enough, and he guides me through the palace at a rapid clip, taking many twists and turns. We climb a set of stairs, then another, and soon I'm completely baffled, convinced I'll never fathom the layout of this cavernous place. I'd always thought Aurelis Palace tremendous, but Vespre is built on an altogether different scale.

Thankfully, Mixael keeps up a steady stream of chat as we go, distracting me from my mounting unease. He tells me that he was born here in Vespre, that both his parents served the Prince as librarians and had done so for several centuries now. This surprises me.

"But aren't you . . . You're human, right?" I ask.

Mixael nods. "I am, as are my folks."

"Are you not Obligates?" I've never heard of an Obligation lasting more than fifty years at the most. Several centuries seems excessive and cruel. But then, what do I know? The Prince of the Doomed City may very well be both excessive *and* cruel. It wouldn't altogether surprise me.

But Mixael says, "No, we're not Obligates. My folks were bound to the Prince for lifetime service, you see. And I was born after their service began, so I've lived here all my life. I'm not bound or anything; I've simply never bothered to leave."

"Do you . . ." I hesitate, uncertain whether or not my next question will be considered impertinent. "Do you ever want to leave? To get out of Eledria and see what life is like in the human world?"

"*Leave* Eledria?" Mixael frowns as though the thought had never occurred to him. "I mean, I've traveled into the human world a few times. Didn't like it much. The air is awfully thick there, and I can almost *feel* Time crawling all over me, aging me with each passing second. Not a pleasant sensation! No, Vespre is my home. Always has been, and I rather think it always will be. I mean, what would *I* do in the human world?"

I don't push him. After all, I've often wondered the same thing, wondered what my life will be like once my Obligation ends and it's time to return to *normal*. Though I crave that return, there's a part of me that simply . . . wonders.

Once Eledria gets into your blood, can you ever purge it out again?

Mixael continues talking, bright and easy, little caring whether or not I'm listening. I learn that he's been training as a librarian since he was old enough to hold a pen, that he aspires to become senior librarian himself one day, if his mother will ever relinquish the title. But he doesn't expect that to happen any time soon, so *junior* it is and has been for a good hundred-some years now.

I'm a little surprised to learn that Mixael is more than a century old. He scarcely looks any older than me! But then, that's how life is in Eledria, even for humans. Were he to spend any great amount of time in his own world, age would catch up with him soon enough. So long as he breathes nothing but Eledrian air, however, he could live as long as any fae. Like Queen Dasyra. She'd lived as Lodírhal's consort for many a long century before her eventual death. And that death, I've gathered, was an accident, and nothing to do with age or sickness.

Mixael stops suddenly. We've climbed a last long stairway and stand before a door. It's as tall as five fully-grown men, carved of solid black stone without any embellishment. The huge door handles seem to be of tarnished silver, shaped like twining snakes. Mixael grabs one of these and, straining a little, pulls one door open. "Step inside, miss!" he says, bowing slightly at the waist and motioning with one hand.

My heart suddenly pounds in my throat and blood rushes in my ears. This is it. This is Vespre Library, home of the Noswraiths. What will I find beyond these doors? What darkness? What danger? The questions storm through my head, but I can't stand here dithering forever.

Swallowing hard, I set my chin and step through the opening. My breath is immediately stolen from my lungs. This place is *enormous*.

I stand in the central citadel I'd glimpsed from the carriage ride. Each floor of the library seems to form a ring around the wall, but down the center is nothing but open, empty space. Only a chest-high rail stands between me and a terrible plunge. I'm too far back from the rail to get a sense of how many stories there are, but I can *feel* the vastness of that space. We've apparently come to the uppermost floor of the library. High overhead arches the huge domed ceiling made from what appears to be a perfectly enormous polished crystal.

Mixael closes the door behind him and steps to my side. I feel the beaming grin he fixes on me, though I'm too busy gaping around to turn and meet it. "Welcome to Vespre Library," he says, his voice fairly bursting with pride. "Not half bad, eh?"

"This place . . . it's full of books?" My voice emerges in a weak little whisper. I can't bear to speak any louder.

"Not on the first floor," he replies with a shrug. "This floor is devoted to workstations. But everything below us, yes. Packed to the gills, as they say."

"But . . . but . . . where do they all come from?"

"Your world. All different times, all different places. But all human, of course. The fae don't write, as you know."

"Are they *all* Noswraiths?"

"Great gods, no!" Mixael laughs at this, a bright, golden sound in this solemn space. "No, they're mostly books on magic—magic lore, magic legend, magic secrets, magic theory, practical and impractical magic, interdimensional, natural, fabricated, and so on and so forth. We've all got to be in tip-top magical shape to do the job we do here in Vespre. Proper mages, one and all!"

He takes my elbow and steers me deftly to the left. I stumble along, numb and trembling. "Time for you to meet the rest of the crew," he says, and takes me around the curving floor. There are no bookshelves here. Instead the walls are lined with desks carved directly into the stone. Each one is a big, curved thing, with lots of crannies and alcoves and shelves for stashing supplies and books. They're inset so deeply into the wall, whoever is seated at one of them couldn't see the desks on either side. Ideal for focused work, I suspect.

My first thought at the sight of all those desks was that Vespre must boast a veritable army of librarians. But as Mixael continues to lead me on, I notice that most of the desks are empty, the cubbies and crannies bare, the seats pushed in.

"Oi! Mother!" Mixael calls out suddenly. "Look who we've got here!"

Up ahead, a chair pushes back from one of the cubbies, revealing a hunched little figure in a faded green gown. Her hair is pure white, but still thick, and tied in a knot right on top of her head, secured in place by several ragged old quills. Over her gown she wears a shapeless sort of smock covered in ink stains. Her hands are both liver-spotted with age and ink-spotted from work.

She sees Mixael and me, and quickly pushes her chair even further back. As she does so, something gives out a rattling bray, and I see what looks like a small blue dragon unfolding itself from beneath her chair. It lifts its head, hissing and showing a forked red tongue.

"Well, if you don't want your tail rolled over, you shouldn't sleep underneath, should you?" the old woman barks in response, even as she puts out a hand and ruffles the upraised crest on the top of the dragon's head. The dragon hisses again, whips its tail close around its body, and slinks out of sight, into the shadows under the desk. Only then does the old woman lean back in her chair and turn to Mixael once more. "Now then, my boy," she says, her voice cracking with age. "Who's this pretty little thing?"

"This is Miss Darlington," Mixael answers with a ceremonious sweep of one hand. "You know, the new librarian the Prince went to fetch from Aurelis?"

"Ah." The old lady nods slowly. "So he managed to snap her up at last, did he? Always was a one for getting his own way, our Prince." She fixes me with a close stare. Her eyes are startlingly blue, pale, and pretty. Sharp despite her age. She doesn't need spectacles.

"Have you any library experience, Miss Darlington?"

I nod, then clear my throat and say, "Yes, ma'am. I mean, Mistress. Senior Librarian." As an afterthought, I bob a curtsy.

"Oh, don't bother with all that." The old woman smiles. Her teeth are all present and accounted for and perfectly white. In fact, other than the thin, wrinkled skin and the shockingly white hair, she doesn't *seem* properly old. "You can call me Nelle. Nelle Silveri. I'm this one's mother," she adds, tossing her head Mixael's way.

I look from mother to son and back again. Mixael has already told me he's more than a century old, but he's not aged beyond twenty or so. His mother need not age either, not if she doesn't wish to. So why has she allowed the wrinkles to creep in? Why has she not held onto her youth?

These are not questions I can ask directly, however. I hold my tongue.

"I suppose you ought to meet the rest of the crew," Nelle says, turning in her seat. "Andreas! Vervain!" she barks down the row of cubicles. "We've got a new one!"

Two more heads pop out from behind the stone cubicles, one five places down, the other a good ten places beyond him. And they are the only two.

Seeing the great spaces in between the desks emphasized like that fills me with sudden foreboding. This library is vast, truly vast. It could swallow Aurelis Library whole and still have room left over. But Aurelis was always peopled with Obligates running here and there, caring for the books and the magic and the knowledge stored within them.

Are there really only four librarians in all of Vespre? Five now . . . including me.

The nearer of the two librarians slowly unfolds himself from his chair and ambles our way, hands in his pockets. He's not quite young enough to be considered *youthful* anymore, but not old enough to count as middle-aged either. His skin is dark, his hair close-cropped, and his eyes are large and solemn, made to seem even larger from behind his round spectacles. His clothing is neat as a pin, and not a single drop of ink stains his fingers.

The figure at the further desk approaches more swiftly. Every move she makes is short, sharp, but not quite what one would call vigorous. It's as though she's propelled by some other, unseen force, not quite her own. She's a very pale woman, a good ten or twelve years older than me, and the dark circles under her eyes look as though it's been a long time since she's had a full night's sleep. Her clothes are unkempt, and her hair hangs in long, limp strands without any attempt to braid or tie it back.

She focuses a hollow-eyed stare on me as she draws near. I feel at once that she dislikes me, though I can't think why. What could I possibly have done in the space of ten seconds to offend her?

"This here is Andreas Cornil," Nelle says, drawing my attention from the woman back to the bespectacled man. "He's been with us a few years now, learning the ropes. Turning into quite a handy mage in his own way. And this here," the old woman continues, indicating the woman, "is Vervain."

Nelle doesn't give Vervain a surname, I notice. Why not? Somehow this omission feels important.

"Pleased to meet you," I murmur, offering a swift curtsy to the two librarians. Then, though I suspect I already know the answer, I ask, "Is that... Are there no more of you?" I glance at Mixael and remember how he mentioned that both of his parents served the Prince. "Where is Mister Silveri?"

Nelle grunts and turns abruptly to her desk, stacking up papers and putting stoppers on several open inkwells, her face pointedly turned away from me. Mixael touches my elbow and bends his head close to my ear. "We had an incident last year," he whispers. "One of the Great Grimoires broke down faster than we could repair it, and a Noswraith got loose. My father died getting it contained again."

"Oh!" I wish I could kick myself, wish I could take back my thoughtless question. Through my memory flashes the image of that one great swath of city seen from the sky, totally laid to ruins. Lawrence had said it was a Noswraith's doing. I cast Mixael an apologetic glance. "I'm so sorry."

He shrugs, though I see pain in his eyes. "We've lost a lot of folks over the years. That's life in Vespre." He nods to his mother. "She took it hard though. Been married a long time and lost him all in a blink. It aged her. I'd never seen her with a wrinkle until it happened, then... this." He heaves a sigh, but quickly sets his jaw and forces his mouth into a determined smile. "But don't you worry, Miss Darlington. She'll recover, and you'll see her like she once was, I'm sure of it. In the meanwhile, the Prince is fixing up our ranks again. We'll be stronger than ever!"

Does he mean me? Do these four lonely librarians expect me to make the difference in their ongoing fight? Gods above, are they in for a disappointing surprise!

Nelle rises, tucks a book under her arm, then pushes her chair in. There's another braying hiss from under the desk, and the little blue dragon emerges, flapping its wings furiously. It's an odd creature, that's for sure. I've never seen a dragon, but I always assumed they had four legs. This one, however, only has two hind legs, and its wings sprout where forelimbs ought to be.

"Oh, leave off your squawking!" Nelle nudges the beast aside with one foot as it tries to lunge at her. Then she crouches and lifts it in her arms with much more gentleness than I would have expected after all her grumbling. Even more surprising, the dragon clambers onto her shoulders and drapes there like a lounging cat. It folds its wings neatly, only flaring them now and then for balance as she walks, and its long tail wraps around Nelle's upper arm.

Nelle catches my curious stare. "It's a wyvern," she says. As though this is explanation enough. She turns to Mixael then and holds out the book she'd taken from her desk. "Here, my boy, finish this last binding of mine if you please. It ain't a tough one. When you're through, shelve it where it belongs, then go on with your duties. I'll take Miss Darlington now, give her a proper tour of the place."

"Sure thing, Mother," Mixael says, and drops a quick kiss on his mother's faded cheek. He casts me a last encouraging grin before setting off down the line of desks and finally disappearing into one of the cubicles. Andreas and Vervain, not yet dismissed, stand awkwardly where they are, not quite looking at me. Neither of them has spoken yet; not social characters like Nelle and her son, apparently.

"Go on with you," Nelle says abruptly to the two of them. "No use gawping at the new girl. You'll have plenty of time to get acquainted."

Thus dismissed, they make hasty retreats. Andreas, at least, tosses me a neat little bow and what might pass for a hint of a smile. Vervain simply turns and, in that same harsh, jerking manner, returns to her desk.

"Well now," Nelle says, drawing my attention back to her. She takes hold of my arm. "Let's start getting you situated, shall we?"

THE PRINCE

I SEE HER FACE AS SHE FALLS. OVER AND OVER AGAIN.

Those wide eyes, shot through with terror. Dark hair whipping about her cheeks. One hand outstretched, desperate, hopeless.

There'd been no thought. No consideration, no weighing of options. Only action. Only the need to reach her, the need to prevent what was happening by whatever means necessary.

I see the moment again. See her plummet, fall. And I dive after her . . .

. . . only to come awake with a start, sitting upright and gasping. Shadows spin on the edges of my vision, and the world around me pitches. I put out both hands, grip a carved stone post with one, a handful of cloth with the other. For the moment, I cannot reconcile the images still flashing in my head with the reality slowly coming into focus around me. I draw a deep breath, then another.

"Ah!" A familiar voice, calm and measured, sounds from somewhere off to my right. "You're awake. Care for a cup of tea, sir?"

I bow my heavy head, give it a rough shake. When I look up again, however, the shadows have retreated. I'm in my own bedchamber. Back in Vespre. Surrounded by my books, quills, scrolls, various items of debris which even intrepid Lawrence can never fully keep in order. On the table nearest my bed sits a thin volume with a moss-green cover. I recognize it; the book I carried with me in the carriage in case need arose for hastily written spells. A writhing aura of fury oozes out from between its pages—all those angry frights, dragged back into their own dimension of thought and idea rather than physical reality. They rail against their captivity, struggling to break down the binding and slip free once more.

I reach out, slap my hand down hard on top of it. The book stills, startled into submission. It'll need a proper binding soon, not this roughshod work I scribbled out in the heat of the moment.

Raising my heavy head, I meet Lawrence's placid gaze. My Obligate stands before me with a tray in hand. He sets it down beside the spellbook and goes about pouring black tea through a strainer. "This will soon set you to rights, sir," he says, "never you fear."

He hands me the cup. I take a sip, wincing a little at the strong, bitter taste. Then I rub a hand down my face. "What happened?"

"Frights, sir, if you recall," Lawrence replies. "Madame Silveri tells me they slipped the wards soon after your departure for

Aurelis. The librarians have been attempting to track them down, but they've laid low up until now. They must have found the new young librarian too tempting a target. Very nearly got her too." He smiles then, a satisfied expression. "But you got them contained again, sir. With quite a dramatic flare, if I may be so bold."

"Why didn't you stop me?" I growl, leaning back into the mound of pillows behind me.

"Well, sir, I did try to remind you that such an exertion might prove rather taxing on your health. But you were in such a state when the wraiths overwhelmed Miss Darlington. If you might recall, you called me a 'damned blackguard,' and threatened to hurl me from the carriage yourself if I did not release my hold on your writing hand, and—"

"Yes, yes. Enough." I set my cup down with a slosh of tea atop the green spellbook. Planting my hands under me, I try to push upright, to rise, only . . . only it turns out I can't. My body simply will not obey me. Cursing through gritted teeth, I fall back on the pillows again. My breath comes hard, and my limbs shake. This is worse than I thought. And all for a little flock of frights! What would one of the Greater Noswraiths take out of me?

"Here, sir." Lawrence slips a bottle from his coat pocket and adds a splash of its contents to the teacup, which he presses back into my hands. "This will help."

I don't bother asking what it is but take an experimental sip and hiss as the bracing burn slides down my throat. I won't say it helps particularly, but it certainly can't hurt. "And what of the librarian?"

I ask at last. "Has she been ensconced in her rooms as of yet?"

"I understand the young lady was sidetracked along the way."

"Sidetracked? How?"

"Do you recall that family of orphan trollings who've been infiltrating the palace for scraps over the last few months?"

"Yes."

"According to Captain Khas, they have claimed young Miss Darlington as their mother."

I groan and slap a hand to my face. "That's the *last* thing we need just now. Gods spare me, she's going to make me regret ever bringing her here!"

"Quite," Lawrence answers with a too-knowing smile. He collects his tray and moves to carry it from the chamber, navigating through the detritus with expert ease.

"Wait," I say just as he reaches the door.

"Yes, sir?"

"Have the girl—the new librarian—join me for dinner. It's time I gave her a rundown of the rules here in Vespre."

"As you wish, sir."

"And Lawrence?"

"Yes, sir?"

"Wipe that infernally smug smirk off your face, why don't you."

"Of course, sir. Immediately, sir."

18

NELLE SEEMS DETERMINED TO CRAM AS MUCH information as possible into my skull at once.

She starts out by showing me the upper floor, including the desks and various doors. Some of those doors may be used both for entrance and exit, but some must be used only for one or the other. She doesn't explain the reasoning behind this, and I don't have the nerve to ask. I'll simply take her word for it.

There's a spiral staircase leading down to the next level, and Nelle guides me that way. As we go, we pass several cages of silver bars suspended on cables above the central drop. "Book lifts," Nelle calls them. "And mind," she adds, with a severe waggle of one finger, "don't you go trying to ride the lifts yourself now! They're meant for books, not folks."

The blue dragon—or *wyvern*, as she called it—lifts its head from her shoulder and flares its crest at me, as though to emphasize her point.

"Yes, ma'am," I murmur obediently.

Nelle and the wyvern both grunt, sounding oddly alike. Then it lowers its head again, and she continues leading me to the stair, the pair of them apparently oblivious to the odd picture they make.

"The library, you'll find," Nelle says, "has a bit of a life of its own. A personality, as it were—most libraries do. You've worked in a library before, I understand?"

"Yes," I answer promptly. "Aurelis Library, at the Court of Dawn."

"Ah." Nelle nods. "I been there once or twice. Quite a bright personality that one has. Vespre, however . . ." The old woman purses her lips a moment before continuing. "Vespre's an altogether different animal. Not a *nice* library, you understand. It's because of the Noswraiths. They've given her a rotten heart. But"—and here she sighs—"we all love her just the same. Like a mother can't help loving even the wickedest of her little ones."

We reach the head of the stairs and begin our descent to the next level. Nelle informs me that she and her fellow librarians confine their efforts to the top twenty stories of the library. She's not entirely certain how many more stories there are—she's never ventured below the twentieth floor and hopes she never will. The bulk of the librarians' work is spent in the upper ten stories anyway.

"And we'll stick to the upper five floors today," Nelle says as we descend. "I'll let the Prince take you below when he's ready. That's a place you're better off seeing for the first time with him at your side."

She goes on to explain that the top floor we just left is considered the primary workspace where the majority of the "scribbling," as she calls it, is done. They call it the *first* floor, even though it is the highest in the citadel.

"And this," she says, stepping off the spiral stair, "is the second floor."

Here at last are the books. Many, many books. The shelves are carved into the wall just like the desks up above. They tower a good fifteen feet tall at least and are packed from floor to ceiling. "Are they Noswraiths?" I ask, breathless.

"No, no." Nelle shakes her head. "Second floor is devoted to Magic of Antiquity. These are all old spellbooks, gathered in every human language, both dead and alive. One of your many tasks as a junior librarian will be to go through these books, searching out references to Noswraiths and their workings. Noswraiths have been around *much* longer than folks originally believed, but they were called by different names in different places at different times, and the various cultures of magic throughout the ages have had different ways of dealing with them."

She leads me along the curved wall, her pace slow and sedate. Now and then she reaches out and brushes her fingertips along various spines. "The Prince," she says, "is trying to compile a master encyclopedia of all Noswraith knowledge. It's his obsession, though he don't get much time for it, what with all the bindings and re-bindings having to be done."

She takes me down to the third floor where the shelves are just as packed as those above. This time, with Miphates Magic. "You know the Miphates?" she asks me.

I shake my head. The word sounds vaguely familiar, but I can't place it in the moment.

"They was the primary magical school of thought back when I was living in the human world some centuries back," Nelle explains. "There ain't much true Miphates magic left nowadays, I'm told, but way back when, they was a force to be reckoned with. Even the fae feared them. The Miphates discovered more about Noswraiths than any magicians who'd gone before." She shivers. "I ain't never had much luck with Miphates. Save one, that is."

At this, her mouth softens into an unexpected smile, a smile that actually reaches her eyes. She absently caresses the wyvern on her shoulder. It closes its eyes and begins to rumble what I think might be a purr. For a moment, they both seem truly happy.

The moment doesn't last, however. The wyvern tries to nuzzle Nelle's cheek, which brings the old woman back to herself with a start. She growls and pushes the creature's nose away, before continuing with her tour.

We venture down to the fourth floor now, also densely packed with books. These, Nelle informs me, are a conglomerate of things, including magic history, lore, and legend. "Not stuff I particularly care for," she admits. "This is more Andreas's passion. He's a *poet*, Andreas is." She says the word like it's an insult. "Got himself in trouble with his poetry. But then, we all of us got ourselves into trouble of one kind or another. Else we wouldn't have ended up here."

At this, she pauses suddenly and shoots me a shrewd glance. Does she know what trouble brought me to Vespre? Does she know the truth of my Pledge-breaking? My mouth opens, the questions ready to tumble forth.

Before I can say anything, the old woman turns and hastens on . . . and I can't help thinking she knew what I was going to ask and avoided my questions.

The fifth floor, to my surprise, is devoted almost entirely to quills. They're mounted in beautiful glass displays, some of them obviously quite fine with elegant nibs. Others are just little sawed-off, ratty things, but every one of them is afforded a place of honor on these shelves.

"We never throw out our quills," Nelle informs me. "The Miphates used to believe that a mage could pour his power into a favored quill. They thought over time it became a sort of channel for him to more easily access the *quinsatra*—the Realm of Magic, you understand—and draw it through into the physical world." She chuckles dryly. "Most of us don't really *believe* it, but . . . in a way, we also kind of do. It's *traditional* is what it is. It's not like it's *real*, but it's more real than simple real."

I'm not sure I follow this at all. But I think of the red quill currently tucked away inside my small parcel. It's more ornate than most of the quills I see in these display cases. I wonder who it belonged to, and why Thaddeus felt the need to give it to me?

Perhaps I should ask Nelle, but . . . something makes me keep my mouth shut. For the present at least.

Nelle pauses at the top of the spiral stairway leading down to the sixth floor. Here she turns and gives me a look. "That might be enough for today," she says consideringly. "You've had a long journey, and no use in overwhelming you, I'm thinking."

"What's down there?" I ask, curiosity piqued.

"Down there?" Nelle indicates the stair with a jut of her chin. "That's the start of the Noswraiths, that is. All the Noswraiths gathered by our Prince over the centuries. There's . . . a lot of them."

A shiver races down my spine. I look at that stair, look at the railing between me and the empty drop down the center of the citadel. Memory of the Melted Man's awful face flits through my mind. That being of sheer horror, sheer wickedness. There was nothing good about him, nothing of value or virtue. He was created evil, pure evil, without even the hope of redemption.

And down there—just below my feet—are more like him?

I feel Nelle's shrewd eyes watching me. I don't like to look at her, don't want to let her see me afraid. Not now, not on my first day. I look up at her, intending it to be a brief glance. Instead I find my gaze caught and held.

"Hmmm." The old woman grunts. "We all feel it at first. The *weight*, as it were. But you get used to it. Faster than you might think."

She begins climbing the stairs then, leading all the way up the many spirals to the first floor. "It's good work," she says as she goes, tossing the words back to me as I follow at her heels. "It's thankless enough, I'll grant you. Fighting tooth and nail to save the worlds every single day, and no one knowing or caring what you're up to. But *you* know. And that counts for something. And you've got companions in the rest of us, folks who know what it is you're doing, folks ready and willing to help you. I still remember when I started out . . ."

She launches into a rambling story about her early days in Vespre, newly married to her mage husband but completely green and unskilled in the ways of magic and bindings. I pick up little bits and pieces of her tale, but don't pay close attention. My mind is far too busy churning over everything I've just seen.

Suddenly I'm tired. So very, very tired. So tired, I'm not sure how I even make it up the last turn of the stair to the First Floor. Once there, I simply stand in place, gripping the rail. Would anyone care if I crawled into one of those cubicles, curled up like the wyvern underneath one of those empty desks, and just slept for days?

"Miss Darlington!"

I groan but turn my heavy eyes to where Mixael stands near the library door, waving at me. Beside him is a tall, pale figure whom I at first mistake for Captain Khas. On second glance, however, I realize that it's a stranger. Another *throwback* troll, but shorter, rounder, and less muscular than the captain. She's shockingly curvy, an exaggerated figure of feminine beauty, and clad in a flowing gown of some translucent material that only *just* offers any real modesty.

"What's this, my boy?" Nelle demands. She's halfway between

me and her son, her brisk pace at odds with her overall appearance of age. "Don't you have work to be doing? And here I find you chatting up the pretty lasses!"

Mixael ignores his mother and instead motions for me to hurry. I sigh but obey, trying not to stare too hard at the beautiful troll woman. "This," Mixael says, waving a hand between me and the troll, "is our new junior librarian, Miss Darlington. Miss Darlington, allow me to introduce Lir. She's your maid."

"My . . . my what, now?" I stammer.

The troll woman flashes a smile my way, a smile so beaming and brilliant, it's almost enough to knock me off my feet. I doubt if I'll ever get used to these magnificent creatures with their godlike stature, their unnatural grace, and their perfect features. "I'm so pleased to meet you," she says. Her voice is silvery and soft, with only the faintest hint of rough growling. "I've been looking forward to your arrival. Will you allow me to escort you to your chambers, Miss Darlington?"

I gape at her, stupidly. Then, with a quick shake of my head, I turn to Nelle and Mixael, both of whom are watching me with amused expressions. "I'm to have a *maid?*"

Mixael nods. "She'll help you get settled in. Teach you about the palace and how we live here in Vespre. You'll find her very useful, I'm sure."

"But I'm an *Obligate*."

"You're a *librarian*," Nelle responds to me with emphasis. "You're charged with a sacred duty to guard and protect the contents of

Vespre Library and, in so doing, to guard and protect the worlds. The least our Prince can do is provide you with a little help along the way."

I should protest. This doesn't make any sense at all!

But then again, who am I to question the ways and practices of life in the Doomed City?

"Please, Miss Darlington," the troll woman interjects, blinking pale eyes framed by long, white lashes. "Allow me to escort you to your rooms. You can freshen up and perhaps sleep a little."

Sleep. Yes! That's what I need. Sleep. More than anything. I nod mutely. Tears prickle in the corners of my eyes, though I can't begin to say why. I'm simply so tired, and the prospect of sleep is so beautiful . . .

The troll woman takes my arm. I don't resist as she leads me toward the door. Just before I step through, I remember to turn and call out a hasty "Goodbye!" to Nelle and Mixael. Then, though it probably doesn't make any sense, I add, "Thank you!"

"See you soon, Miss Darlington," Mixael answers cheerfully.

"Good luck, girl," says Nelle, her voice more ominous than his.

With that, I'm guided through the doors, which shut fast behind me.

19

THE TROLL WOMAN LEADS ME DOWN ANOTHER bewildering series of passages. I think I recognize the corridor of floor-to-ceiling windows without glass where I'd encountered the troll children, but for all I know it might be another corridor exactly like that one but in a completely different part of the palace. Gods on high, will I *ever* get used to this strange, awful, stony, twilit place?

"Your pardon! Miss Darlington!"

I turn sharply, startled at the sound of my name. A tall, lanky form approaches from the end of the stone hall, waving an arm overhead. In the gloom of deep twilight, I don't recognize Lawrence until he is within a few feet of me. The sight of his pleasant, plain face is something of a relief.

He comes to a stop and offers a quick bow, shooting the troll woman a quick glance but addressing me. "The Prince requires your presence at dinner tonight, Miss Darlington. He asks that you present yourself promptly and that you wear something suitable for the occasion."

"Supper?" I blink dumbly, not quite sure what I've just heard. "The Prince wants me to . . . he . . . *what?*"

"Supper. With him. Within the quarter hour."

The troll woman—Lir, if I'm remembering her name correctly—takes a firm step, planting herself between me and the human manservant. "Miss Darlington," she says in a perfectly prim voice that would not be out of place among higher class servants in my own world, "is fatigued. I am taking her to bed now, and she wishes not to be disturbed."

Lawrence has the grace to look chagrined. "I'm sure I do apologize, Miss Darlington," he says, continuing to address me, though he has to lean fairly far to one side to see me around Lir's impressively curvy figure. "But the Prince is the Prince, you know. He will have his way."

I consider the last view I'd had of the Prince being carried off between two great troll guards. He had certainly not looked like a man to be hosting dinner or making demands for company. But who am I to protest? I'm an Obligate. I can't refuse.

"Tell the Prince I will come as soon as I can," I say.

Lir growls something low that I don't hear, but Lawrence nods and offers a relieved smile. "He looks forward to your company, I'm sure." With a short bow to me and a last timid glance for

Lir, he hastens off, disappearing into the gloom and shadows so completely, I have to wonder if the conversation even took place. Maybe I dreamt it.

"Of all the cheek!" Lir mutters, crossing her arms over her substantial bosom. "Imagine, summoning you like that before you've even had a proper rest!"

"Well," I offer meekly, "he *is* a prince, I suppose."

"And *you're* a *librarian*." Lir sniffs, and by her tone, one would think librarians trumped princes any day of the week. "Ah, well," she finishes and shrugs prettily. "One must make the best of one's circumstances, mustn't one?" With this somewhat pedantic insight, she leads me on down the hall before stopping abruptly and opening a door. "These will be your chambers, Miss Darlington," she says, stepping back to allow me space to enter.

I pass through the doorway . . . and very nearly back out again. Surely there must be some mistake! This room is simply too big, too grand. There's a great stone bed with four high, stalagmite pillars stretching all the way to the ceiling, hung with gossamer curtains delicately picked out in silvery threads to create an abstract pattern reminiscent of spiderwebs. A luxurious rug graces the floor, the pile thick enough to lose one's toes in. An absolutely enormous wardrobe dominates one wall—not stone, I note, but a beautiful cherrywood that looks suspiciously as though it's come from Broderick & Son's, one of the premier furniture makers in my own world. Shipping a gargantuan piece like that across multiple worlds must have been a challenging endeavor!

I pull my gaze from the wardrobe, taking in other lovely furnishings, adornments, little tasteful fixtures, and luxuries. The whole chamber, though distinctly trollish in its cavernous shape, rough-hewn walls, and stalactite-studded ceiling, has been fitted out as though for a fine lady.

"There must be some mistake!" I gasp. I turn to Lir, shaking my head. "I'm an *Obligate*. I don't . . . I don't need . . . this isn't . . ."

The troll woman is on her way to the wardrobe but pauses and looks back at me. Her pretty, pale brow puckers. "Is the room not to your liking? I'm sure we can have another one fitted out for you if you prefer. Or is it the furnishings? The Prince likes to see to such things himself, you know."

I look around the room again, trying not to let my jaw gape. "It's . . . I mean, it's very beautiful." I shake my head, almost dizzy. "Is this . . ." I hesitate, then lick my lips and try again. "Is this how *all* the librarians live in Vespre?"

"Well, of course!" Lir offers an incredulous smile and continues on her way to the wardrobe. "The librarians are among the most valued and celebrated denizens of the city, second only to the Prince himself. They bravely stand guard between us and certain doom, after all."

Valued? Celebrated? Those are not words I ever thought to hear applied to *humans* anywhere in Eledria. It makes me more than a little uncomfortable. I'm so used to being treated as nothing, as less than nothing. I'm not sure how I feel about all of this.

While Lir busies herself with the wardrobe, I wander across the room. There's a doorway beyond the huge bed, and when I peek through, I discover a private washroom with a large claw-footed bathtub and every other possible convenience, newer and more up-to-date even than the washrooms in Danny and Kitty's lovely townhouse. There's even a commode—a proper commode with a pull-chain and everything!

I back away, shutting the door softly, and move on to the curtained window dominating one wall. The curtain is made of many layers of the same gossamer spider-web material as the bed curtains, but too dense to let any light through. The room itself would be pitch black were it not for several pale globe lanterns strung from stalactites overhead. How I would reach those lanterns to either extinguish or relight them, I have no idea. Lir will have to teach me.

I find the center of the curtain and peel it back, curious to discover what lies beyond. My eyes widen, and my breath catches. The window offers a sweeping view of Vespre City spread out far below . . . but I am situated directly above the street decimated by the Noswraith. All around it, the buildings shine white under the starlight, making the darkness and desolation of that street so much worse by comparison.

I stare down at that sight. And suddenly all the fineness of the room melts away, all the luxuries and conveniences. None of them matter. What matters is that destruction. That demonstration of raw, unchecked, hideous power. Power which, sooner or later, I will be expected to combat and contain.

I think about Mixael's father dying in battle.

I think about all those empty desks.

How long do I really think I can survive in this place?

Shuddering, I drop the curtain and turn away. Only now do I discover what Lir has been doing—laying out a gown, underthings, stockings, shoes, all pulled from that enormous wardrobe. "There, Miss Darlington!" the troll maid says with a cheerful smile. "This should suit you rather well."

I stare at the gown. "Is that *for me?*"

It's lovely. Truly lovely. Not ornate or exaggerated like the gowns Estrilde liked to dress me in. A simple silvery gray silk with white-lace spiderweb trimming at the collar and cuffs. A round neckline, not too low, but deep enough to emphasize a feminine shape. A tasteful ruffle along the hem. I can tell even just looking at it that it will fit me to perfection.

"The Prince requires a certain standard of dress for meals," Lir says, lifting a soft white chemise and shaking it out briskly. "Come, Miss Darlington! I shall help you dress, then we simply *must* do something with your hair."

Part of me wants to resist. But the truth is, I'm tired. Much too tired. And Lir's demeanor is so calmly insistent, I submit to her ministrations without a murmur. She outfits me in chemise, corset, petticoats, stockings, and gown. The gown fits beautifully, as I suspected, requiring only the barest snugging of the corset to make it flow smoothly. The scooped neckline is flattering to my frame, and the undergarments are perfectly soft against my skin.

With a few deft strokes of a brush, a twist, and a handful of pins, Lir styles my hair. Once she's finished, she leads me to a floor-length mirror and stands me in front of it. "There, now. What do you think, Miss Darlington?" Her tone all but dares me to disapprove.

But I can't. Everything about the gown and the hairstyle is ideally suited to me. And somehow, without the aid of cosmetics, Lir has managed to disguise all the travel-worn exhaustion from my face. Perhaps she used a little glamour without my noticing.

Somewhere in the near distance, a bell tolls. "Ah!" Lir says in her sweetly husky voice. "That's eight bells. Your escort must be here."

"My escort?"

The troll maid doesn't bother to explain but sashays to the door and flings it wide. There, somewhat to my surprise, stand five solemn stone-faced troll guards, complete with lances. "Come, miss!" Lir says, beckoning to me. "You must be on your way at once. No good in keeping the Prince waiting."

My knees trembling more than I like, I lift my skirts and approach the door. The trolls don't look at me. They're so still, so hard, so . . . rocky. If I didn't know better, I'd think they were merely lumps of stone, roughly pounded into shape with a hammer and dressed in leather armor just for the show of it.

But when I step into the midst of them, they turn in perfect unison and set off marching down the passage, hustling me along like a prisoner. Did the Prince think I'd put up a fight or something?

Is that how guests usually react to his dinner invitations?

I cast a last, somewhat desperate glance back at Lir. She smiles brightly and waves as if nothing about this situation is at all unnatural. I wiggle my fingers tentatively in response, then face forward, concentrating my gaze on the broad back of the troll in front of me. I don't even try to keep track of the twists and turns of the palace itself. By now, I'm firmly convinced I'll never understand its layout and there's little point in trying. It's all just one big nightmare.

The trolls eventually come to a stop in front of what at first looks to me like a solid wall of stone. On second glance, I'm just able to discern the outline of a door and what might be a doorknob. The trolls say nothing, offer nothing, but simply stand there, two on each side, one behind me. Apparently, I'm supposed to know what to do next.

Swallowing hard, I step out from among my escort. I lift my hand, prepared to knock, but hesitate. I really hate to rap my knuckles against that hard stone. Instead I clear my throat and call out somewhat tremulously, "Hello? I'm here for . . . for dinner?"

At once, lines of light illuminate the edges of a tall, wide door. I yelp and leap back as it swings outward, and Lawrence's face appears in the opening. "Ah! Miss Darlington," he says warmly. "Do come in. And allow me to apologize for abandoning you on the front step earlier this evening. I hope you found your way about without too much difficulty?"

My perilous encounter with the troll children—and that utterly ridiculous climb out onto the buttress—flashes through my mind. I'd very nearly brought my term of service in Vespre to an abrupt and crashing end!

But I merely nod and murmur, "Yes, thank you, Mister Lawrence."

He takes a step back, motioning me inside. I leave the stony presence of my troll escort gladly enough, expecting to enter a dining hall of some sort.

Instead I step into a bedroom. A completely cluttered, crazed, disastrous, typhoon-tossed mess of a bedroom. In fact, I can only tell it's a bedroom because the bed in the center is so large, one can't miss it, but otherwise, my gaze is completely distracted by piles and piles of random detritus. Books stacked in haphazard towers, papers strewn, ink and quills and trimmings, all the regular accoutrements of a librarian but without a librarian's natural inclination to order. And far more things besides: strange geometrical objects and jointed contraptions of wood and metal the like of which I've never seen, globes and charts and astrological instruments, pieces of what looks unsettlingly like a human skeleton scattered here and there, including a white skull with a large, red, dripping candle balanced on its dome. There are huge disk-shaped things that might be dragon scales, broken tools and pottery, a set of paints long gone dry, gears and gadgets from clockwork instruments, and a completely inexplicable stuffed alligator. Here and there I see signs of tidiness, as though someone had tried to come in behind the room's occupant and impose a little order. Lawrence's efforts, no doubt, and totally useless. The inexorable tide of clutter represented here would be too much for the most intrepid of manservants.

I drag my gaze into focus on the great bed with its thick red curtains and sagging canopy. There, lying propped up on a vast collection of pillows, lies the Prince.

Gods above smite me! A hot blush flares up my cheeks. He's not dressed. Again. Not properly dressed anyway. He wears an ornate dressing gown which is open from the throat all the way to the belt, revealing that muscular torso and abdomen of which I've already seen more than my fill, thank you very much.

I don't know how long I stand there, frozen in place. Finally, I find my voice and blurt, "I thought we were having dinner!"

The Prince, who was idly reading over a sheaf of papers, looks up at me coolly. "Why, yes. That we are, Clara Darling. Do come in. And try to blink before your eyes fall from your skull. I find this goggling most unsettling."

20

I BLINK RAPIDLY BUT DON'T APPROACH AT THE PRINCE'S beckoning. Instead I turn to Lawrence, who is just shutting the door behind us. "I thought we were having dinner!" I repeat, this time in a hissing whisper, though I suspect the Prince hears me loud and clear.

"You are, indeed, Miss Darlington," Lawrence says with a placating smile. "But the Prince is still too much indisposed to leave his bed. You'll dine here this evening. Have no fear! Proper dining arrangements will be resumed on the morrow."

On the morrow? Would I be expected to dine with the Prince then as well?

Deciding not to borrow trouble from the future when the present is plenty complicated as it is, I face the Prince again. He's watching me closely, one eyebrow sardonically lifted. Waiting to see me flush and flutter and make a fool of myself, no doubt. Well, let him wait!

I compose my face into the masking smile. The very picture of serenity, I glide toward the bed, using mincing steps and keeping my hands demurely folded in front of me. Lawrence sets a chair for me, and I sit primly on the edge and arrange my skirts neatly. At last, I turn my bland smile on the Prince.

His eyes glitter. He knows exactly how uncomfortable he's making me, gods smite him. But I see irritation in his gaze as well.

A long silence hovers between us.

"How do you find your room?" the Prince asks abruptly, almost but not quite managing to startle me.

I clear my throat softly. "Very well, thank you."

"Like the furnishings?" he presses. "I chose them myself. Thought to make the space as *human* as possible."

I offer a nod. Nothing more. His eyes narrow slightly. If he's hoping for raptures of gratitude from a lowly Obligate for his unexpected generosity, he's going to be disappointed.

The Prince tosses his papers off to one side, seeming not to care how they fan out across his coverlet. He settles more comfortably against his pillows and folds his arms. "You've met the other librarians by now, I trust. Mixael Silveri was under orders to greet you at the door."

"I have met Mixael Silveri and the others, yes," I reply, taking care that my voice registers no opinion whatsoever.

The Prince's expression grows more irritated by the moment.

"And how did you find them?"

"I found them well."

"All up to your exacting specifications? Or just disappointing enough to allow for a little professional superiority on your part?"

I blink at him. Slowly. I'm not sure what he's trying to get me to say or do. I know only that I won't rise to his bait.

"Hmmm," he grunts and tilts his head slightly to one side. "Not one to betray emotion unnecessarily, are you? Some think such reticence a virtue, call it *restraint* and *forbearance* and the like. Me? I call it *disaster waiting to happen*. I know your kind—all timidity and self-discipline up until the last moment. Up until the explosion. By which time, it's too late for the rest of us."

I pinch my lips ever so slightly.

"Ah! That, I see, has moved you at least." The Prince's eyes sparkle with a cunning light. "Come, Clara Darling! Don't dam up this emotion I see seething in those eyes of yours. Speak your mind before something bursts."

I don't want to give him the satisfaction. Then again, to hold my tongue might provoke him further. I let my smile widen and say in my most demure, ladylike tone, "You have judged my character rather quickly on the basis of a single day."

"I have judged your character on the basis of a great deal more than that," he answers, showing his teeth. Then, with a wave of his hand, he dismisses this topic and launches into the next. "What of Vespre Library? What do you make of it compared to your pretty little book-house in Aurelis?"

Choosing not to let his whirlwind conversation unsettle me, I answer quietly, "It is . . . different from what I am used to."

"How different? Go on, elaborate! I'm agog to know your thoughts."

"Bigger."

He rolls his eyes to the sagging canopy above. "Gods above, you're determined to irritate me, aren't you?"

Now it's my turn to tilt my head slightly. "How so, if you please?" My voice is all innocence.

He growls and opens his mouth to answer. Before any words come, however, someone knocks on the door. "Enter!" he barks, his gaze never leaving mine.

The door opens, and trolls appear, carrying an array of steaming platters and trays with them. Though none of them are throwback trolls like Lir or Captain Khas, they move with a certain solemn dignity and strange silence that I wouldn't have expected from such large, awkwardly formed beings. They set to work arranging the meal before us, laying out lace-edged cloths and setting platters on the bed around the Prince, all within his reach. I get the impression the Prince dines in bed regularly.

One of his servants sets a small table beside my seat, another pours me a tall, clear glass of something red and bubbling, and a third places a large platter which, when the lid is removed, reveals a large meal of nut-crusted seared meat, spiced-wine sauce, various roasted vegetables, crusty bread, and whipped golden butter. Either trolls are more skilled in the culinary arts than I ever imagined, or the Prince has Obligated a chef into his service.

I breathe deep, savoring the delicious aromas. Then, realizing my mistake, I glance the Prince's way and find him smiling wryly. At last, he's gotten a real reaction out of me. Gods blast him and his smug face! I answer his smile with a bland one of my own and sit back once more, keeping my hands neatly folded.

The trolls, having finished their preparations, retreat from the bed, form a line, and bow in unison. It's unsettlingly dance-like and made all the more eerie for its silence. Without ever uttering a word, they file from the room, one after another, the last one shutting the door in its wake.

"Go on," the Prince says, drawing my attention back to him. "Eat!"

I nod and lift a dainty silver fork, resolving to take my time, to be slow, delicate, and sparing. But after the first bite, I am suddenly overwhelmed with hunger. How long has it been since I had a full meal? My mind muddles when I try to puzzle it out, and I end up shaking my head and simply concentrating on the food in front of me.

When my stomach is tight and round, pressing uncomfortably against the corset boning, I finally look up. The Prince, I note, has scarcely touched his own meal. "Are you not hungry?" I ask.

"Ah, well." He shrugs, sets aside his fork, and begins fastidiously wiping his fingers with a linen napkin. "I never have much appetite after one of my *little fits*. But no fear! Lawrence will surely pry my mouth open and force something down my throat at some point."

"Indeed, sir!" Lawrence's voice, distinctly offended, sounds from somewhere across the room. I turn, trying to spy him out, but he's lost somewhere in the clutter.

The Prince chuckles and pushes his plate aside. "Now then, Clara Darling, if you have quite finished . . . I asked you here this evening so that I might give you a basic rundown of the rules in Vespre."

I take a last bite, then lay my fork down and wipe my mouth. "Very well," I say, lifting the tall glass of bubbling drink to my lips.

The Prince laces his fingers across his exposed and muscular abdomen. "First of all," he says, "you must *not* go around adopting troll children."

I nearly spit my drink out. Hastily I swallow and set the glass down. How in the world did the Prince hear about that incident already? He gives me a narrow look. I can't help thinking he looks pleased to catch me once more off my guard.

"I know how tempting it can be," he continues. "I suspect for someone like you—one of those insufferably soft-hearted natures with that destructive impulse to shield and protect—it's nearly impossible to resist. But you'll have all the shielding and protecting you can stomach simply by working in the library. And troll children are *not* your business. They will only distract you from the task at hand. Do you understand?"

I think briefly of the tearful eyes of the three little troll brothers and the defiant, petulant mouth of their beautiful sister. My life will certainly be easier not dealing with them anymore, but I can't deny the pang in my heart at the thought of them all alone. Orphaned. Rejected. Mixael had assured me troll children are practically self-sufficient from birth, but . . . well, they are still children, after all. It seems wrong to leave them to fend for themselves like stray puppies.

The Prince is still awaiting my answer. I meet his gaze and answer calmly, "I understand, Your Highness."

He shudders visibly. "*That* is the next rule—under no circumstances are you to call me 'Your Highness.' If you must address me, keep it to 'Prince.' Nothing more. Nothing less."

"Very well . . . Prince," I answer. "What more can I do to be of service?"

"Your service," he says, emphasizing the word with some bitterness, "will be focused primarily on your duties to Vespre Library. In the effort to make this service as efficient as possible, you will begin training with me every morning at six bells."

I take care not to let any surprise show in my face. Somehow, I'd assumed Nelle or Mixael would handle my training, not the Prince himself.

"You may have natural talent," he continues, "but you're far behind where I need you to be as far as proper understanding of the work to be done here. That work, as I'm sure you've surmised by this time, is simply this: binding the Noswraiths and keeping them bound. Not unlike the little binding you performed the other night."

I hold his gaze for a moment, then lower my gaze to my lap. My smile is still in place, but I know he can see right through it.

"You still don't remember much of the other night's binding, do you," he says.

"Very little," I admit. "Bits and pieces."

He grunts. "Estrilde's restrictions are still in place. I'd hoped they'd fade at once the moment your Obligation was transferred to me, but they're stronger than I thought. They're fading, but they're still present. Which is going to make your training a bit more challenging."

"But can't you simply lift Princess Estrilde's restrictions?"

"Not without causing potentially irreparable damage." He shakes his head slowly, his jaw working with frustration. "No, we'll have to muddle through as best we can until the restrictions fade entirely. There's more than enough for you to learn in the meantime." He sits up a little straighter and quirks an eyebrow my way. "Six bells it is then. You'll have to get used to living your life by the bells here at Vespre, for there is little change in light to help one track the passage of hours. We make do as we can. Lir will help you, make certain you get where you need to go on time. How do you like her, by the way?"

I offer a little shrug. "I don't feel I've had opportunity to form an opinion. She seems . . . efficient."

The Prince considers this. Then, accepting my assessment, continues. "We will begin training at once. Tomorrow morning. You will work under my tutelage from six bells until twelve. From that point on, Clara Darling, I require that you keep out of my way as much as is humanly possible." Since he speaks this last part with the same easy authority he's used for the whole of our conversation, I almost miss the sting in his words. When I do notice, however, it's a sharp, painful sensation that leaves an afterburn.

"As I'll be working in the library," I say, taking care to keep any resentment from tainting my voice, "this may prove difficult."

"Make an effort," he answers curtly.

I nod. "Yes, Prince." Then, though I try to restrain my tongue, I blurt out, "Why?"

"Why what?"

"Why do you hate me? What did I do?"

"Ah!" His expression darkens. Those violet eyes of his become suddenly gray, thunderous, the black pupils dilating. "So you've noticed, have you? I was beginning to wonder; it's difficult to read through that demure façade of yours. But you are insightful, just as I suspected. Dangerously insightful."

He draws a long, slow breath through flaring nostrils, then lets it out just as slowly through full, parted lips. "The memory will return soon enough as Estrilde's restrictions fade. Until then, it's best not to dwell on it. It's all been and done, and there's no fixing it now. All you can do is try to atone for your sin. And what better place to do so than here in Vespre?"

I stare at him, desperately trying to penetrate the many layers of masks he wears as naturally as any fae glamours. But it's no use. My stomach knots, and I suddenly wish I'd not eaten quite so well. But I keep my meaningless smile-mask in place and meet the Prince's gaze, bland and blank as a doll.

"A few other rules," he continues. "You must not leave the palace without an escort. Take Lir with you, at least, but preferably one of Captain Khas's guards. This is for your own safety. For the most part, the folk of Vespre are respectful of librarians, but there are trolls who follow the Old Ways. They think humans make for good eating."

Oh, lovely. Man-eating trolls. So *those* rumors are true after all.

"Yes, Prince," I answer softly. "Anything else?"

"For your own safety," he says, "*never* take any of the books out of the library. Don't even take a volume from the shelf without the express permission of one of the other librarians."

I cast a quick glance around the Prince's disaster of a room. There are more than a few books lying strewn about. I bring my gaze back to the Prince and blink mildly.

His brows draw together in a knot. "Well, of course *I* can take books out if I gods-blighted wish to. I *am* the Prince after all. But you leave them be. Even the simplest of spellbooks, the most innocuous of histories, the driest of genealogies, may prove dangerous here in Vespre. Until you're quite familiar with the library and its nuances, with the workings and wiles of the Noswraith inmates, you must take care not to cause any disturbance. Even the slightest infraction may lead to disaster."

He sits up a little straighter then, and pointedly looks at my plate. I've not touched it for a while now, and my fork and knife lie neatly together to one side. "Are you through with your meal?"

"I am, thank you."

"In that case, you may go."

It's an abrupt dismissal. But it's not as though I particularly want to linger in his company. I rise, bob a curtsy, and, without a word, turn and glide to the door, my dove-gray skirts swishing in my wake. I half hope I'll be able to escape without having to exchange further words with my new master.

Just as my hand touches the door handle, however, he calls out from his bed, "Good night, Clara Darling."

I frown down at my hand, my brow puckering. Then, straightening my shoulders, I turn and face him once more. "It's Darlington, actually."

He's already retrieved his tossed-aside papers and begun leafing through them again, but looks up at me, surprised. "What was that?"

"My name. It's Darlington. Clara Darlington."

He looks puzzled. "No," he says slowly, drawing out the word. "No, I'm sure that's not right."

"Well, it's *my* name, and I should know—"

"I said, *good night*."

I stop, my mouth still open. His eyes hold mine, locked in a sort of challenge. But I have challenges enough ahead of me, don't I? So many challenges, and such limited strength and resources. I must pick my battles with care.

"Good night, Prince," I answer with another little curtsy. Then I turn and leave the room, shutting the door fast behind me.

21

IT'S DARKER OUT IN THE HALL THAN IT WAS WHEN I first arrived. I stand a few moments, letting my eyes adjust, and realize I have absolutely no idea how to get back to my own room. I glance back at the door, uncertain and uneasy. Do I dare knock and ask for help? But no. I have no desire to seem weak in the Prince's eyes. He holds too many advantages over me as it is.

Coming to a decision, I turn abruptly and set off into the dim passage. I vaguely remember turning left at the end of the corridor, so I take a right now. This feels somewhat familiar. But then, all of these carved, stone passages look alike. There's very little decoration to speak of—a few sparce rugs, a ratty old tapestry or two that feel totally out of place. Trolls, apparently, aren't ones for décor.

I wander on, telling myself I'm remembering the way, knowing all along that I'm getting more and more lost. The shadows deepen with every step I take. What's more, I could almost swear there are *things* in those shadows. Things not fully of this world. Things separated from this world by a mere thin veil of reality . . .

Though I try not to, I remember the darkness at the bottom of the library citadel. All those lower levels. Levels even Nelle never ventures into. Are *all* of the Noswraiths safely secured? Are the librarians hard at work even now, making certain of their bindings? Or have they packed away their supplies and gone off for their own meals and beds?

Who watches the Noswraiths at this hour?

"Don't be silly, Clara." Even in a low hiss, my voice sounds strangely loud and hollow in this silent place. I clear my throat and speak again, more firmly than before, letting the sound fill the air around me. "Don't be silly! How can you expect to survive this city if you're going to start jumping at shadows? Cut it out."

I come to a stop and face a particularly dense shadow. My mind is telling me there are figures moving inside it. Several low, squat figures . . . multiple limbs . . . a flash of pale eyes.

"It's just your imagination," I mutter. "It's getting the better of you. So stop it at—"

A rush of movement pours from the shadow.

I scream and turn to flee, but my foot catches in my own long skirts. Falling headlong, my scream cut short, I hit the ground hard. Fear spikes through my jarred senses. I try to scramble upright, but before I can get my limbs under me, weight presses into my back, my shoulders, flattening me back to the floor.

Small voices ring in my ears: "*Mar! Mar! Mar!*"

I turn my head and strain my eyes to stare into the luminous face of Sis, smiling beatifically down at me from her perch on my shoulders. Gasping, gulping, still not quite believing my own eyes, I twist a little further and see the three heavy troll brothers. They grin hugely at me, showing off every one of their gemstone teeth.

Apparently, I'm not about to be devoured by Noswraiths.

With a groan, I drop my forehead to the floor. Much to my relief, one of the troll children slides off my back and scrambles around to sit in front of me. Hard little hands grip my cheeks, and a sweet, rasping voice says, "*Mar?*"

I look up into the ugly, rough-hewn features of the smallest troll boy. He smiles again, even as I shake my head.

"Look here," I say, now that I'm able to catch a breath again, "I can't be your *mar*. I mean it now!"

The other two troll boys clamber off me, and I sit up with Sis still clinging to my shoulders. Before I can rise, however, the three boys jump into the circle of my skirt and sit, pinning me in place as they lean against me. The smallest of them wraps his arms around my middle and presses in close. Sis lets out a jealous shriek and throws her arms around my head, covering my eyes and kicking at her brother with one small foot.

"Here, stop that!" I growl, catching hold of the troll girl. It takes a little effort, for she is much stronger than one would suspect, but I manage to pull her down and plop her in my lap. She glares at her brother and bares her teeth. "Enough!" I snap. My tone is sharp enough to shock her, and she blinks her big eyes and seems to be deciding whether she ought to run. "Your brothers have just as much a right to be here as you. I won't stand for any nastiness; do you hear me?"

She twists her pretty mouth, then leans her whole body into me, tucking her head against my heart. All three of the others press in closer as well, affection rolling out from them like . . . well, if I'm honest, like a spell. A spell strong enough to make me do stupid things. Like climb out on a buttress with a five-story drop on either side. This is dangerous. Truly dangerous.

But when I look down into those four pairs of solemn eyes set in those four faces—three hideous, one too beautiful for words—I find all resolve melting away.

"Gods help me!" I whisper. But what am I supposed to do?

"*Mar?*" says the smallest troll boy.

I sigh. Then, rather than pushing them away and making a hasty exit, I say, "Do you understand me? Do you know my language?"

The three boys nod vigorously. Pretty Sis merely snuggles in closer.

"Well, then, I suppose you might as well tell me your names." I jut my chin at the largest of the boys, who leans against my left arm. "You first. What's your name?"

"*Dig*," he answers in a voice that sounds very much like he's trying to clear his throat.

"Dig," I repeat, and can tell by the way he grins that I got the accent all wrong. Oh, well. No one can expect me to learn trollish in one night. "How about you?" I say, turning to the child on my right.

"*Har*," he answers.

I give it a try. Sis giggles, but the others shush her.

"And you?" I ask the smallest boy, wrapped around my waist.

He smiles sweetly up at me—if a face of broken stone and sharp gem teeth can be considered *sweet*, that is. "*Calx*," he says.

"Calx," I repeat. "Dig, Har, and Calx." I try to growl and rasp appropriately, which only makes Sis giggle again. This time the youngest boy, Calx, giggles as well, and the two older boys cannot hush them. I shrug and look down at the girl. "And you're *Sis*, right?"

She beams at me, her whole face lighting up the darkness like a small moon. My breath catches. She really is the most extraordinarily beautiful creature imaginable.

"Well, Dig, Har, Calx, and Sis," I say, my brow puckering slightly, "I can't be your mother, you know. I'm not a troll; I don't know anything about trolls. Besides, the Prince has forbidden it. So, you see, you're better off returning to the city and your own kind."

By the time I reach the end of this short speech, my voice is almost drowned out by their forlorn cries of, "*Mar! Mar! Maaaaaaar!*" all growled and grated from their rough little throats. Even Sis barks along with her brothers, sounding equally ferocious. I'd be frightened save that the smallest boy, Calx, blinks up at me with such beseeching eyes, it breaks my heart in two.

"I'm very sorry." I try to gently push the two smaller children off my lap but find them stuck to me like glue. "I'm really not prepared to watch over you. I've only just arrived here myself, and I—"

"*Hartorka shar! Kor kor kor!*"

The harsh words ring out against stone walls, startling the four children. They spring from my lap, nearly knocking me over again in their haste. The oldest brother scoops up Sis, and they all scamper fast. I twist my torso to see Lir descending upon them, her hand upraised. She gives chase, swatting and kicking and continuing to spew a stream of angry trollish as they flee around a bend. Her shouts and their giggles and squeals echo against the stone for some while before finally fading away.

A little sore and unsteady, I pick myself up. Odd, but I feel strangely bereft now the children are gone. Perhaps the residual spell they put on me is still wearing off. I straighten my skirts and tuck my hair behind my ears just as Lir returns, her face shining with indignation.

"Oh, mistress, I am *so* sorry!" she trills in that ladylike voice of hers that contrasts so starkly with the troll dialect she just used. "I've been looking absolutely *everywhere* for you. Such an oversight on that awful human Lawrence's part. He must have thought you'd remember the way, but he doesn't always account for the softness of your human minds, unused to troll halls as you are. He's been here so long, he's practically a troll himself, but really, he ought to know better. Are you hurt?"

"Hurt?" I test one shoulder, which had been wrenched in the troll children's scramble to escape. It aches, but nothing bad. "No, no. I'm fine. They're just children."

"Just *troll* children," Lir responds with a sniff. As though she herself wasn't one of their kind. "Wild little waiflings, wholly without respect or decorum. Monsters!"

It's disturbing to hear this troll woman talking so harshly about her own kind. I wonder if it has something to do with Lir being a *throwback*, or if this is truly the way all trolls feel about troll orphans? Either way, it strikes me as singularly cruel.

Oblivious to my discomfort, Lir ushers me into motion, steering me through the gloomy passages and fussing every step of the way. I pay little attention, but when she finally opens the door to my new room, I am relieved. It's still an unfamiliar space, but at least it's mine.

Lir sets to work at once helping me make ready for bed, ignoring all protests on my part. "And how was your dinner with the Prince?" she asks, sitting me in front of a mirror and pulling pins from my hair.

I'm not entirely certain how to answer this. "Um. Fine, I guess."

Lir gives me a look in the mirror glass. "You know, the Prince *never* dines with the other librarians."

I blink back at her. Is she implying that the Prince is showing me some sort of special favor? A laughable thought! The Prince has been very clear about his utter distaste for me and my presence in his life. "He merely wanted to go over some specific rules and regulations," I say. "That's all."

Lir looks unconvinced. Without a word, she finishes brushing my hair and securing it in a braid, then bustles to the bed, pulls back the coverlet, and arranges a hot-water bottle. If I'm honest, all this care and concern is a bit unnerving. But I can probably get used to it.

Feeling a bit foolish, I climb into bed and let Lir tuck me in like a child. My very bones seem to melt into the mattress as exhaustion overwhelms me. This was probably the longest day of my entire life.

"Good night, mistress," Lir says softly and snaps her fingers. Immediately, the pale lamps hanging from stalactites above dim, leaving the chamber suffused in a pale glow like moonlight, dreamy and soothing. "I'll return at five bells and see to it you're ready for the day."

I don't respond. I'm already mostly asleep.

I open my eyes in semi-darkness full of strange shadows and even stranger highlights. It's all so extreme, as though my senses have been heightened far beyond the norm.

My body feels weighed down by inexpressible horror.

Hands are touching me, smoothing through my hair. Gentle, delicate fingers, shivering slightly as they pass over my brow. And a voice—cold, distant, drifting through the shadows—reaches my ear, a bare breath of sound.

He doesn't mean to, you know.

It's not his fault.

He's always suffered so.

No one understands him.

I shudder. Something about that voice is wrong. Something about that soothing touch, which feels almost like subtle razor blades cutting across my skin.

He loves you.

He really loves you.

He loves all of us.

I try to speak. To move my mouth, to shape a single, forceful, *No!* With a wrench, I pull back, and for half a moment, catch a glimpse of something . . . something in the dark . . . something . . . horrible . . .

"Miss Darlington? Miss Darlington, that's five bells now. Time to wake up!"

I crack open my heavy eyelids to see the outline of a voluptuous and beautiful troll woman pulling open the curtains of my one big window. Purple twilight, a far cry from dawn glow, fills the room.

With a groan, I rub the heel of my hand into my tired eyes, one after the other. Gods on high, I am not ready to be awake yet! How many hours of sleep was that? It feels as though I scarcely closed my eyes before—

An image of darkness . . .

A sensation of cool fingers . . . cutting . . .

My eyelashes flutter open, and the images flee my head, fading like fog. I sit up, shake out my hair, try to remember what it was that had filled me with such dread only moments ago. But I can't. Which is just as well, I suppose. After all, I have enough worries to fill my day without holding onto a lingering nightmare.

Lir sets to work getting me ready and makes certain I eat my fill from the breakfast tray she placed on my side table. I don't need much urging. There's more of the same crusty bread I enjoyed at dinner last night, plenty of butter, honey, and wedges of a strange purple fruit I've never seen before. While I eat, Lir pulls a handsome but practical work gown from the enormous wardrobe and runs a bath for me in the washroom.

Before I know it, I'm standing before the full-length mirror, ready for the day. My first day as a librarian of Doomed City.

I meet my own eyes, ringed by dark hollows that good food and rest couldn't quite drive away. "Are you ready for this?" I whisper.

My reflection offers no answer.

A knock sounds at the door. "Ah!" Lir trills from across the room. "Your escort is here, mistress." I nod and turn just as Lir opens the door. "Good morning, Librarian Vervain," she says brightly.

The silent woman I'd met yesterday stands in the doorway, looking at me with her strange, empty eyes.

22

I CAN'T HELP WISHING IT WAS MIXAEL WHO'D COME TO take me to the library. Or his mother. Even the dreamy Andreas would have been welcome. Basically anyone other than this odd, taciturn woman.

Vervain drifts along the passages like one caught halfway in a trance, not fully present, but not fully absent either. I walk beside her, casting her the occasional sideways glance. She's very pale and pinched. Her face is heavily underscored with shadows and dark circles, giving her an almost corpse-like quality; but beneath it all, her features are pretty, delicate. Though she can't be more than thirty or thirty-five at the most, something about her feels aged. Is this what life in the Doomed City does to its librarians?

"How long have you worked in Vespre?" I ask, breaking the silence between us. Vervain starts and shoots me a hasty sideward glance, so I quickly add, "If you don't mind my asking."

She faces forward again. Her lips move several times before any words emerge. I tip my ear toward her. "I'm sorry, did you say *seven* years?"

Vervain speaks a little louder this time: "Seven years. Seventy years. Seventy times seven. What does it matter?"

I drop back into silence and let my pace slow until I'm several steps behind her. If she doesn't want to talk, that's fine. I won't insist. We reach a stairway, and Vervain climbs several steps. I'm just starting to think I recognize this part of the palace when the other librarian spins suddenly and looks down at me, her eyes brighter and more alert than I have yet seen them.

"Are you a mother?" she asks.

I frown, startled. For some reason the faces of the four troll children flash across my mind, but I quickly shake them away. "No. No, I'm not."

"Ah." Vervain turns as though to start up the stair again but pauses after only a single step. Her hand gripping the banister is white knuckled.

"I am a mother," she says. "Always. Forever."

Then she continues, one heavy footstep after the other. As she goes, she gains a little speed. I remain at the base of the stairway, gazing after her. Something about that woman is not quite right. If I didn't know any better, I would almost believe a shadow massed over her like a great, hunched creature clinging to her back.

Hastily I shake my head and rub my eyes. Gods on high, I'm still so sleep-deprived! I must not let myself imagine such things.

Taking hold of the banister, I climb after Vervain. She reaches the top ahead of me, and I recognize the two enormous doors Mixael led me through the day before. Vervain opens one, grunting a little with the effort, and slips inside without a word or look my way. I'm only just quick enough to spring forward and catch the door before it slams shut behind her. The weight is tremendous, but I brace my feet and manage to pull it open wide enough for me to slip through.

Emerging onto the first floor, I look right and left, searching for some sign of the other librarians at their desks. There's no one visible; even Vervain has already disappeared. A frown puckers my brow. What am I supposed to do? The Prince said he would meet me at six bells for morning lessons. How long do I have until six bells?

Uncertain what else to do, I walk along the line of desks, heading away from where I'd seen Vervain sitting yesterday. I really don't want to have to interact with her any more than necessary. I come to one particular desk set a little apart from the others. Something about it makes me pause and look again. At first I'm not sure what it is that compels me. Then I notice the name plaque set front and center: *Soran Silveri*.

Silveri. Like Mixael Silveri? This then must be the desk that belonged to Mixael's father, who died in the last Noswraith outbreak. It's perfectly tidy; I can't see even the faintest ink stain in the wood. Mister Silveri must have been particularly neat and meticulous in his day.

A chill whispers through my bones. It's unsettling to stand before the desk of someone who, until recently, was a living, breathing person. Until the darkness of Doomed City brought about his end. Does the same ultimate end await me?

"Clara Darling."

I make a quick turnabout. The Prince approaches along the line of empty desks, carrying a stack of books under one arm. He's looking much healthier than when I last saw him, the dark circles under his eyes faded almost entirely. I'm pretty sure I sense a subtle fae glamour surrounding him as well, filling out his shoulders, lending him extra height, making his skin luminous and golden even in the pale glow of the library lanterns. He wears elaborate robes of blue and silver, unfastened at the throat, and his hair hangs in luxurious waves across his shoulders. In that moment, I could easily mistake him for one of the lords of Lodírhal's court. There's very little human about him.

He stops before Soran Silveri's desk and gives it a once over. I can't read his expression. Does he feel anything for the loss of one of his librarians, one he'd known for such a long time? It's impossible to tell.

After a moment, he turns to me and smiles. But I know *that* kind of smile: a perfect disguise for all the feelings one does not wish to show. "Are you ready to begin your first day of training, Clara Darling?"

Is there any point in trying to correct his use of my name again?

No, probably not. "I'm ready to oblige, Prince."

A muscle in his jaw ticks. For some reason, my answer bothers him. "This way," he says and, with an abrupt about-face, leads me back along the desks until we reach one with no name plaque. I'm disturbed to see just how far it is from the other librarians' workstations. Am I going to be isolated from the rest?

"We can't risk having an uninitiated librarian working so near the others."

I look up and catch the Prince's eye. He must have noticed the distress in my face, for he goes on, "Until you learn the ways of Vespre Library, you will be a danger to yourself and others. Once you've earned your place—if you survive long enough to do so—you'll be relocated closer to the others."

I nod. His explanation isn't exactly comforting, but it makes sense.

The Prince sets down his stack of books and arranges them on the desk. They are shockingly bedraggled. One of them looks truly on the verge of falling apart, the spine disintegrating, the pages ready to crumble into dust. "Your first lesson and your first task begins, Miss Darling," the Prince says, turning that too-sharp gaze of his back to me. "Have a look at these books and tell me which one is the greatest threat."

I blink. A threat? I look down at the books, and they . . . they're just books. Old books, yes, but books, nonetheless. How can a book be threatening?

The Prince's rasping chuckle grates in my ear. "Don't look so baffled, Miss Darling! You know the books themselves may be just objects; it's what they *contain* that may threaten lives and worlds. The keeping and exchanging of ideas across cultures, across generations, across continents and worlds, is one of the most dangerous acts of humanity. In that respect, each one of the books before you is threatening. But I ask you again, which is the *most* threatening in this moment?"

"I'm... not sure." I bite my lip, then venture, "May I open them?"

"Yes." His grin widens. "If you don't mind having your face bitten off or your mind warped into madness."

My hands, already reaching for the first volume, freeze. I snatch them back, pressing them against my heart. The Prince chuckles again, heedless of my scowl.

"Always remember," he says, "that even to open the cover of a Noswraith volume can be enough to let the Noswraith itself loose if the bindings are worn down enough. You must learn to sense the threat level contained within any given volume *without* opening the volume itself."

I press my dry lips together hard and stare down at the books. There are six total. The covers are all different colors and styles—some cloth, some hardboard, some leather. One of them has lovely gold filigree, much faded with time but still visible, depicting a spreading tree that seems to grow up the spine and spread its branches to both the front and back boards. None of them look particularly threatening, and yet...

My fingers hover over the covers, trailing lightly along leather and cloth. I go back and forth across all six. Am I wrong, or is there the faintest, the absolute *faintest* hint of a vibration in the air coming from the middle volume? A buzzing that doesn't quite touch my fingertips but seems to touch some other, unconscious awareness.

I pick up the book. It's a little smaller than the rest but surprisingly heavy. Too heavy, in fact. Heavy as though it contains something more than mere paper and ink. I glance again at the Prince. He's watching me closely. I can almost feel him silently urging me to *get on with it*. But he doesn't speak.

I study the book in my hand. Why do I feel a sudden *slimy* sensation? As though a large slug is crawling over my fingers while another creeps down the back of my neck. I shudder. "This one," I say. "This one is the greatest threat."

"Well done," says the Prince. I turn just in time to catch a flash of approval in his eye. "And what led you to this conclusion?"

I shrug. I can still feel that slimy coldness crawling over my fingers, but it's not something I can describe. "I . . . I would guess that the physical book is part of the binding spell," I say instead. "That as the spell inside wears, the book containing the spell likewise breaks down. This is the most broken of the selection here, so I suspect the spell inside is also the closest to breaking."

The Prince lifts an eyebrow. "A well-reasoned guess. And, in this instance, correct." He abruptly steps to a nearby desk, grabs the chair and brings it back to where I stand. He plunks it down, takes a seat, and indicates for me to sit in the chair slid neatly into place under the desk. As I obey, he launches into a lecture.

"Noswraiths," he says, "are brought into existence via written magic. In the olden days they were crafted by great magicians known as Miphates, who wrought meticulous spells in the ancient Araneli language. What you *must* understand is that the creation and binding of a Noswraith is one and the same. One must write the binding *into* the actual spell in order to keep the Noswraith contained. Those few mad souls who wrote Noswraiths with no bindings were hard pressed to go back and rewrite the spells, adding bindings into place. But the rewrite is never quite as strong as the original, unbound spell. Which means the original spell tends to *eat* the new one."

I blink at him. Did he just say one spell would *eat* the other? I open my mouth to question this idea, but the Prince is already plunging on, heedless of my confusion. "Volumes in which bindings were added after the fact tend to break down faster than the others. This volume"—he indicates the decrepit thing I'm holding—"was rewritten by Nelle Silveri only a few weeks ago."

I look at the book, frowning. It looks a good century old if it's a day. The spell inside must be strong indeed to have worn it down so completely.

"These fragile spells," the Prince continues, "must be rewritten and rewritten again in fresh volumes before the volumes in which they are contained break entirely. And that, Miss Darling, is the primary employment of the librarians in Vespre—the reestablishing of binding spells, copying out volume after volume. The book you now hold, though only a few weeks old, will soon break apart, unleashing the Noswraith within."

My throat tightens. I think again of the hideous face of the Melted Man. "What happens if a Noswraith is unleashed?"

"In that case, Miss Darling, the brave librarians of Vespre sally forth to create a new binding. But an unleashed Noswraith enjoys the full extent of its power, without even the remnants of its binding spell to restrain it. Creating a new binding is . . . a challenge."

A challenge that cost Soran Silveri his life.

I shiver and turn away from the Prince, staring at the book in front of me. What kind of a monster does it contain? And how soon before it will be turned loose upon this world?

"The other night," I say, choosing my words with care, "when I dealt with the . . . the Melted Man . . . I wasn't copying another spell then, was I?" I don't remember that night clearly, but I seem to recall writing freehand in the book Thaddeus Creakle had pressed upon me.

The Prince shakes his head. "In the case of the *Melted Man*, his binding had entirely broken to pieces, setting him free. Thus an entirely new binding was necessary to contain him. A binding sealed with his name. His *real* name, of course, not the title you ascribed to him."

I seem to remember that too, vaguely: the moment when the Prince snatched the book from my hands and scrawled something on the final page. He'd finished the binding for me. And suffered a physical breakdown as a result.

"The names of the Noswraiths are vital to their containment," the Prince continues. "A librarian must know a Noswraith's *true* name in order to hold it, but unless a librarian is able to find the original records of each Noswraith's personal creator, this can be difficult to accomplish. In the case of the Melted Man, this wasn't so difficult, for he was created by one of our own former librarians."

"What?" My head shoots up and I gape at the Prince, aghast. "One of your own librarians created a Noswraith?"

His lip curls. It's a smile, but also . . . not quite. A cold, almost sinister expression, and the light in his eye is hard. "Of course, Miss Darling. Why else would I bring these people here? It takes a powerful individual to survive the perils of Vespre Library."

I turn from him, unable to bear that gaze. My mind spins, thinking of the librarians I've met—aged Nelle with her bright eyes and sharp tongue—Mixael with his ready smile and easy-going demeanor—dreamy-eyed Andreas and hollow-cheeked Vervain. None of them struck me as *powerful* individuals. None of them seem like the type to go around creating monsters.

And what about *me?* The Prince said I belonged in Doomed City, belonged to the library. Surely he couldn't think me capable of creating a monstrosity like the Melted Man! Could he?

A dark chuckle draws my unwilling gaze back to the Prince. "Don't look so distressed," he says, his tone mocking. "The Melted Man is hardly the worst of the monsters to be found in this library. The one currently resting under your hand is more dangerous by far." He sits a little straighter then and snaps his fingers.

"Now concentrate, Darling! We have work to do. To rebind this particular Noswraith, you will need to copy the spell into a fresh volume. Here." He draws a small book with crisp new pages from some pouch or pocket in his robes and sets it on the desk before me, pushing the other volumes out of the way. He then takes an inkwell from one of the desk drawers, opens it, and arranges it within easy access of my writing hand.

My heartrate quickens. "You want me to try this? Right now?"

"Naturally." He resumes his seat close by. "Best to begin as you mean to continue. You've already proven your knack back at Aurelis. This will be more challenging, but I'm curious to see how you get on." He reaches into the front of his robes and withdraws a simple white quill pen, neatly trimmed. "Here you are. Have at it."

I accept the quill—and briefly think of the lovely, plumy red quill Thaddeus gave me. Was it only just yesterday? Days, hours, even time itself feels like a blur here in this twilit realm, despite the bells' distant tolling.

"When you're quite ready," says the Prince.

I glance his way, pinching my dry lips to moisten them. Then I lick the end of my pen and dip it in the inkwell before carefully opening the blank book. When I reach for the broken-down Noswraith spell, however, my fingers seem to freeze in the air, unwilling to touch that disintegrating cover.

"The first few pages won't be difficult," the Prince says. "As the spell progresses, the Noswraith will sense what you're doing. It will not want you to reassert the binding it's been working so hard to wear down over the last few weeks. You need to be prepared."

"Prepared for what?" I ask in a voice scarcely above a whisper.

I feel rather than see the smile he aims at me. *"Anything."*

I draw a shuddering breath. Then, squaring my shoulders and lifting my chin determinedly, I open the brittle cover.

An overwhelming stench of rot fills my nostrils and clouds my head, strong enough to send me reeling. It's all I can do to grip the edge of the desk and hold myself fast in my chair. My mind whirls and suddenly . . . suddenly . . .

I see a swamp. Grim, desolate. Beneath a heavy, gray sky. Old, decaying trees rise from stagnant pools, desiccated branches clawing for freedom like frozen corpse fingers. And beneath the water . . . down at my feet . . . faces . . . men . . . women . . . children . . .

"Careful, Darling."

The Prince's voice jars through my head, temporarily driving the image out. I'm back in the library, seated at the desk, staring at two open books, and holding a quill pen. I inhale sharply and smell only musty old paper and ink. The Prince stands beside me, having risen from his chair and come to rest a hand on my shoulder.

"You mustn't be drawn into the Nightmare," he says. "Not yet, at least."

Is that what was happening? Gods above, it was so easy! I merely glanced at the first page, and it was like I was *there*. But now, when I look at the same page, I see that it's merely a page of written words strung together to form a narrative. The handwriting is a bit crabby and awkward, but the language is my own, and I can read it with ease. Read it and copy it too.

I can do this. I *will* do this.

Setting my shoulders and brandishing my quill like a weapon, I lean over the desk and begin to copy out the first words into the fresh book. Just one word at a time, that's all. Nothing more, nothing less.

And yet, slowly but surely, my unguarded brain begins to slip . . .

We must cross before nightfall. If not, I cannot guarantee our survival.

I turn in my saddle and gaze back across the company. My men are tired. Haggard. Their eyes are dull with creeping death. Already they have lost hope. Our enemy harries us hard and has at last driven us to this desperate place.

But I am not ready to give up. Reinforcements wait on the other side of this swamp. There will be food, medical supplies, succor for our need. We have only to cross by nightfall . . . by nightfall . . .

"Show them a brave face, Captain," Old Guntor says, standing at my stirrup. His wizened face gazes up into mine, full of the sage wisdom upon which I've come to depend. "Show them what a leader is."

I try. I steel my face into hard lines, assuming the aspect of a warrior. But the men are not fooled. They know I am too young for this position. They know what favors my uncle curried to find me a post with pay appropriate to my birth and station. They know I am a fraud.

But I am their captain. And this is our last hope.

"Forward, men!" I cry, my voice echoing among those dead and dying trees.

The ranks surge into motion. Thirty men, heavy packs on their backs, weapons on their shoulders. Thirty men, the last of my company...

"Mind to the task, Darling."

I draw breath and sit back in the chair, my quill poised over the page. It's a story. It's an actual *story*. Not a spell. Not magic sigils and signs. A narrative, with characters and setting and motivations and... and...

I shift my gaze back and forth between the page of copied words and the original. Or not the original. This is simply a copy done by Nelle a few weeks ago. I have no idea who the original writer was. I know only that, within a few lines, I'm caught. Intrigued. Eager to discover what will happen to this nameless young captain and his command.

The Prince's hand is heavy on my shoulder. He squeezes suddenly, and I turn my wide-eyed gaze up to him. "See the words," he says. "Only the words. Try not to see what they say."

"Oh," I whisper. Of course. Of course, it makes sense that the more I let myself engage with the story, the deeper drawn I will be. This must be part of the magic.

I let a slow breath out through my lips and face the page once more. "See the words," I whisper. "Only the words."

I begin again, writing slowly, precisely. Copying what I see, concentrating on the shape and sound of each word, not on the pictures they create in my head. Generally speaking, my penmanship is not a source of pride. My mother used to despair of my sloppy, hasty hand. She would be pleased to see me so focused in this moment, to see the elegance of the slowly shaped letters taking form beneath my pen.

How

long

have

we

marched

through

this

thick,

and

sucking

mud?

It's slow. It's painstaking. But I won't be drawn in. Not again.

I

turn

once more

in my saddle,

surveying the troops as they

trail behind me in the gloom. One by one I count them. Twenty-nine.

"Sergeant!" *I cry. Old Guntor struggles through the muck to my side, grabs my stirrup for support.* "Sergeant, we've lost a man! Where is little Tomlin?"

"Who?" *Guntor peers up at me, his brow puckered with confusion.*

"Tomlin," *I repeat.* "The drummer boy. He's missing."

But Guntor shakes his heavy head. "Captain," *he says,* "Tomlin died in battle three weeks ago. We buried him with honors. Do you not remember?"

No. This cannot be. I distinctly recall seeing the boy's face there at the back of the line as we marched into the swamp. So small and frail, but brave to a fault.

"He must have dropped behind," *I say—*

"Look sharp, Darling!"

A drop of sweat rolls down my face and blurs the last word I've written. I start and flop back in the chair, breathing hard. "Oh gods," I whisper.

The Prince has drawn his chair up beside me. He sits close, his arms crossed, his eyes narrow. "You were drawn in again," he says.

It was like I was *there*. I wasn't simply *reading* about the young captain—I had *become* him. I felt his tension, his desperation. His horror at the loss of the little drummer. I felt the sweat building up under his uniform, the saddle sores through his trousers. The movement of his horse as it struggled one terrible step after another through the sucking mud. The buzz of flies, the stink of rot, the pressure of that low-hanging sky.

I was there. It was me.

My hand holding the feather quill shakes.

"Last chance," the Prince says, his voice hard-edged. "Continue with the spell. But you must take better care. Even a lesser Noswraith like this will seek to drag you into its world. You cannot let your guard down. You cannot be deceived." He leans in his seat, looking over the words I've already written in the fresh book. "You're doing well," he admits, almost begrudgingly. "You still have time to complete the new spell before the old one breaks. No need to rush. Take it slow."

"Yes," I whisper. "Yes, of course."

I can do this. One word— No! One letter at a time.

I write. I dip my pen and write some more. I write to the end of the page, turn it, and continue writing. One letter, perfectly shaped. Then the next. Then the next.

"

G

u

n

t

o

r

?

"

I

t

w

i

s

t

in

place,

my boots

sunk so

deep, mud pours

over the tops, weighing

me down still more. "Guntor!" I call, casting

my gaze about me. "Where is he? Where is Sergeant Guntor?"

Pikeman Harl takes hold of my arm, his strong grip fighting against the sucking mud. "Captain," he says, his pale, haunted face shrouded in shadows. "Don't you remember? Sergeant Guntor died but yesterday of the red fever. We buried him—

No!

No, I'm not going to be caught up again! I stop myself this time, my quill poised and trembling above the page. Aware of the Prince's gaze on me, I roll my neck and shoulders before dipping the nib again.

Then I'm back at it, shaping the letters. One at a time. Concentrating everything I have on that simple task. My pen scratches across the page, my eyes flick between the old book and the new. I can do this. I can do this. I can—

Something wraps around my ankle.

I look down.

I'm standing in black, brackish water.

I hear the buzz of flies.

I feel the thud of my heart against my breastbone.

"No!" I cry.

The next moment I'm pulled under. Dark water closes over my head.

23

DARKNESS SURROUNDS ME. DARKNESS AND COLD so overwhelming, it seeps into my very soul. I try to open my mouth, to scream, but when I do, more of that darkness, more of that cold, pours down my throat, fills my lungs. I'm going to drown in darkness—

Something grips the hair atop my head.

The next moment, I'm sprawled on the floor beside the stone-carved desk, my quill still gripped in one hand. Black ink flows in rivulets around me, and my stunned gaze slowly comes into focus on an overturned and spinning inkwell.

Heart pounding in my throat, I lift my gaze, turn my head, and peer up at the tall figure looming over me. Strange violet eyes gaze intently into my own. I blink once—and for an instant, in that world inside my head, behind my eyelids, I see it all again. The heavy gray sky. The tortured trees. My horse, wallowing in black mud up to its chest, its eyes rolling. I try to turn, to call out for Sergeant Guntor, for my other men, all of them lost, all of them gone. I'm weeping, sobbing . . .

Then my eyelids rise, and I'm back on the floor again, ink in my hair, staining my hands, my sleeves. Staring up into the face of the Prince.

He crouches and pries the quill from my hand. Then, without a word, he stands and half turns away from me. An open book rests across his left arm, and he begins writing in it furiously. As he writes, the glamour around him melts away. His features, so perfect in their beauty, diminish into a merely human form of beauty without magical augmentation. Then they diminish still more, his golden complexion turning sallow, gray. He sags where he stands but catches himself on the edge of the desk.

At last, he snaps the book shut and looks down at me. "That was close."

I swallow painfully. Part of me still wants to believe my lungs are full of mud. But it's all in my head. I draw a long breath of clear air and then, shivering hard, push myself into an upright position, curling my legs beneath me. "What happened?" I ask tremulously.

The Prince raises one eyebrow. "You were very nearly drawn into the Nightmare."

I shudder, blinking fast . . . and with each rise and fall of my lashes, I see again, in flashing glimpses, that horror of swamp. I close my eyes hard, force the image out of my head, force myself to see only the usual darkness that's supposed to be behind my eyelids. Then, breathing out slowly, I look up at the Prince again. "I didn't see a Noswraith," I say, my voice almost a question. "There was a . . . a man. A boy, really. On horseback. And soldiers under his command. They were trying to cross a swamp. There was no monster. None that I saw."

The Prince's lips—thinner than before and bloodless—curl in an unpleasant smile. "Come now, Darling! You are not such a simpleton as all that. You know as well as I that the worst horrors are not always visible."

I stare back at him. Then I groan and tuck my legs up against my chest and press my forehead into my knees. I can't think coherently, can't do anything but let the waves of shock wash over me.

When I return to myself, the Prince has righted my overturned chair and sunk into it. He's watching me, his gaze deceptively idle. He's got one hand planted on the cover of the new volume, the one in which I'd been attempting to write my binding. He looks almost as though he's holding it shut.

"The Noswraith!" I gasp, fear driving me to sudden alertness. "I didn't finish the binding! Is it . . . will it . . . ?"

"Have no fear." The Prince taps the cover of the book with one finger. "In a pinch, one can always interrupt a struggling spell and use the Noswraith's name to generate a temporary binding. It's not enough to last for more than an hour or so. But sometimes that hour can mean the difference between life and disaster."

So saying, he flips the cover open and shows me a page full of my own painstaking handwriting. The last line ends in an ugly smear of ink that looks unsettlingly like a blood spatter. Following the splatter, a different hand has written in bold, clear letters: *Dulmier Fen.*

I nod slowly, trying to understand what I'm seeing. Then I shake my head and bite my lip before blurting out, "But how? How is any of that a *spell?* It read like a story! A story with characters and plot and . . . and *suspense.*"

The Prince smiles again, that same cold, mirthless smile. "And it drew you right in, didn't it?"

He's right. Despite my best efforts, the words I copied had pulled me in, catching hold of my imagination, catching hold of my heart, making me feel something for that poor young captain and his hopeless mission. The words had crawled into my head and stuck there, images and sensations that became all too real.

"That," the Prince says, shutting the book again and once more planting his open palm firmly atop the cover, "is the way of it with newer Noswraiths. The spell-casting knowledge of the Miphates has been lost in the human world, but the potential for magic lingers on in every human soul. That magic must and will find new ways to manifest. Ways like this. So no, Darling. What you read is not a traditional *spell* the way you've been brought up to think of spells. The magic lies in the writer's ability to make his prose implant in his reader's brain. There it becomes something *real.* It's that interaction of the two—writer and reader—that gives the magic its opportunity to rise. Do you follow me?"

I'm not sure that I do. But I nod anyway.

"Now, this wouldn't be a problem if the story only ever found root in one brain." The Prince continues, reaching out and tapping my forehead with the tip of one long finger. "Even five, ten, fifteen, a few hundred readers interacting with the writer's words wouldn't generate enough magic to spawn a Noswraith. The problem is . . ." He pauses, his lip curling. "The problem is human ingenuity. The problem is the invention of the *printing press*."

He says the words with such venom, it's like hearing him spit out an expletive. I stare at him, uncomprehending at first. Slowly, however, understanding dawns. The printing press—the mass production of literature. The ability to create and distribute stories such as this one to hundreds of thousands of readers all in a very short period. Which in turn means that hundreds of thousands of readers might potentially read the same story on the same day.

And what would happen if they all responded to the story the way I just did? What would happen if they were all sucked into that world, into that fear, into that heavy, gray, slowly mounting terror? All those human minds interacting with words on a page, transforming words into a new reality. A reality that must manifest somewhere . . .

"You see?" The Prince's cold voice draws my attention back to him. I meet his gaze and nod slowly. "This is true magic," he says. "Magic like nothing ever before seen in Eledria, not even in the age of the Miphates. And this one? This small terror you glimpsed today? It is nothing. Nothing compared to the greater horrors my library holds.

"This is why you must learn and learn quickly. Your ability to rebind and contain Noswraiths makes you that much more susceptible to their power. It's a dangerous balance which all the Vespre Librarians must learn over the course of their training. If they can learn that balance quickly, they will survive. Some even thrive. But as their powers develop, so the danger to them grows."

I glance around at all the empty desks ringing this floor. My gaze finds and lingers on the desk belonging to Soran Silveri. He'd lasted several hundred years fighting battles like this, as had his wife, old Nelle. I need only survive ten before my Obligation will end. Then I'll be free to go home.

Surely I can manage ten years!

I pick myself up off the floor. My limbs tremble violently, but I fold my hands tight and force my habitual smile into place. "The Noswraith," I say, hoping my voice sounds measured and calm. "The binding still needs to be completed, correct?"

The Prince nods.

"Then let me try again."

"Try again?" He tosses back his head and utters a single derogatory bark of laughter. My face heats. I open my mouth, determined to press my case, but he stands, picks up the fresh book and the old disintegrating volume, and tucks them both under his arm. He still looks grey and worn out, but not as bad as he was after saving me from the frights.

"There is no *trying again* when it comes to Noswraiths," he says. "One either succeeds or one fails. And if you should survive a failure, you certainly should not attempt the same binding again. The Noswraith will recognize you at once and, like a shark following blood in the water, will hunt you down and end you once and for all. No, no! We will let Vervain finish this particular task."

He turns from the desk and sets off with long strides to the other side of this circular floor where the other librarians' desks stand. He walks close to the railing without a care for that petrifying drop down the center of the citadel. I trail after him, lifting my skirts so they don't impede my progress. "While your powers recover," he says, tossing the words over his shoulder, "we shall make you better acquainted with the rest of the library. Vervain!"

The hollow-eyed librarian is crouched over her work when we arrive at her desk. At the sound of her name so abruptly spoken, she starts visibly and whirls in her chair. Her eyes widen at the sight of the Prince bearing down on her.

"Vervain," he says again, shoving the two books he carries into her unresisting hands. "Be a dear and finish this binding for Clara Darling, won't you? She made an effort, but it proved too much for her in the end."

I want to defend myself, to protest that I'd not done too badly considering how little preparation I'd been given. But all protests sound too much like excuses in my head, so I swallow them back. Instead I study my fellow librarian's face from behind the Prince.

Her expression is very strange and surprisingly open for such a closed personality. In a fleeting instant, I see two extremes of emotion playing in the depths of her eyes—adoration and hatred in equal measure, one unable to dominate the other. "Yes, Prince," she says in her low, tremulous voice, taking the books and adding them to the stack already piled high on her desk.

"Be sure it's completed before fourteen bells," the Prince adds, "or we'll have a real problem on our hands." With that, he turns on his heel and strides back the way he's just come, brushing past me so swiftly, I'm obliged to stagger back several paces or risk being run over.

I cast a last glance back at Vervain. She's staring at the books the Prince has given her, her face fighting that strange convergence of emotions.

She casts an oblique glance at me.

I gasp and pull away to hasten after the Prince. I feel almost as though I've been stung, though I can't quite explain why. Gods help me, I don't think I'll ever get used to Vervain! She's almost as unsettling as the Noswraiths.

The Prince waits for me at the top of the spiral stair. His gaze is both a little too searching and a little too knowing for comfort. I force myself to meet it and to offer nothing but my blandest smile in return.

He narrows his eyes. "Tell me, Darling, how many floors down did Mistress Silveri take you yesterday?"

My heart begins to beat a little faster. "About five, I think."

He grunts. Then he turns and begins to descend, one hand

lightly gripping the rail as he goes. I have no choice but to follow him. Down and down and down some more, in that tight spiral that soon makes me dizzy and disoriented. We pass the various floors without pause. On one level, I glimpse Andreas sitting cross-legged on the floor, poring over multiple stacks of books he's pulled from the shelves and spread around him.

"What-ho, Andreas!" the Prince calls out in an incongruously cheery voice as we circle past that floor. "How goes the search for Archithisulu?"

Andreas raises his head, his expression vague, his forehead lightly puckered. He waves a hand in response, his eyes gliding from the Prince to me before dropping to the open book in his lap.

The Prince glances back at me. "Andreas is trying to find a link between the Noswraith Wumanok and the demon Archithisulu of ancient Serythian lore. He believes the key is in the old poem, the *Epic of Archithus*, of which there are two hundred and five known variations. Should he find the link, the binding of Wumanok will be vastly simplified, making all our lives easier."

I'm not sure if I'm expected to respond to this baffling barrage of information. "Huh," I say, and hope it sounds more intelligent than it does in my ears.

The Prince continues his descent, his feet quick, his robes dragging on the steps behind him. We pass another floor, and I spy Mixael hard at work, loading a series of volumes onto a trolley. "What-ho, Mixael!" the Prince says, raising a hand in greeting.

Mixael looks up and smiles. "Good day, Prince!" He turns that beaming smile on me. "How is our newest addition to the family getting on?"

The Prince pauses, leaning against the stair rail. "She just tried rebinding Dulmier Fen."

"Really?" Mixael's brows rise. "And how did you fare, Miss Darlington?"

I shrug. "I'm fairly certain I nearly got myself eaten by a Noswraith."

A grin splits Mixael's face. "But you *didn't*. And that's the main thing, isn't it?" He shakes his head and chuckles. "If it makes you feel any better, I wasn't allowed anywhere near even the lesser Noswraiths until I'd been in training a good six months. You really do have something special about you, don't you, Miss Darlington?"

I flush, but before I can begin to think of a reply, the Prince rolls his eyes and growls, "Don't go flattering the new girl, Mixael. It'll go to her head. Come, Darling! Now is not the time to dawdle."

I bid Mixael a hasty goodbye and scurry on after the Prince. Turn after turn of the stair, lower and lower and lower still. Soon we reach floor five, which is the lowest level I reached yesterday. Still the Prince continues down to floor six. Floor seven. Floor eight. How deep does he intend to take me? Floor nine, floor ten.

We reach floor eleven . . . and an oppressive darkness closes in around us.

"Here we are," the Prince says, stepping off the stair and onto the floor. He waves a hand, indicating that I am to follow him. I can scarcely see the gesture in the gloom, but his eyes glitter brightly, like two small torches. "Watch your step."

Though it isn't cold, I begin to shiver uncontrollably. I wrap my arms around myself, trying to hold my bones steady. The Prince strides away from me to where a small lantern hangs from a hook on one wall. He pulls another lantern from a nearby alcove and lights it at the first. It's a pretty silver-filigree orb, and the pale white light inside casts patterns of lace on the stone walls around us. Walls which are distinctly *not* lined with bookshelves.

Instead there are doors. So many doors, set approximately twenty feet apart from each other, circling the entire floor. Each door is set with a square, shuttered window and massive wheels that look like heavy and intricate lock-and-bolt systems. Nothing about this floor looks like a library, more like a high security prison.

All around me the air feels . . . *heavy*. And full of invisible movement.

"Come now, don't be shy," the Prince says, holding up his lantern so the light gleams on his face. He beckons again, and I have no choice but to hurry to his side. It takes all my willpower not to grab hold of his elbow and press in close. But I don't want him to know how frightened I am.

"We keep the Greater Noswraiths within these vaults," the Prince says as he leads me past those many doors. "The Noswraiths and every copy of every volume in which they have been bound." He steps to one of the nearest doors and, to my surprise, pulls open the shutters over the window. Glass gleams in the glow of his lantern. He taps it with one finger, then glances my way. "Come.

Have a look."

I hug my arms a little tighter around my shivering body. Forcing my unwilling limbs into action, I approach the door and stand up on tiptoe to peer into the room beyond the glass.

At first I see nothing but shadows. Slowly, however, those shadows seem to solidify, forming various shapes. Books, I realize. Many hundreds of books of all different shapes and sizes, lining the walls and piled in heaps on the floor. Most of them appear to be on the verge of complete disintegration. Are all these books former containments of a single Noswraith, broken down as the spell inside struggled to get free?

A stone pedestal stands in the center of the chamber, rising from the mass of books. Displayed on that pedestal is a single volume, much fresher and newer than the rest.

"That one is the most recent binding."

The Prince's voice in my ear startles me. I jump and back away from the window, my eyes very wide, struggling to make sense of his features in the shadow-laced light. His eyes are unnaturally bright, the violet irises reflecting the lantern glow in eerie flashes. "Soran Silveri completed that binding himself mere days before his death," he says, nodding at the chamber. "These containment volumes are never taken from their vaults. When the time comes for a new binding to be generated, a librarian will enter the vault and create the new one. It's a dangerous business, but far less dangerous than removing the Noswraith would be."

I nod slowly. Then, drawing a shaky breath, I force myself to step back up to the window and peer inside. A strange impression of *movement* fills the deeper shadows within that chamber. Writhing like many tentacle arms or . . . or vines . . .

I draw back again with a gasp. "There's something in there!"

"What did you expect?" The Prince chuckles darkly. "There's something in each of these chambers. Even bound Noswraiths are dangerous. And the Greater Noswraiths, such as the Thorn Maiden here, will always find ways to reach beyond their bounds, however faintly."

"The Thorn Maiden," I whisper. As though in response to her name, something shivers and whispers on the far side of the vault door.

"Yes," the Prince says. "Not her true name, of course; merely her title, rather like your Melted Man. She's a big one. Not the biggest of our collection, but quite a nasty nightmare in her own right. She was originally created by Soran Silveri, one of the most powerful Miphates ever born."

I hope my shock doesn't register on my face. The sheer power emanating from within that vault is tremendous! But worse still is the heavy pressure of evil, a pressure that slowly mounts with every passing second. It already feels nearly strong enough to shatter that huge lock, burst through that door, and fill this whole space with its potency and malice.

And a human created this evil? I don't want to believe it. The idea is simply too horrible.

The Prince watches me closely, gauging my reaction. I turn to him, keeping my expression carefully masked. But I can tell by the glint in his eye that he's not fooled. "Come," he says, turning from the door and continuing along the curving passage. "I have many more such terrors to introduce to you before our time is through."

We pass door after door, and the Prince gives me the title of each one as we go. The Hag of Hillway . . . Boney Long Fingers . . . the Eight-Crowned Queen . . . Old Granny Slack-Jaw . . . the Tall Man . . . and more, a bewildering array. As we pass some of the doors, I feel the inside pressure so profoundly, it's nearly enough to knock me from my feet. Others give an impression of dormancy, and I suspect the bindings in those chambers are more recently written.

We circle the entire floor and arrive back at the stair. For a moment, I entertain hope that the Prince will lead us back up to the higher floors. My hopes are dashed when he steps onto the stair and continues spiraling down to the twelfth floor below. "Keep up, Darling!" he calls out as his lantern light disappears around a turn.

I don't want to stand here in the darkness with all those Noswraiths around me. Gathering my skirts, I hasten after him, my gaze desperately fixed on the bobbing light he carries. The air feels even thicker down lower. It's like there's a tremendous weight over my head; a weight of pure evil, ready to break through all of those floors and send me crashing into the darkness at the base of this towering citadel. I fight the urge to grasp hold of the Prince's elbow and cling to him for strength and support. No, I'll be brave. Even if it kills me.

"You should never venture to the lower levels without a light," the Prince says even as he steps off the stairway onto the twelfth floor. "But likewise, you should never leave a light burning any longer than necessary. Light attracts the darkness like a flame attracts moths. And the darkness is already dense enough down here without our adding to it. Now here, Darling! Have a look."

He's stopped before another vault door and pulled back the shutters. I approach reluctantly, stand on my toes and peer inside. I'm hit at once with that same overwhelming pressure on the verge of bursting free. But along with that pressure is another powerful sense: *sorrow*. Sorrow so profound, it could break my heart in two.

And simmering beneath that sorrow is an uncontrollable, elemental rage.

"The Hungry Mother." The Prince's voice is low, as though even he hesitates to speak in the presence of this being. "True name: *Madjra*."

I want to back away from that window, want to turn and flee straight for the spiral stair. Instead I force myself to look at the central pedestal standing in that vault where the current binding-book lies. Even in that gloom and darkness, I can see how broken down it is. It looks ready to disintegrate before my very eyes. "This one doesn't look so good," I whisper.

"Really?" The Prince takes hold of my shoulders and moves me to one side. I'm suddenly very aware of his proximity, of the strength of his grip, the breadth of his chest at my back. It's a little startling, but it quickly ends when he lets go and peers through the window himself. "Strange. This binding was only just completed a week ago. It should still be strong."

He turns from the window and marches to an odd assortment of tubes that seem to grow organically from the stone wall. I wouldn't have noticed them in the darkness, but by the light of the Prince's lantern, they gleam a reddish copper. He pulls out one of the tubes, scattering bits of crumbled stone at his feet. The end of the tube forms a trumpet shape, which he holds to his mouth. "Vervain!" he says sharply. Somewhere far overhead, I hear an echo of his voice. "The Hungry Mother's binding is compromised. Report to the twelfth floor immediately."

I think of poor Vervain with her hollow eyes and her startled expression when the Prince spoke to her earlier. Not to mention the large stack of books on her desk, a stack which the Prince had already added to with my own failed binding spell. "Don't you think Vervain has enough work already for one day?" I ask.

The Prince turns, swinging the lantern light so that it shines in my face. I wince and put up a hand to shield my eyes. "The Hungry Mother," he says, "is Vervain's own creation. Therefore, her bindings will always be the strongest, surest way to keep it contained."

"That one is *Vervain's?*" Aghast, I turn to the window again. Once more I feel that pressure of sorrow and rage pulsing against the glass window, throbbing just on the far side of the door. Vervain seems so pale, so weak. So fragile. But the power I sense within that vault is the strongest I've yet encountered.

I am a mother . . . always . . .

I shudder as the memory of her words ripples across my mind. What kind of pain lurking in Vervain's history would lead her to create something so dreadful?

"Vervain!" the Prince barks into the speaking tube once more. "Get down to the twelfth floor. *Now.*" With that, he replaces the tube and turns to me once more. "Shall we continue?"

24

To my surprise—and great relief—the Prince begins climbing back up the stair rather than descending to a lower level. Are we done with our initial inspection of the Greater Noswraiths then? One can only hope! I lift my skirts and begin to climb after him, praying he won't suddenly change his mind.

He really loves you, you know.

I stop short.

A cold shiver races from the base of my skull all the way down my spine, stopping me in my tracks.

He really loves you . . . loves you . . . loves you . . .

The whisper rises from the darkness, echoing up from floors below. A whisper so faint, I strain my ears to catch it. Am I imagining things?

Fingers gripping the stair rail, I lean out over the dizzying emptiness of the citadel's center. My eyes open as wide as they can, trying to make sense of the profound shadow. The Prince's lantern is now several turns above me and casts very little glow down here. But maybe that's good. Maybe I'll see better without the light. Maybe if I descend into that darkness, I can make better sense of it.

. . . loves you . . . loves you . . . loves you . . .

"Darling!"

I start and twist my head around, looking up the winding stair. The Prince leans out over the rail, his lantern suspended close to his head, illuminating his face in ghoulish contrasts of light and shadow. "I thought I told you not to dawdle. Pick up those feet. Unless you *want* to be swallowed up by Noswraiths, that is."

I blink and cast a last glance below me. Why did I linger here? What did I think I would see or . . . or hear? I can't remember. All that remains is a feeling like an itch in my brain.

I shrug and hurry on up the spiral until I'm only a few steps behind the Prince. He watches me come, one eyebrow having slid far up his brow. When the light of his lantern gleams full on my face, he studies me closely for a moment. Then, with a grunt, he turns and continues his climb, me trailing at his heels.

We are passing the fifth floor when a sound of scurrying feet draws my gaze upward. Vervain is hastening down the stair, her pace so frantic, I'm afraid she'll fall and break her neck. Seeing the Prince on his way up, she stops, eyes widening, and presses herself against the rail to make room for him to pass.

"Vervain," the Prince says coolly as he draws alongside her. "Take care you secure the binding properly this time. It should not have worn down so quickly." He levels a stern gaze her way. "Do I need to start checking on your work?"

"No, Prince," she gasps, her voice a thin thread of sound, ready to snap.

"I should hope not." With that, the Prince continues his climb. Vervain stays where she is, head bowed, gaze downturned. I have no choice but to hasten on past her, but I hate to brush by without a word. What can I say, though? I shoot her a furtive glance as I come alongside her.

Her eyes flash behind her lashes and lock with mine. For the space of an instant, I'm stopped short, my breath stolen, my heart thudding against my breastbone.

The instant passes. Vervain drops her gaze and hastens on down the stair. I watch her until she disappears around the turn, then listen to the sound of her retreating footsteps.

"Darling!"

I shake my head, tighten my grip on the rail, and hurry on up the stair.

A loud squawk draws my gaze just as I reach the uppermost floor. I turn to the right and see Nelle Silveri approaching, the blue wyvern draped over her shoulders and glaring at me, its crest upraised. Nelle, by contrast, offers a smile, displaying incongruously strong white teeth in her wrinkled old face.

"Morning, Prince," she says, bobbing a curtsy, which the Prince answers with a dignified nod. "How was the first day of training? Is the new girl any good?"

"That," says the Prince, "remains to be seen."

Something in the tone of his voice fills me with sudden inexplicable shame. I don't understand the sensation and try to shake it off, but it holds on like claws gripping my shoulders, weighing me down. Which is ridiculous. Why should I care if the Prince considers me talented or not? I didn't come to Vespre by choice, and I sure as the nine hells wouldn't stay here if I had any other option. If I don't prove to have a knack for Noswraith-battling, that's his problem, not mine.

Frowning, I struggle to concentrate on what the Prince and Nelle are discussing. "Send her down to Andreas," the Prince is saying. "He can drill her for a few hours. She can practice on her own from there."

"I need Andreas to pick up where Vervain left off. Those small bindings ain't going to bind themselves."

"Mixael can manage those."

"Mixael's workin' on Cold Eye's binding this afternoon. Don't you remember?"

The Prince rolls his eyes to the domed ceiling overhead. "Very well. I'll take over Vervain's bindings, and you send for Andreas.

No more protests, Silveri!" He puts up a hand, cutting off whatever Nelle was about to say. "I know my own limits, thank you very much. I can certainly manage a stack of small bindings. It's vital that Darling here begins the drills. She's no good to us until she's mastered them."

"What drills?" I ask.

The Prince doesn't bother to answer. Instead he pats Nelle on the shoulder—narrowly avoiding a nip from the wyvern—and says, "See that it's done." Then he strides away without so much as a word or a look for me. My eyes follow him until he reaches Vervain's desk and vanishes within the carved-out cubical.

"Hmm." Nelle's grunt draws my attention back to her. She's studying me, her brow lightly knitted. It's as if she's reading my thoughts. Hastily I resume my blandest smile, masking my expression. I suspect it's already too late. "He's an odd one, our Prince is. Make no mistake," the old librarian says. "Odd and prickly and enough to send a body bullspittin' mad sometimes. But"—she raises a finger and taps her own temple—"he's as smart as they come. A fellow what's got a *vision*. And let me tell you, girl, it takes an unusual sort of fellow to have any vision when it comes to a place like Doomed City! Most of the High Folk gave up on this realm long ago."

Her voice, though old and creaky as a rusty hinge, is full of admiration. I think again of the adoring look I'd glimpsed in Vervain's eyes when the Prince approached her desk earlier this morning. It seems all the librarians of Vespre harbor strong feelings for their lord and master. All the female librarians, in any case.

That doesn't mean I'll be joining their number. I meet Nelle's gaze steadily and let my empty smile grow a fraction.

"Hmmm," she grunts again, then turns and patters back to the stair up which I'd just climbed. "Come along, girl," she calls as she goes. "Looks like you're running drills with Andreas today."

The wyvern swings its head around to watch me, as though to be sure I'm following. I heave a sigh. The morning has already taken a toll on me, and the prospect of spending the rest of the day with dreamy-eyed Andreas sounds exhausting. Glaring at the wyvern, I hurry after, my legs wobbling a little as I descend the stairway behind the old librarian.

"Andreas!" Nelle calls out as we reach the fourth floor. "Andreas, you're on New Girl Duty today. The Prince wants you drilling her on Noswraith names until some of them stick."

Andreas's bespectacled face emerges from behind a stack of volumes on the floor. He turns his blinking gaze from Nelle to me and back again, before saying in a smooth, faraway sort of voice, "It would be my honor to serve, but . . ."

"No *buts*, my good fellow," Nelle responds crisply. "The Prince has spoken. Your tentacled monster is going to have to wait for another day."

Andreas gazes sadly around at his piles of research. What was it the Prince had said he was hunting for? Some connection between a Noswraith and a demon from ancient lore? It doesn't sound like tremendous fun to me, but Andreas looks as though someone has just snatched his lolly away. Heaving a great sigh, he unfolds his gangly frame, steps out from among his books, and offers me a small but surprisingly graceful bow. "If you will come with me, Miss... Miss... Pardon me, I seem to have forgotten your name."

"Darlington," I supply.

He blinks again. I get the distinct impression that he's already forgotten what I just said. He seems to be the sort of man whose head is so full of very specific kinds of knowledge that he simply has no room to fit superfluous facts into the cracks. "If you will come with me, miss," he says simply.

I glance at Nelle. The wyvern shows its teeth in what looks unsettlingly like a grin, and the old librarian mirrors it. "Good luck, girl," she says, thus abandoning me to my fate.

Andreas takes me to a quiet nook where I'm surprised to see a pair of overstuffed chairs. He takes a seat, sinking deeply into the softness, and waves a hand for me to do the same. It's a relief to sit after all that stair-climbing, and I cross my ankles in front of me. From this angle, I have a clear view of the rail and the huge empty space down the middle of the citadel. Down here on the fourth floor I feel rather too close to the darkness just a few stories lower. I can almost *feel* the pressure beneath my feet, like steam building up, ready to burst.

Shaking off the feeling, I fold my hands in my lap and face Andreas. "Is there a list?" I ask.

"A list, miss?" He tilts his head to one side, his voice vague.

"Of Noswraith names. I assume I'm meant to copy them."

For the first time since I've met him, a flash of real alertness bursts across Andreas's face. "*Copy Noswraith names?*" he says, horrified. "You mean, *write them down?*"

I pinch my lips together. Apparently being new doesn't excuse my ignorance. Trying to keep irritation from my voice I say, "Is there something wrong?"

Andreas pinches the bridge of his nose and shakes his head slowly. "To write down a Noswraith name outside of the binding context is to *bring the Noswraith straight to you.* As in, it will break all current bindings and simply manifest right there, right in front of you. PHHHT!" With this last, expressive sound, he snaps his fingers, making me jump. "And believe me," he finishes, "that is *not* something you want happening to you. *Ever.*"

I stare back at him, meeting his gaze through his spectacles. And I see in his face a whole, shadowy world of horrors I can scarcely begin to comprehend. I feel the pressure from down below once more and know it for what it is: *eagerness.* The desire of each and every bound Noswraith to escape its bondage and wreak havoc on those who dared to bind it. I also feel the frailty of those bindings and the enormity of the task before me, the task these brave librarians confront every single day, every single hour of their lives here in Vespre City.

You were born to be a warrior.

The Prince's words return to me as I face Andreas. As I face this vague, dreamy-eyed fellow, with his long limbs and his shy schoolboy manner, seated in the plush chair across from me. And

I realize how brave this man must be. A true warrior.

"Very well, sir," I say humbly. "Please, teach me."

25

ANDREAS IS PLEASED TO DISCOVER THAT I ALREADY know three Noswraith names and their corresponding titles. I remember the Prince writing the name *Yinzidor* into the binding for the Melted Man. The unseen Noswraith in the story I tackled this morning was *Dulmier Fen*.

"And the Hungry Mother," I say. "I believe she was called *Madjra*. Though I'm not sure how it's spelled."

Andreas spells it out for me and urges me to repeat it several times. When I'm through, he says, "That is a good beginning, Miss . . . Miss . . ." He hesitates, then shrugs and continues. "That is a good beginning. We will proceed with some of the smaller wraiths, for that is where your efforts will be focused over the next few weeks and months."

With that he begins to recite a dizzying list of names and titles, one after the other. I'm lost in a matter of moments, and when he comes to an end and asks me to repeat them back to him, I can manage no more than two or three.

Andreas, however, doesn't seem bothered by my incompetency. "Good, good," he says, nodding, his eyes half-closed. "Now, again."

Hours pass. Andreas, for all his mildness, turns out to be a hard taskmaster. He makes me work until my voice goes hoarse, and only then gives me a brief break for water. At some point, Mixael shows up with bread, cheese, and wine and coaxes us to eat. Andreas only takes a few bites and spends even that time poring over one of the books he'd brought with him, making little notes as he goes.

Mixael takes a seat on the floor beside my chair and offers a sweet smile. "How are you getting on, Miss Darlington?"

I sag in my chair and swallow a bite of cheese that sits like lead in my gut. "It's . . . it's a *lot*." I sit there a moment with my mouth open but can't think of more to say.

But Mixael nods his understanding. "I know. It *is* a lot. And, unfortunately, it never ceases to be a lot. You'll toughen up over time, though, never you fear!"

With that, he clambers to his feet, takes our empty plates and cups, and abandons me to Andreas once more. Soon I'm back at the Noswraith names, drilling until my head pounds.

At last, however, I hear the distant sound of bells. Andreas tilts his head, then stands abruptly. "That's all for today, Miss. You may go."

I stare up at him, a bit dazed and dizzy. "I'm . . . I'm done?"

"Until six bells tomorrow," the librarian says, gathering books and tucking them under his arm. He opens one and buries his nose in it, wafting away from me without a goodbye, lost once more to his studies. I start to call after him, but what's the point? He probably won't hear me anyway.

I find my way to the spiral stair and climb back to the first floor. Nelle is hard at work at her desk and barely grunts when I speak to her in passing. Mixael is nowhere in sight, and from this angle, I can't tell if the Prince is still seated at Vervain's desk. And Vervain? Presumably she is down in the vaults. Working on the Hungry Mother's binding.

I shudder, wrapping my arms around my middle. Am I meant to be working on some other task? Andreas said I may go, but does that mean my workday is through? I hope so. Oh gods! Do I ever hope so! I'm worn to a thread, ready to snap with exhaustion. But I hate to abandon the other librarians.

"Miss Darlington?"

I turn at the sound of my name, and a smile breaks across my face. "Oh! Lir!"

The beautiful troll woman stands in the library doorway. She beckons, and I am more than happy to hasten to her, glad for someone—anyone—to give me direction.

"Oh, my poor little mistress!" she says, studying me as I draw near. "You look quite fatigued. Did they work you terribly hard then?" She clucks, all maternal concern that seems rather at odds with her image of sensual beauty. Putting an arm around my shoulders, she leads me from the library. "And how was your first day?"

I can't find the energy to offer more than a few grunts in answer. Lir doesn't seem to mind. She begins prattling about the other librarians and their various eccentricities, all the while guiding me back through the bewildering array of passages. I scarcely hear a word she says. After what feels like an endless trek, we reach my room, and I stagger to the bed and simply fall across it. Lir burbles and bustles, trying to coax me out of my work gown, but finally settles simply for untying my hair and pulling off my shoes and stockings. She bundles my legs into the bed and covers me with a blanket.

"I'll bring a bite of dinner at nine bells," she says, smoothing hair out of my face. My vision swims, but I try to smile at her. "Rest now, little mistress," she croons, like I'm a kitten in her care. "Rest and sweet dreams."

I don't argue. My eyes close before she reaches the door. I hear it click shut behind her. Then I roll onto my side, bury my face in the pillow, and sink into sleep.

"*Mar? Mar, mar, horarto korar, mar?*"

The stream of grunting, growled words penetrates my dreams, drawing me back to the world of wakefulness. I lie in bed, my limbs numb and tired, and struggle to raise my eyelids.

"*Mar? Mar, mar?*"

"*Horarto korar?*"

"*Mar, torat!*"

Three distinct voices, hard as rocks grinding together. Then a fourth voice speaks with a sweet lisp, "Look! She wake up."

Human words. My own language.

This is unexpected enough that I manage to pry one eye open. At first, the world is blurry, but after a few blinks, it clarifies. I find myself staring at a row of troll faces lined up on the edge of my bed. Three extraordinarily ugly faces, and one more beautiful than the dawn of a perfect spring day.

All four break into huge grins.

I don't have time for more than a short, "Oh!" before the troll siblings spring onto my bed, piling around me. The boys bounce, jostling me so hard I'm nearly flung from the mattress. I utter a cry of fright and cling to the stone bedpost.

"*Jorta!*" one of the troll boys—Calx, the youngest, I think—shouts at the others. "Stop!"

Thin pale arms wrap around my waist, and I look down into Sis's upturned, heartbreakingly lovely face. "*Mar!*" she says, and sighs.

"Oh, no!" I whisper, then shake my head, staring round at the four of them. "How by the seven gods did you find me?"

The boys seem to take this as invitation. They crowd in close, pulling me down between them and piling into my lap in a painful avalanche of rocky elbows and knees. Sis transfers her grip from my waist to my neck and snarls ferociously at any of her brothers who come close to knocking her off. I'm going to be strangled to death in affection.

"That's enough!" I bark.

The trolls freeze. Apparently a strong, authoritative voice works on them.

"All right, off the bed with you," I say and clap my hands for emphasis. "At once!"

One by one they scamper and scramble down. Without being told, they line up in a row before me, arranged from biggest to smallest. I look from one to the next, recalling their names, "Dig," I say. "Har, Calx, and . . . Sis."

They beam with delight, gem teeth gleaming in the light of the pale lanterns overhead. They're so pleased simply to hear their names, it's enough to wrench my heart. But I need to be firm.

"Now see here," I say, "I *cannot* be your mother. Do you understand?" Their grinning faces break into mournful expressions. Sis's eyes brim with tears. But I steel myself firmly, squaring my shoulders. "I'm sorry! It's just the way it is. The Prince has commanded me not to adopt any troll children, and I have to obey him, like it or not. I'm *Obliged*."

Sis begins to howl, throwing her head back and sobbing loud and long. Her brothers immediately cluster around her, casting me reproachful looks. "Say something!" Calx demands, his words strongly accented but understandable. "Say something, *Mar!*"

The desperation in his voice is palpable, as is the sorrow and hungry need in each of those ugly little faces. How can I possibly reject them? I wait for a count of ten, expecting my Obligation to kick in and force me to act against my will. That's the way it's always been with Estrilde. Surely the Prince's command will drive me to comply, and yet . . .

No headache comes. No constricting force around my heart or mind. But that doesn't make sense. I am Obligated to the Prince. He gave me a command. I shouldn't have a choice whether or not to obey . . . should I?

I look into those little faces. Sis has ceased her wailing and now stands in the midst of her brothers, staring at me while silent tears pour down her exquisite face. It's more than I can stand.

"Fine!" I say, tossing up my hands. "Fine, fine, you can stay here tonight. But that's *it*, do you hear me? In the morning, you've got to go back where you came from."

It's anyone's guess whether they heard my last few words, for the little trolls begin cheering at once and pile back into my bed around me, burrowing under bedclothes and forming little nests. Sis, her tears miraculously melted away, tucks under my arm, beaming beatifically up at me.

Gods on high, what will Lir say when she comes back with the promised meal? I glance sideways and see a platter and dishes across the room on a low table. Apparently Lir has already come and gone, and the troll children helped themselves. I sigh and press a hand to my hollow midsection, but then glance around at the children, all of whom have fallen immediately to sleep. The three ugly boys look almost sweet in sleep. Almost. Especially little Calx.

Warmth blooms in my heart. The truth is, I *like* to feel needed.

Oscar's face appears in my mind—my poor little brother, back home in our parents' old house, alone and sinking ever more deeply into his vices and despair. If only I could be there for him. If only I can survive long enough to return and . . . and save him . . . somehow . . .

"Ten more years," I whisper.

Then I wriggle down so I can put my head on my pillow and close my eyes. Lulled by the sound of troll snores, I sink back toward sleep.

He really loves you . . .

. . . you know . . .

I draw a short breath, my eyes flaring wide. I lie in darkness, surrounded by small, hard bodies. The lanterns overhead have dimmed to almost nothing, and the room is full of shadows.

I stare into the deepest of those shadows in a corner across the room. Is something there? Something solid but unseen standing *just* beyond the range of my vision. Something separated by nothing more than a thin veil of reality.

I lie there for a long time, my body tense, my breath tight. Eventually sleep claims me once more.

26

WHEN I WAKE NEXT, THE TROLL CHILDREN ARE gone.

Lir is in the room, bustling around, lighting the lamps, and laying out clothes for my day. She's brought breakfast, gods bless her!

I slug out of bed, cross the room, and flop into the seat by the little table. "Good morning, sweet Mistress!" Lir chirrups. I grunt an answer and shovel food into my mouth. Lir doesn't seem to mind my rudeness. She turns her attention to the bed and begins to make it.

She stops suddenly, however, and her lovely face puckers into a severe frown. Rounding on me, she demands, "Were there *troll children* in your bed last night, Mistress?"

I briefly debate the merits of lying. But what's the point? "Yes,"

I say and take another bite of creamy porridge.

Lir gasps, her pretty mouth hanging open. Then she shakes her head. "You know the rules!"

What follows is a long harangue. I listen, eat, and don't bother to answer as my maid's words rain furiously down on me. I keep thinking about lovely little Sis, sweet Calx, and the others, all piled up on my pillows last night. So peaceful, so comfortable. So confident in my ability to care for them. A totally misplaced confidence, to be sure, but it warmed my heart. If only I could truly help them.

But I can't.

I can't care for anyone. No matter how much I wish to.

My stomach turns over. Suddenly, I have no appetite. I let the spoon drop from my fingers into the half-empty porridge bowl and push the tray away.

Lir gives up on her lecture at last and chooses to vent her frustration by bullying me around instead. She gets me dressed, ties up my hair in a severe bun, all the while maintaining a silent pout. I don't have the energy to care.

While her attention is momentarily diverted, however, I venture to the wardrobe and find my little bundle of belongings brought from Aurelis. Lir never bothered to open it and find places for the contents but simply stashed the whole thing behind the hanging dresses. I untie the bundle now and reach inside to withdraw Thaddeus Creakle's gift.

The pen catches the light from the lanterns, its brilliant

plumage as bright as blood in my hands. I turn it over, looking at it consideringly. Thaddeus gave it to me for a reason, I'm sure. What was it Nelle said . . . that, traditionally, it was believed quills retained the powers of their previous owners? Does Thaddeus think so as well?

If so, who did this quill belong to before it was pressed into my hands?

"Mistress!" Lir calls from across the room. "Your escort is here!"

I hastily tuck the quill into the front of my bodice, then turn about. Lir stands at the open door of my room, her hand on the latch. Vervain waits for me in the doorway.

My heart sinks. Of course, I do need an escort to make my way through this labyrinthine palace, but I'd hoped it would be anyone but Vervain. Repressing a little shudder, I hurry to the door. "Thank you, Lir," I murmur.

"Have no fear, Mistress," Lir says, her jaw firm. "I'll fortify your rooms against any further infestations of troll children. You can count on me."

I want to protest, but what's the point? So I simply nod and fall into step beside Vervain.

We are silent as we make our way through the gloomy, twilit passages. I don't look at my escort but instead concentrate on where I'm going. Am I fooling myself, or am I really starting to recognize some of my surroundings? Not that I'd want to try to find my way by myself, but perhaps it isn't entirely hopeless. For instance, I know we're supposed to turn right at the upcoming intersection. Then there will be a short flight of steps to another level, a long progress down a hall of windows, followed by a left turn . . .

Maybe I'll find my footing here in the Doomed City after all.

I'm just smiling at this self-congratulatory thought when Vervain stops abruptly. She whirls in place, facing me. I meet her gaze and almost wince. There's so much hatred there! Pure, unmasked hatred of . . . of me? No, I don't think so. Hatred without focus. Rage. And underneath it all, sorrow, sorrow, so much sorrow.

"They try to stop us," she says.

I blink and take a half-step back. "I'm sorry, what?"

"They try to stop us." Her hands knot into fists, twisting folds of her gown. "They try to tie our hands. To cripple us, to make us less than we are."

I feel as though I've been dropped into the middle of some ongoing conversation. "I'm sorry, Vervain," I say gently. "I'm not sure what you're—"

"But they can't stop us. Not in the end." She lunges, startling me so that I back up. She keeps coming, and I keep backing away until my shoulders hit the wall. I gasp and try to brace myself. She's neither tall nor heavy, a mere skeleton of a woman. But somehow her presence feels large in that moment, intimidating.

She breathes in short, gasping gusts, her wide eyes fixed, not on me, but on some unseen space in the air off to one side of my face. "They can't stop us," she whispers, the words falling heavily from bloodless lips. "They can cut us with knives, remove our fingers, one after the other. They can bleed us until we are nothing more than husks of our former selves. But deep down . . . deep down inside, we are meant to *make*. Meant to *create*. Meant to give *life!*"

An image flashes through my head—an image of that book disintegrating on its pedestal in the vault. And in the shadows, something unseen. Unseen but real, profound . . . terrible . . . and hideous. Bound, and always, always struggling to be free.

"You did bind her, didn't you?" My voice trembles. I shake my head and try again. "Yesterday, I mean. You re-bound the Hungry Mother . . . right?"

Vervain's nostrils flare. She turns around and marches up the stair leading to the topmost floor of the library. "I know my role here in Vespre," she tosses back over her shoulder. Her voice is no longer that strange, strangled thing, it is merely cold. And heavy. "Don't question me, little initiate. Tend to your own duties instead."

The next moment, she's out of sight.

I hesitate, still leaning against the wall for support. Then, breathing out a long-held gust of air, I push myself into motion, climbing the stair after Vervain. My mind tumbles, unable to form a clear thought. Should I warn someone? The Prince, perhaps? Or Nelle? Should I tell them that Vervain is not herself, that I suspect her of not completing the task the Prince set for her?

But then again, how presumptuous am I? I have no way of knowing if this behavior is unusual for Vervain. I don't know her, and the little interaction I've had with her, she's definitely seemed odd. But the Prince didn't seem to notice anything unusual in her manner yesterday. Surely he and the other librarians would be sensitive to any potential threats to their strange, dark little domain.

Besides, Vervain might simply be blowing off steam. She's carrying a lot of pent-up anger, that's for sure. I don't want to get her in trouble, don't want to get myself tangled up in the still unfamiliar social dynamics of Vespre Library.

I reach the top of the stair to find the big doors open and Vervain already passed through. I hurry after her, stepping out onto the first floor in time to see Vervain's head disappear down the spiral stair. Breathing out a sigh, I look around for the other librarians. Mixael's red head is bowed over his desk, just visible within the curve of his stone cubical. No sign of Nelle or Andreas. It's a big library, after all. They could be anywhere.

Feeling as though I'm being watched, I turn around slowly. The Prince is there. Standing just a few paces behind me. Today, he wears wine-colored velvet, open at the throat and partway down his sculpted chest. All signs of weakness from magic usage are gone, deftly covered in several layers of glamour. If I didn't know better, I'd think he was full-blooded fae.

"Good morning, Prince," I say, hastily pushing my smile into place.

He raises an eyebrow. "Good morning, Darling."

I wince. But there's no point in protesting what I increasingly believe is his willful misuse of my name. I need to pick my battles. My gaze drops to the armload of books he's carrying, and my throat tightens. Something tells me I've got battles enough ahead of me for one day.

The Prince's lips tilt to one side. "Come, along. We've got work to do."

He leads me back to the same desk I worked at yesterday and spreads the array of books before me. "Have a seat," he says, holding my chair. I drop obediently into place. "Now, take a look at what I've brought you."

I inspect the books without touching them. They're small volumes and seem to have only minor wear around the bindings. A faint sense of *pressure* issues from within the covers. "Are these Noswraiths?" I ask.

"Yes." The Prince draws up a second chair and takes a seat beside me. "Little ones, to be sure, but Noswraiths, nonetheless. Tell me, what else do you observe?"

I pinch my lip between my teeth and study the books again. "They don't seem to be on the verge of breaking through. But . . ." I hesitate, uncertain if it's even worth mentioning. Then I shrug. "They all seem to be at about the same level of disintegration."

"Well spotted," the Prince says. Despite myself, I feel a glow of pleasure at his praise. Hastily I stifle the feeling and concentrate on what he's saying now. "None of them are at the point of breaking yet, but they are, indeed, falling apart at the same or similar rate. They also all come from the same part of the library. Which means if they are left until they are a *real* problem, we run the risk of a whole swarm of small Noswraiths breaking out at once. And a swarm of small Noswraiths can be just as dangerous as any Greater Noswraith. Sometimes worse."

He selects one of the books and hands it to me. I hesitate only a moment before taking it and hope he can't see how my hands tremble. "Do you want me to re-bind it?"

"No. Not yet, at least. First, I want you to identify where the breakdown is happening. What exactly is wearing out this book . . . and is it the same for the others?"

It's an odd question. Hadn't he already explained to me that the Noswraiths themselves wear down their bindings? This question implies that outside influence might cause a breakage as well. Not a happy thought.

I open the book and page through it slowly. It's written entirely in a language I don't know. Even the characters are unfamiliar to me. At first, I think this means I'm safe—after all, if I can't read the spell, I can't be affected by it, can I? But after I've turned a few pages, I feel the simmering life underneath. Ideas, existing and vivid and profound. *Real*, regardless of my ability to understand them.

I stop on the sixth page and frown. Something's wrong here. Something I can't quite see . . . but can't quite *un*see as well. A distortion, a warping of my perspective, of reality.

"Here!" I say, holding up the book for the Prince to see. "Here, does this look as though something has . . . has *eaten* into the book?"

A flash of approval shines from the Prince's eyes. "Well done," he says. Once more, I can't stop the little burst of pleasure those words give me. "These books have fallen prey to *sugigoth*—more commonly known as *bookwyrms*. They can be devastating to any library, but here in Vespre? They can be the single snowflake that starts the avalanche. Thankfully, there's a useful spell which can be used to lure bookwyrms out."

He takes up a quill and begins to write in the margins of the page I showed him. His hand is quick, the words flowing from him with ease. As the words of the spell take shape, *things* begin to stir within the page.

The next moment, I gasp and push my chair back. Several horrible, slithering things crawl out from between the pages. They're much bigger than I would have expected, and one of them falls in my lap. I scream, leap to my feet and, on pure impulse, stomp on the writhing thing. It lets out a hiss and disintegrates in a cloud of dark motes, like ash.

"Careful, Darling," the Prince says, continuing to write his spell with one hand even as he holds out the other. The wyrms falling from the book twist and contort, then seem to rise in the air and float into his hand, shrinking as they fall into his palm. Once he's gathered them all, he closes his fingers. A *poof* of dark motes escapes through his fingers, then vanishes.

"*Sugigoth,*" he says in a perfectly easy, conversational tone, "are interdimensional beings. As such, they don't like the air of this world and are easy enough to send back to their own dimension once found. And see?" He holds up the book for my inspection. "How does that feel to you?"

I can't explain it, but somehow the book feels *stronger*. That sense of disintegration is no longer present, and the strange warping sensation I'd felt has vanished. "I don't . . . I don't understand," I say, not liking to admit my ignorance.

"As interdimensional beings, the bookwyrms feast on the *ideas* contained in books rather than the physical pages," the Prince says. Then he chuckles. "Thankfully, they wouldn't dare attempt to devour any of the Greater Noswraiths, or even some of the medium-sized ones like the Melted Man. They only go for the lesser wraiths."

I blink, trying to comprehend what he's saying. "If the bookwyrms eat the *ideas*, does that mean they eat the Noswraiths themselves?"

"Yes. Unfortunately, that helps us very little. Whatever the wyrms manage to eat, the Noswraiths will regenerate swiftly enough. It's the *bindings* that won't regenerate without outside help. Now listen closely, Darling! You need to learn to watch for the signs of *sugigoth* infestation. Locating bookwyrms will be one of your primary duties as a junior librarian while you're developing your other talents."

With that, he launches into another long lecture. As I listen, I can't help but think of my days pixie-hunting in Aurelis Library. I suppose this can't be too different. And it sounds a lot less dangerous than dealing with the Noswraiths themselves.

"Come, it's time you tried the summoning spell yourself," the Prince says at last. He sets a blank piece of paper before me. "You'll learn it first before you apply it to any of our books. Here." He offers me a quill.

"Oh." I reach into the front of my bodice. "I have one of my own, actually." So saying, I withdraw the red plume with its pretty decorative nib. "I forgot to bring it yesterday, but—"

"Where did you get that?"

The Prince's voice is like a dagger, unexpectedly sharp. Startled, I toss him a wary glance. To my surprise, that horrible hatred once more distorts his features. I've been so engrossed in our lessons that I'd half forgotten how intensely he despises me. Now it shocks me like a bolt of lightning. I nearly fall from my chair.

The Prince rises, looming tall and menacing. I feel the power of his fae glamours, only now they seem to distort his features, making him not beautiful but terrible, deadly. His brow is dark as a storm.

"Where," he repeats, each word ground through clenched teeth, "did you get that?"

I gape at him, struggling to form words. "Th-Thaddeus Creakle." My voice emerges in a pathetic squeak. "He gave it to me right before I—"

"It was not his to give." The Prince's jaw clenches. I can see him fighting to master himself, holding back the rage, then forcing it down. Deftly he swipes the quill from my grasp, and before I can even think to protest, it disappears into the front of his robes. He draws a long breath, running a hand through his hair and down his face. Like magic, his expression melts into one of complete indifference.

He blinks, looks down at me. His smile is hard and sardonic.

"The Librarians of Vespre must earn their quills over time. If you apply yourself, you will receive a quill of your own. Meanwhile, you must work with the basic goose-feather pens provided." Once more he offers me the white quill. His hand trembles ever so slightly, but his voice is firm and low. "Come, Darling. Get back to work."

27

I SPEND THE ENTIRE MORNING TRYING TO MASTER THE spell. The Prince tells me I can't simply *write* the words or the shape of the words; I must *connect* with them, let them flow through my mind. For in that connection, he says, I may reach the *quinsatra* and become a channel from it to the physical world.

I honestly have no idea what he's talking about.

I mean, I've gleaned a little information about the *quinsatra* over the years since my arrival at Aurelis. I understand that it's the dimension where magic is spawned: magic that appears naturally in the veins of the fae, but which humans must draw out of that strange realm in order to work and manipulate it.

I've never paid much attention to any of this talk. It's never seemed to apply to *me*.

"Human writing," the Prince informs me, "is a kind of magic in and of itself. Mere scratches and symbols can be made to contain the greatest ideas of the ages. How is this not miraculous? But to truly channel the *quinsatra* requires a mind open to its influence."

I let out a blustering breath through my lips, groan, and pinch the bridge of my nose. I can feel a headache coming on.

The Prince sits back in his chair, folding his arms across his chest. "Am I boring you?"

I roll a sideways glare at him. "Magic doesn't come naturally to everyone, you know. If you remember, I didn't even know I *had* magic until recently. I'm still not entirely convinced, truth be told. I'm not sure I *belong* here."

The Prince's smile is more like a snarl. "Oh, have no doubt, Darling. You definitely belong in Vespre."

"Why?" I push my chair back suddenly and turn to face the Prince straight on. I'm tired of everyone implying and hinting and dancing around while I'm left to play guesswork games. "*Why* do you say I belong here? You've obviously got some reason for all of this. Why don't you *tell me?*"

The Prince looks at me long and hard.

Then suddenly he leans forward, gripping the arms of my chair. His face draws close to mine, and I pull back as far as I can, pinned in place. Not for the first time, I realize how painfully beautiful this man is. The fact is impossible to miss with only a few breaths between us, his vivid eyes boring into mine, his full lips hovering mere inches away. Beautiful like a tiger. And twice as deadly.

"Because, Clara Darling," he says, breathing the words out like poison, "you are a Noswraith-maker. From your mind was born a darkness so terrible, so profound, it could wipe out half a kingdom in a single hour if left unbound."

I can't breathe. I can't think. His words wrap around my head, my throat, filling my lungs like suffocating fumes. I open my mouth, try to tell him to stop, to take it back.

"You may look like a sweet little doll, with your doe-soft eyes and your gentle face," he continues relentlessly. "But I know the truth." He lifts one hand, tapping my forehead hard enough to leave a bruise. "I know the evil that mind of yours spawned. An evil that destroyed . . . destroyed . . ."

A spasm of pain warps his perfect features. He drops his head and closes his eyes, breathing hard. His forehead presses against mine, and I cannot draw back any further, cannot create any space between us.

At last, to my relief, he pushes away, nearly knocking my chair over in the process. I catch my balance awkwardly as he turns in a whirl of wine-colored robes, presenting me with his broad back. For a few breaths I hope he's done, hope I won't have to hear any more of these terrible words he speaks.

But his voice reaches out to me, sharp as a whiplash: "You killed the only person who ever loved me. You killed her. You are responsible. Because of what you carry inside you."

Though he cannot see me, I shake my head. Then I shake it again, harder, as though I can shake away this moment, make it never have been.

"That's impossible!" I gasp at last. How can it be true? How could *I* possibly create a Noswraith? I'm not that kind of person. I'm just little Clara Darlington: daughter, sister, friend. I've never harmed so much as a fly in my life. I'm the caretaker, the reasonable one, the one with the sound mind and calming presence, ready to still troubled waters where I can. I learned from an early age not to raise my voice in anger or my fist in wrath. I learned to make myself humble and small and meek.

"There must be some mistake," I gabble. I know how pathetic I sound. But I can't help it. "You . . . you've got the wrong girl."

The Prince turns, his lips twisted in a ferocious grimace. "There is no mistake. I was there. I saw it happen. Soon you too will remember and then . . ." He nods slowly. "Then we will see how you atone for the deaths you've dealt."

He turns and walks away, staggering a little as he goes. I watch him follow the curve of the rail until he reaches the library entrance, pulls the great doors open, and vanishes from sight.

I cannot move. I simply sit there, braced in my chair, my hands gripping the arms as hard as I can, my heart pounding a staccato rhythm. Despite the huge spaces of the library, the world seems to close in around me. I turn my head, searching for some sign of life. Someone—*anyone*—just to prove to myself that I'm not alone. But they're all gone. There's no one else here, just me and . . . and . . .

And something moving in the back of my mind.

A breath.

A whisper.

He really loves you . . . you know . . .

I don't know how I summoned the strength to rise, but it doesn't matter. Something burns in my breast, hot and terrible and frightening. I can't resist it. It drives me up and away from the desk, away from the stack of wyrm-eaten books. Drives me to the nearest spiral stair.

I grab the rail and descend swiftly, almost running, every hasty footstep risking a terrible fall. Lower and lower I go, past the second floor, third floor, fourth . . . past the seventh floor, eighth floor, ninth . . . down and down until the darkness of the lower levels closes in around me . . .

Down to the thirteenth floor.

I step off the stairway, my knees shaking, my breathing short and jagged. The wall of vaults wraps around the empty center of the citadel, door after door after door. I don't know where I'm going, not exactly. But I don't argue with the sense that drew me here with such certainty.

I pause a moment by the little wall sconce across from the stair where a low, pale light gleams behind a glass globe. I reach into an alcove and find unlit lanterns there. It's the work of a few moments to get the lantern wick to light. Now I'm surrounded in a ghostly aura fraught with filigree shadows.

I walk past vault after vault, door after door. It's as though a memory draws me on. Only it can't be *my* memory; I've never been here before. But I don't question what's happening. Why should I? It's all strangeness and nightmare in this world. Best to accept it.

At last, I reach the thirteenth door. There I stop.

There I set my lantern down.

There I put my fingers to the window shutters, pry them open. And look inside.

It's just like the others. Or so it seems at first glance. A pedestal rises from the center of the room, displaying a large grimoire, the leather cover shut fast and bound with straps and metal buckles. Piles of books surround it—half-disintegrated, littering the floor, jam packed on the shelves. So many books, far more than I would have expected. And there's something odd about them, something I can't quite name at first.

Then it strikes me: they're all the same size. All small, flimsy paperback volumes, nothing like the grimoires in the other vaults. Hundreds of them, thousands maybe.

Why do those books—why does this place—feel so familiar?

He really loves you . . .

. . . really loves you . . .

. . . really loves you . . .

You know . . .

He really loves you . . . you . . . you . . .

That voice. That whisper. Has it always been there in the back of my mind? On and on and on, relentless, whether or not I'm aware of it. Always present, coloring every thought, every deed, every hope, every motivation.

Really . . .

He loves you . . .

Really . . .

Tears brim in my eyes. My lungs are tight, my throat constricted. I grimace and gasp out a breath that emerges in a choking sob. Clenching my fists, I pound on the door.

And I feel the answering pressure from the other side.

Clara . . .

Sweetheart . . .

You know . . .

You know . . .

"You see now, don't you?"

A scream bursts from my lips. I whirl, and my foot kicks my lantern over so that it rolls along the stone floor, stopping at the feet of a thin, dark figure. The light it casts emphasizes the hollow contours of her face, making her look ghoulish, grim. For a moment, I think I'm face-to-face with a Noswraith.

A blink or two more, however, and I recognize her. "Vervain!"

She meets my gaze. Slowly, she crouches and lifts my lantern by its handle. It swings gently from the end of her arm as she offers it to me. For the space of a breath, I can't make myself reach for it. Then, with a quick, darting motion, I snatch the handle.

Her fingers tighten their grip. "You see the truth, don't you? The truth of what you are. Of what you were meant to be." She smiles. It's a smile full of teeth but no warmth.

"No." I tug on the lantern. "I have nothing to do with any of this. It's not . . . it's not who I am."

Vervain holds on a moment more before letting go and stepping back out of the pool of lantern light. She becomes a formless silhouette. "Who you are," she says, her words clear and high and strangely distant, "is a creator. A mother. A giver of life."

Her voice drops an octave: "And where there is life, there must always be *death*."

Death . . . death . . . death . . .

You know . . . you know . . . you know . . .

I stand there, my ears full of echoes, and watch the shadow of Vervain turn and retreat down the passage until she passes out of sight. Then I stand a little longer, listening to those echoes, listening to that voice. Part of me wants to peer through the vault window again. To stare into that chamber, to try to make sense of the being it contains.

Instead I lift my lantern a little higher and, gasping out a prayer, run for the stair. With every step, I expect to meet Vervain again, expect her to jump out at me like a bogeyman. But I meet no one. I reach the stair and climb and climb and climb up to where the lantern is no longer needed and the darkness drops away below me. At last, I sink down on a step in the curve between the fourth and third floors. There I set the lantern to one side and bury my face in my hands.

I can't stop trembling for a long, long while.

28

"MAR! MAR! MAR!"

I wake in the middle of the night, surrounded by smiling troll faces. Calx and Sis bounce at the foot of my bed, while Dig and Har are busy finishing off the platter of untouched dinner I left on the table. I had no appetite when I returned from the library at the end of my workday. Besides, I'd half wondered if I might be visited by these odd little persons again anyway.

Smiling, I sit up and hold out my arms. Immediately, Sis and Calx fling themselves at me, and Calx's stony body knocks the breath clean out of my lungs. The other two boys, seeing affection being offered, abandon their scavenging and scramble onto the bed as well. I try to enlarge myself to accommodate all four small, writhing bodies, so determined to soak up whatever attention I have to offer.

"Naughty little things," I tell them, smiling round at four small faces, three ugly and one startlingly beautiful. "You can stay tonight. But tomorrow you really *must* go. Do you hear me?"

"Yes! Yes! We hear! We hear!" the children chorus in their growling accents. Judging by their smiles, I doubt they plan to pay any attention whatsoever. Which . . . well, honestly, makes me glad.

"All right, time to settle down then," I tell them. They are quick to obey, and I tuck the three boys in on one side of the massive bed, allowing Sis to curl up beside me on the other. I'm right on the edge myself, and one small kick will send me tumbling. But I don't mind.

"*Mar?*" Sis says, stroking my cheek with her dainty hand. "You tell story, *Mar?*"

"Yes!" The three boys echo her request. "Give us story, *Mar!* Story!"

"A story, mmm?" I purse my lips, considering. I used to tell Oscar stories when he was small like this. Stories of danger and darkness and daring deeds. It's been a long time since I thought of those days, thought of those tales. I'd practically forgotten.

Now, as the four children gaze at me with such hopeful expectation, memory stirs. "Once upon a time," I say softly, musingly, "there was a sister and her little brother."

"My brothers all big," Sis says, her lip sticking out in a pout.

"Yeah," her brothers agree. "We all big."

"Well, this brother was little." I give them all a stern look. "Hush, or I won't tell any more. As I said, there was a sister and her little brother, and he was very brave. As long as they could be together, they were both very brave, no matter what happened. One day, their mother asked them to venture into the dark, dark forest . . ."

I let the story spin out from inside me. I feel my way along, remembering each part as I go. The children venture into the forest, searching for something. What is it? A cure, that's right. A cure for their father, who is terribly sick. Mother stays behind to tend him, but the children know it's their responsibility to fix what is broken in him. So they venture deeper and deeper, encountering numerous perils along the way.

One by one, the troll children nod off, lulled by the sound of my voice. I keep on telling my tale until the air around me is filled with gentle snores. Then I close my eyes and nestle into my pillow, Sis's head tucked under my chin. Lying there in the darkness, I see Oscar's face once more; Oscar as I used to know him, pretty and pale and cherub cheeked.

"Will they ever find it, Clara? Will they ever find the cure for their father's sickness?"

"Hush. You don't want me to spoil the story, do you?"

And I'd tell on. Layer after layer of adventure until he fell asleep. The next night, I'd start over from the beginning, creating new perils for the children to encounter, so that the story never truly ended. Sometimes Oscar would beg me to skip to the end, to tell him how it all would turn out. But I put him off each time, because . . . because . . .

Because the truth was, I didn't know.

I still don't know.

He really loves you.

He really loves you.

You know, he really loves you.

I squeeze my eyes tight, clench my jaw. But I can't close my ears, can't silence that voice in my head. It sounds more familiar than ever now. A voice I know better than my own. Is it a memory? Are Princess Estrilde's suppressions breaking down at last? Or is this something I suppressed myself, long ago?

I open my eyes again. The light of the overhead lanterns is dim, but through tear-beaded lashes I can just see the outline of the sleeping troll children. How peaceful they look. Sis snores the loudest of the bunch, her skinny arm thrown across her face. I idly brush a strand of pale hair back from an alabaster brow. Mama used to sit with us like this. She'd come into our room, perch on the edge of our bed, and hold me and Oscar in her arms, one on each side of her, pressed in close. She'd croon and stroke our hair, a warm, comforting presence. How I loved those times! How I long for them even now . . .

My gut turns over, burning with bile. I gasp and sit upright, clutching my midsection. What is wrong with me?

Hastily I crawl out from under the blankets, rush to the washbasin, and dry heave. Nothing comes up. Sweat beads my brow. I push hair out of my face and look around for something to drink. But the trolls have drunk it all. Even the washbasin pitcher is empty.

I rub my arms, trying to rub warmth back into my body. I should get back into bed. Curl up next to Sis, tuck close to her for warmth. Try to sleep.

Instead, barefoot and trembling, clad only in my nightgown, I cross the room to my door and try the latch. I'm not sure why I half expect it to be locked . . . but no! The latch gives at my touch, and I step out into the hall beyond.

The shadows are darker, the twilight deeper than usual. There are no lanterns lit anywhere nearby. I shiver and rub my arms. I need water, but where can I go to find it? I'm afraid to call out, afraid of who might answer in a place like this. Maybe terrifying Captain Khas. Maybe . . . something worse . . .

Like a lost soul, I wander the passages. I take turns at random, or so I think, only to discover myself unexpectedly at the base of the stairway leading up to the library doors. There I pause, a wry smile pulling at my mouth. So I *have* learned my way around after all. Or maybe not. Maybe some force within the library reaches shadowy fingers through the twists and turns of Vespre Palace to pluck at my brain, to draw me to itself.

My throat tightens, and my lips dry and crack. I try to moisten them, try to swallow. I should go back. I should return to my room, climb back into bed with all those snoring children, and go to sleep. I shouldn't let myself be manipulated by the unseen forces of this world. I know better than this.

But somehow . . . it doesn't matter. There are some things I simply cannot resist.

A growl rumbling in my chest, I lift the skirt of my nightgown and all but race up the stairs. By the time I reach the top, my heart is pounding, my breath coming in short gasps. I press on even so, putting my shoulder against the huge door and pushing it open just enough to let me slip inside.

Immediately, I know I'm not alone. Down the line of desks, a single lantern burns, creating a little bubble of light. I can't see who sits at the cubicle, not from this angle.

I hesitate. What am I doing here? If someone asks me, what excuse can I offer?

Before I can come up with an answer, a scaly head emerges from the cubicle and fixes me with a goggle-eyed stare. *"Meeep!"* it says. A most un-draconian sound if you ask me. It flares its crest irritably and repeats, *"Meep! Meep meep!"*

"Right, all right, what's all this racket about?" a sharp voice mutters. The next moment, a chair slides back from the cubicle, and Nelle's white head comes into sight. She holds a quill in one hand, her fingers stained with ink. Strands of hair escape her topknot to frame her face. "Well!" she says, tilting her head like a little bird. "If it ain't Miss Darlington. You look quite ghostly standing there in your nightie. Trying to give us hard-working librarian folk a fright?"

"Oh! No, indeed," I gasp, clutching fistfuls of my nightgown and staring down at my bare feet. "I'm sorry, Mistress Silveri, I . . . I . . ." Now would be a really good time to discover an excuse for my being here. Nothing comes to mind.

I feel Nelle's knowing gaze on me. When I dare glance up at her again, her mouth twists to one side.

Abruptly she stands, steps around her wriggling wyvern, and goes to the next cubicle over. A loud scraping of wood on stone echoes all the way to the dome overhead as she drags a chair back to her cubicle and sets it close to her own. She takes her seat again and turns her gaze back to me. "Well, girl? You've got a talkin' look about you. Might as well come and get whatever it is off your chest."

I hesitate only a moment. Then, feeling oddly grateful, I sit primly in the uncomfortable desk chair and fold my hands in my lap. The wyvern gives me another resentful stare and hisses, rattling its forked tongue at me. "None of that now!" Nelle says, shoving it firmly underneath her desk with one foot. "Sorry. The old worm don't take too kindly to new folks. He'll get used to you eventually." She leans back in her chair, sticking her legs out and crossing them at the ankle. "Well then? What's on your mind? Tell old Nelle all about it."

I let out a long, long breath. Where in the world should I begin? My thoughts are such a tangle, I don't know where one ends and another begins.

Ultimately, I opt for bluntness. "The Prince says I created a Noswraith."

Nelle doesn't look surprised. "Yup." She nods slowly, her expression mild. "Most of 'em have. The librarians brought here, I mean. My boy and I, we're some of the few who ain't. But my husband did."

"Yes. The Thorn Maiden." I recall with a shudder that creeping, slithering *thing* I'd felt in the first vault down below. "He must have been very powerful. Your husband."

"Yup." Nelle twiddles her quill pen around in her fingers, watching the end twirl. "Soran was a Miphato. Back before he became a librarian, that is. Some would say he was the most powerful Miphato of the age." She speaks the words without pride, simply stating a fact. "Didn't do him much good. But he got better. Greatest of the age or otherwise, he was a good husband and a good father, which mattered more in the end."

She turns to her desk where a book lies open, the ink on the pages still shiny and wet by the light of her candle. "I can hear you thinking another question, girl. Out with it. I'm in an answering frame of mind, and I might not be tomorrow, so you'd best ask while you can."

I drop my gaze. "It's just . . . if he . . . if your husband created a Noswraith . . . I just don't understand how anyone *good* can do something like that."

"Well, he weren't so very good at the time he did it, was he?" Nelle chuckles darkly and pops her quill into an open inkwell. The silver nib clatters against the frame. She picks up a jar of pounce and deftly sprinkles the powder over the wet ink to dry it swiftly. Then she leans back in her chair. Her narrow little body creaks and groans as she fixes those vivid blue eyes of hers on me. "He had a darkness in him. Always did. And when he was young, it got out in the form of the Thorn Maiden. He spent the rest of his life fighting that part of himself which he had unleashed. But, as a result of that fight, the goodness in him grew stronger and stronger." The old librarian smiles softly. "He was the best man I've ever known."

How is it possible? How can the man she describes and the creator of that monster I'd glimpsed down below be one and the same? "I don't . . ." My voice trails off.

"Speak up, girl. Might as well say it as not."

I swallow painfully. "I don't *remember*. Making one. A Noswraith. I don't see how I could have!"

"Oh, that's easily explained." Nelle shrugs. "Most of you young'uns are so bursting with uncontrolled power when you're first brought into Eledria, the safest thing to do is to remove all memory of that power and what you've done with it. T'was the same for Andreas and Vervain when they were brought in. As their skills developed, as they learned control, their memories were allowed to return."

I think of Vervain—her strange, solemn, sunken face underlit by my fallen lantern—her voice hollow and full of so much pain, so much rage. In her case, it might have been best *not* to let her memories return.

"Do you know?" I ask suddenly, looking up and catching Nelle's studying eye. "Do you know what I did? How I made the Noswraith?"

"I know some of the story, yes. We all do." Nelle adjusts her seat, looking momentarily uncomfortable. But she doesn't break my gaze. "We've known about you for some time now. My husband was quite keen on getting you over here years ago. But the Prince wouldn't have it. Not until after . . . after Soran . . . Well, when our ranks were so badly reduced, it didn't take a lot to persuade the Prince that we needed extra help. And after what you did, none of us doubted you've got the power in you."

"What I did?" My stomach clenches tight. "You're not going to tell me, are you."

Nelle considers for a long, silent moment. Finally, she says, "It'll come back to you. In time. Meanwhile, don't think it'll do much good for me to try to tell you. You won't want to believe me anyway."

"Do you know who I killed?"

At this, Nelle grunts and shakes her head. "Best not to look at it that way, girl. After all, you didn't *intend* to kill anyone."

But I *did* kill. I have death on my hands. I can see it in her eyes. Even if I can't quite believe it. "How do you know?" I whisper, my voice small and tight. "How do you know I didn't intend it?"

"I don't. Not really." Nelle folds her arms across her flat bosom and sighs. "What I do know is that each of us has darkness in our hearts. I ain't one to judge."

Not exactly comforting. Then again, Nelle isn't exactly the comforting type. But she's honest, I'll give her that.

I look down at my hands. Hands which, somehow, have worked destruction on a level I can't even fathom. Hands that had the power to create horrors, to bring about death. I can hardly believe it.

"Do you know why the Prince hates me?" I blurt the question

before I can stop myself.

"*Hates* you? Hates *you?*" To my great surprise, Nelle tosses back her head and barks a laugh. Quickly she pulls herself together again and meets my confused gaze. "Oh, child, child, it's not *you* the Prince hates."

I frown. "But . . . but sometimes . . . the way he looks at me . . ."

"No, no." Nelle shakes her head slowly, her mouth twisted in a smile that's only just shy of a grimace. "It's *himself* he hates. When he looks at you, he sees all over again his greatest failure. It was *his* job to protect Eledria, to protect the worlds. And he did, ultimately. But not before he lost *her.*"

"Who?" I lean forward in my chair, desperate and frightened, uncertain I want an answer but knowing I can't go on a second longer without getting one. "Please, Mistress Silveri, *please* tell me. I've got to know. Who was killed by the Noswraith I made? Who was it?"

Her brow puckers and her eyes gleam in the candlelight, bright with sorrow. For a moment I fear she won't answer; I fear she will simply send me away. But at last, she sighs.

"Dasyra." The name falls from her lips, heavy as a stone. "Queen Dasyra of Aurelis. His mother."

THE PRINCE

I TWIRL MY MOTHER'S QUILL AROUND IN MY FINGERS, watching how it catches the light from my candle.

How many times had I sat and watched her scratch out magical words and spells with this same quill? Shaping letters, capturing ideas. Drawing all that power straight from the *quinsatra* into this world and binding it with ink on paper. She'd taught me to write using this quill, slowly coaching me to craft the delicate figures that form words and worlds, create realities.

She was strong. So much stronger than most people realized. A human woman, alone in the courts of Eledria. One would have thought her easy prey . . . and one would have been grossly mistaken. She was no one's prey, but a warrior in her own way. A woman of gentle and nurturing heart, yet fearless in the face of peril and champion of all she loved. She was a true queen.

Until I found her body. Broken. Battered almost beyond recognition. Lying in a heap of blood and bone in the middle of Aurelis Library.

I close my eyes. But that's no good. For now I see, not Queen Dasyra—but *her*. The girl, the librarian.

My mother's killer.

I'd already fought a great battle that night, binding the newly-spawned Noswraith. It was a temporary binding at best, for I did not possess its name. But it would hold. For the time being, it would hold.

Now I must concentrate my efforts on finding its source. On hunting down and dealing with the human mage who dared break the Pledge and bring such a being into existence.

Together with my father and my cousin, Estrilde, I journeyed across the worlds, breaking through boundaries, pursuing that vibrating thread of magic which connected the Noswraith to its source. That is how I came to that dark, shadowed street. That ramshackle townhouse, so unobtrusively tucked away among hundreds more of its kind. The air positively reeked of despair. I'd never seen a place I hated so.

Brandishing my sword in one hand, a swell of deadly magic burning in the palm of the other, I burst through that front door.

And she was the first thing I saw. Kneeling before a fire, holding a poker, trying to stoke the few small coals into life.

She leapt to her feet when the door broke into splintering piece. Whirling, eyes widening, she stared up at me in terror as I strode inside. How great and shining and awful I must have been in that small, dirty, altogether mortal space. But she did not shrink away. She did not throw up her hands or duck for cover. No, for even as the two figures beside her—a boy and a man, both rail-thin and pale—collapsed on their knees, she planted herself in front of them, holding out her poker like a weapon.

"Who are you?" she cried, her eyes flashing. "Get out of this house!"

The sound of her voice—the sight of her face—and something struck me. A blow to the heart. Not a physical blow. No . . . it was like my soul was suddenly pierced by a poison-tipped arrow. But this poison sent a jolt of pure ecstasy racing through my blood.

I staggered back, clutching my chest, shocked at first. And then appalled. Raising my eyes, I looked at her again. In that moment, I recognized what she was. The power fairly sizzled in her veins, in her being. I'd just faced that same power in the form of the hideous wraith. I knew enough to recognize it, to know I gazed upon its maker. Darkness swirled in the ether around her. Potent, life-creating darkness. Horror ready to manifest.

I knew what she was. I knew what she'd done.

And yet . . . my heart . . .

Hatred surged in my being. With a roar, I crossed that room, knocked the poker from her hand, and grabbed her arm. When I wrenched her to her knees, the boy screamed and the man shouted.

Neither of them moved to interfere, only retreated deeper into the shadows. While she stared up at me, her face so pale, her eyes riven with fear.

A terrible urge came over me then. The urge to . . . to stroke her soft cheek. To promise her I wouldn't harm her, wouldn't let any harm come to her. To . . . to . . .

Lodírhal stepped through the open door behind me. Great and golden, his soul ablaze with fury beyond anything this world had ever seen. He pointed his sword at the girl in my grasp. "Is this the mage?" he demanded.

"Yes," I replied. "I believe it is."

But my hand, gripping her wrist, began to tremble. I looked into her face again, only to find her lips moving, struggling to form words. "Please," she whispered. "Please, whoever you are, whatever you want . . . do not hurt my brother."

Nothing for herself. Just for him. Just for that boy, cowering in the corner, too frightened to lift a finger in her defense. I looked at him then, really looked for the first time. Magic surrounded him as well. But not the same. Whatever else he might be, he was not the source of the Noswraith.

I turned my attention back to the girl. Tears streaked her cheeks, but she met my gaze without flinching. "Please," she repeated, "he's done nothing. Please."

My lips curled in a snarl. "I'd worry more about your own life, Pledge-breaker."

Even as the words crossed my lips, I hated myself. Hated that I should speak to her thus, hated that I should handle her so harshly. Everything in me longed to stop her tears, to ease her terror. To take her in my arms and . . .

Growling, I hauled her to her feet, dragged her through the door. Out into the street where my father waited, sword drawn.

I open my eyes. Return to my private office, my desk and mounds of books and papers. The tall shelves, the arched windows overlooking the city below. And that quill. Still held in my fingers, red plume catching the candlelight. That quill which had been gripped in my mother's hand when she fell victim to the Noswraith.

The Noswraith that girl brought into being.

How can someone be both guilty and innocent all at the same time? It doesn't make sense. But then, Mother would have told me I'm thinking too much like a fae, everything black and white. Humans, she would argue, exist more in shades of gray.

I turn the quill over. Then, gently, I rest it in a little box on a bed of silk. Dropping the lid, I step away from the desk, go stand at the window instead. Gaze out across the rooftops of my city.

"I won't fall prey to this sickness," I whisper. One hand rests against my heart. It throbs a strange rhythm in my breast. I feel again that wound—that bolt I'd experienced at first sight of her face. It's never recovered. I'm not sure it ever will. I grimace, jaw grinding. "I am master of myself. And what is she but a servant? A human, an Obligate. Nothing."

I am silent for a long moment. Somewhere far away the palace bells toll out the lateness of the hour. The skies over Vespre turn, but the twilight never lifts. Shadows keep the city captive in their perpetual gloom.

"Damn," I whisper. Then I pound a fist against the stone window frame. "I shall overcome this. Gods damn me, I shall!"

CLARA

29

Dasyra.

I can't get the name out of my head.

When I finally return to my room and crawl into bed among the sleeping lumps of troll children, I lie awake for a long, long time. Just thinking that name. Over and over again.

Dasyra.

Dasyra.

Dasyra.

This explains everything. No wonder Lodírhal hates me so. I'm responsible for the death of his Fatebound wife and, therefore, indirectly responsible for his death as well.

This also explains the Prince's hatred. Because, despite what Nelle might say, I'm sure he *does* hate me. He blames me for the death of his mother. When he looks at me, he sees a murderer. An inadvertent murderer, perhaps, but . . .

I close my eyes tight. But I can't stop the thoughts careening inside my head. I created a Noswraith. I killed someone. Possibly many someones; who knows how many suffered for my mistake? Thus I was given fifteen years of Obligated service in Eledria.

I frown. Then I sit upright in bed, clutching the blankets hard. Sis's bony little knee jabs into my thigh, and I gently shift away from her, then slide out of bed and pace to the window. Pulling back the curtain, I gaze out on the city below, but I scarcely see it. My brain is too caught up in turmoil.

Fifteen years.

Fifteen years.

Why is my sentence so short? Some Obligates at Aurelis are serving sentences twice and three times as long, and none of them were Noswraith-creators. Why isn't my sentence longer? I ought to be serving fifty years for my crime, or more.

Something is still missing. A part of this story I don't yet understand.

Eventually fatigue overwhelms me. I return to my bed, crawl back in beside Sis, and drift into a dreamless doze. I seem to still be looking at my room through half-closed eyes, my gaze slowly wandering over the different articles of furniture. There's a strange, shadowy haze over everything, a moving sort of shadow, full of energy, like writhing smoke.

And standing in the corner . . .

By the wardrobe . . .

Just beyond my range of vision . . .

He really loves you, you know.

I open my lips, try to speak. But I'm asleep, and no sound will come. So I simply will the words out from my heart.

"Is that you?"

Yes.

"What are you doing here?"

Waiting for you.

"Why?"

Because you need to know. You need to understand.

The shadow shifts. Something is there, something small, something dark.

"Come out," I say. "Come out where I can see you."

A figure steps out from the shadow. Shriveled. Hunch-shouldered. Head bowed.

"Let me see your face," I say.

The head begins to lift, slowly. Hair falls back, and—

"What is the meaning of this?"

The angry shriek bursts through my brain, startling me awake. I sit bolt upright in bed, heart thudding, and the world around me is full of movement and noise and chaos.

"*Hartorka shar!*" A magnificent pale figure leaps onto my bed and catches a troll boy by his foot. She hurls him to the floor before lunging at the next one, who is just quick enough to avoid her grasp. He springs for one of the bedposts, much nimbler than one might expect for such a solid, rocky little thing, and clambers up like a nimble little squirrel.

"*Kor kor kor!*" My vision clears, and I recognize Lir at last as she whirls about and catches Sis by the hair on top of her head. The troll girl shrieks and twists, kicking, clawing, teeth gnashing. Her three brothers cry out and throw themselves at Lir, the one springing from the bedpost and landing on her back, the others wrapping their entire bodies around her legs. Lir doesn't seem to notice any of them, but springs from the bed and, dragging troll children in her wake, carries the struggling Sis toward the door.

"Stop it!" I push back the covers and all but fall from the bed. Righting myself quickly, I toss hair out of my face and scream, "Stop it at once!"

Lir freezes. She holds Sis a good foot above the ground, and the troll girl twists and flails, hissing like an angry cat. "Put her down!" I growl.

"Mistress!" Lir's eyes widen, and she shakes her head vigorously. "They are *pests*. They *cannot* be here."

"I don't care!" I'm angry now, angrier than I remember being in a long, long while. I cross my arms over my breast and hold Lir's rebellious gaze hard. "I don't care what you call them or what the Prince says or any of it! I *want* them here. Do you understand?"

One by one the troll boys let go of Lir. Calx drops from her back, Har and Dig release her legs, and all three scamper to me, clinging to my nightgown, hiding their bulky bodies behind me. Lir looks mutinous, her jaw set, her fist clenched. But she sets Sis back down on her feet. The little girl kicks her shins, and Lir doubles over, barking, *"Guthakug!"* I don't have to know the language to recognize an expletive when I hear one. Her hand lashes out, catching hold of Sis's hair again before the girl can scamper out of reach. She picks the child right up off the ground again, holding her at arm's length.

"It's not up to me, Mistress," she says, giving the girl a vicious shake. "It's the Prince's orders. It's him you've got to convince."

"The Prince ordered you to serve me, didn't he?"

"Well, yes—"

"And I'm ordering you to put that child down. What's more, I want you to bring breakfast. For all of them. Do you hear me? *All of them.*"

Lir's brow knots furiously. "The Prince won't like it."

"That's my business, not yours."

We stand facing one another for a long moment, fighting a silent battle with our eyes. Finally, Lir opens her hand and lets Sis drop to the floor. With a squeak, Sis hurtles to me, nearly knocking me from my feet as she flings her arms around my knees. Lir turns on her heel and stomps to the door, banging it open and shut again in her wake. Presumably gone to fetch breakfast.

A flood of exhilaration rushes through me. I've never felt more powerful, more in charge in all my life! I look down at the smiling troll children, who immediately begin their chorus of, *"Mar! Mar!*

Mar!" all over again.

"That's quite enough of that," I say in my firmest mothering voice. "If you're going to stay, you must learn to behave with proper decorum. And baths! You're going to have to learn about baths. But not"—I add, as bells ring out in the distance, five tolls echoing along the stone passages—"not just yet. For now, I want you to stay put in this room. Try not to cause too much mischief, and *don't* attract the Prince's attention. Not until I've had a chance to speak to him."

The children chorus a noisy agreement as I pry myself free of their arms, grab my old work gown, and slip into the bathroom for a little privacy as I prepare for the day. They stay just on the other side of the door, babbling and occasionally trying the latch. I stand in front of the mirror, taking several long breaths. Unexpectedly becoming mother to four troll children might be a bit more than I'm prepared to handle, but . . . but at least it's something I can *do*. Something good, something kind, something right.

Something that might make up for some of my sins.

I dress quickly, braid my hair, and wrap it in a bun at the nape of my neck. Despite my restless night, I feel strangely invigorated. At least now I know why I've been Obligated, and that knowledge is power in itself. I'm not entirely certain how I'll use that power, but I'll hold onto it, nonetheless. I finish pinning up the last few strands of my hair, then give myself a firm smile in the mirror. I'll face whatever the day has to offer, whether it's more terrifying library tasks, more of the Prince's hot-and-cold treatment, more revelations of my own history . . . whatever. I'll face it all. And I'll triumph. Seven gods help me.

A sudden awareness of quiet pricks at my senses. Frowning, I step to the bathroom door, open it a crack and peek out into my room. It's empty. The children are gone.

"Calx? Har, Dig? Sis?" I peek under the bed, into the wardrobe. I even return to the bathroom and check the enormous bathtub and behind the mirror. Nothing. They've vanished like a dream.

I stand in the middle of the room, looking around at the large empty space. All of that determined enthusiasm I'd felt moments ago seems to have melted away. But really, what did I expect? That four busy younglings would stay cooped up in my room all day long? That's not a life. They would be better off returning to the city and their own kind. It's one thing for me to make bold speeches to Lir. But the truth is, I'm not equipped to care for four children of a species I know next to nothing about.

Lir has not returned with breakfast yet. I don't want to wait around, so I leave the room, shutting the door behind me. No escort awaits me this morning, but I retrace my steps of last night and make my way back to the library on my own. Just as I push open the heavy doors and step through, Mixael comes barreling past at a quick pace.

"Watch-ho!" he yelps when I nearly collide with him and jumps back several paces. Three books fall from the stack he's carrying and land with dull thuds on the floor.

"Oh, I'm so sorry!" I exclaim and bend to pick the books up.

None of them simmer with life or evil energy, so I guess they aren't Noswraith bindings. "Busy day?" I ask, eyeing Mixael's armload.

"Always!" he responds with a grin. "Go ahead and pop those back on top, why don't you?"

"I don't mind carrying them for you."

"Well, in that case, fall in step, Miss Darlington! I can use the extra hands this morning."

I obey, matching Mixael's easy stride as he makes his way to the nearest of the book lifts Nelle pointed out to me on my first day. As we go, I cast a glance back toward the desk where I've worked these last two mornings. There's no sign of the Prince.

"The Prince won't be in today."

I meet Mixael's gaze, and he smiles at me from behind his stack. "He sent word earlier, claims he's *otherwise engaged,* whatever that means. You can work with me instead today, learn what you can from my sage wisdom." He waggles his eyebrows.

"Sage, eh?" I smile, and my heavy heart lightens. "And just how sagely are you, Mister Silveri?"

"Oh, the sageliest, to be sure," he replies and places his stack of books in the already-full book lift. "Though, to be honest, our work today will be of a rather un-sagely nature. We're cataloguing. All the books you see before you need to be returned to their proper places."

I glance at the lift, which contains a good twelve or more precarious stacks of books, all different shapes and sizes. None of them *feel* possessed, but there's an awful lot of power condensed into this small space. "I'm happy to help," I say. "I need to learn where everything goes, after all." Honestly, compared to the last two days, cataloguing books sounds like a welcome break.

"Excellent." Mixael waves one arm. "Hop on board. It'll be a quicker ride and save you some knee-aching stairs."

My eyes widen. Nelle was absolutely clear that the book lifts were *not* for riding. Besides, I don't particularly like the idea of sitting in that little cage suspended over the vast drop down the citadel center. "Is it strong enough to bear my weight?" I ask, taking a half-step back.

Mixael's grin widens. "A little bird like you doesn't come *close* to the poundage of books Andreas likes to load into the lifts! It'll be fine; you can trust me."

I pinch my dry lips together. But I don't want Mixael to think me timid. So with a quick nod I climb into the lift. It lurches unsettlingly beneath me, and I quickly take a seat among the books. Here, with the stacks surrounding me, I'm much more aware of the power and magic simmering within these volumes. There's such force, such *life*. Human magic.

Mixael turns a crank, and the lift begins to descend in short, jerking intervals. I choke back a little scream and fight not to close my eyes. Though I can't see over the edge, I feel the enormity of the drop beneath me. Oh, why in the seven gods' names didn't I listen to Nelle?

The ride is ultimately uneventful, however, and I reach the third floor in one piece. Hastily, I scramble out of the lift, then look back up to the first floor. Mixael's face peers down at me over the rail. "You all right, Miss Darlington?"

"Yes! I'm all right!" I call back, hoping he can't hear the quaver in my voice.

"Great! Be down in a flash."

To my horror, Mixael swings suddenly into full view, gripping the lift cables in his hands, hanging out over that terrible drop. With absolutely no protection between him and a deadly fall, he slides down, hand over hand. Before I can catch my breath, he reaches the top of the book-lift cage, hitting the bars with a clatter.

The next moment, he scrambles over the side of the lift and over the rail onto the third floor beside me. One look at my shocked face, and he laughs. "Remember, I grew up in this place," he says with a wink. "I know all the tricks of the trade!"

We set to work loading the books from the lift onto a trolley, then I spend a relatively enjoyable few hours trailing after Mixael while he shows me where each volume belongs. Our work concentrates primarily on the second and third floors, and I can almost imagine I'm back in Aurelis Library, working with books that won't actively try to kill me should I ever let my guard down. Now and then I feel the weight and pressure of the Noswraiths rising from the deeper levels, but a joke or a laugh from Mixael quickly dispels even that. He never once seems bothered by his proximity to the worst horrors humanity has ever invented. His ease gives me confidence, and for a little while I can almost forget where I am . . . and what I've done to bring myself here.

Nelle finds us at twelve bells and makes us break for lunch. Mixael and I join her and Andreas on the first floor to feast on bread and cheese and some salty cold meat that I don't recognize. Nelle launches into haranguing Mixael about using the book lifts as his own personal elevator, and he takes her scolding with good grace, offering no more than a few teasing remarks in response. He does not, I notice, repent of his wickedness. Neither does he promise to mend his ways.

Eventually Nelle gives up and asks Andreas after his research. Andreas merely blinks dreamily at her around his mouthful before offering, "The Learned of Trotholeus did badly misconstrue the effects of *dulderium* on the subconscious will."

We all stare at him, letting this baffling revelation echo in our ears.

"Anyway!" Mixael says, turning to Nelle. "How is that binding of yours coming along this morning, Mother dearest? Have you got old Bloody Hands back under control?"

The rest of the meal passes enjoyably enough. As we finish up, Nelle mentions to Mixael that she noticed signs of bookwyrms on the sixth floor, and will he look into it? He agrees and passes me off to Andreas, saying I'd probably best spend a few more hours drilling Noswraith names. Andreas gives me a doleful look, no doubt reluctant to give up his afternoon with the Learned of Trotholeus. But he doesn't complain.

So my day passes. I work with Andreas, pleased to discover how many Noswraith names and titles I remember from our last session. After a while, Nelle steals me away to show me the records she keeps of which Noswraiths have recently been rebound, which are likely to need rebinding soon, and so on. When that lesson ends, I'm handed off to Mixael again for a few more trips up and down the book lift.

Not once do I so much as glimpse Vervain. At one point I ask Nelle where the other librarian is.

"Oh, she's resting," Nelle answers easily. "She's on overnight shift tonight and needs to sleep. Not that there's any actual *night* here in Vespre, of course," she adds with a chuckle. "But we do have darker hours, and in those hours, the Noswraiths are always stirring. It's best to keep someone on hand, just in case. Tomorrow night, Mixael is on task, and I believe the Prince intends for you to accompany him on his rounds."

"Oh?" My heart shudders at the thought. But of course, I'll have to learn all of this eventually. Sooner rather than later if I'm to survive in Vespre.

Eventually my workday draws to a close, and Nelle dismisses me. I rise from crouching on the floor to shelf a row of somewhat battered old histories, and gingerly stretch my aching back. Yet I find myself strangely reluctant to go. While working in company with the other librarians, I've been able to keep my thoughts firmly in check, to focus only on the needs of the moment. Now, with another evening alone looming before me, I'll have to face my own thoughts again. Face the revelations of yesterday.

I grimace while climbing the spiral stair, then make my way to the exit. Pausing in the doorway, I look back into the library. Nelle bends over her desk, scribbling away at something. Mixael is out of sight, but I can hear his cheerful whistling rising from a floor or two below. Andreas is at a table, shifting through a stack of loose-leaf papers, his brow furrowed, his spectacles pushed up on his forehead. Apparently, none of them are finished for the day yet.

I sigh and step through the doors, which close heavily behind me. The stairway is gloomy, with few lanterns lit at this hour. I wish Lir would come to escort me again. But she's probably still angry at me about this morning. Setting my chin, I descend the stair alone and make my way back through the palace.

Am I wrong, or is there a strange atmosphere in the air this evening? Ordinarily it's a relief to leave the library behind and the constant pressing, overwhelming presence of the Noswraiths that weighs so heavily on the soul. Now it feels as though some of that pressure has followed me. As if the Noswraiths themselves have caught hold of my spirit and somehow *ridden* me out of their prison, out into these open passages. I can almost imagine them flitting as half-seen shadows, escaping through the open windows, making their way down to the lower city, there to prey upon the dreams of the city's denizens.

But that's ridiculous. The Noswraiths are all bound. Everyone is fine. Safe. The Prince has seen to that. The Prince and his librarians.

Of whom I am now one. Or *almost* one.

It's funny how drastically things can change in such a short amount of time. Just days ago I would have balked at the idea of actually *wanting* to become a Vespre Librarian. Now I feel a swelling of pride at the prospect. This, after all, is good work. Noble work.

You were born to be a warrior.

Well, that might be an exaggeration. I'm still just little Clara Darlington after all. Meek and well-mannered and soft-spoken. But . . . maybe I could learn . . .

I reach my room and step inside, half hoping to be met by a chorus of small growly voices and enthusiastically rough hugs. There's only silence. The lanterns suspended from the stalactites overhead gleam on the tray of still-steaming food left on the table. Lir has come and gone but didn't care to stay and visit with me.

I eat a lonely meal. Then, with nothing else to do, I change into my nightgown, sit at the vanity mirror, let down my hair, and begin to brush it. The long rhythmic strokes are soothing, and I take care to count them slowly, all the way to a hundred. I try not to think the many pressing thoughts trying to break through to the forefront of my mind.

But as I count brushstrokes, as I fall into the rhythmic motion, thoughts slip back in anyway.

One, two, three . . .

Dasyra . . .

Twenty-five, twenty-six, twenty-seven . . .

Noswraith . . .

Forty-nine, fifty, fifty-one . . .

Creator . . .

Death . . . death . . . death—

The world erupts in a cacophonous clamor of bells.

A jolt of terror shoots through my veins. These aren't the bells I've become used to, announcing each hour. This is something dire. An alarm. An alarm for what?

I don't have to guess. Not here. Not in the Doomed City.

I stand, drop my brush on the vanity, and turn in place. Should I dress? Of course I should. I can't face whatever is about to happen clad only in my nightie! But the pounding bells seem to freeze me in place. I cover my ears, close my eyes, try to scream, try to drown out the sound.

There's a pounding at my door. I don't know how I hear it over the bells, but I fixate on that sound as if it's a lifeline thrown to me in the midst of a storm-tossed sea. Whimpering, I stagger to the door, grip the latch, and fling it open.

The Prince is there. Staring down at me.

Suddenly the noise and mayhem retreats, giving way to a roar of blood throbbing in my temples. I'm painfully aware that I'm wearing only my nightdress. I open my mouth, not sure what I want to say, not sure that my voice will even be heard above the thundering bells.

Before any words come, the Prince reaches out and grasps my hand. A bolt of lightning shoots up my arm and explodes in my chest. I gasp for breath, my gaze caught and held by his.

"Quick, Darling," he says. How strangely calm and level his voice is, yet somehow audible over the deafening bells. "A Noswraith has broken loose from the vaults. We need you."

30

A NOSWRAITH. BROKEN LOOSE.

I can't seem to make my brain grasp this information. I'm simply in motion . . . motion without purpose, pulled along by the greater forces of this world. Or at least by one powerful force embodied in the Prince, who still grips my hand as he drags me along after him.

The bells continue ringing. My feet seem to be moving in time with each *clang, clang, clang.* And as I go, the pounding in my head becomes words:

Doomed, doomed, doomed.

You are doomed.

The city is doomed.

Seven gods above, I am not prepared for this! Whatever Noswraith has slipped its bindings, it's got to be something much greater than the Melted Man. No, this alarm would not be sounded for a lesser Noswraith. This is something big. Something terrible. Something like . . .

Is this *mine*?

I stagger. The Prince's grip on my hand tightens. He looks back at me, his strange violet eyes flashing in the lantern light. "Come, Darling!" he growls and yanks me after him, up the stairs to the library doors, which stand wide open.

We rush in, and I see Nelle, Mixael, and Andreas congregating, their arms full of lanterns, quills, books. But I scarcely glance at them before my gaze is drawn elsewhere . . . up . . . to a great, gaping hole in the skylight.

"Oh," I whimper. My whole body seems to go slack. "Oh, no."

"Nelle!" the Prince barks.

Immediately his senior librarian darts up to him, saluting smartly. In that moment she doesn't look as old or bent as usual. It's as though in her fear, she's forgotten her age and allowed some of her youth and vigor to seep back into her limbs. She looks strong, wiry, and grimly determined.

"It's from the vaults, Prince!" she says, her voice trembling only slightly. "The Hungry Mother."

My stomach plunges. It's *not* my Noswraith. Relief floods my veins, and I'm able to take my first long breath in a while. That relief is short-lived, however, as I realize: *Vervain!* Vervain was supposed to bind the Hungry Mother. Vervain, who was acting so strangely, and . . .

"Where is Vervain?" the Prince's voice breaks through the throbbing fear in my head, echoing my own thoughts.

"I saw her," Mixael volunteers. "There was a rush from below, and the dome broke. Soon after, I saw Vervain race up the stairs. She was out the door like a flash, and I'm fairly certain she had a book and quill with her. I think she was going after it."

"By herself?" Nelle cries in dismay.

Before Mixael can respond, the Prince interrupts. "There's no time to worry about her. We must work together." His voice is firm, confident. In that moment, I don't believe he feels any fear. I latch hold of his courage like a shield against my own calamitous fear. "We need to pair up. Nelle, you take Andreas and make for Jorlok Sector. Mixael, you have Darling. Don't let her out of your sight. I want you to cut through Tuvortoj District. None of you are to face the Hungry Mother alone, am I understood?"

"Yes, Prince!" the other three answer in unison. I nod mutely.

"I, meanwhile, will search for Vervain," he continues. "She mustn't be alone out there either, and she's our best chance at getting this thing rebound without incident. Does everyone have a quill and book?"

"I don't," I say softly, not sure I'll even be heard. But Mixael leaps into action and soon provides me with both. I grip them hard, the book pressed to my chest, the pen in my hand. They feel like such flimsy weapons, but they're all I have.

"Now remember," the Prince says, "to catch the Hungry Mother, you don't need a *complete* binding. You simply need a basic bond and then seal it with her name. I can create a stronger, more permanent binding once she's encased, but I don't want any of you trying something beyond your skill."

His gaze fixes on me. I nod. My mouth is dry, my tongue cleaving to the roof of my mouth.

"Stay alert," the Prince says, addressing the others now. "Stay awake. Do *not* let her draw you into the Nightmare. Follow the signs of her presence, but whatever you do, *stay on this side of reality.*"

"Don't worry, Prince," Mixael says, his voice bright and cheerful as ever. He steps to my side and loops an arm around my shoulders. "I'll watch after the new girl."

The Prince's gaze slides from Mixael to me, pinning me in place. "Remember, Darling: you are not, under *any* circumstances, to engage the Hungry Mother. Not on your own. Stay close to Mixael and let him do the binding."

I swallow. Then I nod.

The Prince takes a step back and sweeps an arm as though to encompass all of us in that one gesture. "May the gods be with us tonight," he says. Then he turns and marches from the library.

We follow after, swiftly descending the stair and racing through the palace corridors. The Prince soon disappears, outpacing the rest of us. Nelle and Andreas peel off next and slip down a side passage. When I turn to follow them, Mixael catches my elbow. "This way, Miss Darlington," he says, his voice still determinedly upbeat.

The bells have ceased their clamor by now, but the palace is not quiet. There are shouts and growls and noise from every corridor, though I see no one else until we reach the huge circular entrance hall. There, Captain Khas's voice booms as she barks orders. I spot the beautiful captain standing at the front of a formidable assembly of armed trolls.

"Gods curse it," Mixael mutters.

I glance his way and, for the first time that I can remember, see tension lining his face. He looks much older suddenly. "What's wrong?"

He shoots me a swift look, his jaw working. "It's Khas. She always feels obliged to take her troops into the city during an attack like this."

"Can they do anything?"

"Some." Mixael shrugs and grimaces. "They can fight. They can distract and deflect, draw the wraith away from city folk. But they can't actually *stop* a Noswraith, not even a little one. Definitely not one the size of the Hungry Mother. And they put themselves in grave danger." He breathes out another curse, then catches my arm. "Come on, Miss Darlington. The sooner we get this thing contained, the better."

He casts Khas one last look before dragging me with him through the open front doors. I think she looks at him as well, but we're moving too fast for me to tell for certain.

I clamber awkwardly down the enormous front steps, trying to move quickly without breaking my neck. I clutch the book I was handed against my chest and hold tight to the pen. It's a simple quill, I notice with some concern. How am I supposed to write anything without an inkwell? But then, I suppose I'm not meant to write anything at all. I'm supposed to stick close to Mixael. That's it.

"Hurry!" Mixael urges as we spring down the last few steps. He leads me into the city streets. I've never been in the city before, and I find the tall, carved-out buildings eerie, the deep shadows between them terrifying. A starlit sky arches overhead, offering all too little light. It's easy to imagine Noswraiths leaping out of every gaping doorway, spying at us from each dark window.

Screams break out from other parts of the city. Deep, guttural screams from the trollfolk denizens of Vespre. We tear down the center of a main street, Mixael leading the way directly toward that sound. Then we take a turn, and suddenly I'm faced with a wall of large, rock-hard bodies rushing like an avalanche straight toward me. I stop dead in my tracks, my eyes rounding.

The next instant, Mixael latches hold of my arm and yanks me to one side. We duck into the doorway of a building just as the stampede of trollfolk rolls by. My heart pounds in my throat. I would have been trampled to death, crushed beneath the weight of those terrible bodies. I try to make sense of them, try to see individuals amid the mass. But in the twilight gloom, they seem as featureless as rolling boulders.

And what about *my* little trolls? Dig, Har, Calx, and little Sis? Are they out here somewhere? Are they safe?

The rushing crowd passes, leaving the street clear once more. In the stillness that follows, I hear Mixael's panting breath close to my ear. "Come on," he says grimly, pulling me from the doorway.

Once more, we're out in the empty street, running hard. I'm wearing nothing but bedroom slippers, and I shiver as the cold air whips through the thin fabric of my nightgown. But I don't slow my pace, sticking close to Mixael's heels. I wonder how he knows where to go. Other than the distant screaming of trolls, the city is dreadfully silent. Perhaps he has some developed librarian's sense that helps him keep track of—

We turn a corner.

I stop short.

Mixael is gone. I'm alone, standing in that strange world of stone buildings and deep shadows under twilight. I'm alone, and I'm . . . I'm . . . I'm frightened . . .

"*Mama?*" I call, tentatively. My voice is quavering, small. The book in my hands is too heavy. I drop it and the quill, take several toddling steps. "*Mama?*" I call again. "*Mama! Mama!*" Tears brim in my eyes, spill onto my cheeks, drop from my chin.

All around me, the world is dark. This isn't the dark of twilit Vespre nor even the dark of night. This is a *living* darkness, full of chaotic movement and energy that overlays everything in a nightmarish film. Part of me recognizes this darkness. I seem to remember seeing it before in Aurelis Library, staining everything, seeping deep into my perceptions.

I sob now, my mouth hanging open, my eyes swollen. "*Mama!*" I cry. "*Mama! Mama!*" Why doesn't she hear me? Why doesn't she come to me? Why am I alone in this terrible dark place, why—

Mama's here.

Mama's right here, sweetness.

Come to Mama.

I turn toward that voice, swallowing back a sob. Something lumbers into view around a bend in the street.

It's huge—over ten feet tall, bent over, hunched. Long hair falls from the crown of its head, hanging lank over its ears, covering its face. It's totally naked, with huge sagging breasts and a distended, limp belly that jiggles with every heavy step it takes. Its overlong arms drag on the ground behind it, knuckles bouncing over stone.

Blood trails from its fingertips.

31

EVERY SENSE, EVERY REASON, TELLS ME TO BE SILENT. To turn, to flee.

Instead I open my arms wide.

"*Mama!*" I cry. My voice is babyish, pathetic, but loud. It echoes off those strange, writhing, living shadows, against the stone walls of the buildings around me. "*Mama! Mama!*"

The huge thing turns its head. Through dark strands of hair, I see a huge, bloodshot eye fixed on me.

Mama's here, sweetness.

I stand there, caught in the hypnotic spell of that eye, my arms outstretched. My face goes slack; my mouth drops open. I try to blink but can't.

The dark figure squares its shoulders and draws itself up to its full height, its long, bent spine slowly straightening. Its hair wafts to one side, revealing a second eye, this one pitch black. I'm caught in that gaze, unable to move.

"*Mama?*" I breathe.

It lunges.

Before I have a chance to cry out, something strikes me from the side. I fall hard, roll, and feel the *whoosh* of a huge arm pass over me, dragging an icy blast of wind in its wake. My senses reel, my limbs flail as I struggle to pull myself upright.

I'm lying on stone cobbles beneath a twilit sky. The writhing darkness is gone, replaced by less threatening shadows. My eyes are bleary with sleep, but I shake my head hard, shaking sleep-fog from my brain.

Someone lies on the ground beside me. I turn and see a woman pushing up onto her elbows. Her shadow-ringed eyes catch my gaze.

"Vervain!" I gasp.

She scrambles upright, latches hold of my arm, and yanks me to my feet. "Come on," she growls. "We're not safe."

I try to protest, but I'm still dizzy from my fall, and my head aches where it hit the cobbles. She pulls me into a narrow space between two tall buildings, pushing me behind her. Her back pressed against the stone wall, she peers out into the street. With a gasp, she draws in again. Her breast rises and falls with short, panting breaths.

Slowly, my brain clears. I look down at my body, which is once more that of a woman, not of a toddling infant. Was it a dream?

Had I dreamed that I was a child once more, lost and searching for my mother?

No, not a dream . . . a nightmare.

And it's still close.

Darkness moves out in the street. I look around Vervain and see the moving, writhing, energy-filled shadows crawling along the ground, spreading across the walls of the buildings. The Nightmare Realm slowly pervades the waking world, dragging everything down into its depths. There the Noswraith waits. Hungry.

It lurches into sight on the far side of the street. I can't really *see* it so much as *feel* it. But the feeling is as strong as sight, filling my head with the image of that huge, lumbering, knuckle-dragging form. Something plucks at my brain, like a song that bypasses the ears. A keening, wailing song, full of longing.

Vervain's hand finds mine, grips fast. "Don't listen!" she hisses. "Don't let her draw you back in!"

The wraith's shadow flickers around a bend and vanishes into the next street over. The moment it's out of sight, the song fades from my ears.

I exhale, closing my eyes in silent prayer. Then I turn to Vervain. "Where is Mixael?"

Vervain shakes her head and reaches for a satchel she wears slung from her shoulder and across her breast. She pulls out a book and quill. "You should get out of here," she says, opening the book to its first blank page. "You're not ready. You'll only make trouble."

"I can't just leave—"

"Get back to the palace before you get someone killed." Vervain's eyes flash in the starlight. Then she whirls away and slips from the alley, running out into the open street in pursuit of the wraith.

Gods on high, Vervain is right! I'm not ready for any of this. I want to crouch right here in this alley, wrap my arms over my head, and simply wait for someone to find and rescue me, wait for the horror of this hunt to be over.

But the Prince called on me to help. He obviously thought I could do *something* at least.

Biting back a curse, I peer out into the street once more. My book and quill lie abandoned where I dropped them, the book open, pages wafting in a light breeze. No sign of the Noswraith close at hand, however.

I spring from hiding, sprint out into the open, and snatch up both book and quill. For a moment I stand in the middle of the street, uncertain what to do. More screaming erupts from a few streets over. Are the trolls being dragged into the Nightmare, falling prey to that monster I'd glimpsed? Or are these screams coming from those who are awake, discovering the damage left in the wake of the wandering Noswraith? Either way, I can't let this mayhem continue.

I hurry to the end of the street and the corner around which the lurching figure of the Hungry Mother had disappeared. It takes every ounce of courage I possess to round that corner and peer into the next street.

It's empty.

My heart thuds painfully in my throat. What should I do? Do I dare continue? I don't know which way the monster went or even if Vervain followed it. I'm so vulnerable, so ignorant. Vervain was right; I'm nothing but trouble, liable to get someone killed. I take a step back.

Then, squaring my shoulders and growling deep in my throat, I lunge into the street. I won't abandon Vervain or Mixael or any of them. I may not be able to do much, but I can offer what little I have. If nothing else, I might prove a distraction, might draw the Noswraith's attention my way and give some other poor soul a chance to escape.

My bare feet slap on the cold stone street. One step, two steps, three steps, four . . .

I stagger, stumble.

All around me, writhing shadows close in.

The quill drops from my fingers, and the book is suddenly so, so heavy. I stare down at the plain leather cover, my eyes brimming with tears. Why am I carrying this thing? I let it fall from my hands and cram my knuckles into my eyes, sniffing harder and harder as a wail builds up in my throat. My lip quivers as I try to form a single word. *"Ma—"*

"Mama!" another thin voice cries out.

I look up, surprised.

A woman stands at the end of the street. A woman I know . . . with pale, sunken cheeks and long, loose black hair. Vervain? Is that her name? I'm not sure. I'm not sure of anything.

"*Mama!*" the woman cries out again, but her voice is that of a child. She lifts her arms, her hands open and grasping, as though desperate to be lifted off her feet. "*Mama! Mama!*"

Something appears at the end of the street, pouring out from the shadows between two buildings. It looms huge, even with its shoulders hunched. Two eyes—one bloodshot, one black as a void—fasten on the woman.

Mama's here.

The voice is full of soft, gentle poison.

Mama's always here.

I gasp . . . and suddenly I'm myself again, standing in my own adult body. Somewhere not far off, I feel myself crouching, picking up the dropped book, opening the cover, turning to the first blank page. Somewhere not far off, I feel my hand deftly setting the quill pen's silver nib to the page, beginning to shape the first letter, the first word, the first sentence.

But here, in this world . . . *I run.*

The same moment I spring into motion, the Hungry Mother springs as well. We're both aimed at the same target: Vervain, standing transfixed in the middle of the street, her jaw sagging, her eyes wide, her arms reaching out to the monster she created, to the death bearing down upon her in great, lumbering strides.

I reach her just seconds faster.

My arms wrap around the rail-thin librarian, knocking her tumbling just as the Hungry Mother's swinging arms slash through the air over our heads. I land hard, my hold on Vervain broken, and roll several feet away from her. The Noswraith staggers on, carried by its own momentum, and crashes heavily to its weirdly jointed knees. Its head rears up, swinging around until it fixes its horrible gaze on me where I lie.

Immediately, I'm a child again. An infant.

This time, I'm aware of the change. My waking self—somewhere close in the world outside the Nightmare Realm—tries to resist. She struggles to write another word, just one more! But the draw of the Nightmare is too strong. Her arms go limp. The quill drops from her lifeless fingers, spins to the ground.

And here, inside the Nightmare, I clamber to my knees and hold up my arms. *"Mama! Mama!"* I cry, desperate and terrified and trapped.

The Hungry Mother looks at me. Then she opens her mouth, displaying immense bloodstained teeth. Her limbs gather for a final, deadly lunge.

A roar splits the air.

My awareness fluttering between child and adult, I whip my head about to see a pale white figure in golden armor bearing down on the Noswraith. She heaves a massive ax overhead and brings it crashing down straight into the Hungry Mother's skull. I watch, horrified, as the monster crumples beneath that blow.

For a moment, Captain Khas stands above her fallen quarry, lungs heaving, arms still gripping the haft of her ax.

The next moment, the darkness of the Nightmare gathers and whirls around the broken figure on the stones. A great arm spasms, rises, plants a hand firmly on the ground. The shoulders hunch, the bony back arches. The heavy head lifts, hair hanging to hide the wretched face. I watch the split in the skull repair itself before my very eyes.

The Hungry Mother twists her long neck, fixing her gaze on Khas.

The troll captain takes a step back, her eyes widening. She shoots me a swift glance even as she takes a battle stance. *"Bind it! Bind it, human!"*

The Hungry Mother lashes out with a long, muscular arm, fingers flinging an arc of spattering blood that splashes across the captain's breastplate. Khas is only just swift enough to dance out of reach. She whirls and darts in close, her ax blade flashing, and cuts the Noswraith's arm clean off its body in a single powerful stroke. Dark liquid like ink spews from the gory wound.

But the Hungry Mother reaches out, picks up her own arm, and shoves it back into place. It reattaches in an instant.

Mixael was right. Khas might be able to enter the Nightmare Realm, her mind strong enough to resist the Noswraiths' spell. But without written magic, nothing she does here *matters*. Every blow she lands will simply heal. Eventually the Noswraith will overpower her.

I've got to do something. I've got to help.

I close my eyes, forcing my awareness back into the waking world. The darkness of the Nightmare fades, and I open my eyes back in the twilit world. There, lying at my feet, are my book and quill. I pluck them up fast, opening the book to the page where I'd left off writing in an ugly scrawl. The Prince had said never to go back to a failed spell . . . but is this a spell? I hardly know. I don't even know exactly what it is I've been writing.

Off to my right, I see Captain Khas. In the Nightmare Realm, she fights for her life, but here, she's caught as though in a trance. Vervain lies close to her, a broken heap in the middle of the street.

I stare back down at the page, at the words hastily scrawled in my own rushed handwriting. "Just a story," I whisper. "Tell a story."

Is it really so simple?

Yes. And simultaneously not simple at all.

My hand moves, my quill dancing across the page. The quill itself must be magicked in some way, for ink flows freely from its nib as though it were a fountainpen. I don't bother to question this but simply keep on writing.

As I write, I let my mind sink back into the Nightmare.

I stand in that writhing darkness, my awareness split between two realities. Part of me is in my waking body, writing fast—but most of me is here, now, watching Khas and the monster circling one another.

"Khas." I whisper her name, realization dawning. In this world, she's a weapon. A weapon I can use as I like if I can only . . .

Khas lashes out with her ax.

I write the words swiftly, little caring if they're legible. Neatness doesn't matter, not in a moment like this.

*Her powerful arms bring the weapon swinging in an arc—*I write—*neatly slicing off the Hungry Mother's hand.*

The Noswraith howls as the blow lands. She quickly snatches up the appendage and shoves it up against the stump of her wrist. I see the Nightmare beginning to reform, mending the wound.

Only this time it doesn't work, I write. *The hand disintegrates through her fingers, turning to dust and floating away on the wind.*

I watch the words I write come to pass, watch the little dark motes that were part of the Noswraith's essence whirl and dissipate in the air. The Hungry Mother stares, aghast, her horrible mouth sagging with disbelief.

Then her head comes up, her horrible mis-matched eyes widening. She turns and looks straight at me.

She knows what I'm doing. She *knows.*

Horror stabs my gut. I concentrate, forcing my hand to steady, forcing my waking body to write a few more words. In the Nightmare, I simply stand where I am, mouth open, stupid with fear.

Khas lets out a vicious battle cry and assaults the wraith again. This time, the Hungry Mother knocks her aside with a single swipe of her bloody, handless arm. The troll captain hurtles to the ground and lies there as though broken, her arms and legs spread wide. I can't tell if she's breathing.

I don't have time to worry. The Hungry Mother lunges at me next.

She comes at me on all fours, leaning heavily on her knuckles and her bloodied arm stump. Her bare, sagging breasts sway from side to side, and her dark hair streams behind her in a ragged cloud. Though she's awkward and hulking, she covers the distance at blistering speed.

I try to write another word, just one more word: *Khas.*

As though answering a command, the troll captain picks herself up off the ground. She sways, shakes her head. She casts about for her ax.

Khas picks up her weapon—I write—*and hurls it at her enemy.*

Responding to the words, I write, Khas swipes up the ax that suddenly appears at her side. She arches her back, her whole body, her arms swinging the ax high above her head. Then she hurls it, spinning end-over-end. It plunges into the Noswraith's spine.

The Hungry Mother roars and staggers to one side, her arms flailing in her effort to dislodge the blade. It's buried deep, and she cannot reach the haft. I take advantage of the few moments granted me and scrawl a few more hasty sentences:

Khas reaches for her belt and unhooks a coil of rope.

The troll captain, her eyes wide with surprise, obeys, discovering the rope on her belt where I placed it. It's a silvery, shining thing, woven from moonlight and strands of unicorn hair.

She wraps the rope around the Hungry Mother's neck, I write.

Khas hastily loops strands around her hands, pulling the length of cord taut. Then she runs at the Noswraith, her powerful legs carrying her through the Nightmare in a few swift strides. She leaps and twists the rope around the monster's neck, just as I had written, once, twice, then springs free and readjusts her grip. With all her strength she pulls, her muscles rippling, her armor flashing. The Hungry Mother chokes on a howl. Her hand and bloody stump scrabble at her neck, trying to catch hold of the rope, trying to loosen it. Her legs sag, buckle. She sinks to her knees.

Bind her. I've got to bind her. This is working, but I must fix the spell in place with her name . . . her name . . .

Oh, what is her name?

"Madra!" I shout.

The Noswraith, still pulling at the rope, turns and looks straight at me.

In the waking world, my hand flies, the quill nib shaping the word on the page: *M . . . a . . . d . . . r . . .*

The Hungry Mother utters a terrible roar. She lets go of the rope around her neck and hurls herself instead straight at Khas. The troll captain only has time to turn and take a single step before the Noswraith snatches her up in her one good hand and lifts her over her head. The silver cord falls free. Khas utters a single, desperate shout, before the Noswraith flings her. She flies through the air and lands hard many yards away. I see her try to push up onto her elbows once before her shaking arms give out, and she sinks back down again.

The silver rope falls free of the Hungry Mother's neck, landing in coiled loops like a dead snake. The Hungry Mother turns to me once more. She smiles, showing every red-stained tooth.

*I'm here, sweetness. I'm here to hold you. To cradle you. To comfort you.*ungr

I try to fight. I try to resist.

I can't.

Even as I back away, I sink back into that small, frail, infantile version of myself. My little feet stagger, stumble. I fall to my hands and knees. I'm weeping uncontrollably, desperate with fear and with need.

The Hungry Mother draws near, her arms outstretched. Black blood flows freely from her cut stump, but she doesn't seem to feel any pain. Her face warps before my eyes, the hideous visage transforming into something softer, gentler. A vaguely familiar face, though I cannot quite place it.

Come to my arms. Come to my arms and rest, my sweet. Come to my arms and sleep. Forever and ever sleep.

I open my mouth. I try to scream.

Instead I say, "Ma . . . ma . . . ?"

A flash of silver whips in front of my eyes.

I start back, shocked into my adult form, and see the rope

I'd written into being encircle the Hungry Mother's throat. The moment it touches her skin, she transforms back into the monstrous thing with the lank hair and the mismatched eyes. She opens her mouth, gagging on her own roar, scrabbling with her one hand to loosen the rope's hold. It tightens, the cord vibrating in the air.

I turn to discover who holds the other end. And I gasp.

The Prince stands over Khas's fallen body. He's huge—huge like a hero of old, like a god come down from the heavens. Huge and shining and ferocious, with mighty wings blazing at his shoulders, filling this whole nightmarish world with light.

He yanks on my rope, pulling the Noswraith off her feet.

The Hungry Mother screeches, her hideous face twisted with wrath. She writhes. Her one good hand grapples with the rope, trying to get purchase and pull the Prince off his feet.

His hands move in a swift configuration I can't quite follow. Suddenly, there's another loop of rope. He throws that as well, his aim perfect, lassoing her wrist and yanking the loop tight. Then, holding both ropes with one hand, he creates a third noose, and with that one snares the Hungry Mother's legs.

She's caught like a fly in a spider's web, twisted in shining silver. She screams, spasms, gyrates, the sounds issuing from her throat utterly inhuman. More ropes appear and twist around her body, until her limbs are bound fast, and she lies immobile on the ground.

The Prince approaches her. Slow, powerful. He plants a foot on her head, and leans down, staring into her eyes.

"Madjra," he says. "*You are bound.*"

He waves his hand. More ropes appear out of thin air, winding around the monstrous body until it totally disappears in a cocoon of moonlit strands. When it's through, the Noswraith is nothing but a lump of silver.

The Prince stands beside his catch, his wings outspread, his hair flowing dark and thick in the breeze of this Nightmare Realm. In the darkness, his golden skin seems to glow with its own inner light, and his eyes flash like stars. He is, in that moment, overwhelmingly beautiful. I cannot tear my gaze away.

As though suddenly becoming aware of my presence, he turns and catches my gaze. His mouth tilts in a smile. "Well met, Clara Dar—"

Before he can finish, a wrenching gasp breaks from his lips. His hand presses to his chest as though trying to catch hold of a terrifying pain. His eyes seek mine once more, holding my gaze with desperate intensity.

Then all the blood drains from his face, and he collapses in a dead faint.

32

I OPEN MY EYES.

I stand once more in the waking world. Bodies litter the ground all around me. Khas and Vervain lie close to each other, the one flat on her face, the other spread-eagle on her back.

And right at my feet, holding my own book in his hands . . . the Prince.

He looks terrible. Nothing like the vision I'd glimpsed just a moment before in the Nightmare. His golden skin is gray and sallow and sunken, his eyes mostly closed but not quite. I can just see a gleam of violet irises, but they are dull and unseeing.

I sink to my knees beside him and hastily press my ear to his chest. A heartbeat! Faint but definitely present. I sit back, pushing hair from my eyes. "Prince!" I say, my voice shaking more than I like. "Can you hear me? Please, answer! Can you hear me, Prince?"

I pat his cheeks, rub his wrists, shake his shoulders. Nothing works.

Shivering, I slide my book from his grasp. At once I feel how the *weight* of it has changed. When I carried this little volume into the city, it was merely a blank book ready to be filled with words.

Now it's possessed. I feel the Hungry Mother writhing inside.

I bite my lip, swallowing back a bitter curse. The Prince finished my binding for me. Because I failed. But how? I know the story I wrote was a bit on the feeble side, but it was working. I really thought I had her right up until . . .

Until I tried to write her name. Until I tried to finalize the binding.

What went wrong? Did I forget the spelling? Perhaps. After all, I'd never seen the name spelled out before. I'm tempted to open the book, to inspect my work, to compare it to the Prince's. But I can feel the power straining inside those two feeble covers. I'd better not indulge my curiosity. It would be all too easy to let the Noswraith escape again.

I press the book tight to my chest, then cast about for the quill I brought with me, the one that miraculously wrote without needing to be dipped in ink. It lies broken beside the Prince. At least it worked long enough to get the job done. Perhaps it earned its place in one of those little display cabinets on the Fifth Floor.

Movement to my left draws my attention. I turn to see Khas pick herself up. The troll looks my way. For a moment, her face radiates fear. Then, breathing hard, she shakes her head, shuts her jaw, and offers me a firm nod. Does she realize how I used her as a tool to fight in the Nightmare? Hopefully she won't hold it against me. After all, while I'm not at all opposed to *writing* the thrills of an epic battle, I'm certainly not equipped to take on the role of action heroine myself.

Khas moves to Vervain's side, crouches over the prone librarian, and checks her pulse. "Is she all right?" I call out, my voice thin and a little too loud in the stillness of that street.

Before Khas can answer, a cacophony of voices erupts behind me. I turn to see Mixael, Nelle, and Andreas rounding a bend. They cry out and rush toward me, but at sight of the Prince crumpled on the ground, their cries change in tone.

"What happened here?" Nelle demands, falling on her knees beside the Prince, nimble despite her apparent age. She cups his face in her hands. "Oh, he looks bad, he does! Tell me, is the Noswraith . . . ?" She looks up at me as though afraid to finish her question.

I brandish the book. "It's contained."

Mixael takes the volume from my unresisting fingers. His brows rise in surprise as he flips through the pages. When he reaches the end, he closes the book and passes it to Andreas before offering me an approving nod. "Not bad. Not bad at all! Looks like you almost had her—"

"Enough of that now," Nelle says sharply, cutting her son off with a glare. "You can enthuse over technique on your own time. Right now the Prince needs our help."

Mixael immediately kneels beside his mother. "What happened to him?"

"I . . . I tried to bind the Hungry Mother," I say, not liking to admit my failure. "It was . . . It didn't work. She was coming for me, and then the Prince was there. He finished the spell."

"And used an awful lot of human magic in the process," Nelle says grimly. "Look at the boy! Positively drained."

He looks bad, I must admit. I remember how he fainted in Aurelis after a small display of human magic, finishing my binding of the Melted Man. That was nothing compared to the magic he wielded tonight.

"Will he recover?" I ask, afraid to hear the answer.

Nelle merely grunts, then turns as Captain Khas approaches our little cluster, Vervain draped limply in her arms. "Are you all right?" Mixael asks the captain, his tone a little too revealing in that moment.

Khas casts him a swift glance but doesn't answer, for Andreas has stepped to her side and is checking Vervain's pulse. His brow is uncharacteristically stern. After a few concentrated moments, he looks round at us. "Alive," he says, his voice dark and deep. "But I'm afraid she may be lost."

Lost? What does that mean? I shudder at the horrible possibilities whispering in the back of my head, but when I open my mouth to ask, I can't force the questions out. I simply can't bear to know. Not yet, anyway.

"Right," Nelle says, getting to her feet and drawing her little aged body upright. "Mixael and Andreas, I want you to carry Vervain between you. She's slight enough; you can manage. Captain, if you wouldn't mind bearing our Prince?"

Khas nods and, after passing Vervain to Mixael and Andreas, lifts the Prince in her arms. He suddenly looks much smaller, narrower, and weaker than I ever would have believed possible. So human, and no more than a few inches taller than me, slender and delicate boned. In contrast to the powerful bulk of the troll captain, he seems almost comically frail.

With the Hungry Mother's temporary binding tucked under her arm, Nelle shoos the boys ahead of her then sets out after them. Khas falls in step behind the old librarian, and I follow last of all, holding my broken quill tenderly. We progress back up the silent street, a strange little procession. Along the way I glimpse flashing eyes peering out of various upper-story windows and a few dark doorways. They aren't friendly eyes . . . and they definitely aren't human.

I shiver and hasten after the others, back through the unlit streets to the palace. My knees tremble and my stomach roils, but I can't deny the faint glow of triumph in my heart. I survived! I survived against one of the Great Noswraiths! And while I didn't succeed in binding the monster on my own, I came close.

Not close enough to spare the Prince, however.

That thought dampens my triumph significantly. Will the Prince be all right? If not . . . if he died of this overexertion of magic . . . what would that mean for my Obligation?

Would I be free?

Guilt stabs my heart. How could I even think such a thing at such a time? Quickly I tuck my chin and hurry on after the others, determined to outrun this all-too-pressing thought.

Everyone disperses upon reaching the palace. Mixael and Andreas carry Vervain off one way, Nelle and Khas disappear somewhere else with the Prince.

And I'm left standing alone in the middle of the massive entrance hall, my heart pounding, my chest heaving, my blood racing.

I have no idea where I'm supposed to go or what I'm supposed to do next. I'm not even sure how to get back to my own room from here. Not that I particularly *want* to return to my room. The thrill of battle still pulses in my veins. How could I possibly sleep after everything I've just seen and done?

I drift along the passages, vaguely aware of hurrying shapes in the darkness, always just beyond my range of vision. A few days ago, my imagination would have jumped and shivered with terror, assuming those shapes were Noswraiths escaped from their bindings. Now, having encountered the Hungry Mother face-to-face, I know better. Those shadowy figures are just trolls going about their business in the dark, taking care to give me a wide berth.

Are they avoiding me simply because I'm human? Or do they know what I have done? What I am capable of doing?

You were born to be a warrior.

I pause before a floor-to-ceiling window without glass to survey the city below. My wanderings have led me to the same hall in which I first encountered the troll children. That dizzying drop doesn't frighten me as it once did, and I step right up to the edge, lean against the sill, and gaze out over the buttress and the hunched shoulders of the stone gargoyle, out across the starlit view. A faint pink glow tinges the horizon, the closest thing this world ever sees to sunrise.

I let out a long exhale. Could it be that the Prince was right? Am I truly everything he says I am?

"You're no warrior," I growl. The words sound overloud in the silence of this starlit dawn. But I repeat them with emphasis, my voice harsh in my own ears. "You're no warrior! Don't forget who you are, don't forget what you want. You want to get home. *Home.* To Oscar. To Danny. You want . . . you want . . ."

A thin gleam of sunlight crests the horizon, turning the topmost towers, spires, and domes of the city to gold. My breath catches. It's so beautiful! The white stone glows in that unexpected light, and all the harshness of Vespre City melts away, momentarily transforming into a city not of nightmares, but of dreams.

Doom is warded off. For one more day at least.

And I was part of that. A small part, perhaps, but still . . . *I* began the binding that even now holds the Hungry Mother at bay. The Prince finished the story *I* created. He didn't dismiss it and create his own—he used *my* work. Which means . . . which means . . .

I'm not sure what it means. But a spark of pride glows in my heart, nonetheless.

"Miss Darlington?"

I turn, startled, one hand gripping the edge of the stone window frame. A figure stands at the end of the passage, a lantern in one hand. I blink, letting my eyes adjust from the dawn glow back to the interior gloom of the palace. "Oh, Mister Lawrence! How is the Prince? Is he all right?"

Lawrence approaches, his lantern swinging, the light wafting strangely across his face. I've never seen him look so solemn. "He's bad off," he says as he draws near, casting sidelong glances into the shadows as though afraid of being overheard. "Just about the worst I've seen him. The curse he carries . . ." His voice trailing off, he clenches his jaw and shakes his head. Then, with a sad shrug, "He wants to see you, Miss."

"Me?"

Lawrence nods. "He's awake. And he's asking for you."

I don't know what to say. I open my mouth, but every word that comes to mind sounds lame and limp. Besides, it's not as though I can protest. I am an Obligate. If the Prince wants to see me, then see me he will.

I nod and step away from the window, folding my hands demurely. "Lead on, then."

To my surprise, we arrive at the Prince's chamber within a few turns. Lawrence approaches what looks like a bare stone wall, turns a hidden latch, and the door appears as though by magic.

Lawrence steps inside, the lantern he carries the only light to be had. "Miss Darlington," he announces quietly.

I follow him to stand just within the doorway. Lawrence carries his lantern across the room, navigating piles of detritus to the massive bed in the center of the room. The pale light flashes across the Prince's face.

I suck in a breath. He looks like death. Pale, drawn, his eyes closed. His cheeks are deeply sunken in, his eyes hollow, and the flesh on his bones tight and almost transparent in that lantern glow. If I didn't know any better, I would think I looked upon a corpse.

His eyes flicker open as Lawrence sets the lantern on a nearby table. He lifts a weak gaze to his servant's face. "She's here, Prince," Lawrence says, his voice hushed and gentle. "I found her. Would you have her approach?"

The Prince swallows painfully. I watch the muscles in his throat spasm with the effort. When he opens his mouth, no words emerge. He closes his eyes again and, rather than speaking, simply nods.

Leaving the lantern on the table, Lawrence crosses the room to where I stand in the doorway. "He's very weak," he says, ducking his head to speak close to my ear. "Try not to . . . well, try not to let him speak if he doesn't have to."

I nod. The next moment, Lawrence sidles from the room and shuts the door behind him. I remain where I am for some moments. I can't quite find the will to move my feet, to cross the space and approach the Prince's bed. My heart is pounding, though I'm not altogether certain why.

At last, the Prince opens one eye, fixing me with a stare. Though he's still ghoulishly pale, that look packs enough force to galvanize my limbs. I cross the room, stumbling over unseen debris until I reach his bedside. There I stand, gripping my nightgown tight and looking down at him.

He slowly opens his other eye and holds my gaze. A long, long silence follows.

At last, he lifts his head a few inches off the pillow and opens his mouth. I see his lips move, see his tongue flicker, as though he's trying to form words. The effort is too much for him. With a shake of his head, he sinks back onto the pillow and simply motions with one hand. Does he mean for me to speak?

"The . . . the binding." I stop, clear my throat, and bite my lip. But as I can think of no other reason why he would summon me here, I continue. "I'm sorry I got it so wrong. I . . . I tried. I hope you know I really, truly tried. I'm not certain what went wrong, if I spelled the name incorrectly, or if I simply—"

His arm moves. To my utmost shock, he reaches out and catches hold of my hand.

I stare at those long, cold fingers of his gripping mine. What is this? What is he doing? Why am I here? There's very little strength to that grip, but I feel him squeezing, holding on even when I try to pull away.

I lift my gaze back to his face. His eyes are closed again. I would almost think he'd fainted if not for the continued pressure of his grip. It's as though he's using all the strength remaining to him to hold onto me, to keep me here.

Several times I try to speak, to no avail. When words finally come, they emerge in a small shuddering whisper: "I know what I did." I wait for him to react. He doesn't. So I continue. "I don't know all of it. But I know enough. I . . . I killed your mother."

For an instant, the pressure on my fingers tightens. It's almost painful. I gasp but don't pull back. The pressure loosens, but he still doesn't let go.

"I understand now why you brought me here," I say. "Restitution. For my sin. For what I've done to you." I study his face, searching for some sign of understanding. His features are perfectly still, his breath ragged.

"I'm sorry," I whisper at last. "I know it's not enough. I know it can't be enough. But I'm sorry, and I will do what I can to atone. I swear it."

There. I've said all I can say.

But he doesn't let go of my hand.

So I stay where I am, beside him in the flickering lanternlight. I stay until at last his grip loosens, his fingers slide from mine and fall.

Gently, I pick up his wrist and drape his hand across his slowly rising and falling chest. I hesitate again, gazing into his sunken face, trying to tell myself that I see a little bit of life returning to his features, a little color.

Then I turn and hasten back across the room to the door, fighting the urge to look back.

33

Several hours later, I make my way to the library. There, to my surprise, I find Nelle, Andreas, and Mixael all gathered around one desk and so absorbed in whatever it is they're looking at that they take no notice of my arrival. I don't bother to announce myself but tiptoe up behind them, listening to their talk.

"This is the new way though, ain't it?" Nelle says. "And it's stronger, honestly, than the old spell-writing of my day. Once it can be honed, that is."

"But how strong is it, do you think?" Mixael asks. "The Prince's binding, of course, should last. Will the rest of it hold up?"

"I give it about a week," Nelle answers with a shrug. "Not real long, but not bad for a first effort."

"Extraordinary." Andreas's mild voice is soft and low but

expresses more emotion in that single word than I've ever heard from him.

I take a few more steps, craning my neck, and see what it is they're looking at: a book. *My* book, the one I carried into the city last night, the one in which I wrote the binding. It's my own work they're analyzing so intently.

A hot flush rises in my cheeks. I shouldn't be here, eavesdropping like some common snoop. Should I retreat? Slip back through the doors and flee to my room? But no, that won't do any good. I need to face the Vespre Librarians eventually.

I clear my throat loudly. "How is Vervain?"

The three librarians jump and whirl about as though caught in some illicit act. Nelle deftly shuts the book while Andreas and Mixael sidle closer together, shoulders touching, hiding it behind them. "Vervain?" Mixael echoes. Then with a quick shake of his head, "Oh, yes! Vervain, of course. She's . . . she's not well, I'm afraid."

I wince. But it's not as though I'm surprised. I saw how Vervain looked after the battle. She took the brunt of the Hungry Mother's attack, that's for certain.

I pull out the chair from the nearest cubby and take a seat. "She tried to stop it, you know," I say, addressing myself to Nelle.

The old librarian nods. "Yes. She did all right." One eyebrow slides up her forehead. "*After* she let it go."

"Let it go?" A stone drops in my gut. "You mean . . . you mean she released the Hungry Mother on purpose?"

Andreas and Mixael exchange a glance. Then Mixael shrugs and turns to me once more. "It happens sometimes. It's that bond, you see—the bond between creator and creation. As time wears on, it can be harder and harder to continue binding something you've made yourself, something that's a part of you."

I stare at him, horrified. "But the Hungry Mother is a monster! Why would she ever want to turn it loose? Even if it's part of you, wouldn't that make you want to hide it that much more?"

Nelle clucks softly. She's reverted to her old-lady form, losing that youthful vitality I so briefly glimpsed last night. "Oftentimes we love most those things of which we're most ashamed." Her eyes take on a faraway look. "My Soran was the same way. At times."

A slithering sensation creeps over my mind, memory of the Thorn Maiden down in her vault. Is it possible that Soran Silveri had sometimes been tempted to set his monster free as well? More importantly . . . will *I* ever feel tempted to unleash whatever Noswraith I created? No. No, that's simply impossible! I can't imagine any circumstance in which I would do such a thing.

Shaking that unsettling thought away, I ask, "Where is Vervain, then?"

"She's in a holding cell on the other side of the palace," Mixael replies. "When the Prince recovers, he'll try to work with her, see if her mind can be restored. But after last night . . ." He shrugs. "I don't know that anyone can bring her back."

I shudder and rub my upper arms as though to drive away a chill. "What *is* the Hungry Mother?" I ask quietly, not at all sure I want to hear the answer. "I mean, I know it's a Noswraith, but . . . how did someone like Vervain go about creating something like *that?*"

Nelle and the other two exchange glances. Mixael raises his eyebrows, and Andreas merely blinks softly. "Fine," Nelle grunts, folding her arms. "I'll tell her." She turns to me, her lips twisting as though whatever she's about to say tastes bitter.

"The Hungry Mother," she says at last, "is an outpouring of Vervain's own sorrow. She was, you must understand, a very sad woman. A woman who had suffered a great personal loss."

"What loss?" I press.

"Babies." Nelle's response is so blunt, it feels almost like a slap. "She had babies. Two of them, I believe. The first of which she did not want. To have a child at that time of her life—unwed as she was, you understand—well, it would have ruined her reputation, her career. The poor girl was trapped. She didn't feel she had a choice. So she took steps to see the child was not born."

Her words fall on my ears like funeral bells, full of sorrow deep and reverberating. I remember the look in Vervain's eye that day on the stair, when she gripped the rail and spoke those words that had seemed so strange at the time: *I am a mother. Always. Forever.*

"Then came the second baby," Nelle continues. "Vervain was married by then and no longer feared a scandal. She hoped this one would live, would make up for the one she lost. But . . . her body never fully recovered from the first time . . ." The old librarian stares down at her hands twisted together in her lap. "The poor girl! Something like that, it changes a person, changes the shape of the soul. And later, when that soul needs an outlet for the pain . . ." She sighs and, looking up, catches my eye. "She was a gifted writer in her day. A novelist of some standing among the literary circles in Seryth, or so I'm told. You may have heard of her—Vervain Keldi."

"*Keldi?*" My mouth drops open in shock. "Wait. Wait a moment. You're telling me that Vervain . . . *our* Vervain . . . she is Vervain Keldi? Author of *The Blue Oblivion* and *Crow's Peak* and *The House of the Fallen?*"

"So you've heard of her."

Have I ever! Vervain Keldi's three novels are considered masterpieces of gothic horror. The authoress herself was believed to be dead for some years by the time I discovered her work, but her name was still celebrated. *The Blue Oblivion* has not ceased to be a bestseller since it was first published forty years ago.

How many times have I read that book aloud to Oscar and Mama? Sitting cross-legged with my back to the fire so the light could fall on the pages. And they would lean in close, eyes shining, breath catching, listening to the dreadful tale as it unfolded, relentless in both terror and gore. We loved every spine-chilling sentence.

Nelle studies me closely, noting my shock. "She wrote a fourth book, you know," she says quickly. "Her last work, her *great* work, some said."

"She did?" I frown. "No, that can't be right. I would have heard of it, surely."

"No, you wouldn't." Nelle smiles, a mirthless smile that doesn't reach her eyes. "You wouldn't because all recollection of it has been purged from human memory, and every last printed copy—every last page of every last variation of every last manuscript—is contained in a vault down below. The Prince hunted them down, one after another, and brought them here for safekeeping."

I stare at Nelle. Her words ring inside my head, a revelation I can scarcely begin to fathom. But of course, if anyone was going to create a Noswraith, it would be a writer like Vervain Keldi. Not even my father's darkest, most popular tales had ever matched Keldi's for true horror. Horror that embedded itself in the minds of her readers until the sheer power generated by all those minds brought something new to life from the darkness . . .

"So the Prince brought her here," I say softly. "He brought her here to fight her own Noswraith. To contain it."

"Some wanted to kill her for her crime," Nelle continues. "But the poor woman was so broken, so sad. And she obviously had no idea what she'd done. She merely wrote from her pain, from her sorrow. From her fear."

"The Hungry Mother," I whisper and close my eyes. Vervain's voice rings in my head: *"They can bleed us until we are nothing more than husks of our former selves. But deep down . . . deep down inside, we are meant to make. Meant to create. Meant to give life!"*

Her natural ability to make life was taken from her—first by the cruelty of the society in which she lived, then by the betrayal of her own weakened body. But she found a way. She created. She gave birth by the only means remaining to her.

I am a mother. Always. Forever.

"Vervain has served at Vespre Library ever since." Mixael's voice breaks through my thoughts. "Once she was made to understand what she had done, she was more than willing to enter into service. She's not an easy person to know. But her heart was in the right place. Most of the time."

Andreas heaves a heavy sigh. "It's sad that her story should come to an end tonight."

"Now, now!" Nelle clucks and shakes her head. "We don't know that do we? The Prince might yet be able to help."

"If he recovers," Andreas responds dolefully.

At this, the three librarians look very solemn. They don't meet my gaze but seem very interested in studying their own hands. I realize suddenly how much they depend on their Prince to govern and guide them in their ongoing efforts. If something happens to the Prince, how long before the Doomed City suffers its final fall?

"Enough of these long faces!" Mixael says suddenly, flashing a determined smile round at everyone. "We have cause to celebrate, remember?"

"Yeah?" His mother gives him a look. "And what cause is that exactly?"

Mixael throws his arms wide. "We all survived the night, didn't we? Disaster was averted and not a single life lost." He looks at me, his smile growing. "Thanks to the quick action of our newest member."

I flush and duck my chin. "I didn't really—"

"No, I won't hear any false modesty from you, Miss Darlington," Mixael says, waving his hand in a shushing motion. "Your spell-writing saved the day, regardless of who put the final binding in place. In fact, I think it's only fair to make things official."

With this enigmatic statement, he darts across the floor to the nearest book lift. Ignoring his mother's protesting squawks of horror, he leaps over the guard rail, grabs the cables, and descends, nimble as a squirrel.

Nelle tosses up her hands and exchanges looks with Andreas. "I swear, that boy will be the death of me!" she mutters. Then she turns to me and taps the book lying on the desk before her. "It *was* an impressive bit of spell-writing, girl. Not *proper* spell-writing, mind you. But undeniably powerful. Over the next few days, I'll teach you some tricks to strengthen your technique, and, of course, a more long-term binding must be established. But until then, it's not bad at all."

Before I can answer, Mixael's puffing breaths announce his return. We all turn to see him climbing the spiral stair. He waves something over his head like a flag.

It's a quill.

Hastening to rejoin the rest of us, Mixael drops on his knees before me and offers up the quill in both hands as solemnly as a squire offering up a blade to his liege lord. "Clara Darlington," he says, "allow me to humbly present you with this token of our appreciation and admiration. The quill-bonding ceremony will be held shortly hereafter, and you will be officially instated as one of our number."

"Bullspit," Nelle mutters. "Such nonsense! Quill-bonding ain't nothing more than an old Miphates superstition. Don't have any real merit to it."

But I can scarcely hear the old librarian's grumbling. I stare at that quill, and my heart seems to swell in my breast. Fingers trembling, I reach out and pluck it from Mixael's hands. I turn it over gently, reverently. It's certainly not as fine and flashy as the red quill Thaddeus gave me. It's a simple gray feather with a nice silver nib, no engravings or embellishments.

But it's mine.

I feel eyes upon me. Slowly I look up and around at the others. First Andreas, then Mixael. Then Nelle, last of all. "I don't know what to say," I breathe.

Nelle smiles. "Welcome to the Doomed City, Clara Darlington. Something tells me you're going to fit in just fine."

DON'T MISS BOOK 2 OF THIS
BREATHTAKING ROMANCE!

ENTANGLED

HE MIGHT HATE HER. THAT DOESN'T MEAN HE'LL LET ANYONE ELSE HAVE HER.

For five years, Clara has wanted only one thing—to survive her fifteen-year sentence of servitude to the fae and get home to her beloved brother. But she can't afford any . . . distractions.

Like Danny, her handsome childhood sweetheart, who longs to set her free. Or Ivor, the devastatingly beautiful fae lord, who desires to whisk her away to his own bright court of scheming and danger.

Most of all, she can't be distracted by the complicated and intriguing Prince himself... who may or may not be her enemy.

HOW ABOUT A BONUS SHORT STORY?

ENTICED

Five years ago she devastated his world.

Now he needs her to help him save it.

Want a little more of the Prince's point-of-view on events? This short story offers some tasty insights into his perspective . . . particularly when seeing her in *that* dress.

Download your free short story at www.sylviamercedesbooks.com/free-book-4

A CLEVER THIEF. A DISFIGURED MAGE.
A KISS OF POISON.

THE SCARRED MAGE OF ROSEWARD

For fifteen years, Soran Silveri has fought to suppress the nightmarish monster stalking Roseward. His weapons are few and running low, and the curse placed upon him cripples his once unmatched power. Isolation has driven him to the brink of madness, and he knows he won't be able to hold on much longer.

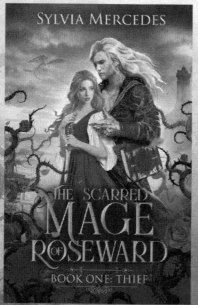

When a sharp-tongued, uncouth, and undeniably beautiful young woman shows up on his shore, Soran resolves to drive her away. He won't be responsible for another death.

But Nelle is equally determined not to be frightened off by the hideously scarred mage. Not until she gets what she came for . . . .

Can two outcasts thrown together in a tangle of lies discover they are each other's only hope? Or will the haunted darkness of Roseward tear them apart?

ALSO BY SYLVIA MERCEDES

This arranged marriage romance about a human princess forced to wed a dark and desperate Shadow King is sure to entice!

BRIDE OF THE SHADOW KING TRILOGY

Though she is the oldest daughter, Princess Faraine lives in the background, shunned from court and kept out of sight. Her chronic illness makes her a liability to the crown, and she has learned to give place to her beautiful, favored younger sister in all things.

When the handsome and enigmatic Shadow King comes seeking a bride, Faraine is not surprised that her sister is his choice.

Though not eager to take a human bride, King Vor is willing to do what is necessary for the sake of his people. When he meets the lively Princess Ilsevel, he agrees to a marriage.

So why can't he get the haunting eyes of her older sister out of his head?

The first book in a new fantasy romance series, this sweeping tale of love and betrayal is perfect for readers looking for a touch of spice to go with the sweet in their next swoony, slow-burn romance.

ABOUT THE AUTHOR

SYLVIA MERCEDES makes her home in the idyllic North Carolina countryside with her handsome husband, numerous small children, and the feline duo affectionately known as the Fluffy Brothers. When she's not writing she's . . . okay, let's be honest. When she's not writing, she's running around after her kids, cleaning up glitter, trying to plan healthy-ish meals, and wondering where she left her phone. In between, she reads a steady diet of fantasy novels.

But mostly she's writing.

After a short career in Traditional Publishing (under a different name), Sylvia decided to take the plunge into the Indie Publishing World and is enjoying every minute of it. She's the author of the acclaimed Venatrix Chronicles, as well as The Scarred Mage of Roseward trilogy, and the romantic fantasy series, Of Candlelight and Shadows.

Made in the USA
Middletown, DE
29 August 2024